THE LOOP

"*The Loop* is as amiable a crime novel as one is likely to find. Burnett's sympathy for the 'other side' of those who engage in criminal activities… The better parts of the natures of the heisters get a 'slice of life' handling with no attempt to exaggerate the good or the bad of their conflicts and decision making… Burnett consistently worked against the demonization portrayal of criminals prevalent in movies and much of popular crime fiction, so a valuable counterpoint in the genre..."   —Bill Kelly

"It stands beside Burnett's greatest work as another variant of the hard-boiled, noir, or crime novels that will forever define him as a major American writer. It offers a new, fresh angle that will not disappoint either new or old readers of his work."

—David Laurence Wilson from his introduction

"His novels are not mysteries, but crime novels, powerful, accurate cynical explorations of criminals in their own environment: at their best they are important additions to the honor roll of hard-boiled fiction."
—George Grella, *20th Century Crime & Mystery Writers*

"One of the most important American fiction writers of the twentieth century."   —H.R.F. Keating

"Burnett knew his characters and the worlds in which they lived, and he wrote about them in a clean, hard style."   —Elgin Bleecker, *The Dark Time*

The Loop
Man With a Thousand Enemies

W. R. BURNETT

Introduction by David Laurence Wilson

Stark House Press • Eureka California

THE LOOP / MAN WITH A THOUSAND ENEMIES

Published by Stark House Press
1315 H Street
Eureka, CA 95501, USA
griffinskye3@sbcglobal.net
www.starkhousepress.com

ISBN: 979-8-88601-154-8

Book and cover design by Mark Shepard, shepgraphics.com
Proofreading by Bill Kelly and David Laurence Wilson

First Stark House Press Edition: July 2025

7

W. R. Burnett:
"Outside Everything"
by David Laurence Wilson

17

The Loop
by W. R. Burnett

133

Man With a Thousand Enemies
by W. R. Burnett

234

W. R. Burnett
Bibliography

W. R. BURNETT: "OUTSIDE EVERYTHING"

By David Laurence Wilson

"Although Allen hadn't published anything for twenty years, he hadn't stopped writing. He did a daily stint, sometimes two, just to keep his hand in. He had worn out the vanity of publishing. So you published, what happened? If it was a novel, it had to be a book club choice or it just laid there, gathering dust on the shelves of various bookstores across the land.

"If you were lucky, the newspaper reviewers pawed it over, and many of them took the opportunity to display their superiority to the author: Why had he written this book? Why hadn't he written another book, like the one before? . . . And so there you were, with months of work—for what?"

—From the unpublished novel, *Cafe Nowhere*, by W. R. Burnett.

I

Pinch me, if I appear to be sleeping, because if you are reading this volume a long-running dream has come true. I want to take notice before the moment passes. As it is it is one of my very best dreams.

The two novels you have here, *The Loop*, and *The Man With a Thousand Enemies,* are the first "new" novels from W. R. Burnett in nearly half a century. These well-populated stories weren't written yesterday, or even during the last four decades. They weren't composed by psychic, invisible hands . . . they have simply been overlooked, set aside, their existence almost unknown and forgotten.

But not forgotten by me. These old, fading manuscripts were on my list.

□ □ □

I was a Southern Californian and I was hooked on words on paper. There was no obvious path for a career freelancer. The culture of the southern coast was built on sand, literally, and on the provenance of good will and shifting relationships, umbrage, collegiality and immersion. You had to be active and you had to be able to talk. One step follows another. You cash a check and then repeat.

At the time life seemed to be one long adventure novel in real time with the names and dialogue of real people, high and low. In those years the greatest virtues . . . were those that opposed one another: ignorance and curiosity, persistence and patience.

□　□　□

In Southern California the film industry rolled across the land like tumbleweeds, over and through the schools, streets and parks. Those within this cult-like profession became our acquaintances, lovers and fantasies. But it wasn't a shock to see a movie actor sitting in a car or a restaurant. I could be cool about that.

In 1971 the novelist and screenwriter Niven Busch (*Duel in the Sun* (1944) and *The Postman Always Rings Twice* (the screenplay, 1946), was a guest lecturer at the University of California's Irvine campus. Busch had broken in with the *New Yorker* by writing about speakeasies and, eventually, producing profiles, which were later repurposed into his first book, *Twenty-One Americans*, published in 1930, one year after W. R. Burnett's *Little Caesar* (Dial, 1929). (Coincidentally the book only featured twenty Americans, the last of the tally presumed to be Busch himself, a conceit that nobody seemed to understand or appreciate at the time.)

Busch trained me to read his handwriting, type fiction, and drive in San Francisco but I was also tutored by Burnett, who in my mind occupied the position of a guru on a hill, bearded or otherwise. There was a great confidence and purity of focus and intent in the rhythm, pacing and the staging of his scenes, his transitions so smooth that his hardly needed a plot. Reading one of his novels was like an upper-division fiction seminar.

Both Busch and Burnett were known as "mavericks." Neither ranked high in the "Literature" section but they were notably present in the aisles of "Fiction," conveniently side-by-side. Busch was three years younger and a few years behind Burnett when he landed in Hollywood. He admired the way Burnett was able to manage both a literary and a Hollywood career. Busch managed this same trick capably, but nobody did it better than Burnett, who was adamantly a writer of prose—while simultaneously posing as a crack screenwriter.

The two writers followed the same trails in Hollywood, the same studios, on occasion, the same actors populated their stories and they worked with a handful of directors who were simpatico: Raoul Walsh, John Huston and John Sturges. Busch delved into executive functions, as assistant and producer. Burnett remained a maverick, only occasionally making an effort to rework another writer's script.

□ □ □

In 1981, on the eve of the publication of *Goodbye, Chicago*, the last novel published during Burnett's lifetime, I found his phone number, wrangled an interview with him and a review for the short-lived magazine *Mystery*. Such presumptions seemed easy in the early nineteen-eighties.

Burnett had a real good answer to the age-old question: "What have you been doing lately?"

We talked about sports, about running. Both of us had run track but he was a sprinter. He recalled an occasion when he raced—and lost— to Jim Thorpe.

During our interview Burnett hinted that he had unpublished novels in his office upstairs, along with his current dog. It was crowded. "I'm always working on a book," he said. "I've got novels stacked upstairs, some of them that I've never even copied. New ones and old ones. I write constantly. I'm not methodical at all, Just the opposite."

I was incredulous that the writing industry could let a new novel, let alone a full shelf of new stories from Burnett pass by without notice, without grabbing it and throwing it in a safe. It was a slap in the face to thirty years of almost unimaginable critical and popular success. Where did Burnett's readers go? Were there no more seats in the cinemas? Was it an unfortunate glitch that could one day be repaired, to not even be published . . .? In any scenario it seemed an injustice to writers and readers alike.

Burnett didn't like to edit, or rewrite, and his vision was failing. Flushed with the skittish confidence of youth (always under—or over— confident) I asked him if he'd like me to help out. I had already served an apprenticeship with Busch. Under the circumstances, it was something to consider. Ask a writer what is more intimate than working on another fellow's novel!

By the time the interview was published I was also able to review *Goodbye, Chicago*. It was: ". . . a pleasant afternoon of reading with a master," I wrote. ". . . There are so many interlocking characters that one is tempted to reach for a scoreboard."

A year later Burnett died. I continued to assist Busch on his novels

Continent's Edge (Simon and Schuster, 1980) and *The Titan Game* (Random House, 1989) until his death in 1991.

That was almost fifty years ago. My first son was named "Niven" after my friend. In recent years, however, it has been Burnett, rather than Busch, who has been the greater presence in my own career. I have published seven essays on Burnett, hailed his worth in at least three languages. I have edited excerpts from his journals and contributed photographs to the record of his accomplishments. And now this . . .

II

At a certain point in life, the to-do lists of goals, chores and responsibilities become a "bucket list"—tasks of a greater scale and urgency, a tapping on the shoulder and whispering that it's now or never, a confluence of wishes and dreams, chance and capricious destiny. It has something to do with "kicking the bucket."

On my bucket list I have travel plans to Iceland, Niagara Falls and the Ausable Chasm in upstate New York. Would Atlantic City be going too far? Like every writer of history I would like to acquire a gently-used, well-oiled time machine . . . before I get too old to enjoy it.

But there has also been a shadow, a pile of books in silhouette, phantom words on aging paper. I wanted to read Burnett's unknown novels. I wanted this volume to be published. This was on my list too. Did those stories still exist? Were they anywhere near as good as his published novels? Read on.

□ □ □

It was years later when the postman rang twice for me, gently, but insistent, the occasion of my second cancer diagnosis.

There was still a chance, however, to set aside the verdict of history, that for whatever reason, these novels by Burnett would not be published. I wanted to contradict fifty years of judgment bearing a casual thumbs-down. Burnett's words have always been a pleasure. I wanted more of them.

Circumstances and opportunities change. After all, the fabulous novel *Little Caesar* was rejected, almost forgotten until it wasn't.

Again, I reached for the phone, and it was time.

□ □ □

Things had changed for Burnett in 1961.

After the Bel Aire fire in 1961 and the loss of his library, correspondence, papers of all kinds—everything—after twenty years of routine and security, the next twenty years would offer financial insecurity and frequent relocations.

The Burnett family moved to the mid-Wilshire district. Despite a lack of new credits the screenwriter Burnett could still plausibly pass as part of the Hollywood community. After all, Mae West—another major shaker of the nineteen thirties—had her own apartment across the street. Then for five years the family lived in Pacific Palisades, followed by five more moves, each for a shorter period and a smaller house as age and assets determined their trajectory. The great writer stayed in the vicinity like an old handbill blown against a fence.

Filmmaking is a collaborative art and there was (ain't there always?) a generational change going on in the Hollywood studios. Burnett was on the wrong side of the divide.

Burnett continued to write—he always continued to write, though now his stories lay unpublished. They "stacked up." And Hollywood did not call.

Despite a cool reception from both publishers and filmmakers, Burnett completed novels, short stories, and plays. He submitted outlines and stories to H. N. Swanson, his agent for film sales, but in many ways it was as if Burnett was simply going through the motions of a professional career. He became a writer whose primary impulse was not economic.

In the end he wrote because he was a writer. Period. Burnett was no longer engaging in employment or an act of commerce. He had lost both hope and interest in the gamesmanship of the system. At home his journals were produced with the same effort, the same observation and insights that he had once reserved for his fiction. He remained truly a maverick.

"I've never used people's suggestions," he told me. "I don't write that way. . . . And I never had any editors, or anything like that. Harper's . . . Knopf . . . They just took the books and set them up and published them."

In his later years Burnett was also interviewed by Ken Mate and Pat McGilligan for a story that appeared in *Film Comment* in 1983, reprinted in *Backstory 1: Interviews with Screenwriters of Hollywood's Golden Age* (University of California Press, 1986).

They asked: "Do you see yourself as an outsider?"

Burnett replied: "Yes, definitely."

"Outside the literary establishment?"

"Outside everything."

It seemed like Burnett was writing to an audience of one—himself. He had simplified the act of writing to its essence—words on paper.

During this new era he had time and opportunity for self-doubt. He noted: "Something is trying to get itself written but I don't know what it is—it gets mixed up with what I'm trying consciously to write."

Burnett believed that his work as a screenwriter had limited and tainted the quality of his prose. It had dulled his instincts.

Too often he was regarded as a genre stylist of crime fiction. Really, in the breadth of his writing he fit no category. In the fifties, when he wrote five novels of the early West, did that make him a "Western" writer?

We talked about Ben Hecht and McKinley Kantor, Simenon and John Fante. Burnett talked philosophy, and his strategies, as a writer and wage earner. Once it had been good luck that poured down upon Burnett.

"I never had any idea of making a career out of writing for movies," he said. "I never took that seriously. I did the best possible work that I could, but it was merely a way to make money so I could write novels. A lot of novels don't make you anything. I was a well-known writer, yet some of my novels didn't make anything outside of the advance on the first go-round. Then we'd make some money on the paperbacks, and if I sold it to the pictures . . . but there's nothing more precarious than novel-writing."

□ □ □

Burnett's last home was a condominium in Marina del Rey. This was where he lived when *Goodbye, Chicago* was published. His fortunes had begun to change and it was not a shabby last stand.

□ □ □

Despite *Goodbye, Chicago*, Burnett the private man had outlasted the career of the fabulous, well-honored and well-paid writer W. R. Burnett. After over twenty years of editorial oblivion the heavy-handed hinges of destiny had begun to turn and in that Indian summer Burnett's enthusiasm and love of craft was returning.

Finally, today, in a reverse, with this publication of these "new" novels, the writer and his work have returned to the conversation while the man himself, regrettably, is missing. Of course there remains a sadness in that fact.

In any event, twenty years of frustration did not lead to the abandonment or destruction of those later manuscripts. Burnett kept them during his moves and they were passed down after his death to his widow, Whitney Burnett, and then to their son James, who bundled them around during his own moves in California, New Mexico and Oregon.

These stories that were left behind are full of excitement and character, wonderful staging and agile plotting. The story of the manuscripts themselves was not. Their survival has been a simple matter of respect, luck, and a family of guardian angels. They were never abandoned. It is simple and at the same time, considering the inherent fragility of paper—extraordinary.

Truly, Burnett had left many gifts behind. Among the complete but unfinished novels in the family's collection was *The Loop* but also *The Pilot's Seat*, a story about events following the sighting of a "flying saucer;" *Men In War*, a Viet Nam novel; *The Cabana Crowd*, *The World Is Square* and *Cafe Nowhere*. None of these other novels fell into the category of Burnett's stereotyped specialty, the crime novel—but they all feature Burnett's large, memorable casts and complex plotting.

Among these unpublished manuscripts was something new for Burnett, a manuscript originally titled *Babylon U. S. A.* This was a collection of short stories that were written around a common theme: the events taking place during one day in the life of a city. This was begun, most likely, in the early nineteen-seventies and Burnett was working on a revision, as *City People*, at the time of his death.

"There's another one of these that I love that everybody else hates," Burnett told me. "It's called *The Limelight*, about a famous Hollywood actor who goes downhill and ends up owning a supper club in the Midwest. He's deserted his family and his son is searching for him."

Like the father in the story, that manuscript has not been found, may never be found.

The Loop is a survivor that fought for its life, a book that simply had to be published. In fact, more than once it had become so close to publication that it was included as a published book in Patrick McGilligan's bibliography for *Backstory 1*.

On April 11, 1982, an interview was published in the *Los Angeles Times* two weeks before Burnett's death, at the age of 82. It claimed Burnett had five novels in progress, all in various stages of completion, also that St. Martins would be publishing *The Loop* in 1983 and that it would be the second piece of a trilogy set in Chicago, begun with *Goodbye Chicago*.

The article concluded, rather macabrely: "'My God, I have 60 screen credits,' (Burnett) says disbelievingly, as if he can't figure out for himself how he's been around so long."

□　□　□

Despite the premature announcements, when *The Loop* did not appear it seemed that it was truly the end of Burnett's career. Those last manuscripts could have easily been lost, misplaced . . . destroyed. Stuff happens. Remember the fire that took everything.

This *Stark House* volume represents the first publication of an "Unknown Burnett." The "new" novels in this collection are finally being published nearly forty-five years after the author's death, a quiet interval that has lasted longer than Burnett's most productive (and published) period between 1930 and 1963.

Today, a half century later the easy-going, loquacious Irish Burnett gives us another plot twist: the long-awaited publication of *The Loop*. It remains the gem among these unpublished stories. It is out of fashion in the very best sense and it is honest enough to read as an accurate enactment of an age. It stands beside Burnett's greatest work as another variant of the hard-boiled, noir, or crime novels that will forever define him as a major American writer. It offers a new, fresh angle that will not disappoint either new or old readers of his work.

This volume also includes *The Man With a Thousand Enemies*, which reads rather like a movie treatment. This manuscript's survival and discovery is even more of a surprising event than the appearance of *The Loop*. This slimmer manuscript was found in the estate of Burnett's agent, of H. N. Swanson, after Swanson's death in 1991. It was purchased by *Royal Books*, of Baltimore, Maryland, where this manuscript also sat in obscurity during the past three and a half decades. Burnett himself did not have a copy of this one, which is episodic and character-based, including a colorful "dame," a clever, sassy gold-digger who would have fit Joan Blondell just right in a 1933 Warner Brothers' production. It was probably intended specifically for a film sale.

This is a belated return to worldwide readers of one of this century's finest American authors, a grand moment, and no better moment for a master of ceremonies to thank the ushers and step off stage. The pages of Burnett's last great crime novel are already rustling under your fingertips.

—Portland, Oregon
April, 2025

David Laurence Wilson has written for many magazines and newspapers and has written about crime and noir fiction for nearly 50 years, including introductions for Stark House editions of W. R. Burnett, A. S. Fleischman, Gil Brewer, Arnold Hano, Day Keene, Wade Miller, William R. Cox and Harry Whittington. He has also been preparing a history of American stuntmen and daredevils. He lives in Portland, Oregon.

The Loop
....
W. R. BURNETT

CHICAGO
1928

There is nothing in this world as empty and dismal and deserted-looking as a Chicago L station platform at around three in the morning. As Dooley crossed to the down-stairway he was accompanied only by his own lonely footfalls. The lighting was both dim and bleak. No wonder there was constant mugging late at night. The whole setup was an invitation. But Dooley was not worried about mugging. It was done mostly by scared young punks, or junkies trying to get enough dough for a fix. Dooley was a pro. They were all amateurs. It would be like a bush league pitcher throwing at Babe Ruth.

Dooley descended into The Loop which was as deserted as if nobody lived there. Empty boulevards stretched off to further emptiness—the street lights glowing in isolated loneliness; the big buildings towering over all like frozen colossi.

Hamm's hotel was in a little side street, hardly more than an alley, but Dooley found it without trouble, and following Hamm's instructions he ignored the guy nodding behind the desk and climbed to the second floor, where he found number 28 and tapped three times. He got no response. He waited. Then after a moment he listened at the door. There was nothing but a throb of silence, the pulsations of an empty place. He cautiously tried the door. It was unlocked. He opened it slowly—then gave a start. Hamm was laying on his back in the middle of the room, with blood all over his shirt, obviously dead. Dooley noted an open window beyond, that gave onto a fire-escape, then he closed the door and went back down the stairs.

The clerk seemed to be sleeping now, with his head hanging forward. Dooley went out, taking his time about it—out into the empty streets where not even a cat was prowling, the garbage and trash cans lined up for collection. He was absolutely baffled.

He came out into a main boulevard and noted a lone taxi parked far down the street. So it cost him five or six dollars—he didn't want that bumping swaying ride on the elevated again. Somewhere a big clock banged four a.m. The whole city seemed dead.

The taxi-driver looked at Dooley warily as he approached. Dooley was not reassuring to look at. He was above average height and very heavy about the chest and shoulders, with long arms to which were attached big, powerful, hairy hands. His brow was low and heavy, and opaque-looking dark eyes glanced out from under thick black eyebrows, with a look that some considered hardly human. Among his confreres his code name was Gorilla. But nobody had ever called him that to his face. Nor was his name Dooley. A former cellmate had hung it on him many years ago. The cellmate insisted he looked like an Irish ditchdigger he'd known as a boy—Dooley—and the Gorilla had been Dooley ever since. Believe it or not his born name was Arthur Robert Mundhenk. He was called Dooley Mundhenk now—and even signed his name that way, when he wasn't signing it some other way as an alias.

Dooley got into the cab and gave the address—a small North Side hotel, miles from The Loop. They rode for a while in silence through the deserted Chicago streets. Finally the taxi-driver asked: "You know Joey Singer?"

"Who?" asked Dooley grudgingly. He had other things on his mind, very serious, puzzling things.

"He lives at that Northland hotel. Former hackie."

"Never heard of him," said Dooley, as much to say, shut up.

The taxi-driver got the message, and continued the trip in silence. But it was lonesome at night on this beat, lonesome and dangerous, and he liked to talk, to ease the loneliness and edge the interminable hours along. He hadn't liked the look of Dooley, now he liked the look even less: surly bastard!

The driver finally couldn't keep still. "Some town," he said. "Christ, I think I'll go home to Elkhart. You know what the gag is now? Young punks drive along the street in broad daylight. They see a woman or a girl in a fur coat. They knock her down—grab the coat and beat it. Right on the street in broad day. Christamighty, what are we coming to?"

Dooley said nothing.

The driver said: "I've been stuck up twice in the last month. Both times, young punks with knives."

"I'm not going to stick you up," said Dooley. "You'll probably stick *me* up with that hot meter you got."

The driver leaned against the wheel to laugh.

"I guess we're all on the take," he said.

"Yeah," said Dooley.

And to the driver's surprise, the surly tough-looking monkey gave him a pretty good tip that would make up some for his long trip back, with no fare—nobody out at this hour.

Dooley made himself a pot of coffee and sipped a cup, staring out the window into the empty street below. This didn't make sense, somebody

killing Hamm. It didn't make any sense at all. One week out of stir—
and pow! Couldn't have anything to do with stir or he'd have been
killed there—even on the Honor Farm (called the Play House by the
cons), where he'd spent the last six months of his armed robbery
sentence . . . being "rehabilitated." It just had to have something to do
with the job, but what . . .? It seemed so unlikely. After the job you
might have trouble, or during the job. But before it had even got started
. . .? No damn way. Could Hamm have merely been robbed, and killed
when he resisted? Hamm must have had some money stashed for
coming out. But Hamm was such a wily old bird. No—it didn't make
sense.

Dooley went to bed, with his clothes on, and lay trying to think it out.
It was a jolt of course to kiss fifty thousand dollars or so goodbye—
Hamm had promised he'd net at least that much. But the real jolt was
the death of Hamm—and the mystery about it.

Dooley had very little worry about being involved. It's true he visited
Hamm once at the Honor Farm—but he could be connected with
Hamm in no other way. And of course Hamm had not named him to
the clerk, who had seemed at least half asleep anyway. All the same—
that clerk would bear looking into. Dooley snapped his fingers and
bounded off the bed. Mahaffy! Skip! A young sharpie, a police informer,
who turned the fringe guys in and worked with the big ones. One
trouble . . . a junkie. And who trusts a junkie? But Skip hadn't blown
the whistle on anybody big yet.

Dooley called Willie's exchange, identified himself, and got several
numbers for Skip. It was usually like trying to find a flea—but Dooley,
who was using the pay-phone in the deserted lobby of his hotel, got
him at once. Skip could be insolent, insulting, wheedling or even kind,
but with the Gorilla he was respectful. Dooley gave him the tale—and
whistled. "I've got two bills for you," said Dooley, "and get right on it.
Anything you can find out—with the clerk or at the station."

"Among my law-and-order friends?" said Skip, giggling. Skip could
go anyplace. He looked like a college youth. Old ladies liked him. He
was something, thought Dooley.

Feeling relieved, Dooley returned to his room and climbed into bed.
Lighting a cigarette, he lay back, stared at the ceiling and thought. No
other way: Hamm's death had to be connected with the job. It was big,
it was sensational, it was the Big Money. But . . . what . . .?

He'd had one cautious letter from Hamm—from the Honor Farm,
nothing: just come and visit me on a stated Sunday. Dooley was free in
the State, no warrants, not wanted for anything he knew of—in other
States it wasn't so cozy, but he never worried about that. So he went to

the Honor Farm that Sunday and talked to Hamm in a huge ramshackle room, like a small airplane hangar, where dozens of other visitors, men, women and children, were talking to other inmates. Hamm, heavy-set and cheerful-looking as usual, tanned and well-fed, talked very very cautiously. But it was so big he'd guaranteed Dooley fifty thousand dollars minimum, for his part, which usually consisted of supervision and handling the others. Dooley was utterly ruthless. Hamm was not—he could be taken advantage of, and was inept at handling the toughies he often had to deal with. Hamm was known as a Brain, but a fool otherwise, if you can figure that out. (In fact his "closest friend" had turned states on him, putting him behind bars. "I trusted him," Hamm had said sadly.)

And now it occurred to Dooley suddenly that Hamm had maybe trusted somebody else. Things began to clear. Had Hamm talked to others? Had he given them—or maybe one individual—the whole plan, the whole layout? And then had he been erased, no longer necessary to the project? If Hamm hadn't merely been killed for his money, this was the only thing that really made any actual sense—

Dooley was so relieved, he turned over and fell asleep.

He met Skip in a North Side bowling alley that was crowded with team bowlers and their families; it was one shop or store against another and much rah-rah and yelling and carrying on. There was a row of double benches at the far end of the place, away from the uproar. Skip and Dooley sat with their backs to each other and talked prison style—a straight john wouldn't even know they were conversing.

"With the clerk— nothing," said Skip. "He don't hear good and I'm not even sure he's all there. He didn't give the law much of anything, except a guy he hardly noticed came in and went out. He's not smart enough to be mixed up in anything. Who would trust him for big? Right? But how about this: the laws found over twelve hundred dollars stashed around Hamm's room . . ."

That cinched it. Long silence. Then Skip asked: "You want to hit one for the dagos? They are looking for an outside man; big-money."

"I don't hit. Let 'em do their own dirty work."

Skip snickered uncontrollably for a moment. He was a tall thin rather baby-faced young blond guy who looked as if he should be at the prom, even to his dark-blue suit, white shirt and dark tie. He'd got hooked young and fallen among thieves, as he occasionally explained to an adoring whore. He could have made a fine living just as a pimp, but that was too uncomplicated for Skip. He liked to be on the run—foiling pursuit.

After a moment Dooley spoke again: "It's big, very big. If you hear of a very big one . . . you know. And another thing. Who did Hamm talk to? Did he talk to anybody since he's been out? Anybody big—possible?"

"I gotta go slow on this, you know, Dooley," said Skip. "The cemetery is cold, they tell me."

"Don't go too slow," said Dooley, then he got up and left.

Skip, noting the chill in Dooley's voice, got the message. Don't monkey with this character. It was well known it was not healthy.

Myrta met him at the door with the usual smile. She was a rather large woman with natural red hair and something sort of soft and nice about her that attracted men, though she was no beauty. Dooley had known her for over six months and the relationship was mutually convenient—and hardly much of anything else. Women did not think much of Dooley—"Who's that ugly jerk?"—and Myrta, deserted by her husband and hampered by two small kids, a boy and a girl, had her problems.

They'd met in a North Side bar, or speak. A neighbor was baby-sitting for Myrta and she was out looking for "fun." Dooley was merely having a quiet and lonely drink. Two drunks started to manhandle Myrta and make fun of her, calling her "Mama" (both were considerably younger) and also making obscene suggestions of what they would like to do to her. The bartender kept saying, "Please, fellows." Dooley minded his drink. But the drunks ignored the bartender and tried to forcibly remove Myrta from the bar. Dooley glanced at her. She looked hopelessly terrified. Then he noted the smirk on one guy's face. A pretty boy type. Punk!

"If she wants to go with you, she'll go," said Dooley. "If she don't, she can stay here with me and have a drink."

"Please, fellows . . ." begged the bartender.

Technically he was carrying on an illegal operation. He was selling beer, wine and something that passed for whiskey. The Chicago cops gave him no trouble—in fact the best-man often dropped into the back for a free beer. But beefs were out. Hoodlums were overrunning the town at night and the CPD had declared war on them—and on hangouts where they were tolerated. "Please, fellows . . ." pled the bartender.

The two guys had Myrta by the elbows now, moving her toward the door. "I want to stay with him," cried Myrta.

Dooley got up and went over to them. "OK, ma'am. Come on."

One of the guys swung at Dooley, who blocked the punch by raising his arm. The guy winced at the contact—but he tried it again. Dooley blocked it as before but with something added and the guy howled and grabbed his arm in pain; but at the same time the other guy hit Dooley a glancing blow, and Dooley turned and hit him with a vicious punch in the belly, and the guy fell and rolled around, howling. Dooley then calmly knocked his first assaulter down with a short punch to the chin.

"Please, mister . . ." pled the bartender, his face white.

Now Dooley took Myrta by the elbow. "Let's get out of here," he said. Myrta stared down in horrified surprise at the two guys writhing on the floor—then at Dooley. What did he remind her of? For a moment she was more scared of Dooley than the damned young fools on the floor. God, she'd been warned often enough to stay out of Chicago speaks when she was alone. Maybe this would cure her . . . the next moment she found herself outside in the cool, deep Chicago air and Dooley was saying: "They might go get a gun and come back. I saw that happen once. And I don't want to kill anybody."

But she found she had nothing to fear from Dooley. He was a perfectly normal man—according to Myrta's lights, and in fact you might even say, the answer to her prayers. No more lonely prowling around in bars and movie theaters and dance halls. They slept together two or three nights a week—it was almost like being married to a traveling salesman—and they went out to eat and to movie theaters and speaks, and as Myrta explained to herself, lived a "normal" life.

She often wondered that Dooley did for a living, but he always seemed to have money, never talked about himself, and she was not of a very curious nature anyway. And why look a gift horse in the mouth? But from observation she thought he must be an expert workman of some kind. He could fix anything: lights, plumbing—one night he fixed her electric iron. It was a wonderful relief for Myrta, who couldn't fix anything, to have a man like that occasionally around the apartment. He even fixed Bobby's toy fire engine. And Bobby asked: "Is he our pop now?"

The other pop never fixed their toys or even paid any attention to them. He always had "headaches," as Mommie explained, and when he did he sang and laughed and acted silly or snored on the sofa or yelled at Mommie. He was a real weird pop. Bobby and his sister Shirley often talked about it. They were 7 and 8, but growing up fast.

Dooley had no feelings about kids one way or the other; he neither liked or disliked them. One night he said to Myrta, surprising her: "The trouble with kids is, they grow up to be bastards like us." Myrta never forgot that remark and from time to time she'd look at Bobby and Shirley with different eyes. What would they be like? The sum total of their parents, the father an alcoholic, the mother abnormally susceptible to the opposite sex . . .? Could it possibly be? Dooley often unsettled her with throwaway comments, but that comment had unsettled her most—

Yes, Myrta met Dooley at the apartment door with the usual smile; they pawed each other briefly and said, "Hi"—then Dooley asked: "Why haven't you got your coat on? It's cool out."

"We can't go," said Myrta. "Millie fell down the backstairs and sprained her ankle. It's all swole up."

"Nobody else around here . . .?"

Myrta shook her head. But Dooley had been looking forward to dinner out—he had an aversion to Myrta's canned food—and he'd been looking forward to a movie. He liked movies. For a couple of hours he could forget everything, watching the silly characters on the screen, yak, yak, yaking.

Especially the shoot-em-up westerns—action, action.

So to Myrta's surprise they wound up in a Chinese restaurant with the children—who had a wonderful time, especially with the fortune cookies—and then later they went to a movie and saw a cowboy and Indian picture that delighted Dooley and the kids—and bored Myrta almost to collapse . . . in fact she kept falling asleep.

That night when she was putting the kids to bed, Bobby said: "We like our new pop." Shirley concurred.

The Polack lay back in his big padded chair, staring steadily at Shamus, who was telling him the tale. Shamus was Selby Reed, a former policeman, who's been busted for being too openly on the take when he was a member of the vice squad; out of a job, he'd contracted the drug habit, done time, straightened himself out, and was now an underworld shadow. He followed people for pay. It was not an activity that had a tendency to prolong life. But Shamus was deeply experienced and wary. And he worked for cash only, on the line—in advance. "If I'm going to get killed for it, I want the money in my pocket," he explained. And in this case he had a very good chance of getting killed or at least maimed: it was not healthy to follow the Gorilla.

"Give me that again," said the Polack, lighting a cigar and putting his feet up.

Shamus laughed and then said: "Since I've been watching him he's done absolutely nothing except go out for something to eat or for a drink. Except for last night he took his woman and her two kids to Wung's on the North Side for dinner and then to a movie— a western, ridemcowboyhellforleather—it was terrible. I ought to get extra pay."

"You know the woman?"

Shamus wagged his head. "She's just a square. Cashier in a cheap little eating-joint. Just his lay, that's all."

The Polack considered for a long time, then he took out his wallet and handed Shamus a bill. "There's your extra pay."

"That's it?"

"That's it."

"Yeah. I'd say he was marking time—or rather killing time. Doing nothing."

"I'll call you if I need you."

Shamus gestured and went out. The Polack turned to the silent man leaning against the wall, smoking a cigarette. "What do you think, Goggles?"

"I think you worry too much. Dooley's always got something on the fire. If it's not this, it's that."

The Polack nodded to himself, confirmed.

When Dooley got back to his hotel the man at the desk motioned for him to come over and gave him a number to call. It was eight o'clock in the morning, so Dooley caught Skip in bed, and not alone, as he heard giggling.

"I'm earning my money," said Skip. "You're being tailed."

"Who?"

"Too dark. Couldn't see him. But he's a real shifty one."

"Shamus?"

"Or one like him."

Dooley thought for a moment, then he said: "I'll run up to Milwaukee for a couple of days. Maybe they are waiting for me to make a move. If they are, me going to Milwaukee ought to throw them off—they'll think I'm casing."

"Yeah," said Skip. "Why else would anybody go to Milwaukee?"

"Yeah," said Dooley, not laughing, he never seemed to laugh or even smile. "Think you can get anything out of The Shamus, if it's him?"

"Maybe. He likes broads and he doesn't drink too good."

"OK. You may be in for a bigger cut than you think. Just keep your nose clean."

Skip giggled, then Dooley heard him urge: "Say hello to one of my best friends."

"Hello, one of your best friends," said a girlish, not exactly sober voice.

Dooley hung up. Skip and his whores. It was said Skip came from a good family in Southern Illinois. Some good family, thought Dooley.

Shamus kept eyeing the brunette and Skip kept eyeing him. Beyond them a jazz band played in the smoky supper room while the girls danced and shrieked out a song. "Some broad," said Shamus.

"I'd like to do you a favor," said Skip. "But she's got a dago hood on the string and he's a real bad one. Dope running for the Mob. Money falling out of his ears."

"They don't scare me," said Shamus. "They just make the newspapers."

"I'll see what I can do."

He would pick that broad, thought Skip: Queer as a three-dollar bill and having a thing with the club owner's wife—money, furs—you name it. It was a Mob protected club and coining money.

They went out and walked around in the cool night air, then down the street for a couple of good Denver sandwiches at Chiggi's. Over the second cup of coffee Skip said: "Picking a broad like that, you must have been doing some fancy shadowing."

Shamus showed a roll under the table.

"Whoeeee," said Skip. "Big stuff, eh?"

"Big, boy, big."

But otherwise he wouldn't crack, except to say the shadow had been called off—but only temporarily, he hoped. And Skip kept wondering about what to do about the brunette charmer, Dixie.

On the way back from Milwaukee on the inter-urban Dooley had a sudden flash of memory. Doc! During their conversation at the Honor Farm Hamm had mentioned something about a guy in Chicago named Doc . . . a real one, a right one: a hundred per cent, out of the rackets now but . . . something like that. He hadn't paid much attention to the time as he had expected to talk everything over seriously in Chicago. Doc. Maybe he knew something.

It took nearly all of one day for Dooley to locate Skip, the flea; but he finally ran him down (he had five numbers to call now). They met just as night was falling over Lake Michigan and the street and house lights were just coming on. Not too far north of them was the Edgewater Beach hotel, looking enormous and brilliantly alight in the descending dusk of an early fall evening. They stood leaning on a barrier, looking off at the lake. Skip gave Dooley a full account of his dealings with Shamus. "It was a big one and it's been called off, temporarily," Skip explained, "and I think he was tailing you. But he won't crack otherwise."

"Keep trying," said Dooley, then he gave Skip some more money. "This is getting expensive. Don't stiff me, don't soldier."

"Are you kidding? I'm too young to die," said Skip; then Dooley brought up the matter of Doc and gave Skip all he knew about him. "He was big once, I'm sure. He's out now. But he's in the area some place. Ring a bell?"

"No," said Skip, reflectively. "Doc? Doc? Maybe I can find out."

Finally Skip gestured and walked away toward the boulevard to pick up a cab. Dooley stood staring at the lake. It looked cold and strange with the wavering lights playing across its gray waste of waters.

Dooley had got back a day ahead of schedule. It was a Monday. Myrta's restaurant was dark on Mondays and she was usually home on that day with the kids to save the expense of a day school. She was off on Thursdays, too, but she generally saved that day for herself, shopping and whatever other errands had to be taken care of, like the paying of small bills. Myrta found the minutiae of life excessively boring and often wished she'd never met that big drunk, Charley, with his false charm and geniality, and worst of all married him and encumbered herself with two children. Charley had been no help at all. He passed from job to job, drinking himself out of one after another, and taking practically no responsibility at home: she raised the children, she looked after the house, she worked. Was this what life was all about? At first when Charley deserted them she'd almost gone to pieces. What in God's name would she do? But it had all worked out much better than she'd expected—with a better job, more pay—and now Dooley.

Well, it was a Monday so Dooley dropped over to see Myrta. Nobody answered the bell for a long time—though Dooley could hear the kids tearing around inside. Finally Myrta opened the door. She looked flustered. Just beyond her stood a tall young guy, hat in hand, forcing a smile.

Dooley hesitated but Myrta gestured him in. Ignoring the adults and their mysterious problems, the kids tore through the apartment, chasing each other and yelling.

The young guy studied Dooley rather uneasily. Couldn't make him out. He was well enough dressed, in respectable conventional clothes, his attitude was mild, but there was something vaguely brutish about him that disturbed the young guy's equanimity.

"This is Ken, a friend of Charley's," said Myrta.

Dooley nodded. "Hi."

"Hi," said Ken. "I was just leaving."

"Don't go on my account," said Dooley.

But Ken didn't know how to take that remark. There was no smile accompanying it, nothing. "I've got a few calls to make. Just dropped in to say hello to . . . yes, a few calls to make. Insurance, you know."

He finally managed an exit, bowing rather awkwardly to Myrta. Dooley sat down and lit cigarette. The kids swarmed in, yelling. "Hi, pop," said Bobby.

Dooley looked at the kid in mild surprise, then gestured negligently.

"He's just one of Charley's friends," said Myrta. "I haven't seen him in years."

"All right," said Dooley.

"Fix you a drink? Mr. Antonelli sold me some good stuff. Canadian whiskey. The real thing."

"Sure, fine," said Dooley, not bothering to explain to Myrta that the Mob was bottling "Canadian whiskey" at half a dozen distilleries spotted around the North Side. Expensive bootleggers were selling it to rich clients as "right off the boat." It wasn't bad, at that. As for the raw stuff, half the Italian families in Little Italy were making mash for the Mobs, in the bathtubs, it was said. As an old pro Dooley had contempt for this trade. Selling booze was not his idea of living. Several guys he'd known in the old days had got into it—as muscle. One with the Italians; one with the Poles; and one with the Irish. All were pushing up daisies now. All had made the Chicago papers. Big deal— the true pro remained anonymous, unknown, unheard of—at least as far as possible.

Dooley often studied Myrta when she wasn't looking. What she didn't know would fill a Carnegie Library. She'd been a square john all her life, knew nothing else; she lived, actually, in a kind of fairy-tale land. Dooley's relations with such people were strictly limited. He usually wound up with a girl from the inside, or a whore; if anything, they knew too much. Myrta was in many ways a pleasant experience for him, and here she was, square that she was, very worried because he'd come unexpectedly and caught her with a very good-looking young guy. Charley's friend? Hell, the guy obviously didn't even know her name, or couldn't remember it—which didn't point to long acquaintance.

She handed him his drink and sat beside him on the couch.

"How about Chinese food again with the kids?" asked Dooley, trying to say something that would allay her fears. After all, she'd seen him beat two guys up pretty good.

"Oh, fine, said Myrta. "Kids, kids . . ."

They came running.

"And a movie," said Dooley.

The kids danced and yelled and Shirley kissed Dooley on the cheek. He almost smiled.

Now the kids disappeared into a back bedroom and Myrta said: "I was lying." Dooley just looked at her. "I met that guy in the supermarket," she went on. "I had the kids with me. He carried all my packages home for me. I think he was on the make. That's all there was."

"Look, Myrta," said Dooley, "you don't have to explain anything to me. I don't own you."

Myrta studied his face, then said nothing more. She wasn't sure whether she liked this or not. She remembered back to the time when Charley was so jealous it was embarrassing. He had even called her his Red-Haired Queen—though toward the end he'd been referring to her as "that fat redheaded bum."

Dooley was a strange one. Myrta just didn't understand him at all.

It was about midnight when Dooley turned up at Chez Roma. He had plans in regard to Shamus who was the best there was, and Dooley knew that if things turned out a certain way, no cinch by any means, he could use him. Dooley dealt only with the best when at all possible— like Hamm. He wouldn't listen to even a very big proposition from some jumpy crum he didn't trust. No matter how big, what good was it if bungled? And more big jobs were bungled than not—by guys who really didn't know what they were doing.

Chez Roma was a safe place for Dooley, who didn't appear very much in public where others of his kind gathered. It was a Mob owned, Mob protected joint and the pros avoided it. It was not their type of place, and the diamond-studded hoods were not their kind. Most of the hoods avoided it, too, except on special occasions. It was strictly a place for rich city suckers and out-of-towners, like those who attend conventions. It was run tough. No trouble. No beefs. Any outsider was safe there.

Dooley had a drink at the crowded bar. Booze was sold openly, the CPD ignoring the operation. Once it had been raided by the Feds who smashed up over fifty thousand dollars' worth of property. But the Mob redecorated and reopened almost immediately—and they hadn't been raided since. It was a well-known fact the CPD and the Feds did not exactly see eye to eye . . . so maybe somebody in City Hall had been able to put in a fix with somebody in Washington. Nobody really knew— or cared. So Chez Roma roared on.

The stage show was on. A guy in top hat, white tie, and tails was doing a wild dance, backed by six glittering, half-naked girls, who were shrieking out a song. The brunette Skip had told him about, Dixie, was on the end away from the bar. She was a picture broad, thought Dooley. She even frightened him slightly. Too delicate to handle; she might break. Slimmer than the others, less exuberant, rather disdainful, as she kicked up her long, slim legs, with the other girls grinning in piano keyboard smiles. Dooley had never had a girl like that. He wasn't sure he even wanted one like that—but he was sure Shamus did. Skip had managed to get him into conversation with her twice, but there were lynx-eyes about and it wasn't easy.

Finally the show was over. Then Skip and Shamus ran into Dooley by "accident" at the bar. The Shamus studied Dooley's gorilla-face narrowly. Did the brute know Shamus had tailed him. He didn't miss much. But Dooley merely nodded, and gestured carelessly, and Shamus heaved a sigh of relief.

They had drinks together and talked about nothing, while a fill-in piano player played and nobody listened. Later Skip and Dooley met in the men's room, where they stood side by side in the stalls and talked prison style.

"It don't make much difference whether he lays this broad or not," said Skip. "He's hooked. It's all he thinks about. And he loves me like a brother. He'll talk eventually."

"Good!" said Dooley.

"Now about Doc. There's only one Doc I can get anything on. Doc Pace."

"Yeah . . ." said Dooley, interested at once. Doc was a very big one who had disappeared from the scene after allegedly knocking over an armored car for God knows how much loot. The case was still pending— nobody had even been arrested. It was a slick knockover; the kind only the best pros could manage—and get away with.

"But he's been straight for two years or more," said Skip. "He's out. Runs a big used car place—over on the West Side some place. I'll get the location for you."

Dooley merely grunted.

"I'm invaluable, you know, Dooley," said Skip.

Dooley grunted again, and later handed him some more money. If this turned out to be as big as he hoped, Dooley would have to maybe raise a loan for front money. He could make it two ways: with a loan shark executive he'd known in stir or with a bail bond guy, who had the biggest outfit in Chi. Dooley was good for big money with them. He had the right kind of record.

They were back at the bar. Shamus, striking out for the evening, had gone home—or out on the tail. Dooley thought things over for a while, then he said: "If this is as big as I think, do you want in all the way?"

Skip smiled broadly. "Yes, sir. All the way."

They shook hands on it.

Later that might homicide detective, Dave Santorelli, just "happened to run into" Skip at an open-fronted diner not too far from Chez Roma. It was a cool, dampish fall night, with heavy moisture in the air that appeared as small crystal globules in the beams from the lights. It was so late the big street-sweepers were rumbling past. But Skip was in his element: night and the city. He was a prowler at heart, a predatory prowler. He had no more use for daylight than an owl.

Dave had a cup of coffee and a chili-dog with Skip.

"What's this with you and Dooley?" asked Dave, mildly.

"You and your two-bit finks," said Skip.

"It's murder one."

"Don't kid me," said Skip. "Dooley knows nothing."

"How do you know?"

"I asked him."

"Why?"

"None of your business," said Skip.

"George Hamm's the kind of guy he would know."

"Sure, he knew him. That's why I asked him. He don't know and he don't care."

Dave nodded to himself. Probably true. Nor did Dave care. The more Hamms that get knocked off the better. Just like the hoods. Three hundred and fifty of them had got knocked off last year and nobody was crying. But it was routine, on the books; homicide. You had to at least ask around. There were more important matters, like the rapes and muggings where the communities began to yell and make trouble for the police. The sharpshooters were actually doing the police a favor—and as long as they kept it among themselves . . .!

"This is not my department," said Dave, trying to salvage something, "but it's an uproar at the station. Know anything about the guys knocking girls down and grabbing the fur coats? Right on Michigan Boulevard the other afternoon."

"That's trouble," said Skip, complying with alacrity; if he could help the police in anything like this he always did. "It's not organized. It's just a bunch of young guys grabbing. Don't take that angle. Try the fences."

"Anybody in particular?"

"Try South Side Mo."

Dave patted him gently, then said, "I'll pop for another chili-dog."

"It's worth more than that," said Skip, giggling.

"You have my gratitude," said Dave, laughing.

No police vouchers for Skip. When it was something big, they slipped him cash. But this was on the house, though it might turn out to be mighty "big" for South Side Mo. But Skip was not going to cry about that. Once South Side Mo had stiffed him with a cheap fur coat—for his girl. A week later the hair began to fall out and the girl openly called Skip a lousy cheapskate. Let South Side Mo look to himself . . . if he happened at the moment to be dealing in street-clouted fur coats, which he no doubt was—that was just too bad.

Anyway, Skip liked to keep a few favors ahead of the laws, just in case he got into a jam of some kind, like the time he'd almost killed a pusher who had sold him a big load of bad stuff. The police never cried over pushers anyway and Skip was not even tried . . . as a matter of fact, technically, he was not even booked.

"You want some dough?" asked Dave.

"No," said Skip. "It's on the house."

Now they sat eating their second chili-dogs in silence as the huge street-sweepers droned distantly on the side streets. The empty boulevard shone like a river of black glass, sharply reflecting the lights. Electric signs winked to emptiness. Occasionally a nighthawk taxi ripped past, and Skip felt completely at ease.

Dooley went to the West Side on a city two-decker bus, riding on the open top in the mild sunshine of a pleasant fall day. You could hardly miss the "Alvin Pace—Used Cars: We Deal Fairly" sign—as it must have been fifty feet across and stretched between two telegraph poles and billowed gently in the occasional breeze. Below it was what looked like a city block full of heaps, in various states of decrepitude. Dooley walked across the lot, in between cars, to a small cluster of one-story offices in the middle of it. A few people were looking at cars and of course, kicking tires. No salesmen were in sight—so it didn't appear to be a quick-hustle joint.

As Dooley approached, a husky tough-looking young guy, maybe thirty, came out of the largest of the small offices. His hair was cut very short and he was wearing what looked like a Marine fatigue shirt. He regarded Dooley coldly.

"Looking for somebody?" he asked.

"Mr. Pace," said Dooley.

"That's me."

Dooley studied him, noting the steady unfriendly grey eyes and the thrust-out jaw. This boy was a toughie, no doubt about it.

"It must be your father I'm looking for."

"I generally take care of business," said the guy, stubbornly.

"This is a personal matter."

Dooley wasn't annoyed. The guy didn't know him from Adam and was rightfully cautious.

"Just tell Doc I'd like to talk to him for a minute or two. Tell him it's Dooley."

The young guy studied Dooley briefly, then crossed back to the office and disappeared. In a moment he reappeared and gestured for Dooley to come on.

It was very dim in the outer office except for a couple of desk-lights where two girls were working at typewriters. Dooley was gestured into a small private office at the rear, hardly large enough for three people. Doc, an older heavier version of his son, was sitting behind the desk. The son stood beside him, warily, as if to guard him.

"Shut the door," said Doc, and when Dooley had complied, Doc said: "It's about Hamm, isn't it? Sit down."

Dooley sat and lit a cigarette. The atmosphere was not exactly unfriendly, but it was bleak. These were obviously two guys it was not wise to monkey with unless you knew exactly what you were doing.

Dooley nodded, then: "Do you know me?"

"I know of you," said Doc. "And Hamm mentioned your name."

"And did he talk to you about the job?"

"Only vaguely," said Doc. "You?"

"Vaguely. But it's my thought he talked to somebody and told them too much."

The Paces exchanged a long look. Then Doc said, "That never occurred to us. We just figured it was a personal matter of some kind, or robbery. I liked George Hamm—hadn't seen him for years. So we went down to the morgue to claim the body—Chuck and I—(Chuck nodded coldly)—in case nobody turned up to claim it. I didn't want George buried in no potter's field. But an old woman claimed the body. His mother, I think."

Dooley nodded. The more he saw of the Paces the better he liked them.

"Did he mention anybody else but me?" asked Dooley.

"Not by name. He just said he had backing, a guy with a lot of money."

Dooley thought this over for a moment, then he said: "I think that's the answer. That guy was going to put up all the front money—apparently Hamm only had about a thousand or so—and on the strength of that Hamm must have given him the whole layout. So the guy didn't need Hamm any longer—why give him front money? So he had a pro kill him. In and out the window—and nobody saw a thing."

Dooley noted that Doc's heavy, rugged face had turned red. "I'd like to get my hands on that moneyman."

"It's possible," said Dooley. "Are you in?"

"I'll kill him myself," said Chuck.

"I don't mean that," Dooly said snidely. "No killing. If I finally figure out who the man is I'll have him watched around the clock and if they are working on the deal we'll be able to figure out what it is—or at least where."

Both Doc and Chuck began to smile.

"And if we can't figure out what the job is, we'll let them pull it and then hijack them."

Both Paces were laughing now. They loved the Gorilla. What a shifty bastard!

"I never heard of one like this," said Doc. "And I've pulled some dandies. The last one was such a doozy I bought this lot, that makes money for me—and I've never heard a rumble."

The Paces took Dooley to dinner at a German rathskeller where they had good beer, and guys in short leather pants danced and sang with buxom girls in peasant costumes. And the band played umpah, umpah.

"It's kind of lonesome for us," Doc explained. "We've got no women folks. My wife's dead—and Chuck's divorced. So we like this place— it's homey—and one of them cute girls is a friend of Chuck's. Right, Chuck?"

Chuck grinned, as if ashamed of himself, and his father laughed. "Chuck's always been kinda bashful with girls, but Ingeborg's got him straightened out now. Right, son? She's the one with the blonde pigtails."

Dooley looked. Ingeborg was quite a buxom broad. She could really straighten you out, that was for sure.

"Yeah," said Dooley, enjoying his beer and the heavy but delicious German food.

As they said goodnight, Doc spoke. "We're in. Whatever you say, Dooley. Big or small."

"It's got to be very big," said Dooley.

On his way back on the top of the bus, moving through the night streets of Chicago, Dooley reflected: "Well, we don't have to worry about muscle."

Around midnight the night clerk hammered on his door and told Dooley there was a call for him on the payphone. It was Skip who was giggling and chortling.

"I may deliver tonight," said Skip. "Anyway, there's a possibility. Shamus is having supper with Dixie and falling all over himself— from soup to nuts and what they call champagne in Chicago. Oh, it's funny as hell. This guy was once on the vice squad—and he's acting like a convention Hoosier. Broads, man. You can't beat 'em. He's not getting in the hay, if that's what you think. Not a chance. But I don't think he cares. He's got hopes, hasn't he?"

"How did you do it?"

"I find out things. Found out something about our friend Dixie. So she's kindly doing me a favor. It's not a big thing. But it might hurt her with Madam Chez Roma. She's married." Skip exploded into giggles.

"Well," said Dooley, "we're about ready to move. As soon as we find out from Shamus who he was tailing me for."

"Right. Sleep tight."

And Dooley did, the best sleep he'd had in weeks.

It was what might be called a quiet night at home. It was after midnight. The kids were in bed. And for the time being Myrta was incapacitated, so she and Dooley were sitting in front of the big gas grate staring at the welcome flames, drinking beer, and occasionally talking. Outside howled a fall storm. They'd just made it home in time. While Myrta was putting the kids to bed, it began to blow, then howl, and finally hail began to rattle against the windows—then came the blowing, cold rain. It was a King Lear night and Myrta, Dooley and the kids were well sheltered from the pelting of the pitiless storm.

Shirley had amused Dooley at the movie by her comments on the love scenes. "Why do those people act so silly?" she asked Dooley, who didn't have a ready answer. He thought they were acting pretty silly himself. They couldn't find a Western so they'd gone to this big ballyhooed movie about love in New York. Women agonized over love. Men agonized over love. Everybody agonized over something—and then everything came out fine after all. It bore absolutely no relationship to reality whatever and even the kids knew it. But Myrta had loved the show. She'd even cried a little, while Dooley sat in painful boredom, trying not to fidget so much.

"Kissing, kissing, kissing," said Shirley. "They're silly."

"Yeah," said her brother.

Myrta had finally got really annoyed with the kids and told them to shush. And she was secretly annoyed with them on another matter. Dooley seemed to be taking more and more interest in them and seemed to prefer having them along when they went out to the movies. At first he'd hardly noticed their presence. They had stood around looking at him big-eyed and he'd gone right on talking to Myrta as if they were no more than phantoms. Charley had really disliked the kids; they'd meant nothing to him outside of being damned nuisances he'd saddled himself with. But Dooley paid attention to them now, fixed Bobby's toys, and even helped Shirley put one of her dolls back together. Bobby had stepped on it in a fit of temper. And the kids could run through the house and yell and fall down and fight and Dooley would never turn a hair. Charley used to say: "If you don't shut up those brats I'll kill them." Myrta wanted the attention. She was hungry for attention. Had been all of her life. And she did not appreciate its diversion.

"I know just how that blonde girl felt," said Myrta. "I had a boyfriend just like that when I was in high school. No good bum."

Dooley didn't know what she was talking about. "What? What girl?"

"In the movie." Myrta talked on, telling him the story of her high school days in East Chicago, Indiana. He neither commented nor listened. He felt very comfortable sitting there in front of the fire with the wind howling outside, and it was a kind of new experience for him. He almost never felt comfortable. He seldom felt anything but tense, waiting for tomorrow.

"Where did you go to school, Dooley?" asked Myrta, after a long rambling incursion into the past.

"What?"

"School? Where did you go? You falling asleep?"

"In Toledo. I didn't finish high school."

He left it at that. Myrta rose to get them some more beer. At sixteen Dooley had got into trouble over a little matter of what belonged to who and had been given a suspended sentence by juvenile authorities; this had brought on a lot of trouble with his surly, working-man father— and finally Dooley had run away from home, and he was still running, after quarter of a century. He had worked at many jobs in between, mastering none—except the one of handling men and hitting various institutions or stores for very large amounts of money.

He had served time twice—one a stretch of five years, the other the kind you do on your head—18 months in a correctional institution. He had not been "rehabilitated"—like most pros he considered that all just one big square joke. The shrinks and the welfare workers and the preachers and the correctional officers—what did they know? They had secure jobs. What kind of a secure job could he get, supposing he wanted one, which he didn't? He was no Doc Pace—who was part pro and part chamber of commerce. Outside the pro ranks, Dooley was unskilled labor. What else?

He sipped his second beer in silence. Finally Myrta fell asleep with her head on one side. The wind howled.

"This is OK," Dooley told himself, then he lit a cigarette, crossed his feet, and settled down in his chair.

Shortly before one the phone rang. Myrta woke with a start. "Who in God's name could be calling me at this hour?" She answered it, then turned and looked in surprise at Dooley: "It's for you."

"Thanks," said Dooley. "I gave this friend your number. Was it OK?"

"Of course it's OK."

"We're promoting a small real estate deal," said Dooley, "and I guess the guy we're expecting just got in town."

Myrta felt pleased. Real estate was it? Dooley must be doing all right. He always seemed to have plenty of money. Once she had noted a very big roll.

He talked briefly on the phone, showing a kind of grim satisfaction, almost smiling, then he said to Myrta: "I've got to call a taxi. This won't keep."

"It's raining and howling out," said Myrta, like a dutiful wife. "You'll get soaked. Wait, I'll get you my umbrella."

So Dooley rode the taxi northward, with Myrta's umbrella between his knees and the wind howling, the rain pouring and the pavements slick as glass, with the taxi-driver cursing to himself at a few slight skids.

Dooley got down at a small suburban apartment building in Evanston. It was on a tree-lined side-street, very respectable, mostly small houses with small lawns—the normal habitat of the square johns. Trust Skip. This was his main headquarters, far from the toil and moil and danger of The Loop. He lived in a small one-bedroom apartment on the second floor. Skip had busted his cover. And this was a gauge of how important he thought this meeting was; of course, if there was a slip-up, he could move at a moment's notice. He paid his rent by the week—no lease.

Skip let Dooley in. Then Dooley stared. In his shirtsleeves Shamus was sitting at a small studio piano, playing—and pretty good. His curly black hair was all ruffled and he was so shook up that he was still wearing his gun under his armpit. With him a gun was a necessity. Dooley never carried one, except on jobs. Then it was a .45 in his belt, and a chopper, or what the troops in World War One called a she-she gun. Chuck would know all about that. He'd fought in France with the Marines.

"Hi, Dooley, you old rascal," called Shamus, and Skip gave Dooley a wise look. "I'm in for the money. I'm in all the way. But I wish I was in Dixie all the way."

"You may make it yet," said Skip.

"I'll do my best."

"You've done good, son, good," cried Shamus, rattling out "Yes Sir, That's My Baby, No Sir, I Don't Mean Maybe."

Dooley sat down and patiently smoked a cigarette. No hurry. Shamus would eventually come down off the ceiling. Dooley masked his curiosity. He was about to find out who had hired Shamus to tail him, which meant he would probably find out who killed George Hamm, or had him killed. Finally Shamus relaxed and threw himself into a chair.

"It was a guy nobody knows much about," said Skip, jumping the gun.

"The Polack," said Shamus. "Mike Ivan. He runs a small trucking company. Everything looks legit—except that creep, Goggles, who's always hanging around."

"Gunman?" asked Dooley.

"I don't know what," said Shamus. "He gives you goose pimples. He never says a word. He just stands there. He wears these big crazy-looking glasses—very nearsighted."

"It was a foxy killing," said Dooley. "In and out the window and nobody saw or maybe even heard a thing. And old Hamm was no amateur, you know. Took him completely by surprise."

"Here's all I know about Mike Ivan," said Skip: "He's from Detroit. He's been here about a year—not much longer—and he runs a regular independent trucking company—and as far as I know he's not running dope. And I'd know. No Mob connections. At least none I know of."

Shamus said: "So why would George Hamm trust . . .?"

"Detroit, eh?" said Dooley, thoughtfully. "Yeah. Maybe that explains it. Hamm's from the area—and he used to go back there a lot. Maybe Mike Ivan was one of his 'friends'; like the one who blew the whistle on him, turned states and got him sent up."

"Sounds reasonable. Must be," said Skip.

Now Dooley turned to Shamus. "I've got an idea. Reed, why don't you drop in on The Polack and do him a favor? On the house, you know. Tell him about my trip to Milwaukee. You just found out about it. And you think I'm casing a big job of some kind there."

Skip giggled. The Gorilla didn't look smart, but he was.

"Fine," said Shamus.

"And for your information . . . Mike Ivan is walking around on borrowed time. If anything slips, the Paces will definitely take him. They liked Old Hamm. The went to claim his body."

Skip and Shamus exchanged a long look. They were now in the very big time, not on the fringe, committed. This was not kid stuff—cheap pushers and guys who wanted other guys and sometimes wives or girlfriends followed (oh, yes, the boys in the underworld, whatever that is, as Shamus always said with a laugh, also had woman trouble just like the squares in suburbia). In this area a slip could be very costly indeed.

They studied Dooley, who sat with his feet crossed, calmly smoking a cigarette. Then they looked at each other again. Dixie was forgotten for the moment. Shamus suddenly noticed he was wearing his gun. With an apologetic laugh, he unbuckled the strap and took it off. Dooley said nothing more.

Dooley went crosstown on the double-decker, inside this time, as it was misting rain from a low dark cloudy sky, and had a meeting with Doc Pace at the rathskeller. He explained the situation and he noticed how grim Doc looked about the mouth.

"Now," said Dooley, "I've got a couple of very expensive guys on my payroll and we can't do without them. We're lucky to have them in this set up. We've got expenses. I can't afford the front money, but I can borrow it."

"I'll front," said Doc. "For a reasonable amount. If it gets bigger, I'll borrow."

"Fine, Doc."

"And if anything goes wrong, if we miss—I want that Mike Ivan."

Dooley thought for a while. "I haven't worked the whole thing out yet—but you may get him anyway, Doc."

"Fine," said Doc.

The next afternoon Shamus sauntered into Mike's Wabash Trucking Company yard and looked about him at the activity, smoking a cigarette. The weather had cleared. Blue skies overhead. Fine day. Shamus felt good as he whistled to himself, "Oh, I Wish I Was in Dixie."

Goggles looked out of the office, then pulled his head back in. Shamus thought that Goggles would do very fine for one of the gargoyles on the Church of Notre Dame in Paris. Shamus had been there with the American Army, World War One—Army Intelligence.

He crossed to the office and Goggles motioned him in. Mike Ivan's desk consisted of a large drafting table, covered with charts—behind it was his huge padded leather chair, and Mike was in it. Shamus curiously studied the man who was living on borrowed time (but aren't we all, Shamus asked himself?). He was heavy-set, with sandy, rather fuzzy hair, beer-colored eyes and a look of implacable immovability, a great contrast to Goggles who was slim to the point of skinniness, and dim, except for the glasses.

Shamus gave Mike the tale, indented a quickly suppressed look of relief. "Just as a favor," said Shamus. "You paid me well. He's definitely got his eyes on Milwaukee. He's been there twice already." Shamus padded it a little, gilded the lily, now that he was sure the mark believed him.

"I told him already," said Goggles, disdainfully. What—could the gargoyle speak?

"You told him what?" asked Shamus.

"That he worried too much."

Mike Ivan studied Shamus's face for a moment. "You're not curious about this business?"

Shamus held up both hands as if in horror, or to ward off evil. "No. What you don't know can't hurt you."

"Right," said the Polack, with a heavy laugh.

The general meeting at Doc Pace's boneyard of ailing cars was hours away so Dooley had dropped by to take Myrta and the kids to dinner, but he had called first, as it wasn't a regular night, which was usually Monday or Thursday or both, and to his surprise he found her cooking, and the kids running around in sleepers. Not just opening cans: cooking, and she looked sweaty and irritable, brushing back her thick, luxuriant red hair with an impatient gesture—meanwhile, the kids were playing some kind of running game, falling down and shrieking.

"My God," cried Myrta. "You really walked into a madhouse."

"Hi, pop," called Bobby.

And Dooley gestured, then said: "What do you think you're doing?"

"I'm cooking you a real dinner for once. I used to know how. My mother taught me well. But you don't cook for a drunk. Drunks don't eat; they drink. So I got used to eating out of a can. But I've lost my touch. I've even burned myself twice."

Things smelled good. Dooley sat down on a kitchen chair and smoked contentedly, noticing the well-set table in the dinette. There was no dining-room in the apartment, only a living-room, two small bedrooms, and a good-sized kitchen with a small dinette. It was on the first floor of a very old building that had been refurbished several times. Myrta always said: "It's a good thing we are on the ground floor. If we were on any other floor they'd throw us out of here with those damned kids running around and falling down all the time."

Dooley smoked in silence. The kids ran and fell and even fought briefly—and Myrta burned herself again and cursed with feeling, impatiently brushing back her hair.

"It's almost ready," said Myrta, heaving a long sigh of relief. "Do you want beer, coffee or buttermilk?"

"What are you running, a restaurant? Coffee."

Now the kids insisted on playing in the kitchen around Dooley's feet, and Myrta finally turned and in exasperation said: "Put 'em to bed,

Dooley. It's time."

"Put 'em to bed . . .?" said Dooley, as if she'd asked him to jump off the roof.

"Well . . . can't you see how busy I am?"

Dooley stood up. "Shoo, shoo," he cried, as if handling chickens. "To bed."

They just stood looking at him.

"You've got to make them go," said Myrta, irritably; she was hot and tired and wished to God she hadn't had the brilliant idea of cooking Dooley a "nice" dinner.

So Dooley grabbed one under each arm, carried them kicking and laughing into the bedroom, and roughly threw Bobby on one bed and Shirley on the other. They giggled and laughed hysterically.

"What's the matter?" asked Dooley.

"Wrong beds," said Shirley.

So Dooley shifted them, throwing them like rag dolls. They loved it. He started out.

"You forgot something," called Bobby. "The lights."

"Goodnight," said Dooley, and switched them off.

"Goodnight, Pop," called Shirley, then she got down under the covers and hid her head.

Crazy kids, thought Dooley. He'd been a crazy kid himself once—but he'd had a tough old man who hardly ever acknowledged his existence except to belt him occasionally "for the good of his soul." His old man was a shopworker who worked ten hours a day, sometimes thirteen, when the shop was unusually busy—three hours overtime, and the old man got paid for overtime and he was very proud of that fact; though the three hours amounted to no more than five dollars. Big deal! Dooley remembered his old man as tired, sweaty, and surly. Strong as an ox. Proud of his ability to bend horse shoes with his bare hands and tear up telephone books. Dooley had inherited that strength but what else? Nothing he could think of. Dooley was not aware of the inherited surliness. That's the way he appeared to others; not to himself.

The dinner turned out to be fine, though Myrta kept apologizing: Swiss steak, hominy, creamed peas and a good salad, with fresh corn bread. Dooley ate until he had to unfasten his belt. He weighed two hundred and twenty-five pounds but no one would have been able to guess it. He wasn't fat—he was just big. Finally he pushed his plate away and lit a cigarette.

"Well," said Myrta, pleased. "You cleaned it all up. Want some beer?"

"Couldn't handle it," said Dooley. "I'm packed."

Myrta cleared the dinette table, then they sat sipping their coffee in silence. Finally Dooley spoke.

"Remember that phone call I got here? Well, the deal's on, I think. But it's going to take some doing and I may not be seeing so much of you as I've been . . . till it's all set. I may have to go out of town for a day or two. I don't know what."

Myrta studied his face. Was he just trying to break it off in an easy way? It was possible. "Well," she said, "I wish you luck, Dooley."

"Now you understand if anything would come up here. I don't know what. But anything. Just call the hotel. If I'm not there, the guy will take a message. And he's good at it. Understand?"

"Yes," said Myrta, feeling a surge of relief and looking back briefly on the bleak days before she'd foolishly gone to that dirty speak in a fit of terrible loneliness. Life had been pretty nice ever since.

Now Dooley took an envelope from an inside pocket and held it in his hand as he spoke. "We've sure had some fun times, Myrta. And once in a while I felt like I was freeloading, eating here and taking up your time . . ."

"Don't be silly," cried Myrta. "All the money you spent on us, taking us to movies and dinner and to the park that night and the kids spending all that money in the penny arcade and everything . . .!" She felt both embarrassed and apprehensive. It sounded like the finish after all.

"I know you don't make too much money at the restaurant," said Dooley, "and you've got bills and the kids . . . here!" he added suddenly, handing her the envelope.

She took it. "What's this? Money?" asked Myrta, flushing slightly.

"Now don't get on your high horse," said Dooley. "Put it in the bank. You may need it."

Myrta hesitated, torn between outrage and gratitude (she was always short of funds), then she counted the money in kind of a daze: one thousand dollars. She'd never had more than a couple of hundred dollars at once in her whole life.

"My God, Dooley . . .!" she cried, staring at him in amazement.

"I want some more coffee," said Dooley, hurriedly.

She heated the coffee, poured two cups and sat down again.

"You must make a lot of money, Dooley," she said, staring at him as if at a new man.

"Well," said Dooley, "you know how it is in real estate. May not make a dollar in a whole year, then the next year I may make a lot of dollars. I just sold a property for a friend of mine now we've got this big deal coming up, industrial property. If it sells, I'll have a lot more money. But if it doesn't, I'm out all my expense money." Dooley had done time with a real estate guy who'd got caught with his hand in the till, and he'd picked up some of the lingo, and had used it from time to time ever since on curious straight johns.

"Well, I don't know what to say except thank you, Dooley. I know you mean it right."

"Good," said Dooley, the corner of his mouth moving slightly in what was almost a smile.

On the way to the meeting Skip suddenly felt the need for a jolt so he got off the bus and took a taxi back a mile or so to the Candy Store. Candy Store was right: candy and sodas and hot fudge and such in the front, and you name it in the back: cocaine, heroin, hash, whatever— as long as you were known to The Greek or one of his helpers or sons. There was no way you could get serviced otherwise. It was said The Greek had heavy protection but Skip knew nothing about that, didn't want to know. The Greek's was very expensive, off limits to cheapies. Skip very seldom used it—but he was well known there.

He had the taxi-driver let him off a block away, paid him, and walked. Halfway there a heavy shouldered guy stepped out of a doorway and Skip shied off like a skittish horse. But he never worried too much as he had the difference under his left armpit.

"Well, fancy seeing you here," said the guy, who turned out to be Detective Tom Brenner.

"What are you trying to do—scare me?"

"I'm on stakeout. If you were prettier, I'd kiss you."

"What are you on—H?"

"We busted South Side Mo—with over a hundred stolen fur coats. You ought to see the broads coming into the station and screaming when they don't get their coats back. Evidence, you know."

"You guys are cruel savages."

"Santorelli told me all you got from him was a couple of chili-dogs."

"I'm a public-spirited citizen. What have you got staked out?"

"I'm not saying. But stay out of the Candy Store."

"Thanks, pal," said Skip, and flagged down another taxi. It wasn't the Candy Store that was to be hit but some wanted character who was expected to turn up there. Skip decided he could stand the strain without a jolt; he'd be home in a few hours.

And while the quick moved from different directions toward meeting at Doc Pace's used car lot, the dead lay at peace in a little funeral parlor in a small town about forty miles from Detroit. George Hamm Ziegler had run his course. He looked very natural lying there in his casket, not very much different than he'd appeared at the Honor Farm in his last meeting with Dooley. The only difference was, something had fled, and he'd hold no more hopeful meetings on this earth.

In a little frame house on the edge of town, Uncle Louis and George Hamm's mother, old Cora Ziegler, as she was known in the neighborhood, were looking through a dog-eared book of snapshots, picturing George in various phases of his youth. Mrs. Ziegler, now over 70 years old, was one of the fortunate oldsters. Her husband, and one son, Phil, had died, leaving her quite a large amount of insurance. Neither had been anything like wayward George. Both had been hard workers, steady as rocks. George had been more like her brother, Uncle Louis, restless, impatient, unable to hold a job for any length of time. And with Louis it was complicated by drink. But Louis had never got into any serious trouble, while George had been in serious trouble since he was eighteen years old.

Well . . . he was dead and now it was all one, and nobody really cared but Mrs. Ziegler and Uncle Louis who lived together now in this small frame house on a little tree-lined street. In his 70s Uncle Louis had mellowed. He drank beer and minded his own business. On good days he sat in the park and fed the birds. Some evenings he even played a game of pool at Mackey's, around the corner.

"This is when he began to put on weight," said Mrs. Ziegler. "See? It's at the Lake. He was about nineteen there, I think."

"Yes," said Uncle Louis, drawing on his pipe. "Chunky. Always ate too much."

"Yes," said Mrs. Ziegler. "Remember how he used to love those pies I baked for him? Rhubarb was his favorite."

"And lemon cream," said Uncle Louis. "I never saw a boy who could eat so much pie."

They sat turning the pages. But they didn't sit up too late. Tomorrow morning was the funeral and they wanted to be up and dressed and fed and ready at an early hour. Besides, cousins were coming in from Lansing, Michigan, and had to be met at the station.

Meanwhile, in the little funeral parlor George Hamm, big time pro, slept on, oblivious.

The meeting was held in the fairly large outer office of Doc Pace's used car lot. Doc and his son were strangers to Shamus and Skip and vice versa, and there was a good deal of surreptitious sizing up; finally Doc asked Skip: "How old are you, son?"

"Old enough," said Skip. "Twenty-five."

"You don't look it."

"It's the clean athletic life I lead," said Skip.

Doc regarded him grimly, then glanced at Chuck, who seemed equally grim. At this point Dooley arrived and almost at once there was a different atmosphere. All relaxed.

"Want me to talk?" asked Dooley, and they all nodded.

"You talk," said Doc.

"Well, first," said Dooley," this is a very tough one, but very big and worth the trouble. Second, it's going to cost money. Third, it's going to be a lot of hard work. Let's not kid ourselves. And last, we may blow it."

He looked around him. Nobody said anything.

"Now," said Dooley, "about the money. Let's get that settled before we do anything. I've put my own money in; Doc is putting his own money in. And we may have to borrow. Doc and his son and I are taking nothing out now. Shamus and Skip are getting paid. And that's only right because this is going to take up all of their time. Am I right, boys?"

Shamus nodded. Skip said: "I'm losing money right now."

"All right," said Dooley. "Now—if any of you don't agree on this say so now, because beefs about money cause one hell of a lot of trouble and even shootings and rumbles. The front money, no matter what the amount, comes off the top . . . and Doc and I will both keep books. Right Doc?"

"Right," said Doc.

"Whatever is left over will be split five ways."

Shamus and Skip tried to keep their faces controlled. They hadn't expected this. Good God, they might be in for small fortunes.

Nobody said anything.

"No objections?" Dooley demanded. "If anybody's got any, speak now. Or this is it." He paused briefly and then added in an odd-sounding voice: "And I'll see that it is."

And they all knew that he would. There were no objections; there was amity all around. Shamus and Skip hadn't expected to be cut in, neither had Chuck. He generally operated as a unit with his father. Dooley always knew what he was doing. If you've got a dissatisfied crew you've got trouble to start with and possibly continued dissension. Just plain dissension had blown away a big job. Three or four times Dooley had backed out of jobs . . . because he saw it coming. In every case the job was bungled, either before or after the take. In one case it had led to a shootout over the money, with two dead and two later grabbed by the police, and all the money recovered. Dooley always insisted he could "smell" them.

"Now—how do we operate?" Dooley went on. "Shamus is known to Mike Ivan and has to be careful. Of course he could work inside but that's too dangerous and might make Mike suspicious. Skip is not known to Mike as far as I know . . ."

"Right," said Skip.

"But Skip is well known around town and if he was seen in Mike's area too often it might cause talk and give Mike an idea maybe all was not well. But nobody knows Chuck in this town. Am I right?"

"Nobody," said Doc. "For over two years we haven't touched a thing— never, around here."

"So Chuck is elected," said Dooley. "He will keep an eye on Mike and his operation. And I'll leave the doing to Doc and Chuck. There's nothing I can tell them that I know of."

Doc chuckled, pleased.

"Now—Skip and Shamus. For the time being this is your job. Find out anything you can about Mike Ivan. He's going to need pro help and he'll be talking to them, some place or other. And keep your ears peeled for any noise of a Big One. It almost always gets around, one way or another. Otherwise I don't need to tell you guys anything. You know how to operate—that's why you are being cut in—for big."

Skip and Shamus nodded and smiled. It was nice to be in top company for a change.

"Now, cars," said Dooley. "Doc and I have talked it over and he'll furnish them: for Skip, Shamus and me—just cars, sound but nothing fancy; nothing about them easy to remember. Doc makes out legitimate rental slips—in case anybody gets nosey. Doc is absolutely clean in this town. No problem."

In Chicago cars were a luxury more than a necessity. The Loop was compact, the distances short, and transportation was excellent all over the city; streetcars, buses, the elevated and taxis—it was no big deal to get any place in a reasonable amount of time. In fact it was much cheaper not to have the responsibility of a car at all.

But at the moment they needed one ready at a second's notice.

"One more thing," said Dooley. "Guns. I've got a chopper and my own .45. Doc?"

"We've got choppers and plenty of ammunition. No problem," said Doc.

"Good," said Dooley. "I'll see my chopper gets over here and you can store it for me. All right?"

"All right," said Doc.

And that about did it. Chuck went out and got sandwiches and coffee for them, then he said: "If you don't need me . . ."

"He's got to see Ingeborg every night, right?" said Doc.

"Not after tonight," said Dooley, and they all looked at him. There was a moment of tenseness.

Then Chuck grinned and said: "That's for sure."

He left, gesturing rather awkwardly.

They ate their sandwiches and drank their coffee in silence, all thinking over what had just happened. Dooley kept studying Shamus surreptitiously. He seemed to be changing, more spruce, more careful of his appearance—Dixie, no doubt. Dooley supposed Shamus was what women would think of us good-looking or handsome; the only one in this outfit. Doc and Chuck, aside from their toughness, were ordinary looking. Skip was thin and gangling and there was something comical about his postures and expressions. As for Dooley he knew he's never win any beauty prizes—"who's that ugly jerk?" But Shamus was different. He had curly, coal-black hair, a fair complexion and blue eyes, and a sort of graceful build on a six-foot frame. His features were regular, almost classically so, and it would have taken an insider to note the wary toughness and cynicism in his eyes. Nor would you peg him for a cop, which is what he really was; a cop declasses. Actor, might be a square john's estimate.

Dooley decided he'd have a little talk with Shamus later.

"Don't worry about Chuck, Dooley," said Doc. "He's all business. I was only kidding him."

"I don't worry about any of you," said Dooley, which was not strictly true. "Or I wouldn't be here. All I'm saying is, this is a twenty-four hour a day job for all of us from here on in."

They smoked together desultorily for a while, then Dooley decided to break it up, and rose.

"I'm taking a room in The Loop tomorrow," said Dooley, "and I'll give you all the number. I'll be there most of the time. All of the time if necessary. This is very big so I figure it's in The Loop where big things are. We'll take it from there."

They went outside. Three small cheap cars, but in perfect condition, were waiting for them side by side. And Doc pointed out the slips. They were the kind of cars driven by those with small to moderate incomes, the right kind.

"Chuck's been working on them for three days," said Doc. "And Chuck's the best."

"How about me?" said Skip. "A mac on wheels. I used to be hell in a rumble seat in the days of my youth."

Doc stood shaking his head over Skip as he drove off. "He looks like a punk kid, not dry behind the ears."

"Don't worry about him, Doc," said Dooley, then he shook hands with Doc, and slid in beside Shamus in Shamus's car. Shamus glanced at him in surprise.

"Reed," said Dooley, "watch the Dixie stuff, till later . . ." Shamus was going to protest, but Dooley went on: "I know how you feel. But she's got some bad connections, and anyway it's not going so smooth as all that, is it . . .?"

"Well . . . " Shamus hesitated. "No."

"But with fifty thousand dollars or more it would go a lot smoother, wouldn't it?"

Shamus turned and stared at Dooley. "It sure would. It sure would."

"And the way to get that big hunk of dough is to think about it and work and don't think about anything else. She's not going to run away. And what's a few weeks?"

"You worrying about me, Dooley, when now you've got me hoping for a rainbow? I never expected to be cut in."

"I'm worrying about you."

"Well . . . don't. I'm worrying about that cut. I'm tired of working for cheap punks."

Dooley patted him on the shoulder and got out. Shamus drove off.

"Well . . . good hunting, Dooley," called Doc, as Dooley drove off.

It was after one a.m. and the streets were clearing. Not used to driving, Dooley had some trouble at first then little by little it all came back to him. Crossing the Wacker Street Bridge in a car was very different from crossing it in a big bus; it all looked closer, more intimate, with the black water, dancing with city lights, passing under him as he drove northward. Sometimes the bridge was up, as a huge freighter passed under it, and you had to wait. But tonight there was no river traffic. Dooley moved off toward the only "home" he had; a cheap hotel room on the fourth floor of a cheap North Side hotel.

He was just getting ready to roll up the carpet and get out his arsenal when a thought occurred to him. He glanced at his watch—nearly two a.m.; well . . . he'd just have to wake her up. He went down to the bleakly deserted lobby and called Myrta on the payphone. She sounded sleepy and bewildered.

"Dooley!"

"Sorry to wake you up. But I'm leaving town tomorrow for a few days. I'll call you when I get back. Now listen to me: don't get overnight rich with that thousand bucks. Put it in the bank and let it alone, unless you have to touch it."

"Sounds like you're not coming back. Why don't you just say so,

Dooley?" Myrta sounded apprehensive, deeply worried.

"No, no," said Dooley, "nothing like that. I just got back from a business meeting and I got thinking. Just do as I say."

"Okay, Dooley; except I've got to pay some back bills."

"Good. Well . . . "

"Can I call you at the hotel?"

"Yes," said Dooley, "but I won't be here for a couple of days. But leave a message. I'll call in from time to time."

Myrta sounded relieved. Then he thought he heard her say, distantly: "What are you doing . . . "

"Hello, hello."

"Kids!" said Myrta. "Shirley heard me talking on the phone and now she's up." Then he heard her say: "He doesn't want to talk to you. Go to bed. Oh, all right."

"Hi," said Shirley, over the phone.

"Hi," said Dooley. "Go to bed. Don't bother your mother"

"All right," said Shirley.

Myrta came back on, laughing. "She'll mind you, but she won't mind me."

They talked for a little while longer, then Dooley hung up and returned to what he'd been doing before the thought of Myrta crossed his mind. And as Dooley rolled back the carpet and lifted up a square of the floor he'd cut out with his small power-saw, he was thinking vaguely that out there in the world it was kinda nice to have somebody you could call on the phone—neither a whore, nor one of his own clan, worrying about the next job, or hiding from the police.

Below the square hole were a couple of joists and on the joists rested a heavy-duty canvas duffle-bag, bound in leather, and inside the duffle-bag were his tools, his .45, his chopper, plenty of both kinds of ammunition, and a big money belt full of packed large bills: the result of a quick-bust bank robbery in Wisconsin when he'd been short of funds. No rumbles. It was put down to locals. Dooley and his two men had been in the state and out within a few hours—a local had done the casing. A good knockover—but peanuts—compared to what they were working on.

He packed the towel-wrapped chopper and several boxes of ammunition into a small suitcase; then he returned the other stuff to the hole, put the lid on, and rolled down the carpet.

Then he went back to the lobby and called Skip. Finally he got him.

"It's a strange night," said Skip. "I'm sleeping alone. Makes me nervous."

"Can you pick up a suitcase here at noon and take it to Doc?"

"I'll be there."

Dooley returned to his room, undressed and went to bed. He felt tense. The only time he didn't feel tense was when he was with Myrta and the kids—and there was no future in that. If there was anything he didn't need in his crazy world it was the burden of a woman and two kids.

The best laid plans of mice and men . . . and so forth. They were stymied. Dooley spent most of the day pacing in his new hotel room, like a caged animal in a zoo. And although Chuck Pace had taken a room in a working-class neighborhood near the Wabash Trucking Company he had nothing to report. With Skip and Shamus it was worse. They had to be extremely careful. They could not ask questions or seem to be interested in anything in particular: all they could do was listen and listen and listen. Meet people here and there and listen. Finally they became convinced there was no rumble of anything big any place.

But they hated to tell Dooley this. They were working for big pay and had big prospects. With an ordinary client in such a situation they would merely have lied, insinuated, promised that very shortly, etc., etc. But lying to Dooley was not a very healthy thing to do and he was very shrewd; besides, lying to Dooley now would be lying to themselves. In this job they were both employees and clients. It was a little confusing at times. Both were experts at stringing people along for profit. But why string yourself?"

Skip finally brought himself to call Dooley. "Nothing, not a thing," he said. "My God, last night I only slept three hours. I'm getting punchy."

Not much later, Dooley received similar reports from Shamus, then Chuck. He said the same thing to all three: "Keep trying", then he banged up the phone. Was it all a myth? A dream? Had he gone wrong in his calculation? Had Hamm been killed for some other reason? Did Mike Ivan suspect Dooley of it? What? What? Meanwhile, the front money rolled out.

At night Dooley lay listening to the clang of downtown Chicago; taxis roared in the narrow street; and one night there was a shooting—he could clearly hear the sounds of an automatic weapon, and later police-car sirens; he ignored it. Shooting them and leaving them around in the street for the cops to clean up was a way of life with the Chicago hoods. And all over what? Beer. Booze. Who was the Big One? Stupid.

Dooley had kept his hotel room on the North Side. It was cheap, and when you were working on something like this it was just as well to have a couple of places, at least, where you could light. Besides, messages might come in there for him. In his new place he was registered as Arthur Roberts and nobody knew about his presence there but his four co-workers. When Dooley wanted to lose himself he was nearly impossible to find—as the police in various states had learned the hard way.

The little four-story hotel was wedged in between two larger buildings on a side street, almost as narrow as an alleyway. It was old and rundown and full of whores, who gave Dooley the eye on the stairway. It was noisy. The plumbing was old and badly in need of repair and the pipes gurgled and banged, and at night this made a very loud sound. But all this was as nothing to Dooley. At a time like this, peace and comfort were the least of his worries. He was like a committed soldier at a listening-post. Nothing else mattered but word of the enemy. The elevated station was only half a block down the narrow alleyway street, and if he needed to move fast and couldn't reach his car soon enough he could duck out for the L. The hotel was a very well-placed little headquarters, noisome and noisy as it was.

Dooley had called Myrta once to reassure her. He wasn't just certain what his plans were in regard to Myrta and the kids. What could they be? If this one was as big as he hoped, it would make a big noise and he'd be a fool to stay in Chicago. In fact, he had his mind set on Southern California. He'd never been there—and there wasn't a want on him in a single far Western state.

As a rule Dooley slept fitfully, while the city hummed on, taxis, police or fire sirens, the clanging of trash and garbage cans as the collectors made their outrageous rounds—always at three or four in the morning; boat whistles all dominating for the moment the constant rumbling undertone of a huge city at night—breathing steadily, like a monstrous beast.

Dooley's normal tenseness grew. He countered it by drinking a lot of beer, which he bought by the case and kept in the hotel's refrigerator. A few bucks had made a bedeviled day-man his willing slave. Dooley drank beer, waited, sweated, and hoped. His main characteristic was a kind of patient craftiness, or crafty patience—he had the patience of the devil, when necessary. And right now it was very necessary. The others were all active, Shamus, Skip and Chuck, while Doc ran the used car business just as if nothing was happening. But all Dooley could do was sit, stand or lie—and wait. Another guy might have gone stir-crazy and blown the whole thing. Not Dooley.

Time passed. The first snow fell. It was November now and soon the murderous Chicago winter would set in, with an occasional blizzard and at times temperatures as low as 25 below zero. At least the snowfall quieted the town and Dooley managed to sleep one night for six uninterrupted hours.

Skip was making his rounds, with no hope in his heart, after all this time. Finally he turned up at Chez Roma and from his vantage point at the end of the bar saw Dixie standing down a narrow backstage hallway, leaning against the wall, smoking a cigarette and tapping a foot impatiently. Problems?

When the bartender looked away, Skip slipped around the end of the bar, ignoring the sign: FOR CHEZ ROMA PERSONNEL ONLY, and went to have a little chat with Beautiful. To pass the interminable time away, what else?

She was wearing a Japanese kimono over her scanty costume. She merely looked at Skip, without expression or comment. She was, as Skip said, a sight to behold. As tall as himself, slender and graceful, she had natural midnight-black hair, black eyebrows, long black lashes and strange-looking green eyes, like marbles or jewels, accentuated by dark-green eyeshadow. She looked, in her make-up, like an idol or a queen—or something out of this world.

"Whatever happened to Pretty Man?" she asked.

"Reed? Busy. Up to his ears making money."

"That's nice," said Dixie. "Money is so nice. Don't you think?"

"What would we do without it?" said Skip, looking into those dreamy eyes, wondering what was behind them. Stupidity? Brains? Craft? What . . .?

She couldn't be too smart at that. She'd married a bum of an actor who never worked and seemed to spend his time lying around with other broads. Apparently he didn't like perfect form and green eyes. Skip had seen him with some real pigs. In this world you never know!

Skip studied her. There seemed to be a little tightness about her pretty mouth, that looked as if it had been carved by a very fine sculptor. He had noted the tapping foot previously.

"Something wrong, honey?" asked Skip.

"What could be right about this style?" asked Dixie. Why Dixie? It was an unsuitable name. No class. This kid had class.

"You need a laugh?"

"Do I ever."

"I'm your man," said Skip. "I just heard a funny one. In fact I told it to Pretty Man and he almost blew his cork. There was this Englishman on the boat that runs between France and England. He was coming back home. On the boat he'd met a very pretty girl named April. As the boat was nearing the Cliffs of Dover, what did the Englishman say . . .?"

"How do I know?" said Dixie. "You're telling it."

"He said, 'Oh, to be in April now that England's here.'"

"He said what?" demanded Dixie, irritably.

Dumb, thought Skip. Dixie, the beautiful idol, was just plain dumb. But don't try to tell that to Shamus; in fact he didn't care whether she was dumb or not.

"That's what we call an inside joke," said Skip.

"Well, I should think so," said Dixie, impatiently.

"Pretty Man ought to be checking with you soon. OK?"

"Why not?" asked Dixie, indifferently. "Though he's rather boring."

He *is* boring, thought Skip; but he smiled politely.

Dixie started slightly. "Oh, God," she said. "Here comes the Peacock."

Madam Chez Roma appeared from the back. She was a tall slender woman, in her forties, with high-piled blond hair (it had once been black), and the air of a *grande dame* of the court of Louis the Quince.

"You'll catch cold out here, dear," she said.

"I was just going," said Dixie, and with a gesture, she did just that.

"Madame, good evening," said Skip, inclining his head slightly.

"This is only for Chez Roma personnel," said Madame Chez Roma. "Didn't you see the sign?"

"I'm sorry. I did not."

"Well, don't let it happen again," she said, meaning more, thought Skip, than she was saying. There were big-muscle hoods in the back rooms.

"I'm very sorry, Madame," said Skip, and returned to the bar.

And later Skip always said talking to Dixie had brought him luck. If it hadn't been for her he'd have been long gone and he could have missed Schikel Benjamin. Why he was called that, nobody knew. Was it a name or what? He was a very tough but amusing Jewish hood who'd been absent from the scene for quite a while. He came over to Skip at once and took him aside.

"What's going on around here? I no sooner land and I run into a couple of Detroit hoods, who pretend they don't know me—and duck out."

"Here?"

"No. At Clancy's across the street."

"You never know."

"You usually do."

"So— what if they are here?"

"They are big time. So there's a caper, man. Somebody is already dead—or there's a class knockover and I'm looking for work. Wouldn't even speak to me, them bastards."

Skip could hardly wait to get to a phone. "I'll see what I can find out for you, Schik . . . "

"On the house? I'm busted, Skip. Could you spring for a twenty?"

Skip gave it to him. He might be useful.

"I love you," said Schik. "Who do you want killed?"

"I'll give you my list."

"Where can I reach you?"

"Call Willie's exchange. He'll give you a number."

"Still as cagey as ever."

"You live longer that way."

Skip had a hard time getting rid of Schikel Benjamin, who seemed lonesome and disoriented. He'd probably been doing time.

Skip made his phone call. He spoke and heard Dooley grunt with satisfaction, then he hung up. Dooley immediately called Doc Pace so he'd warn Chuck to be on the lookout, but Doc seemed to want to talk himself: "Good news, Dooley. Chuck's got a job at the trucking company—mechanic. And he's the best, so it's fine."

Things were moving. Dooley drank a bottle of beer, took off his clothes and went to bed. He had a feeling it wouldn't be long now.

They had a meeting late at night at Doc's used car lot. While Skip told about his meeting with Schikel Benjamin, Dooley noted that Doc and his son seemed to be having a hard time holding themselves in and listening; they seemed to be bursting with something. Shamus said that after talking with Skip he'd done a little scrounging around and it appeared that a Detroit big-timer, Billy Lacy, had arrived. The information hadn't come from the police but from the honky-tonk grapevine, but it was very likely true.

"Doc," said Dooley, "you've got something you want to say?"

Both Doc and his son started to chuckle and laugh, then Chuck opened a drawer and got out an envelope from which he extracted various snapshots, and spread them out on the desk-top. All crowded around to look.

"Good Christ, there's Goggles," cried Shamus, staring. "And Mike Ivan. And who are those two guys?"

"You tell us," said Doc.

"They got to be the Detroit hoods," said Skip. "I could get an identification but it's too dangerous."

"You mean Schikel Benjamin?" asked Dooley, and when Skip nodded, Dooley said: "No."

"Right," said Skip.

"How about this Chuck?" said Doc, laughing, proud of his son. "Take the magnifying glass. You can read the license plates. See the Michigan license? Also the plates on the one Goggles is standing by, and the one Mike Ivan generally uses. Drives it himself."

Skip, Shamus and Dooley made notes, taking down the make, year and license plates of the three cars. They took their time carefully studying the very good pictures of the two strangers: Mike Ivan and Goggles.

Dooley finally slapped Chuck on the back in a familiar gesture, very unusual with him. "Fine. Swell," he said. "That's what I call know-how."

Skip and Shamus both felt embarrassed and ashamed; they were professionals and they'd been outdone by this ex-GI grease-monkey.

But Dooley turned and said: "You're all doing fine. But don't relax—not for a second. Keep it up. We're getting there."

Skip and Shamus were partially mollified; at least they felt a little better. They'd actually been hating themselves for quite a while now. A pro is supposed to produce. If he can't do that, what can he do?

"How did you get those pictures?" asked Dooley.

"Had a little camera inside my jumpers, hanging around my neck. Nothing to it," said Chuck. "Simple. But Mr. Dooley . . ."

"Not mister," said Dooley.

"OK," said Chuck, grinning. "But there is one thing I've got to tell you about. I made a slip . . ."

They all turned and looked at him, all sharply attentive.

"It's nothing," said Doc, quickly.

"Let him tell it," said Dooley.

"Well, it was like this," said Chuck, slowly, as if groping for words. "I was taking off my jumpers in the back, getting ready to leave. We don't have any locker room, or anything like that—just a small can or two, so you dress where you're able. I thought I was all alone. There's this guy, Bart—Bartolozzi—another mechanic. He's a creep of some kind. Good mechanic, but a creepy guy. I'm not sure he's not a stack shy. Always grinning in a funny way. Little guy, very thin—Mike calls him The Shadow because you can hardly see him. Well, I was taking off my jumpers—and there's Bart looking around a car at me. And I'm wearing a gun . . ."

Shamus and Skip and Dooley all exchanged glances. This was bad.

"So I had to tell him something. So I gave him the big lie. I told him I was having woman trouble and that the woman's husband was a great big muscle man that I couldn't handle—and he'd been threatening me . . ."

"That's a pretty good tale on the spur of the moment," said Doc; but the others said nothing.

"Well, I'm pretty sure Bart believed me; he even said he'd keep an eye out for any really big guy hanging around. I asked him not to say anything around the places as it might get me in trouble and I needed my job. Fine. Except the next day I'm working on a car and I feel somebody starring me. You know what I mean? I turn—and there's Goggles looking at me. Bart spilled . . ."

"Goddamn it," said Dooley.

"And Goggles said, 'Hello there, gunman.' And I gave him the tale. He just stared at me for a long time, then he went in and got Mike. I gave Mike the tale, then I said: 'I don't want to give you any trouble, Mr. Ivan. So I'll just quit.' But he said: 'You will like hell. You're the best mechanic I ever had working for me. We just don't have them breakdowns anymore, costing me money, and if that big son-of-a-bitch comes on this place he'll be sorry.'"

Doc lay back in his chair and laughed, but Dooley was not amused. "Maybe you got away with it, and maybe you didn't," said Dooley. "Those guys are smart. Maybe they just want to keep their eyes on you. And if you leave, just disappear, they'll really smell a rat."

Doc had sobered. "Yes, maybe Dooley's right."

"I'm sorry," said Chuck. "I should have been more careful with that gun."

There was a long silence. Finally Skip gave a jump in his chair. "I got it. We'll have him arrested."

All stared at Skip in utter amazement.

"Wait, wait," said Skip. "I haven't blown my cork. He's done his work, right. Do we need him there any longer? We've got the guys nailed. We've got the licenses. It's all tailing them now, right? And that's our job, Shamus and me. So we have him arrested. I've used this gag before. And I got the guy for it, badge and all."

"Oh, no!" said Shamus, putting his head down and laughing almost uncontrollably.

They all began to laugh, except Dooley. Doc pounded on the desk in his mirth. Finally the uproar subsided.

"What charge?" asked Dooley, startling them.

"Well," said Skip, "wanted for questioning in an assault case—in a bar."

"Good," said Dooley. "Arrange it. It gets Chuck clear, out of a joint where he might get killed. And I think it will put them off the track."

The next morning Chuck was "arrested" at the trucking company and handcuffed. City Detective O'Brien was very persuasive and efficient and entirely convincing, and he apologized for causing Mr. Ivan any trouble. O'Brien should know his part; he played it many times on and off the stage. He was well known to all con artists in the area, and they'd used him many times, in frightening suckers.

"Son-of-a-bitch," said Ivan. "The best mechanic I've ever had around the place. Has he got somebody to bail him out?"

O'Brien took Ivan aside. "Confidentially," he said, "this guy's for the cooler. Half a dozen charges."

Ivan went back into his office swearing and stamping his feet. Goggles hadn't appeared. He was allergic to coppers.

Dooley was back in his cage, but with an entirely different viewpoint now. They weren't hopelessly fumbling in the dark. Slowly the whole picture was becoming clear, and Mike Ivan, at least according to his lights, was playing it smart. Apparently he was as clean in Chicago as Doc Pace—Mike also obviously was part pro and part chamber of commerce, a mysterious breed to Dooley—and he had no doubt brought Goggles with him (he was unknown around town) and he was also bringing unknown pros from Detroit.

It was a very good way to operate. Except that the pros hadn't been smart enough to stay out of the local dives; where they'd been seen by Schikel Benjamin—the lead that broke everything open. (You could never be too careful, thought Dooley; and the tip-and-tear bunglers never were; that's why so many of them wound up prematurely in drawers in the morgue.) And that it was big was obvious. First there was Hamm's word—and Hamm was no fantasist—but what made it even more obvious was the apparent care that Mike was taking; no rush, hardly a move as yet, except for some seemingly aimless driving around Chicago by the Detroit hoods, either familiarizing themselves with the locals or starting to map out their escape, or getaway routes, all dutifully reported by Skip and Shamus.

And they seemed to be driving mostly around an area not too far away from Dooley's listening post. That is, in the general area of the Wacker Street Bridge and the river embankment. But here there were nothing but commission houses and warehouses—but on the street that they backed were two banks, several savings and loan buildings, and a couple of large stores—and on the corner toward one of the downtown L stations was the plushest travel agency in the city, Travelon, Inc. with its "smart-looking" plate-glass windows, in which were displayed very large and intricate models of several of the world's finest luxury liners, American and British.

Dooley began to worry. Banks? Loan companies? Stores? What could they be getting at? Certainly not a rip-and-tear bank holdup; what was big or unusual about that? Certainly not a tunneling job. They were a dime a dozen. And in both cases the percentage of failure was very high. Anyway, it wasn't Hamm's style—after all the caper was Hamm's. Like Skip, Hamm had imagination—time after time he'd come up with the unexpected: like the traditional, the landmark jewelry store—part of the town's history—that had never been tapped over fifty years—Cleveland, Ohio—that Hamm had successfully knocked over. Dooley was not in on that caper, but he'd seen some of the jewelry and it was unbelievable. A fence in St. Louis offered to sell him some of it cheap—as an investment; and Dooley could have turned a big profit— but he had been short of ready cash at the time.

No. If it was Hamm's and big, it wasn't routine.

The day passed slowly. Dooley drank beer, smoked and sat staring out at Chicago, clear as crystal in the light air of a sunshiny November day. He had a radio now and occasionally listened to a program or two: he was much amused by *Amos and Andy* and *The Three Doctors*, and now the time passed less slowly.

Toward evening, hearing nothing from anybody, he called his North Side hotel and asked for messages. There weren't any except a call from Myrta. Dooley restrained a very strong impulse to make a hurried trip out to see Myrta and the kids. Hell, they could reach him there if they needed him; Skip had sense enough to call till he got him; but Dooley resisted the impulse. It might take precious time to find him and besides who was he to lecture Chuck and Shamus if he couldn't restrain himself? No good.

So he called Myrta on the phone.

"Dooley!"

"Is everything all right?"

"Well . . . yes; except we are getting lonesome for you."

Dooley couldn't reply for a moment. Nobody in his whole life had ever said anything like that to him before. He didn't know how he felt, but he felt strange.

"I'm calling from Milwaukee," said Dooley. "I checked with my hotel and they said you'd called."

"Well, you told me it was all right," said Myrta, defensively.

"Of course it's all right. I just thought maybe something was wrong."

"No. I just wanted to talk to you."

"Are you taking care of that money?"

"I've spent only a little over 70 dollars, paying back bills. What a relief!"

"How are the brats?"

Myrta laughed. "The brats are in bed … no! Here they come, ready or not."

Dooley talked to the kids on the phone and finally Bobby asked: "When are we going out and get some more of them fortune cookies with the little writing inside?"

For some reason both kids had been much impressed with the fortune cookies. They'd never seen any before.

"Get your mom to take you," said Dooley.

"No," said Shirley. "It's more fun when you're here."

Suddenly Dooley began to swear to himself. What the hell did he think he was doing tying up the phone like this, talk about Shamus!

"Well," he said, "I've got business to look after. Call the hotel if you need anything."

They all kept talking but finally he managed to get off the line. "Dooley," he said to himself, "you are a goddamned old fool. What's the matter with you?"

The phone rang almost immediately. "There," Dooley told himself, "you see?"

It was Skip. "Dooley, I've been trying to . . ."

"I know, I know," said Dooley, irritably.

"Something wrong?"

"No. What do you want?"

"I'm not going to talk about this over the phone," said Skip. "It's a shaker, boy. How about Doc's, in about an hour or so?"

"I'll be there," said Dooley.

As he got ready to leave, he said to himself: "You see, you fool? You might have been on your way out to Myrta's."

And as he drove out to Doc's through the busy Chicago streets of early evening, he sat rigidly grim, thoroughly disapproving of one Dooley Mundhenk, alias Arthur Roberts, not to mention Arthur Robert Mundhenk.

They were all there, Shamus pacing nervously and seeming very upset.

"Well," said Dooley.

"I don't believe this," said Shamus, running a distracted hand through his curly hair. "Do any of you guys know about Travelon, Inc.?"

None of them did; Doc and Chuck were relative newcomers; Dooley was in and out of Chicago, hardly part of the scene; but even Skip didn't know.

"Travelon, Inc. is legit," said Shamus, "the biggest travel agency in the Midwest. But it is also a front . . ."

"For what?" asked Skip, breaking in. How come he didn't know? This irritated him.

"For the biggest bookie operation west of New York."

"Good Christ," said Dooley. "That Hamm—you can't believe him."

"Mob protected?" asked Doc, as Chuck just sat staring.

"All sit back. Take careful hold of the arms of your chairs. The Mob has nothing to do with it. Once they tried to cut in and three of them died before they got the idea. It's politically protected. How high it goes nobody knows—or they are not saying. Did you ever hear of Fort Knox?"

"Go on," said Dooley, his spine crawling slightly. Sometimes you can get too big.

"After all," said Shamus, "I was once a member of the force. The other night an old friend of mine and I had a few drinks together. He's an acting lieutenant who should have been a captain long ago and he's not happy about it. Well, since we've been watching the hoods I haven't seen a thing in that area where they are fooling around that could be . . . you know, an unusual knockover. The kind Dooley's expecting. But I noticed Travelon, Inc. I had heard rumors about it, you know; big time bookie joint, where the rich kids chunk it in. I always figured it was just a tale somebody had started. So I got my friend on the subject. I never mentioned Travelon, Inc. Just bookies in general. And he told me the tale. Even the lieutenant doesn't know how high up it goes."

"It may not be the hit," said Dooley.

"You're right," said Shamus. "And I hope it's not, because it's going to cause an uproar to end all uproars. I think we ought to figure it is, then prove it's not by watching those guys."

"I'm for that," said Dooley.

"Now let me give you the rest of it. If you'll remember: the building's on an angle, the ground slopes down in the back. It's one-story in front, and two stories in the back. The travel agency takes up the whole first floor—so the bookie joint's got to be in the back, down below. With an alley entrance, or a side stairway entrance from the travel agency. Maybe they've got a door upstairs marked Private for the guys in the know. Or maybe they've got both. All right. Well, I saw that creep Goggles drive down that alley. For what? In at one and out the other."

Long silence. "This may be it," said Dooley, not liking it. "But we must keep checking."

Another long pause.

"A place like that would have heavy security, mugs, everything, wouldn't it?" asked Doc.

"I'm not so sure," said Shamus. "Even the Mob didn't try to knock it over. They tried to use muscle—to intimidate. And they got the hell shot out of them. Maybe they feel safe now. Maybe they are careless."

"I don't know," said Dooley. "Don't forget it's a Hamm job—with weird angles, right down to the last T. And Mike knows those angles and we don't—and never will . . ."

"What are you saying?" asked Shamus, as if afraid to hear the answer which he feared was: we blow this one out; too much.

"Well," said Dooley, "first we make sure this is it, which it may not be. If it is, we let them make the take then we hijack them. It's the only way."

Shamus heaved a long sigh of relief and sank back into his chair. There was no joking tonight. All were solemn, even Skip.

The routine started all over again: Dooley at the listening-post, Doc minding the store, and Chuck, Shamus and Skip watching the enemy. Chuck and Shamus worked at the spying only at night—as both could be identified, by Mike or Goggles. Skip worked the day shift—and it was killing him, as he was a nightbird at heart and didn't ordinarily get fully awake until the sun set.

Lucky for them all, the weather held. It was an unusually fine November, neither heavy rain nor heavy snow since the first big storm. But at night when the wind was blowing from the lake, it cut like a knife, as if blowing off arctic snowfields or glaciers. And Shamus and Chuck often shivered in their heavy coats as they drove around the night-city.

Dooley waited patiently, alleviating the boredom by listening more and more to the radio. He'd never been a radio-listener before, except for the local news, trying to hear something, anything, that would give him a lead or word about a confrere or an enemy—with Dooley it had always been the "commercial"—never the casual, the merely interesting, entertaining or amusing. But now he was even looking forward to *Amos and Andy*. But his tenseness grew and he drank more beer than ever. It seemed to have little effect on him except to relax him a little; he sweated it out nearly as fast as he drank it.

"What a crazy life," he said to himself one night as he was trying to go to sleep. It was cold. The city was noisy. The old steam radiator was clanking dismally in a corner of the room. And some place in the hotel a woman was singing, a high full soprano—probably one of the whores, drunk. He fell into an uneasy doze. Everything seemed to turn into a nightmare, blending the natural noises into a weird cacophony of sound, dominated by the soprano. Dooley jerked awake with a start. Then he rose and paced the room, smoking a cigarette.

"I'm getting the jim-jams," he told himself. "This is dragging on too long." It never occurred to him to ask himself, "Is it worth it?" To him it was, it always had been; he'd never known anything else. Even in prison his head had been full of plans and stratagems and cons, and moves of every kind that could be profitable to him. One day a guard said to him: "Dooley, why don't you join a circus and be a strong man for a living and stay out of trouble?" Dooley hadn't even replied, though this screw was not a bad guy, one of the few not in the black book of the cons.

The phone rang and Dooley gave a jump. It was Shamus.

"Just thought you'd like to know," Shamus said, his voice sounding tired, weary. "The grapevine was right. It's Bill Lacy, and the guy with him's name is Novak or Kovack; he's a heister who joined the Detroit Mob for a while. It all fits, Dooley."

"Looks like it."

"And we ought to have some more news soon if I don't collapse," said Shamus, trying to laugh it off.

After he'd hung up, Dooley went to the window and stood looking out. Over the rooftops he could see the upper stories of gigantic buildings, their elevator shafts alight—the whole scene dwarfed by these towering monsters. Nothing like them had ever been seen in the world before. Tall towers, yes. Pyramids, ziggurats; but not monstrous house piled on house in which people worked a thousand feet above the pavement, and took it all as a matter of course. When he was younger, Dooley, who had been raised in a small town where five stories was high for a building and there was plenty of open space all around him, in fact, far horizons, had felt vaguely intimidated by his first sight of these colossi. Now they were merely part of the cityscape; yet now and then he noticed them directly and had the same tight feeling in the chest.

Dooley turned on the radio and sat listening to it; jazz music—not of much interest to Dooley, but company nonetheless.

All were tired and irritable and trying to restrain themselves. Shamus was late—and he'd called the meeting. But finally he arrived with what looked like a portfolio under his arm and without preamble he opened it out on Doc's desk. He had spent the whole day collating the information gathered by himself, Skip and Chuck—and here it was, and he patiently explained it in a series of charts.

"No doubt about it," said Shamus. "Their getaway route is back to the trucking company. Their alternate route leads south—and then maybe bends westward. But the getaway route is straight west to the trucking company. If they get a big rumble they might go south. Another thing, there is no doubt in my mind that Travelon, Inc. is the hit. How, I don't know. Rip-and-tear is out. In the daytime it would cause such an uproar they wouldn't get two blocks away till the coppers had them in their gunsights. So it's night—so it must be a break in—and maybe a safe job. So that means very late at night."

"Well," said Dooley, "if it's a safe job they need a peterman—and a big one. So if one arrives, and we tag him that will be it."

"Yes," said Shamus. "That will be it."

All fell silent. The strain was telling heavily on every one of them. It was like a nightmare that they couldn't extricate themselves from. Normal life was simply impossible, even for Doc, who found himself almost unable to keep his mind on business. Ed Weed, his sales manager, an old-time used car man Doc had practically picked off the street, wondered what was the matter with Doc, but he held his peace. Ed was very grateful to Doc; to him Doc could do no wrong. Doc had given him new hope. At sixty-five where do you look for a job—no matter how well you know a business?

Dooley gave a long sigh and rose. "Well . . ." he said.

The others rose also. A lengthy silence. Dooley looked about him at the long tired faces and said: "I told you it was going to be a tough one."

Then he gestured and left.

"Well," said Chuck, "here goes nothing. Goddamn am I getting sick of them streets."

Shamus handed Doc the portfolio. "Will you keep it for me?"

"Right," said Doc.

Chuck left. They heard him drive off. Dooley had already gone. Shamus and Skip went out side by side. Doc put his head down on his desk, stretched out his hands and fell into a doze. He'd had a hard time sleeping lately.

"What do you say?" asked Skip, as they moved toward their cars.

"I can't repeat it," said Shamus.

"I was in talking to Dixie. She asked about you."

"She what?"

"Right. And I gave her a build. You know what she calls you? Pretty Man."

"You're kidding," said Shamus, amazed.

"You might have it made . . . later," Skip added hurriedly. "She's a little lady who likes money. And you'll have some, boy. And I think she's fed up with that place. The Madame practically threw me out."

"That's a bird, the Madame," said Shamus. "I heard she runs the place, has the money. Giovanni just goes along for the ride. He used to be a table-captain at Weinrath's."

"I know," said Skip.

"She's got a cousin in the Mob, so I hear. That started it all. Now look at Chez Roma. Like a license to steal."

"Well . . ." said Skip.

"Back to the mines," said Shamus.

Another night and a dismal one, with clouds that almost touched the tall buildings, and a steady drizzling rain. After a frustrating night Shamus came out of Clancy's into a wet, dripping, but shiny world. The wet pavements gleamed with many-colored reflections, straight lines of light, zig zags, ripples, as in a tipped-up wet watercolor picture. And across the street from him glittered the mauve electric sign: CHEZ ROMA.

Shamus glanced at his wristwatch. Past showtime, but not much past. It might still be on. Shamus was tired, bone-weary, dragged out, and his will was tired also; he'd been punishing it for weeks. He wanted to see Dixie. For Christ's sake, he could at least go look at her! What would that hurt? "Pretty Man," he said to himself, reminiscently; Shamus had no high opinion of his personal appearance; in fact he would have preferred to look more like the other guys in the station— in the old days. "She must have been ribbing," he told himself. "Yeah, ribbing. What else?"

Nevertheless, he wound up in Chez Roma. It was packed and noisy and the guy in the top hat, white tie and tails and the six girls were doing the blow-off number, the finale. Shamus felt a slight tightening in his chest at the sight of Dixie, languidly kicking up her long slender elegant legs. What a doll!

He crowded forward to the end of the bar and reached a spot where the performers would have to pass him to get into the back. There was milling, quite a crowd. The number concluded and the performers hurried off the stage—no encores, no return for applause at Chez Roma. Dixie was the last down the short stairway to the club proper. To Shamus's surprise Dixie's green eyes flashed at the sight of him, as if lit up from inside. She came to him immediately, grabbed a lapel, got up close to him and whispered: "Got a car?"

"Yes," said Shamus, baffled.

"Meet me outside in fifteen minutes," she whispered hurriedly.

"But . . ." Shamus began.

She cut him off. "It's important. You know, the alley behind—right at the street corner." Then suddenly her manner changed, she gave him a phony professional smile, and quickly disappeared into the back with the rest.

Shamus stood there for a moment like a man who'd just been hit with a club, then he hurried out into the rain, recovered his car from Clancy's parking lot, drove down the side-street and pulled up by the stage-alley, a dead end.

"Oh, God," thought Shamus. "Dooley will have my hide for this."

He waited. From time to time he glanced at his watch. It seemed to have stopped. Just ahead of him, near the curb, was a CPD sign that read: NO PARKING HERE AT ANY TIME. It was a very congested area with narrow, one-way streets. At times there was an almost hopeless tangle of traffic. But tonight, nothing. Rain, wind.

More time passed. Shamus began to worry, then a thought occurred to him that bothered him very much. "Was it a gag? Had she set him up? When would the wags appear and ask, "Waiting for somebody?" It was an old rib, pulled many times on stage-door johns. But on him? It didn't make sense.

He stood with his mind in confusion, getting wet. He was so physically exhausted and beat he began to wonder if he hadn't dreamed the whole thing . . . the flashing green eyes, the eagerness—it had given him goose-pimples. It was what you called being really wanted—and it happened to few men . . . especially with a doll like Dixie.

He was about to give up when he saw her coming toward him up the dingy alley wearing a bulky man's raincoat and carrying a large overnight case, almost as large as a regular small suitcase.

Shamus felt stunned. Could it be?

He helped her in, then ran around to the driver's side, slipping and almost falling on the wet pavement. Boy, he was shook.

He got in and stepped on the starter: it coughed and died, coughed and died. "Where to?" he asked, over the unsettling noises of the rebelling engine.

"Where to?" cried Dixie. "Haven't you got a place?"

The world seemed to recede then come closer, then recede again. "Sure," Shamus finally replied.

"Well . . ." said Dixie, settling back.

Shamus had an old apartment on the northern fringe of The Loop and on the fringe of Little Italy. Not too many blocks away from it was Five Corners, the bloodiest spot in the city, the legendary battle ground of the booze barons. To the east loomed the expensive towers of the Gold Coast luxury hotels. It was quite a spot—rich and poor within throwing distance of each other—but never meeting, or even acknowledging the presence of the other. Shamus lived in a kind of No-Man's land. His apartment was on the fourth floor, with a wonderful view of the Gold Coast and the Lake, and no view at all of Little Italy.

The apartment was in a huge old Chicago mansion, built in the 80s and remade into an eight-unit dwelling. It was said that it was full of ghosts, but Shamus had never seen any of them. In fact, he was seldom there, except late at night, and then only to sleep. He often made up his mind to give up the apartment, save expenses, and move to a cheap hotel room. But somehow he just never got around to it.

In the car there was a long silence. Shamus didn't know what to say and Dixie seemed unwilling, or too tired, to talk.

Finally out of the blue, she cried: "Well, if you want to know, I'm fed up! With my stupid no-good bum of a husband and with Chez Roma and those crumbs and with Angelina and with the whole bit. I'm fed up!" she screamed, then she fell silent.

Good God! thought Shamus, have I got her on my hands? He couldn't believe it. (Oh, I may get killed for this, thought Shamus. But resist it he could not.)

The little modern self-serve elevator looked strange, fitted into its incongruous surroundings of the splendor of the past, but it worked and it was better than walking up four floors.

"Say," said Dixie, "this is a weird place. I like it. How did you ever find it?"

"A real estate guy I know."

And when she saw the apartment she was more than pleased. It consisted of one huge room, with a very high ceiling, none of your box-rooms, the kind they were building now in the new hotels going up; a large bedroom; a surprisingly large and modern bathroom; and a dinette, with an electric range. Dixie, the bulky raincoat removed, was like a cat moving about in a new place, testing, looking, seeking, evaluating.

Shamus drew the curtains and showed her the view of the Gold Coast—there wasn't much to see tonight; it was all blurred and misty, and little showed but lighted windows, hundreds of them.

"Fix me a drink," said Dixie. "Could we talk?"

"Might be a good idea," said Shamus.

He returned with whiskey and soda and they sat side by side on a huge overstuffed lounge.

"Well, I powdered," said Dixie.

"So I see."

"I don't know what I'd have done if you hadn't come in. Cheap hotel, anything, I guess. I'm fed up. I can only stand so much. I've always been that way. People get too much for me, I run. I've always had people after me, goddamn it," Dixie added. "And it gets tiresome. I like you. You're not a creep. My husband is a stinking creep, and lives off me, sleeps around with bums, and slaps me around if I say anything. And Angelina is a worse creep, a creepy creep, a super creep! I'm fed up!" screamed Dixie.

Who was Angelina? Madame Chez Roma?

Shamus sat studying Dixie carefully. This beautiful doll was not very far from the screaming meemies. A real problem. But Shamus didn't care, he just didn't care. Imagine—Dixie sitting right there on his sofa, drinking his liquor. So dreams did come true after all!

And he was in no hurry with Dixie. She was in a state—all she needed at the moment was some oaf pawing her. To hell with that. He'd waited a long time for her. He could continue to wait.

He freshened their drinks.

"I know what you mean," said Shamus. "I get fed up myself. It's a rough world. What you need is a rest. No peace. Two shows a night. God knows what all. All right. You can rest here. Sleep in the bedroom, make yourself at home. I'll sleep on this couch. It's big enough for four." (In fact, he'd seen four on it, at times—but now that was only a memory—of the past, he hoped.)

Dixie studied his face for a moment, her green eyes puzzled, then clearing; then she put down her glass, leaned over, kissed Shamus, patted his face and said: "You see what I mean. You are no goddamned creep."

"Only one thing," said Shamus. "Do me a favor. Stay in. The place is yours. But stay in."

Dixie laughed. "You think that's trouble? I'll be glad to, after what I've been going through. A week, a month, a year! Oh God, lead me to that bed. But first, a bath . . ."

"Help yourself," said Shamus.

Dixie gave what almost sounded like a giggle. "Happy, happy," she said, then she went into the bedroom and in a moment reappeared, wrapped in a sheet and disappeared into the bathroom.

Shamus poured himself a straight one and gulped it down, then he went to the window and stood looking out at the blurred lights of the Gold Coast. Finally he said: "Selby Reed, I just don't know about you."

Faces began to swim before his eyes: Dooley's, Doc's—but the dangerous one was Skip's. The disappearance would be noted—and Skip would hear about it as soon as anybody. Sooner.

In the bedroom the water was gurgling loudly for the bath. Shamus still couldn't believe it. Dixie in his tub? Incredible!

The next night found Dixie luxuriating in Shamus's apartment. It was Dreamsville. Hours to herself. Nobody to say do this, do that, come here, go there—hop in bed, hop out. Hours of silence and solitude. Shamus had dragged in a huge amount of groceries, and he had brought her *Vogue, Harper's Bazaar*, and half a dozen movie magazines. They'd had two meals together and much desultory conversation. What a relief Shamus was after the childishly egotistical company of her husband, Ty—known to his friends as the "mirror-fighter." Ty thought he was beautiful and irresistible. Actually, he wasn't nearly as good-looking as Shamus, who didn't act as if he thought he was good-looking at all. But the real difference was that Ty was a big child, and Shamus was a man.

Now Dixie was lying stretched out on the sofa, which to her resembled a boat, reading *Vogue*, staring at the models—thinking, "well, she's not so much"—and smoking one cigarette after another. If she only had some candy. Of course, we could run down and get some, but Shamus had cautioned her again and again not to go out. And it finally occurred to Dixie that he must have a damned good reason for all the caution— so she willingly complied. She could speak to Shamus about the candy.

Delicious, relaxing hours passed. Dixie dozed for a while, woke, started on *Harper's Bazaar*, dozed again—then finally slept. The ringing of the phone woke her. She let it ring. Shamus had told her that under no circumstances was she to answer the phone.

"But supposing it's you?" asked Dixie.

"It won't be me," said Shamus. "Just don't answer the phone—never."

"Fine," said Dixie. "I'm not expecting any calls."

And they laughed over that one.

The phone rang on and on. Finally it broke off. But in a few minutes it started ringing again. This happened three times. The third time Dixie crossed from the sofa and took the phone off the hook.

"Now try to ring," she said, and went back to the sofa.

An hour later Shamus appeared.

"Hi," said Dixie.

"Hi," said Shamus. Then he just stood and looked at her lying there at ease on his big sofa—that had pillowed quite a few, but none like this—and thought to himself, "I still don't believe it." She seemed so pleasant, so relaxed, so at ease . . . maybe tonight . . .

"That damned phone kept ringing and ringing so I took it off the hook," said Dixie.

Shamus quickly hung up the phone, then said: "Don't do that, Dixie. Just let it ring."

It rang—Shamus grabbed it up, showing a certain amount of nervousness.

It was Skip. Who else . . .?

"Look pal," said Skip. "I've been trying to get you for . . ."

"I'm having trouble with my phone," said Shamus. "The repair guy's coming over tomorrow. If you can't get me here try the other numbers."

"I tried, I tried. OK. Brace yourself, pal. Dixie has disappeared. It's a stink."

"What?" cried Shamus, trying to sound "sincere." "What do you mean?"

"You haven't heard anything about it?"

"I don't even know what you're talking about."

He turned and winked at Dixie and put his fingers to his lips, indicating silence.

"Well, I'll give you the tale. I'm working days and I can't sleep at night—one of these days I'll just throw an old-fashioned fit—so I made the second show at Chez Roma. Only five girls on the stage; no Dixie. So I ask around; I've got friends, you know. So . . . this is it. Dixie didn't show up for work at all. And she didn't call in. And nobody knows where she is. Even her husband; he's looking for her, too. And Madame Chez Roma has reported Dixie missing to the police—and now the coppers are looking for her."

"They won't look very hard," said Shamus. "They got more important things . . ."

"The point is, where is she?"

"How should I know?"

"You don't sound very upset."

This sobered Shamus. "Boy, you can't see inside me."

"Well . . ." said Skip, "I just thought I'd let you know in case you hadn't heard. And Shamus—don't let it upset you too much. Remember? Money, moola, gelt, mazuma, loot, silver eagles, legal tender? So . . . I'm not going to say anything about this to Dooley. He's got enough to worry about."

Shamus secretly heaved a sigh of relief. "Don't worry about me," he said.

"Stout fella," said Skip. "Now I'm going to try to get some sleep. Sleep? What's that?"

He hung up. Dixie was waiting to hear the news and as he fixed drinks for them he told her all about it.

"Well, f . . . 'em," said Dixie.

"Which reminds me," said Shamus.

Dixie began to laugh. They drank in silence. It was going to be all right, thought Shamus; all right indeed—

Shortly after eight o'clock the next morning Dooley's phone rang. It was Skip.

"Dooley, I hit it. The safe man's here, I think."

"Tell me about it," said Dooley sitting on the edge of his bed in pajamas and fumbling for his cigarettes.

"It was a hunch—I don't know what. I'm so punchy now maybe I'm psychic. Couldn't sleep so I took a little run out to the West Side and prowled the streets around the trucking company. Finally a car drove out with a hood in it, Kovack or Lacy. And I followed it. Very little traffic so I could give him a block or so leeway. No problem. Well, he drove to the bus station and picked up a weird little guy—no bigger than a jockey."

"You've done it, Skip," cried Dooley, in triumph. "It's Menzies." Then after a pause: "It's too bad."

"Too bad? Why?"

"He's a harmless little guy. Nitro expert—the best. And this could turn out to be his last job."

"So what do you think?" said Skip after a long pause. Skip had felt a sudden chill, but why comment? "Travelon, Inc.?"

"Has to be. Tough safe. It's obvious. So now get busy while I move. I spotted a perfect spot. Nearly behind Travelon. I'll let you know. Call Shamus, and Doc and Chuck. The four of you find an apartment on that side-street and move in. Let Doc and Chuck handle the renting. You and Shamus slip in at night. The guns have to be moved. But Doc knows all about that. And we haven't got much time. I doubt if it'll be tonight; talking to do. It might, but more likely tomorrow night. Naturally call off all tailing."

They talked on for a while, taking care of other matters, then Dooley hung up with a faint grim smile of satisfaction.

"We might do it," he said. "We just might."

Shamus's phone rang to an empty room. Shamus was blissfully asleep in the big bedroom, and Dixie, also asleep, was curled round him, with her bare arm flung across his back.

Finally the ringing penetrated and Shamus opened his eyes and said: "Oh, Christ . . ."

"What's the matter, honey?" asked Dixie, cuddling into his back.

Shamus finally made it to the phone.

"What's the matter for Christ's sake!" yelled Skip, who was burned. "You dead? What? This is it—so get that slow ass of yours . . ."

Shamus listened to the instructions in silence. After all this hopeless time, this finally was it. A sense of dread began to nag at Shamus. He looked up. Dixie was standing in the doorway, sketchily attired in a bedsheet.

"What is it, honey?" she asked in a low voice.

Shamus put his fingers to his lips for silence, and Dixie disappeared. It wasn't curiosity, Shamus knew. She had thought it might have something to do with herself.

Skip was still burned when he hung up. Lack of sleep was really getting to him—and the usual fix just wasn't doing the job, and he hated to step it up. He'd seen too many addicts make the funny farm—

Shamus sat down on the edge of the bed and studied the Sleeping Beauty for a moment, then he gently shook her awake. "Baby," he said, "how much do you know about my work?"

"Work? What work?" she said, sleepily. "Do you work?"

"All right," said Shamus. "I get paid for following people. So now a very big job has come up and I've got to go out of town for a few days."

"Big money?"

"Very big."

"Then go, go," said Dixie. "I'll mind our castle. I love it. I love *you*— you saved my life."

"What do you mean?"

"I was ready for anything. Even the sleeping pill bit; goddamn it, I was! So you go. Don't worry; I'll stay in. I won't answer the phone. I'll be like a bear. What do they call it?"

"Hibernate."

"Yes. I'll hibernate."

It was not yet noon and Dooley had already moved to his new location, and Doc had just called to say they had found a perfect spot on the side-street that led down from the Travelon, Inc. corner to the street that paralleled the Chicago River. Skip and Shamus had been alerted and would slip into the beat-up old furnished apartment through the back as soon as it got dark. They'd even found an empty garage where they could park the cars face out and ready to move. (Dooley's car was in a similar position at the side of a cement ramp, by the hotel, where the dayman, slipped a buck, had let him park it.) All was as well as it could be, given the circumstances. Would the enemy spring a surprise of some kind? Dooley hoped not. It was tough enough, speculative enough, as it was.

Dooley's room was at the side of the hotel, and from his window he had a good view of the back of Travelon, Inc. Better yet, Doc had furnished him with something called night-glasses. Doc was originally from Fond du Lac, Wisconsin, and apparently he knew all about fishing and boating. One day, during a lull, Doc had talked to Dooley about Lake Winnebago, and cabin cruisers, and pike, pickerel and muskalungs—and apparently he'd used the night-glasses on his boat. According to his conversation, Doc had been in the car business several times—in Fond du Lac, in Oshkosh and finally in Chicago. Doc was the kind of man who baffled Dooley; half straight, half pro—apparently he couldn't really make up his mind which side he was on—though he looked steady enough, God knows: a smart, shrewd, tough, able guy. But how he had got into the pro ranks baffled Dooley. It took years, years, from petty to big. How does a guy go from running a car agency to one of the biggest armored car knockovers in history—and get away clean . . .? Like Hamm, Dooley was all pro. On the other hand Mike Ivan, trucking company executive, seemed to be another Doc Pace.

Under Dooley's bed now was his chopper, and his ammunition, and beside it his money belt. He intended to wear the belt on the job. You never knew. If for some reason you slipped up, if there was a rumble, if the coppers got into the act and you had to lam, it might not be convenient to get back to your headquarters; and there you'd be out in left field with a few dollars of spending money in your pocket. But with the belt, if need be, he could lam to California, or Europe, for that matter.

Having time to spare now, Dooley sat on the floor and loaded the chopper. He didn't really like what he was going to do, not out of compunction, but because it was rip-and-tear and extremely dangerous. But this was a must. Mike Ivan had not only done him out of a very big job; he'd had Hamm killed. Without a doubt by that creep, Goggles. Dooley declared himself judge and jury. Mike was guilty by any canon you could name: underworld or straight john. If caught for complicity in the murder of Hamm, the Illinois authorities would, without compunction, try and hang him. So Mike did not really have a leg to stand on. Nor did Dooley in any way regret Mike's coming demise; he merely deplored the necessity and the method.

The chopper loaded, Dooley rose and tried the night-glasses in daytime. They worked fine. Satisfied, Dooley got out a bottle of wine and a tissue-paper-wrapped ham sandwich and had his lunch, like a workman knocking off when the noon whistle blew.

From time-to-time images of Myrta and the kids swam before his eyes—and the peace of sitting there that stormy night, with the wind howling, the rain pelting, the kids snugly in bed and Myrta by his side talking, then dozing . . . but, hell, he told himself . . . the whole thing was impossible, except for moments, and moments were not for real life, they were for dreaming . . .

In the beat-up old apartment, Doc was stretched out on a couch and

Chuck was listening to a turned down radio and cleaning and oiling a .45 revolver.

"I was thinking," said Doc.

"Yeah?"

"I was thinking we should move on."

Chuck turned and looked at his father. "Move on? You're kidding."

"I'm not kidding," said Doc. "Win or lose, we won't starve. I was thinking last night, I'd just turn the operation over to Ed, let him run it, as he's running it now, and pay me off as he goes along and when he can. I don't really need the money and I like old Ed . . ."

"I'm tired of moving on," said Chuck. "I've been moving on all my goddamned life."

Doc sat up and looked his son in surprise. Chuck was the least rebellious guy Doc had ever met, but this sounded like rebellion.

"What are you talking about?"

"I'm talking about Fond du Lac, Oshkosh, Cleveland, Youngstown, Pittsburgh and Chicago."

"You want to get stuck in one lousy place, Charles?"

When the Old Man was getting sore at him he always started calling him "Charles". Chuck said nothing, went on cleaning the gun and listening to the radio.

"You didn't answer me," Doc insisted.

"Look," said Chuck. "I got Ingeborg—and I'm not moving on and leaving her here, that's for sure."

"Oh, for God's sake," said Doc in disgust. "A big broad-assed German broad— there are broads all over the place. That's what this country has got the most of, broads."

"You do your way, I'll do mine," said Chuck stubbornly. "This time I get my own cut. Dooley said so."

Doc lay back and stared at the ceiling. This was just no time for a family argument. After a while he took out a cigar, puffed on it slowly, and finally amused himself making perfect smoke rings.

"Well," he said at last, "I guess you're tired of your old man's company."

"Did I say anything like that?" Chuck protested. "I said I wasn't moving on and leaving Ingeborg behind, that's what I said."

Chuck always dreaded a clash with his old man who was smarter and tougher than himself—he'd been backing away for years. But goddamn it, he was thirty years old and it was time he spoke out. This was his big opportunity. If the job worked out, he'd have his own money, big money—and if he walked away on his own, he wouldn't starve, that was for sure.

And Doc was aware of all this. Tough as he was, Doc feared loneliness, aloneness. Chuck was the only relative he had in the world. Without Chuck, he didn't have a link to anyone—he would be Doc All-Alone . . .

"Well," said Doc, tentatively, "it was just an idea. We'll see. I was figuring if I went to Los Angeles or San Francisco, I might be able to buy up a Cadillac agency and run a class business again, as we did in Fond du Lac. We'll have plenty of money—I hope."

"Cadillac," said Chuck. "Good idea. So what do you need with me? You can hire grease monkeys."

Doc sat up again and stared at his son, who was giving him one surprise after another. "I thought you liked to work with cars. And you keep saying you're no salesman."

Chuck was being unreasonable and realized it. He had no ready reply. All his life he'd lost every argument with this father. This time it had nothing whatever to do with argument, or logic; it was a feeling, a pervading feeling, an unreasonable feeling. Actually he had very little to complain about. The old man had always done well by him. When other guys were walking or hitching rides, he had his own car, a present from Doc—even when he was 14 years old and couldn't get a license to drive. He drove anyway, and Doc encouraged him. He'd lived well in every respect. And when he'd decided to volunteer for the Marines, Doc hadn't argued with him but had tried to help him. Oh, Doc was an all right old man—that is, if you didn't try to oppose him when he had his mind set on something. Then—he was trouble, much trouble.

"All I'm saying is," said Chuck, "I don't like moving around all over the place like a gypsy—and I'm not leaving Ingeborg here. That's all I'm saying."

Doc rose, walked to the window and stood looking out. This would take thought, much thought. He decided to pass it for the time being. There was an outside chance they'd all get killed or at least maimed, so actually this was a very minor matter at the moment. And it was not good to have Chuck unsettled over it.

"All right," Chuck," he said. "I won't press you. Time will tell."

Chuck said nothing. He was sure this wasn't the end of the argument—not by a damned sight. He just had no intention of going back to the old stooge relationship, and that was that.

Skip was hiding out till nightfall in the little downtown apartment of one of the call girls he knew and occasionally placed, if the money was big enough. Her name was Patsy and she was from Butte, Montana— the only person Skip had ever met from that city. She was known as Ride-Em-Cowboy, as she kept talking about her brother who was a rodeo rider. Patsy was very cute and very tough. She looked like a doll and she'd take the shirt off your back. Fiftyish executives of various companies, attending conventions, were fair game for Skip and Patsy—they nearly always flipped over her. She was close to 30 years old and at times looked 16. The old guys probably felt they were committing a mortal sin: she had a slim boyish figure and big brown eyes that got red when she was mad, and that was often. But she thought Skip was wonderful. He made her laugh. He never pressured her, nor did he try to steal her money. He was fair.

So Patsy slept on in the big bed, and Skip sat by the window trying to contain himself. He was jumpy—but though you'd never guess it from his appearance his will was strong and he refused to step up the fix. He'd take it and like it. It was a tough enough roller coaster he was on. Why connive at his own destruction.

Skip often thought vaguely of a cure. But how? He was always up to his ears in business, petty or large; he seldom had time to sleep. So why dream about a cure? To take the cure you had to go away and hide—no bright lights, no excitement . . . Skip sighed and tried not to think of what they were all in for. The only reassuring thought was of Dooley; Dooley would manage it. The Gorilla would come through.

Night fell early, and Dooley sat by his window, looking down at the back of Travelon, Inc.—though the hit might still be at least ten hours off—and listening to the uproar of the rush hour, as working people moved homeward from the Loop in every direction but east, on buses, streetcars, the L, taxis and private cars, causing such a jumble of noises that they lost all individuality and seemed to blend into one great noise, a combination hum-clang-shriek. Soon the Loop would be all but empty and very still, until the theater and nightclub crowds began to show up, and the uproar would start all over again, but it was a minor noise compared to the cacophony of the rush hour.

Dooley had listened to the whole performance the night before, not expecting the hit to be made but sitting up till dawn nonetheless—then sleeping like a dead man for nearly eight straight hours.

Tonight was different. This should be it. Menzies had been in town long enough to be exhaustively briefed—and rested, and prepared. No point in calling him in at all unless they were ready to go. The preparatory part, the casing, the mapping of getaway roads were none of his affair. His only affair was to blow the safe quickly and efficiently, take his pay and go. It was unlikely that he was cut in for a full share—but Menzies came very high, and he wouldn't even look at you unless you said $10,000 and that had to be a simple one that took up only a moment of his time. For something like this, Menzies could write his own ticket—say, $50,000.

Dooley was ready. Beside him on the floor was the chopper, a box of ammunition, his .45 and his money belt. Around midnight he intended to put on the belt and holster his .45—just in case; although he didn't expect the hit much before three a.m., maybe a little earlier—but he didn't want to lose an extra second when it came time to leave. On the window sill were the night-glasses and from time to time he'd pick them up and study the back of Travelon, Inc., and the surrounding streets that weren't blocked from his vision by buildings.

So? So you just sat and waited. What else.

Skip was asleep, stretched out on the couch where Doc had been sitting the day before. Exhaustion had finally caught up with him. Shamus was reading a Chicago newspaper, the sports section, and occasionally wiping non-existent sweat from his brow. Actually it was cold in the room, the clanking steam radiator doing little to warm things up. Chuck just sat and stared into space, while Doc kept vigil at the window. Occasionally Doc would wander out and see that the two cars they intended to use were OK. All they needed was for some punks to steal the cars—or strip them, as was being done all over town. Doc and Skip would be in one car; Shamus and Chuck in the other. Doc considered Skip to be the least steady of the outfit so Doc wanted him where he could watch him and see to it that he did his part. Chuck he never worried about and Shamus seemed solid enough.

In fact Doc thought highly of Shamus, particularly since the exhaustive briefings Shamus had given them all in regard to streets, turns, angles, red lights, alternative routes—and finally just how the two cars should proceed, when the time came. Well, after all, Shamus was a former cop, and he must have been a good one, thought Doc.

Time passed. Skip woke with a start, looked about him wildly for a moment before he remembered where he was, then he got up and stamped around, trying to wake up his right foot that had fallen asleep. Finally he sank down in a chair beside Shamus, and lit a cigarette.

"Sleep, sleep, glorious sleep," said Skip. "I've just had two hours of it and I feel better, much better."

Shamus said nothing.

"I figure you're pretty upset about Dixie," Skip went on, "but don't let it worry you too much. I think she just got fed up and blew. She was pretty sick and tired the night I talked to her. She'll turn up."

"I hope so," said Shamus.

"Oh, she will," said Skip. Long silence. Chuck stretched out on the couch. Doc was in and out. Time ticked on inevitably but the hours passed as slowly as drops from a Chinese water torture.

Shamus rustled his paper and tried to concentrate on the football news. Rah, rah! Chicago U! Big Deal! All he could think of was Dixie all alone in the apartment, hibernating. During that long (but very short) night together they'd talked occasionally, desultorily, small talk, throwaway, nothing—but during the course of one conversation they'd discovered that both had been born in Chicago—which was odd as NOBODY was born in Chicago; everybody had come in from some other place. Now Shamus remembered: he'd said he didn't even know her name—only Dixie.

"Are you sure you want to know?" asked Dixie.

"Of course. Why not? I want to know all about you."

"That'll be the day," said Dixie. "Well—if you can stand it—my name is Ludmilla Polakov or Polakova?"

Shamus had a feeling she was kidding him. "Don't you know which?"

"Polakova is the feminine."

"What are you, a Russian spy? We shoot them at dawn, you know."

"I'm Polish," said Dixie. "But I wasn't born in Poland; I was born where you can smell the Stockyards very strong."

"Chicago born, eh? Me too. I was born on North Halsted Street."

Two Chicagoans! Shamus sat thinking this over, then he turned to Skip.

"Where were you born, Skip?"

Skip gave him a look. "You mean 'why' don't you?"

"I just got thinking," said Shamus—about Dixie, what else? "Nobody is born in Chicago. I was."

"I was born in Belleville, Illinois," said Skip. "In fact, you might say I'm a St. Louis boy. It's across the river. Why?"

"I told you why."

"Shamus, this is a dull conversation."

They fell silent, as had the city. Doc kept prowling. Chuck was now asleep.

"Shall I read you all the news about Alonzo Stagg and good old Chicago U.?" asked Shamus.

Skip got up and walked away and out into the cool air of night-Chicago. He breathed deeply several times and felt much better as the result of the ozone intake. It was nice to get out. The beat-up old apartment stank; there were probably mice and rats and cockroaches. It was not exactly a plush spot. Well . . . it would eventually all be over, one way or another. Skip had no faith in fate, or luck or Providence or whatever you wanted to call it, but he did have faith in Dooley.

The drops continued to fall at long intervals from the Chinese water torture.

Dooley was ready. In fact he'd been ready for nearly two hours, the money belt around his waist, the .45 in its holster and the loaded, towel-wrapped chopper on the floor at his feet. It was nearly two a.m. and the city was enveloped in a kind of vast silence except for a few individual noises of strayed revelers and taxi-cabs and an occasional huge truck, starting on a night journey.

It was the hour of the silent prowler. Houses all over the huge Chicago area were being robbed, women raped, men shot—as the police knew only too well; as they heard it all, in a delayed replay, on their own radios. The Chicago of the straight johns slumbered on oblivious—feeling safe and sound and God's in his heaven, all's right with the world . . . meanwhile, the creeps and prowlers came out of their caves and crevices, the nuts, the rapists, the impoverished junkies looking for a fix—the whole large army of night people that hid from the day and from the sun. Dooley knew that world only too well; it was part of his own, though as a pro he never acknowledged it as such.

Another drop fell from the Chinese water torture. Dooley looked away to light a cigarette; when he looked back he saw a rather small nondescript panel truck coming down the street at the side of Travelon, Inc. He waited tensely, with a hunch this was it. The truck turned into the alley and stopped just behind Travelon, Inc. Dooley felt a sudden surge of triumph, picked up the night-glasses and centered on the truck. A legend read: CHICAGO PLUMBING AND HEATING CO. Four men got out, one after the other, two from the back. Two were tall and broad; the Detroit hoods; one was tall and very slight—Goggles, no doubt; one very short, little taller than jockey-size and carrying a square case or satchel—Menzies. Dooley studied them for a long moment—to be absolutely certain—then, still looking, he called the switchboard downstairs.

The nightman was a drunk, who by the time he went off duty was plastered, though cold sober when he arrived for work. He was Dooley's slave because Dooley had seen to it that he was; with money and liquor. Earlier in the day he'd warned the nightman he might want to make an important late call, to stay by the switchboard. And the nightman had saluted and said: "Yes sir, colonel. You can count on me." (An ex-GI, as he would occasionally brag when he'd had a few too many.)

The nightman was as good as his word, and the connection was made in a matter of minutes.

Doc came on.

"They're here," said Dooley. "Now keep this line open. I'll give you every move while your guys get ready."

Doc turned and nodded to the others who were all standing, hoping and even fearing that this was it.

Dooley put down the receiver and took up his vigil. One hood was apparently working on the car, as a blind—he was the lookout. Menzies stood by, suitcase in hand, waiting, like a CPA in a bank line. Goggles and the other hood were making an entry of some kind. They were in the shadows so Dooley couldn't quite make them out. All were in work-jumpers, except Menzies.

Whatever the entry was, it was part of Hamm's plan and maybe one of the major parts. Hamm was a genius at finding weak spots, shortcuts: an unconsidered ventilating system, a goof by architects, leaving an egress exposed, any small slip or folly in security precautions—this was Hamm's meat. And no doubt he'd found one here.

"By God, he sure has," thought Dooley. Goggles and the hood were already inside; they disappeared from view. In a moment Menzies also disappeared. The other hood went on fooling with the car, and occasionally looking all around him at the silent city and its silent streets.

From time-to-time Dooley relayed the information to Doc, who finally said: "We are a hundred per cent ready, Dooley."

"Good," said Dooley. "But be patient. It will be some time yet."

In a moment Skip came on the phone: "Doc's checking. I'm here. How's it going?"

"It won't be too long now," said Dooley.

He kept the night-glasses trained on the big curtained windows of the lower floor of Travelon, Inc. and in a little while he saw what looked like a very dim glow. At first it was so vague he thought it might be a reflection or that he was imagining it—but finally it came dimly clear in the glasses. It was a work light. What else?

Another drop fell from the Chinese water torture. Such a long time seemed to pass that Skip asked: "Anything wrong?"

"I don't think so," said Dooley. "It takes time."

He'd no sooner got the words out of his mouth when there was a dull, heavy thud that rattled Dooley's window slightly, and what looked like a dim-reddish flash showed against the Travelon, Inc. curtains.

"They blew it," said Dooley.

"Yeah," said Skip, in an odd voice. "I felt it. I thought maybe it was the L. The goddamned L is practically over our heads here."

It was the kind of powerful dull thud that would wake sleepers in the area, who would turn over in bed, stare, and say, "What was that?"—

listen for a moment—then go back to sleep.

Doc came on; for once Doc sounded excited. "Mike Ivan's prowling the area in a car," he said. "He just went past."

Dooley thought for a moment, then said: "Good. I was wondering where he was. He will either lead the truck or follow it. If he leads it, let him pass. I'll take care of him. And if he follows it, I'll still take care of him. Understand? If he leads the truck let him pass."

"Right," said Doc.

"Okay," said Dooley. "Go, Doc."

Doc hung up. Dooley did likewise, then he rose and gathered up his towel-wrapped chopper but kept his night-glasses on Travelon, Inc. The hood was no longer fooling with the car; he was in the driver's seat now, waiting.

In a moment Menzies emerged from the shadows, carrying his case, then he turned, and after a brief gesture to the hood, walked off down the alley, like a workman on his way home from a night job. Dooley felt an almost wild sense of relief. Menzies had done his job and had been paid and now he was on his way to the bus station or a cab stand. Menzies was not only exceptionally clever at his job, he was also very cagey and smart. Dooley had worked with him twice and in both cases had hardly laid eyes on him—except for the moment of truth. Menzies almost never said a word. He was a mild-appearing little men, but Dooley had noted a steely flash in the blue eyes that were generally hidden by tinted-glasses. It was said his eyes had once been injured in a nitro accident and that he'd been nearly stone-blind for a year or more.

Dooley waited, his excessive patience taxed now by a violent desire to act. In a moment Goggles and the other hood appeared, carrying what looked like a mail sack and began to open the back of the truck. Dooley turned and left abruptly—out, and down the stairs, carrying the chopper heavily wrapped in dirty bath towels. He gestured to the nightman.

"Thanks, pal," said Dooley. "I got a woman kindly does my laundry." He indicated the bundle. "And she works odd hours," he said.

"Sure, sure," said the nightman, laughing. He didn't know what was up and he didn't want to know. But it wasn't laundry, that was for sure. With him Dooley could do no wrong. Friend in need was a friend indeed, thought the ex-GI returning to his bottle of "Canadian" whiskey, provided by Dooley.

Dooley drove out into the side-street, taking it slow. Up ahead of him the truck was just turning west on the boulevard, which was a straight shot to the trucking company except for a few turns and bends—and it had one rather circuitous bend that would be, Dooley hoped, their undoing. And Shamus had placed "the spot" far enough along, so if they got off scot-free from Travelon, Inc., as expected, they would no doubt feel safe and be laughing and congratulating each other on a very big knockover.

Dooley looked about him cautiously. Not a car in sight. So he cut his lights. He could see perfectly with his lights out. Far up ahead of him gleamed the truck's red tail-light, and as they moved along through the hush of the dead hour an occasional taxi appeared out of a side-street—and that was all. Nothing. And as Dooley knew, radio-cars were very scarce in this area where there was little if any real trouble at night. The trouble was where the teaming thousands lived in each other's laps—or in the far-scattered clubs and speaks and in their immediate neighborhoods. Late at night The Loop was as deserted as if the population had fled before an invading army that would soon arrive.

Far up ahead a car came out of a side-street and cut in front of the truck. Dooley had a moment of worry and then he relaxed. Mike had picked them up and he was leading the way. Dooley muttered to himself. In the excitement, had Doc understood him? Would he let Mike pass? Both Doc and Chuck wanted personally to settle Mike because of Hamm. But that was all nonsense when it came to the big knockover. There was no room for sentiment here. Business was business. Dooley kept worrying as time passed slowly.

Mike, half a block up ahead, led them at a moderate driving speed, no muss, no fuss, no haste. They were clear—oh, what a knockover!— but this was no time to get hilarious about it and go tearing off through the city, whooping, like Hoosiers. The time to whoop was later.

In the truck Goggles sat making a strange sound that was a mixture of chuckling, giggling and hysteria. Like robbing a blind cripple— apple-pie—and for God knows how much; Goggles was still shook from the sight of all those hundreds of stacks of bills—good Christ!—by the bushel. And once things cleared, Goggles was for Costa Rica. He had a friend there who kept writing him—a beach bum. Weather great; broads great—and so cheap a guy could practically live for nothing. With the kind of money Goggles foresaw, he could retire—for good, period. Rich as Rockefeller. How about that? Goggles kept making that sound, and finally tough-faced Frank Kovacs turned and looked at him.

"All right, all right," said Goggles, and subsided.

Inside the truck, Bill Lacy sat congratulating himself and occasionally patting the fat mail sack jostling there beside him. "Christ, what a load of moola," he thought, then he began to whistle. That Mike Ivan— what an operator!

Goggles woke up first, as the car slowed and swung round a long bend. Wasn't that a car without lights . . .? What was it doing . . .? And on the far side there was another car without lights . . . But Mike had gone safely past . . . he could see the twinkling of Mike's tail-light up ahead. Well . . .

"What the hell . . .!" cried Kovacs.

And then the shooting started. Choppers shattered the quiet night and the truck was raked fore and aft by a merciless fire. Goggles was shaking with fear; he froze; then acting in a kind of instinctive way he turned on the big flashlight in his hand and for one fleeting second, as in a nightmare, he caught a glimpse of the contorted face of Shamus with a chopper in his hand, firing. Then Frank Kovacs slumped, dead, against the wheel, and the truck slithered around and hit the curb a very hard wallop—and came to a shuddering stop. Goggles, untouched, fell out of the open car door into utter darkness and the back doors burst open and Bill Lacy staggered out, badly wounded, took two steps forward, then fell on his face in the middle of the street, writhing. Another burst was fired and Lacy lay still.

Goggles came to with a start. He was wedged down between the wheels and a wide cement storm-drain that carried the heavy rain runoffs that accumulated in this area and guided them down to the Chicago River. Suddenly he seemed to slip, fall quite a ways, then land hard on cement in a few inches of water. He lay frozen with terror and panic—

He heard somebody say, as in a dream: ". . . son-of-a-bitch fell down the storm drain . . ." Then he blacked out.

Mike had been riding along, congratulating himself and calmly smoking a cigar. This was the knockover to end all knockovers. What a noise it would make—and himself completely clean in the city. Then he heard something. Christ, it sounded like shooting. He glanced into the rearview mirror. The truck's headlights seemed to be wobbling all over the place—over half a block back. Blowout? What the hell . . .?

He threw the wheel over to make a U-turn, and at that moment a car without lights came plunging out of a side-street and before Mike could make up his mind what to do, he was dead, across the wheel . . . and his car was taking a wildly erratic course which carried it over a curb, across the sidewalk and into the front of a small brick building— there was a wild clashing of metal and the shattering sound of falling glass.

Dooley put his chopper on the car floor and headed for the Alvin Pace

Used Car lot—where Alvin Pace dealt fairly, according to the sign.

Dooley and Doc looked grim, Chuck unconcerned, but Shamus was very pale and kept mopping his brow and running his hand across his face. Skip was frozen into silence. He fell down into a chair and kept staring at his hands, as if they didn't belong to him.

"All right," said Dooley; "of course you couldn't stop and dig him out. Was he hit?"

"How could he help being hit?" said Chuck. "We shot the hell out of that truck."

"All right," said Dooley, again. "That's one we can't help. I hate loose ends but . . . Come on. We've got work to do. Chuck, will you sit on the outside—just in case?"

Chuck went out.

Now Dooley turned and noted the attitudes of Skip and Shamus. "All right, guys! Get over here. We've got to count this money, and then scatter as fast as possible."

So the four of them counted the money, each making a separate tally—all surprised by the amazing bulk of the take. A moderate-sized mail sack was nearly full of wrapped bundles of bills—of various denominations, some them large; some of them very large.

Little by little the tension and shock died down as the men became so absorbed in their work that it grew to be just a job, something to be got through.

At last each had his own tally. The tallies were handed to Dooley who sat figuring, then Doc and Dooley got out their lists of expenses— the front money—and checked with each other. Finally they were satisfied.

"Let's make it a good round figure," said Doc. "Minus front money, the take is eight hundred thousand dollars—which is one hundred and sixty thousand dollars apiece. Any complaints?"

Shamus and Skip were not astonished by the figure as they'd helped to do the counting—even so they couldn't quite believe it. They believed the figures, of course, but emotionally they simply did not believe that they'd soon have one hundred and sixty thousand dollars in their own possession to do with as they pleased.

Chuck was called in, and Skip went to sit in one of the cars. Chuck, who had had no part in the counting, almost fainted, literally. He sat down in a chair and just sat there. This was impossible!

Now Doc and Dooley counted off the shares and Doc got out three very large briefcases from the bottom drawer of his desk. "Here you go," he said. "Something to carry your ill-gotten gains in."

Dooley and Shamus packed their money away. Skip was called in and Chuck went out again, to sit in a car and keep an eye on the night-city.

Doc said: "This has been what they call a very profitable association, so I'll tell you what I'm going to do. I'm going to make you three guys a present of those cars, if you want them."

They all wanted them.

"Fine," said Doc. "So just leave the rental slips on. No problem."

"Thanks, Doc," said Dooley; then: "All right. Let's get out of here and scatter. It's getting late."

And one by one the three of them left: Skip, still in a state of shock, for Evanston; Shamus for his Gold Coast apartment, where Dixie was hibernating; and Dooley for his old spot at the North Side hotel.

Chuck waved to them then came back inside.

"Well, Chuck," said Doc, "we've got over three-hundred and fifty thousand dollars."

"No we," said Chuck. "I've got one hundred and sixty thousand."

Then he crossed to a cabinet at the back of the office, got out a briefcase and began to pack his money into it.

"I noticed you only bought three of these," said Chuck, "so I got one for myself."

Doc sat down and lit a cigar and propped up his feet.

"What are you figurin' on doing?" he asked.

"Well, first I'm going to get my own apartment. I've got one already picked out."

"Fine," said Doc. "Maybe it's time."

Chuck paused and turned to look at his father. What was this—some kind of trick?

"I mean it," said Doc. "I've been thinking. Time I took a vacation. Maybe up to Lake Winnebago. You and Ed can run the place till I get back. I might even go up to Canada, like I did one year when you were a kid, and do some hunting. On snowshoes. I learned it then. OK?"

"Well . . . sure," said Chuck. "But I don't want to get stuck with this place. I'm figuring I'll buy up a couple of filling stations and run my own business."

"Good idea," said Doc, then he leaned back in his chair and blew perfect smoke rings.

This big hunk of money had given Doc new courage. Doc, with a clear take of a hundred and sixty thousand dollars, was not the Doc All-Alone who had been suffering from nervousness and tension before the big plunge ...

Goggles lay in the storm drain trembling with fear and rage. Coppers all over the place—noise, voices, lights and flashing weird reflections along the sweating wall above him. He'd lost his gun and his glasses— he could hardly see his hand in front of his face. But he could see that vision of Shamus's fierce grimaces as he pulled the trigger of the chopper very very plainly—as plainly as if it had been painted on a wall. "Oh, you dirty conniving bastard," thought Goggles, as he continued to tremble with fear and rage. Goggles had no idea who had been with Shamus, nor did he care. The others, whoever, were mere shadows, with no connection to Goggles—but Shamus had taken Mike's money and some way had managed to sell them out to . . .?

Goggles gave a wild jump. Dooley! Shamus had sold them out to the Gorilla!

He heard a voice say: "Here comes Murtaugh!"

Sergeant Murtaugh was the field boss of the Metropolitan Hoodlum Squad and he was a very tough hombre, who rode around in an open Cadillac with a mounted machine-gun in the back. He was supposed to be as tough as the toughest hoods. Tougher—everybody said.

There was a loud squeal of brakes, a car door slammed, and Goggles heard the heavy footfalls of Sergeant Murtaugh.

He was merely swearing, then: "Will some bastard inform me what the Holy Jumping Jesus Christ is going on around here? Three stiffs lying in the street. A lousy panel truck. What in the . . .?"

His voice trailed off as he moved farther up the street.

Calming himself, Goggles settled down for a long wait. Could he climb out? Maybe.

The dead hours ruled the city as three cars on different boulevards and at a staggered pace moved toward their destinations: Shamus toward the near North Side, Dooley toward the far North Side, and Skip toward Evanston, which was much farther north even than Dooley's goal. Meanwhile thousands of uneasy sleepers, all about them, turned in their beds already partially awake and dreading the morrow, the alarm clock, the cold bedroom, the rush to work, the crush and crowding—just another day. What else?

Shamus arrived home first, noting that the briefcase was as heavy as if he'd been carrying bricks. He still couldn't quite believe it—One hundred and sixty grand . . .? Incredible! As he opened the apartment door he was greeted by what seemed to him like a deserted silence. Dixie? Had she lammed? He hurried to the bedroom door and opened it—but there was Dixie sound asleep, curled almost into a ball—a dim, lovely picture in the whitish-yellow reflected light from outside. Shamus felt such a tightness in his chest that for a moment he could hardly breathe. Everything was OK—OK.

He quietly shut the door, put away the briefcase in a strongbox he kept on the closest floor at the back—actually a stout metal locker with a system of triple locks—then he went to the little wet-bar in the corner, poured himself a large hooker of "Canadian" whiskey, and drank it slowly, staring out at the lights of the Gold Coast hotels, clear tonight.

Shamus didn't know how he felt. Violence was no new thing to him: he'd seen a God's plenty of it in the war and when he'd been a member of the police department, and yet never before had he taken part in an ambush and the withering destruction of guys who never knew what hit them. Shamus felt very tired and very shook—and kept wincing away from pictures that insisted on jumping up before his eyes: the hood falling out of the back of the truck and writhing on the pavement— the crashing shattering noise: the surprised cries of anguish . . .

"What are you—chicken?" Shamus demanded of himself sternly.

But it was no good. The problem was, he was just worn out, from weeks of relentless tracking, from uncertainty, from tension, from suspense, and finally he thought: "I wouldn't do it again for double the money. I'll be goddamned if I would."

Maybe penny ante was better. In the final analysis you'd live longer that way.

He heard something and turned. It was Dixie standing in the bedroom doorway, wearing one of his shirts, her black hair all tousled—not the elegant Dixie of Chez Roma, a vulnerable looking, a younger Dixie—

"I thought I heard . . . what's the matter, honey? You look so pale and tired. God, you look pale! What is it?"

"I'm worn out," said Shamus. "Haven't slept."

"Well, there's the bed in there," said Dixie. "Get in it and sleep. And I'll let you alone . . . I think."

Shamus tried to laugh. "OK. Well, anyway, baby, we're in the money."

"Good, good," said Dixie. "Now put that drink down and come to bed. I'll be quiet as a mouse and you sleep as long as you like. Sleep like the dead."

"Yeah," said Shamus.

The nightman was surprised to see Dooley enter at this hour, carrying a briefcase and what looked like a bunch of dirty bath towels. But he was also pleased; he'd missed that good "Canadian" liquor and the two or three bucks here and there. Mr. Dooley was a great tenant—one of the few.

"Well, I'm back," said Dooley. "And I even brought my dirty laundry."

The nightman laughed. "Glad to see you."

In his room, Dooley rolled back the carpet, lifted out the panel and put away his tools, his accoutrements, his money belt and his briefcase. This time he shifted the furniture and moved a huge wardrobe over the spot where the panel was. Not that he was really worried about it, as the cleaning woman was as incurious as any human he'd ever seen (probably stupefied with drink) and never gave his room more than a "lick and a promise", as they said in his youth in Toledo, Ohio. She generally made the bed, gave a few whisks with a dust cloth, made a stab at sweeping, then stumbled out. As for moving something like the wardrobe—forget it.

It was just that the Big Money called for further precautions. He now had nearly two hundred thousand dollars buried under the floor. Now what . . .?

He undressed and took a long soak in the shower. He had no tub in his room, only the shower. He felt very tired, but some of the tenseness was gone and his main feeling was one of grim satisfaction. He'd pulled it off. He'd pulled off the near impossible, and they'd all got off scot-free, with their money. What any of them did now was no concern of his. He had no intention of seeing any of them again. It was his normal method of procedure—his MO, as the cops said. The preparation, the take, the scatter. Even pros sometimes went in pairs or even small groups. It was always a mistake in Dooley's opinion. Look at Menzies. He'd taken his fee and left. Otherwise he'd now be in a drawer in the morgue.

Ties were dangerous. And Dooley had avoided them almost from the beginning.

He put on his pajamas and then stood at the window, smoking a cigarette and looking down into the empty street. A late fall dawn would soon be creeping as usual over the house-tops. Everything in the universe worked like clock-work. How and why Dooley did not know nor did he care. On a prison farm with time on his hands he had once wondered vaguely about it. Why did the sun rise every morning on the dot? Who set up the mechanism?

Dooley yawned widely and went to bed. Almost at once he fell into a dreamless sleep as into a black pit.

Skip was shaking so badly he almost dropped the briefcase as he unlocked his apartment door. The whole town was dark and silent— nothing stirred, as if everybody had moved away. Skip was on the verge of hallucinating. The people *had* moved away. He was the only one left—he was certain of it. Good God, what would he do all alone in a dark world like this . . .?

He stumbled into his apartment, almost falling, threw the briefcase on the floor, and made himself a normal fix, then he hesitated and doubled it. "Just this once," he told himself. "Just this once. Good God, what a night! Guys falling around all over the street. Jesus, what a mess!"

He lay down on the couch. It seemed to sail away into the darkened sky—where there was nothing, nobody, emptiness, eternal silence . . . time ticked on like an old watch that needed cleaning. Skip didn't know where he was—then he didn't know who he was. He lost all sense of identity—he was a thing, something . . . a what . . .?

But slowly the world came back into focus. Sweating like a bull, but feeling fairly steady now, Skip rose from the couch, locked away the briefcase in a desk, lit a cigarette and sat down and slowly forced himself to think about the future. He wanted out. But he couldn't go home; his father hated his guts—"You've disgraced us all," were the last words his father had ever spoken to him. And the lamsters always went either to New York or to the Coast. He wanted no part of either. He wanted a quiet place—where he could get himself together and take a cure—a remote healthy place, like Denver, Colorado, for instance. He'd been there once as a boy, with his father—and he could still remember the marvelous air, the views, the Rocky Mountains. He had the money now. No use to scrounge in the city anymore, at least for a good long time. And who in his right mind worried about ten years from now?

Suddenly Skip was assaulted by a terrible fear—of being alone. He had a strong desire to get out of the apartment, take his car and drive someplace—any place. Soon day would be here, he kept telling himself, and there'd be people everywhere . . . so why run? It didn't make any sense at all—but the fear grew and he could hardly control himself. He wanted to shake hands with somebody—he wasn't sure exactly what he wanted except an alleviation of his loneliness.

Finally, swearing at himself, he called Patsy.

A last she answered sleepily: "Skip? Do you know for Christ's sake what time it is? What do you want, Skip? I'm beat, I'm getting some rest, and here you . . . What is it, Skip?"

Skip hung up. He felt like crying. He felt like climbing the wall. He started laughing. The phone rang. It was Patsy.

"What the hell is the matter with you, Skip?" she demanded. "You wake me out of a deep sleep and then you hang up. Got a hot one? What is it?"

"Sorry," said Skip. "Call you tomorrow."

Reality was slowly returning. Skip finally decided he'd take a bath and go to bed.

Goggles was making it on foot. He'd found his glasses and his gun, and he'd managed to climb out of the storm-drain after a long struggle that almost brought him to total exhaustion. He'd get so far, then slip and fall back. Once he'd almost been clear and was grasping for the outer rim of the drain when his foot slipped and he fell all the way back and for a long time lay stunned. The barrel of his gun seemed bent; he'd have to examine it closely when he got a chance, and one lens of his glasses was smashed. He was a sorry sight, dragging himself along a West Side street in the early pre-dawn hours. The sky was graying slightly and so it would be day. And what a day! Not the one he'd been looking forward to for so long a time now: that rosy day that would bring him much loot, enough to slip away to Costa Rica and never come back to these crummy streets and this crummy life.

His body ached all over, his left leg was encrusted with dried blood, and his clothes were soaking wet, and clammy. And he was still weary blocks away from the Wabash Trucking Company where he had a small room at the back of the office complex. What would happen to the company? Mike was the brains. Without him it would fold. Knolte, the manager, was a yes-man who never made a decision on his own; and the foreman, Patrick, was a drunk who had bottles hidden around the place. Goggles had kept tabs on all of them, for reasons of his own. It was an art he had. He also had the art of appearing and disappearing, of silent pursuit, of craftiness, of surmounting physical obstacles. For instance, not one man in a hundred would have been able to climb, unassisted, out of that storm drain. Goggles had talent, many talents, all dubious, but talents nonetheless.

At long last, just as it was beginning to get light he reached his destination. The big front gates were locked; it was too early for anybody to be there—and Mike had let the night watchman go several days ago, as he didn't want anybody around the place when they arrived back from the big job. Which was a sorry laugh, thought Goggles.

Grimacing with pain, he slowly and carefully climbed the high fence, dropped into the yard, then crossed to the office complex, past big trucks waiting patiently for drivers and the start of a new day.

He let himself in through the back with a key, went to his room, undressed, handwashed himself, dabbed iodine on a long cut in his left leg, put on fresh clothes, quickly packed his small handbag; then he examined his gun—it was all scratched up but not bent. It was OK. He counted his money. A little over a hundred dollars. Footloose with a hundred dollars? That wouldn't do.

He went down the hall and jimmied the main office door. Inside was a small safe, but that was of no use to him, as there was no way he could open it. But there was a drawer under a counter where Mike often carelessly kept money. He'd seen him more than once throwing a handful of bills into it. Mike, unlike most guys Goggles had known, was careless with money. Easy come, easy go. Mike had once been a sucker gambler but had finally broken himself of the habit, after twice going broke.

Goggles jimmied the locked dresser and found over four hundred dollars in small bills—and a load of silver he couldn't handle, though he took a handful of it. Now the first step was to get out of the trucking yard before anybody arrived—the windows showed morning to be near. The next step was to find a taxi. The next was to get his glasses fixed. As for the rest . . . a place to stay, and time to think in peace, and nurse his murderous hatred.

Dooley rose about nine o'clock, feeling more like his normal self after an absolutely blank sleep of more than four hours, dressed and went down into the lobby, where the dayman was now on duty. He smiled and gestured to Dooley. "Andy told me you were back," he said.

"I forgot to ask for messages last night," said Dooley.

The dayman looked. "Just one," he said, handing Dooley a slip of paper. There was nothing on it but Myrta's phone number.

Dooley gave a long sigh, gestured and went out. He'd almost forgotten about Myrta and the kids in the uproar of last night, from which they were so far removed, so incongruously antithetical, as if living on a different plane, in a different world, members of a different species. What would he ever do about them? What could he do? He'd already done his best to ease Myrta's mind with a little money.

He went down the street to a diner where he often had breakfast. They always had good little pig sausages and he ate them with scrambled eggs, buttered toast with marmalade, and coffee. On the way in he picked up a morning paper. Probably nothing in it. The knockover was on too late, at least for this edition. He went through it slowly, while he ate. Nothing. He finished his breakfast and with his second cup of coffee lit a cigarette. What were his plans? He didn't really know. Somehow he felt strangely lethargic, with all responsibility lifted from his shoulders. What did he *want* to do? He didn't know, and was surprised to discover he didn't really want to know or to bother with it at all. As he drank his coffee and smoked the cigarette, he began to feel sleepy again. God, the sleep he'd lost. Maybe that was it . . .

"Did you hear about them gangsters in The Loop?" asked the counterman, a cheerful-looking red-faced guy in a chef's hat.

"No," said Dooley. "What happened?"

"Three of them got the hell shot out of them. Good riddance, I say. It came over the radio."

"Three, eh?"

"Yeah," said the counterman. "They been identified. From Detroit. Police say it's probably a gang war, with the Detroit guys trying to cut in, in Chicago. Jesus, ain't we got enough of them bastards of our own?"

"You'd think so," said Dooley.

Although Goggles was not aware of it, he'd left the yard none too soon. An hour or so later the police were swarming all over the place, questioning everybody who showed up, a lot of bewildered guys who had no idea what the police were talking about. Mr. Ivan? What the hell did the police mean? And then the news began to come over the radios . . . gangsters, muscling in, Detroit hoods, it was preposterous. Knolte and Patrick just stood shaking their heads, as the police talked to them. It was stupid. Mr. Ivan was a legitimate business man.

The police combed the place and found many things they didn't understand. A pair of ripped and worn pants, with a big bloodstain. A jimmied door. A jimmied drawer—full of silver. What the hell had been going on here?

It was three o'clock in the afternoon. Dooley was sleeping on his back, snoring. The dayman had to knock several times before Dooley opened his eyes.

"Call for you, sir. On the payphone."

Dooley roused himself with difficulty and went to the lobby. It was Shamus.

"I heard this junk over the radio while I was having breakfast," said Shamus, "so I decided to see what I could find out. I contacted my friend the lieutenant. That's the official story. Ivan, Kovacs and Lacy— the two hoods well known for muscle in Detroit—came into Chicago and tried to cut into the West Side take. And the Irish or the Poles wiped 'em out. Gang war. The papers are going to give it a big play . . . they believe it, naturally. And gangster headlines sell beaucoup newspapers—all over the country . . ."

"Do the cops believe it?"

Shamus laughed shortly. "Could be. But Dooley—not a rumble from Travelon, Inc. Not a word. Apparently open for business as usual."

"Are you sure?"

"Well, watch your papers. Listen to the radio. Wouldn't you think a million-dollar robbery would make the big time?"

Shamus laughed and hung up.

Throughout the day, between naps, Dooley listened to the radio. The news was full of stories about Detroit gangsters trying to "take over"; there was even learned comment about the Purple Gang. Nothing about the robbery in the evening newspapers. And little by little it became clear to Dooley that all news of the robbery had been suppressed—not by the police, not by the newspapers, but by those running (and protecting) Travelon, Inc. A million-dollar robbery in a travel agency? Hardly bloody likely. And then why scare off the rich clientele? And why bring about an investigation? Wasn't it best after all to swallow your loss? It would all flow back in again from the pockets of willing suckers.

About ten p.m. Skip called on the payphone. "Have you been talking to Shamus? Has he given you the unbelievable tale?"

"Yes," said Dooley.

Skip giggled hilariously, they talked for a moment longer, then Dooley hung up. There was no heat. No heat at all. They were all clear.

It was another night and a night like all other nights—to Skip. He'd regained his spirit and his confidence and he hardly even remembered his panic and his crackup. When occasionally the memory of it came in a flash, he winced inwardly and felt a fleeting moment of shame. Calling a whore for comfort—that was pretty far down!

However, that was a thing of the past. Skip's money was now resting in a safety-deposit box in an Evanston bank; minus a few hundred he'd held out and deposited in his usually quite large checking account. And as Dooley had pointed out to them, it was not hot money. It couldn't be traced. It was not the kind usually floating around the underworld— money that had brought the thieves maybe fifty cents or less on the dollar—money they'd had to "sell" to fences or others. Every dollar of it was worth a dollar. Good God, what a smart knockover! Skip said himself: "If I knew where Old Hamm was buried, I'd go put flowers on his grave."

And so . . . Skip continued his life as before. He'd even had a call from the bell-captain at the Blackstone for "something choice" for a "big guy"—which meant an old guy with money—and he had promptly dispatched Ride-Em-Cowboy, who had even apologized for "being mean" to him when he'd called.

Skip decided to see what was cooking at Clancy's. He made up his mind he'd stay out of Chez Roma till the little matter of Dixie's disappearance was cleared up. He'd been seen talking to her; his profession was no doubt known. It might get embarrassing.

Clancy's was roaring, as usual: with the Mick at the piano singing requests, usually for Irish songs—though those making the requests were often Italians, Poles, Czechs or Germans. They were known along the boulevard as "Clancy's Irishmen."

Skip moved to the end of the bar and ordered. The place was loaded with familiar faces, the night crowd; some were known personally to Skip, some only by sight. They were a motley lot of squares and others. Sports writers and pro athletes often came there and bumped shoulders with dope pushers, muscle men, pimps and armed robbers. But it was a friendly place. In fact it was friendly, or else, as Clancy said. Clancy and his two big sons, not to mention the Mick, who sang in a high falsetto, but was tough as well, would unceremoniously bounce out on their ear anybody who insisted on trouble. The hoods did not frighten them—and the fact that Clancy was loved by the police, especially by Sergeant Murtaugh, a mick himself, also helped. If you wanted a safe convivial evening go to Clancy's. If you did not, don't go.

Skip sipped his drink and looked about him while the Mick sang "Galway Bay" to vociferous applause. It was a male place, though women occasionally appeared, but always with escorts. As Clancy said: "I don't want none of them hoors in here." And the women who did appear were not the usual boulevard types, like the clientele of Chez Roma, but wives, or girlfriends of long standing, many of them dowdy. It was not what the magazines called a "smart" place. Chez Roma was "smart."

Skip was just about to order again when somebody pushed beside him, somebody big and bulky. He turned. It was Franco, a hood from the backrooms of Chez Roma.

"Hi," he said.

"Hi," said Skip.

A pause; they both ordered. Skip kept looking at Franco sideways. Very unusual for him to be in Clancy's.

"Fellow," said Franco, "you get around. Ever hear anything about Dixie?"

"Only that she blew."

"Well . . . the Madame, she's all . . . you know how dames get."

"Yeah," said Skip.

"She saw you talking to Dixie one night."

"Right," said Skip.

"Well . . . she knows you hustle big. Now you didn't by any chance hustle Dixie out of Chez Roma, did you, pal?"

Skip felt a slight chill. This was not good. And he realized how smart he'd been to stay out of Chez Roma where guys were occasionally worked over in the back rooms, or so it was rumored. In Clancy's, nothing could happen to him. The Chez Roma boys were helpless here.

"I'll give you a tip," said Skip. "The night I talked to Dixie she was all upset about something. I had the feeling that she was fed up and wanted to blow the joint. I told her a few jokes, trying to get her to smile, then the Madame came along."

Franco thought this over. "You know that punk actor husband of hers?"

"Only by sight," said Skip. "I see him around."

"He was in there the other night, crying. Big slob. Seems the broad was keeping him and now he's out of money and he was trying to collect her salary."

"Maybe she's running from *him*."

"Yeah," said Franco. "We been thinking about that. Tell you what. I got my eye on you; I still think you hustled her. Big money, boy—they'd pay for that one. But you get us a lead and maybe I'll think different. OK?"

No good, thought Skip. Franco had put him in the middle. But before he could say anything, there was a disturbance of some kind out in front, then talking, laughing, and a man entered, surrounded by other men, who were pushing and shoving, trying to get a word with him.

"It's Murtaugh," said somebody.

Skip turned. When Skip turned back, Franco had melted out. The Mob was allergic to Sergeant Murtaugh. He gave them the shivers.

The sergeant was a medium-sized guy in his forties, broad and heavy, with a craggy-looking face and bushy black eyebrows. He spoke in a bass voice with the suggestion of a croak and also with the suggestion of a brogue, though he'd been born on the South Side of Chicago.

He pushed his way through the crowd and went over to shake hands with the Mick at the piano. "I know what you want," said the Mick, and he began to play the "Irish Washerwoman"—and the joint began to jump.

Clancy's Irishmen, Italians, Poles, Czechs and Germans, all began to pound and stomp—and one of Clancy's big sons hustled a drink over to Murtaugh, who drank it right down, wiped a hairy paw across his mouth, then stomped and pounded with the rest.

Later, he took Clancy into a back room. It was not a social visit, as Skip well knew; he'd probably come to ask Clancy's help in keeping an eye out for any more "Detroit hoods"—the police definitely believed the gang war theory, no doubt of it. And hoods were Murtaugh's problem and his meat.

Skip had a sudden inspiration. Did he have guts enough to do it? He crawled inside at the thought of bracing Murtaugh . . . but if he'd listen . . . Skip moved through the crowd to the back, and stationed himself near the door through which Murtaugh and Clancy had exited. "After all," thought Skip, "my name's Mahaffy, so maybe he'll listen."

He had quite a wait, but finally Murtaugh came out talking, followed by Clancy.

Skip got in front of Murtaugh, who glared at him, with discolored-looking yellowish eyes.

"Sir . . . Sergeant . . . excuse me . . . my name is James Mahaffy and . . ."

The Sergeant blinked. "Well . . .?"

"I got something important that I'd like to . . ."

"You know this man?" Murtaugh asked Clancy, and Clancy turned and whispered to him.

"A pimp?" said Murtaugh. "What could you have to say to me . . .?"

"It's about Chez Roma."

Murtaugh blinked again and motioned Skip into the backroom. Clancy went on about his business. Skip was trembling inside at this confrontation with Murtaugh but he struggled to keep his composure.

"Mahaffy, eh?" said Murtaugh. "That's a hell of a name for a pimp."

Skip swallowed but immediately launched into the Dixie tale, from his conversation with her to the business with Franco.

"She's missing?" asked Murtaugh.

Skip nodded. Murtaugh opened the door and yelled—and in a moment one of his men appeared. Tom Boyle.

"Hi," said Skip.

"Hi, Skip," said Tom.

"You know this man?" asked Murtaugh.

"I sure do, Sergeant. He busted a big case for a friend of mine. The fur-grabbers."

Murtaugh studied Skip. "Well . . . good! Now, son, are you telling me that a hood named Franco from Chez Roma came into Clancy's and threatened you?"

"Yes sir."

"Very well. Now you give Tom here all the details of this missing person case and I will walk across the street and have a little talk with the Mob."

He went out banging the door. Tom laughed: "Any excuse," he said.

They sat down at a table and Tom took out his notebook. "I know a little about this case. I saw some pictures of her. Yow, what a doll!"

"Yeah," said Skip.

Skip filled Tom in, giving him all pertinent details, but naturally not mentioning the name of Shamus. Suddenly Tom began to laugh. "I'd like to see the faces of the hoods across the street. They know the Sergeant would kill them as quick as look at them."

Murtaugh's descent on Chez Roma had not gone unnoted. In fact it was all over town along the grapevine within an hour or two. And there was much speculation. Was it tied into the "Detroit gang war" business? Feverish crime reporters were milking this "Big Story" for all it was worth—for far more than it was worth, because there was no truth to it at all. But how could their eager readers know that . . .?

But Skip had made a very smart move. He'd cleared himself. Chez Roma wouldn't dare touch him now.

Things were not going nearly as well as Chuck had expected. Of course there was the money, but that was in a safety-deposit box and even in the case of such a sum as that, out of sight can be out of mind. There was the business to run, the responsibility. Ed Weed was a good man, knew his work, but he was also an *old* man, who tired easily, and sometimes seemed to avoid the niggling details out of shear weariness.

And then Chuck missed his own Old Man. At first he wouldn't admit it to himself but little by little he was forced to. If you had a problem you took it to the Old Man and he said yes no, do it, or don't do it—and it was that simple. Now he took a problem to Ed Weed and Ed said, "Well, now let me see . . . first we've got to consider the . . . and then . . ." And so forth—and then finally, "Now what do *you* think?"

Doc had gone to Fond du Lac—and it was more than a pleasure trip as he was known there by his true name, Evan McKinley—(Pace was his mother's maiden name), and he'd never broken his cover—as far as Fond du Lac knew he was still the respectable car dealer and member of the chamber of commerce—and with him he was taking fifty thousand dollars of the job money which he intended to deposit in a savings account in a bank where formerly he'd been well-known. Call it fall money, call it a secret stake, call it anything you like: it would be comfortable to have it there, far from the clutches of any authority if a contingency arose, unlikely, but always possible.

Very little was known about Doc Pace. Practically nobody knew he'd served time for armed robbery at the age of 22 and had received a five-year education in a maximum-security prison in Arkansas. Even Doc himself was not sure how he'd got involved in armed robbery. He'd been working steadily but also running around with a bunch of guys he's met in this town in which he was a stranger. They were a bad lot. The next thing Doc knew they were knocking over stores here and there for laughs and for spending money. If Doc had been in his

Wisconsin hometown, he would never have got mixed up in anything like that. But he was far from Wisconsin and he had felt footloose; it was a kind of adventure. Then they attempted a big one; they bungled it, and all were busted, tried and convicted. Doc was a first offender—at least it was the first time he'd been caught—but the judge took no notice of that. He gave Doc the jolt—and that was that. Armed robbery was frowned on in Arkansas.

At 27 he returned to Wisconsin, where nothing was known about his time in prison, and got a job selling cars. He prospered at once: he was a natural born salesman. But in his opinion the money came too slow, and remembering his five years of education in prison, he began to put it to good use—in forays far from the town where he was working. Doc had managed to elude the law, and he hadn't done a day of time since his stint in the Arkansas prison.

His marriage hadn't changed him in the least, but his wife had known nothing about his extra-curricular activities. They lived well, had plenty of money, and always a prosperous business, small or large. Ten years later his wife died in a typhoid epidemic. Doc raised Chuck himself. And when his son came home from France, nursing a wound, sour and disillusioned, Doc had leveled with him. Chuck hadn't batted an eye. He was in. And he'd been in ever since.

Yes, Chuck missed the Old Man. Things weren't as simple as they'd appeared in his imagination. He'd wanted to be free—that was all, free. What did that mean? Chuck wasn't sure now; and he often wondered what he'd been griping about. He had his own apartment now. He did as he pleased. He had his own money. But he just wasn't happy. And then there was Ingeborg, who had given him quite a shock.

Now that Chuck had his own money, his own apartment, his "Freedom," he decided to ask Ingeborg to marry him. Chuck's relationships with girls had consisted to a series of disasters, culminating in his wife running off with another man. Chuck was awkward with girls, bashful, uneasy, inhibited; he'd always been that way. You might say girls frightened him. Worse yet, sex seemed "dirty" to him—he couldn't explain it—it just did. He was a kind of embarrassed fumbler. But Ingeborg, big, healthy, laughing, cheerful, had changed all that. With her it seemed like the most natural thing in the world.

So he'd asked her to marry him—and she had refused.

She was helping him move and put his new apartment in order.

"For what?" asked Ingeborg. "No!" Chicago born, she nevertheless had a touch of German accent.

Chuck was amazed. "Wasn't it the right thing to do, to marry the girl? That's what he'd always heard. Besides, he wanted her permanently. He didn't want to go through all those grinding embarrassments again.

"Have you some complaints?" asked Ingeborg, smiling. She had large, very white teeth, and a kind of Sunny Jim grin that everybody liked. She was not fat, but heavily made. Ingeborg was no beauty but on the other hand it would have been an odd kind of guy who would have refused her advances. She really stirred Chuck up.

"Complaints?" said Chuck. "I just asked you to get married."

Ingeborg sat down for a serious talk. "Chuck, I'm only 21 years old. Why should I get married? I don't want to get married. My sister Elsa is married and already she has three children. Always children, children, diapers, crying—what for?"

"Did I say anything about kids?"

"They come, they come," said Ingeborg. "My mother had ten. What did she do with her life? Children, children, children. Now she's dead. Is that a life?"

Chuck didn't know what to say. He sank down into a chair, lit a cigarette, and stared at the wall.

"I like to sing and dance and make fun," said Ingeborg. "Like at the rathskeller. I get paid—yes but I would sing and dance anyway. Marriage? I don't like it. Aren't we very happy this way?"

"I guess we are," said Chuck.

"Well . . . then we will stay that way," said Ingeborg, "till you get tired of Ingeborg . . . or maybe Ingeborg gets tired of you."

Chuck said nothing. What could he say? It was the very last thing he'd wanted to hear. So Chuck was making the painful and surprising discovery men had struggled with for millennia: that money wasn't everything.

Shamus and Dixie were having what might be called a "night at home."

Shamus was slumped down in a chair, reading the latest edition of his favorite Chicago paper and Dixie was lying on the big boat-lounge, reading a movie magazine and eating chocolates from a five-pound box Shamus had bought her, at her request.

Finally he looked up. "If you don't stop eating all that candy, you'll get fat."

"Would you love me if I was fat?"

"No," said Shamus. "You wouldn't be Dixie."

"I would be, inside."

"It's the outside that counts."

Dixie laughed. "You know, it's a funny thing," she said. "I almost never eat candy. I almost never eat, period."

It was true. Shamus had never seen anybody in his life before who ate so little. The old gag did not apply to Dixie:

> "She eats like a bird."
> "Yeah, a pelican."

Dixie actually did eat like a bird. A little of this and a little of that—and that was it. A couple of grapes for dessert. Amazing!

"All of a sudden I get an urge for chocolate candy," said Dixie. "Maybe twice a year. So don't worry. I won't get fat."

Shamus went to the bar and mixed a couple of drinks. It was a cold clear night and the lights of the Gold Coast hotels were twinkling like little yellow stars in the thin air.

"Dixie," said Shamus, giving her the drink and sitting opposite her, "I think we should talk."

"I don't want to talk," said Dixie. "I just want to hibernate. God, this is lovely! You don't know what I've been through."

"Come on now," said Shamus. "Let's face things."

"I'm tired of facing things. Want some candy? Try these with nougat filler."

"No, thanks."

"Could I interest you in something else?" asked Dixie.

She stretched out on the lounge and dared him.

"Well," said Shamus, "we can talk some other time."

Dooley had taken to sleeping a lot. He'd rise about eight or nine o'clock, go down the street to the diner for his breakfast, then come back to the hotel, read the morning paper, listen to the radio for a while, and then nap. He began to realize he was no longer twenty-five but closer to forty-five and that he had taxed himself physically throughout the long course of the Big Knockover. He now had an enormous appetite for sleep, which was not his usual way at all. In the past he wasn't able to blot out the world with sleep, for hours on end, even when he was doing the five year stretch in prison. Sleep is the prisoner's best friend. It helps lead-footed time to pass. But in prison Dooley had slept only in short intervals and had then cat-napped, only too conscious of what was going on around him. Now he blacked out at night—he heard, thought, felt, and saw nothing.

He was taking another nap, sitting in a chair with his feet propped up. It was a little past three in the afternoon. He woke with a start, feeling a certain uneasiness he couldn't account for. What was it? He was a type not given to premonitions, nervousness, nor fear of the unknown, or of the what-might-be. He just felt uncomfortable for no apparent reason.

To pass the time and maybe change his mood, he took a shower, shaved and put on fresh clothes—but that vague demon kept nagging at him. Was it time to go? In his heart Dooley was aware that he should have gone long ago; he should have left the morning after the take. That was always the best way. But three things had checked him; the fact that they were in the clear in a comical turnaround that was hard to believe; secondly, a strange physical lethargy and weariness; and thirdly, vague thoughts of Myrta and the kids.

Well . . . maybe it was time to go. But where? Maybe to New York where he could lose himself in the anonymity of the biggest jungle in the country. Or maybe to the Coast—an exotic place, in Dooley's imagination: he'd never been there. New York he'd seen, once—after the Spaulding knockover when things got very hot indeed in Youngstown, Ohio. In fact the police, some way or another, had busted Red Nolan and he'd been tried and convicted. Dooley hadn't even been named as part of the group, though he'd managed the whole business. But taking no chances, he'd fled to Cleveland and then managed to get a compartment on the Twentieth Century Limited, which thundered all across the northern Ohio countryside without a stop between Toledo and Cleveland. It had been quite a trip. The porter couldn't make Dooley out, though he was a quiet passenger and conventionally dressed. To the porter Dooley had the kind of face that went with broken noses and cauliflower ears, and yet the gentlemen's nose was not broken, but only slightly flat from birth, and his ears were no more mutilated than the porter's. Dooley said little or nothing, but was good for considerable judicious tipping. The porter was practiced in these things and he realized Dooley knew how to ingratiate by the use of money. Once Dooley convulsed the porter, as they were traveling up the Hudson in the morning hours, by identifying West Point as Sing Sing.

Yes, it had been quite a trip. Dooley had stayed at a little theatrical hotel in the 40s, filled with actors and others, to him all *rara avises*—occasionally he'd even see them in make-up. And in this hotel he'd made the acquaintance of an out-of-work actress of about his own age, Isabel, who had taken him around to clubs and little French restaurants, and helped him spend his money. They'd had quite a good time. Isabel was a realist and expected very little out of life. Dooley was a kind of light in the forest. He even paid her hotel bill, when one day he found out she was in trouble with the management and in danger of being locked out of her room. Isabel had never before in her life met a guy with whom money seemed to be no object. She settled down to a long stretch of unaccustomed bliss. One day Dooley simply disappeared and she never saw him again. Later, she explained the whole odd business to an out-of-work actor friend of hers and he'd said: "Sounds like a guy on the run."

Isabel took it big—the take-um! "You mean a criminal?"

"Sounds like it. Did you know anything about him? Did he have any friends?"

From then on, this became Isabel's conversation piece. My God, did you ever hear about the time I got mixed up with a criminal?

Dooley enjoyed wandering down Broadway at night.

He's heard about it before, of course, but it turned out to be nothing like what he'd expected. The Great White Way? It was a crummy place, with barkers and con men, Chinatown tours, and penny arcades and hash houses—and crowded? At certain times you could hardly move along the pavements.

Yeah, why not New York for a month or two? A stranger, out of the blue—completely unknown, just one of the jostling crowd. And this time he could board the Twentieth Century Limited in Chicago, where it made up, and take the whole long journey in the peace, solitude and privacy of a compartment.

A guy he'd known in Youngstown had recommended the little hotel in New York to him. It was not well to land in a strange city with no idea of where to find a place. Very easy for a stranger to find the wrong place. Well, if he did finally decide to make his objective New York, he had a "home," the only kind of home Dooley knew. (The little North Side hotel where he was now staying had also been recommended to him by one of his own kind.)

Dooley decided on New York—but how soon could he leave? Could he leave? And what would he do about the car? Could he store it in the little hotel garage for a moderate fee? He had every intention of coming back to Chicago, eventually; over the years it had become a kind of base for him.

"I'm getting out of here this week," Dooley told himself, firmly. "I think I need a change anyway."

The money didn't worry him. He was used to carrying and managing large sums. His method was dangerous—what in his life wasn't—but he'd seen too many guys get chased away from their carefully hidden hoard, or from their non-reachable safety-deposit boxes. Anybody who took Dooley's money would have to kill him first. But suppose the hotel caught on fire? Yeah—thought Dooley, suppose the sky falls.

Suppose you get hit by a car? Suppose you take a spill in the bathtub and break your neck? Life was full of danger, even for straight johns. Dooley just was not a worrier.

He ate dinner at a little Italian restaurant, not far from the hotel. It was checked tablecloths, sawdust on the floor, red wine that tasted like rosin, and the best chicken he'd ever eaten anyplace—even in his home country where frying chicken was an art. This Italian chicken apparently wasn't fried, but maybe roasted and served with a wonderful vegetable sauce. Dooley put away quite a dinner, then he sat back and lit a rare cigar. Live it day to day, and life is tolerable. But it was something Dooley had never been able to do. With him it was always, what's next?

The fat Italian waitress recommended an expresso, but she had such a spaghetti accent he could hardly understand her—finally the idea came through that it was coffee, and he agreed. It was brought to him by a very pretty young Italian girl in a peasant blouse. She looked so Old-World Italian that Dooley asked her if she spoke English; God knows the fat waitress didn't.

"Oh yes," said the girl, amused. "I work here part-time. I'm going to Northwestern University."

Dooley felt like an idiot. It spoiled his cigar. He left shortly, after the expresso, which was so strong it hurt his throat.

As he was walking back to the hotel, it suddenly occurred to him that it was a Monday and Myrta would be home with the kids. Why not drop in and see them for the last time? Not that he intended to tell them it was the last time; he'd merely state he was going away on a business trip and might be gone for a month or so. As a rule he just melted away from people he'd been connected with, like Isabel in New York City. But Myrta and the kids were a special case, really the only one in his whole rackety life.

As Dooley was parking he noted the pleasant glow of the yellow lights behind the curtains of Myrta's apartment, and it gave him a good feeling. And he remembered the stormy night, and the kids in bed, and he and Myrta sitting by the fire and drinking beer and talking leisurely about nothing; it was a memory he would retain for the rest of his life. There was just something "right" about it.

He rang the bell, there was quite a delay, and then a tall man with curly, light, almost whitish hair opened the door. He had a ruddy face and round blue eyes. He was large, raw-boned, but looked soft, slack.

"Yes?" he said, neither friendly nor unfriendly.

"Excuse me," said Dooley. "Is Myrta here?"

The man eyed Dooley carefully, surprise showing in his gaze. More than surprise, puzzlement.

"Are you Mr. Dooley?" he asked.

"Yes."

"I'm Charlie Hansen."

Dooley had no immediate reaction to this name. Should he have?

"I'm Myrta's husband."

It was a shock. Dooley didn't know what to say. Over Charley's shoulder, he saw Myrta come into the room, then the kids, in sleepers.

"Come in, come in," said Charley.

"I can only stay a minute," said Dooley. "I'm going out of town on business and as I was passing this way . . ."

Dooley took off his hat and stepped in. Myrta was looking at him with an odd expression, and the kids were back to their big-eyed look, still-faced, non-committal.

"Well," said Charley, "you're younger than I imagined."

"I told Charley how kind you were to us and how much you helped us while he was away."

"Yes," said Charley. "And don't think I don't appreciate it."

"Yes," said Myrta. "I told Charley how lucky I was to meet you in the supermarket that day and how you took us to the doctor to have my ankle treated and everything and how nice you'd been to the children . . ."

Myrta was giving Dooley the con-tale so he'd know how things stood and so he wouldn't make any goofs. Dooley looked at the kids again; they were poker-faced. Smart or scared? He couldn't make out which. Well, they had a father now, such as he was, and that was the way it should be.

"It wasn't anything," said Dooley. "Glad to help."

"Won't you sit down?" said Charley.

"No, thanks," said Dooley. "I'm short of time . . ."

"It's always real estate," said Myrta. "Isn't that right?"

"That's right," said Dooley. "And I finally pulled off my big deal for that industrial property. Of course, I may have to wait a while for my money."

"Well," said Myrta, "Charley got his old job back, and . . . I think maybe everything's going to be all right."

"That's good, that's good," said Dooley; then: "Well . . ." he offered his hand and Charley shook it, smiling a rather forced smile; a "sincere" smile, like a salesman who is about to take you for long dough.

"Did you say you were going out of town?" asked Myrta.

"Yes," said Dooley. "But I'll be back at the hotel eventually, I think. Goodbye, kids," he said.

They seemed to shift about uncomfortably. "Goodnight, sir," said

Bobby, rather sadly. Shirley merely waved, wriggling the fingers of her left hand, and clutching the doll Dooley had mended, in the right.

"Bye, Dooley," said Myrta.

Dooley left. Charley shut the door after him, then turned and said: "Go to bed, you kids."

They went, without a look or a word.

"He sure is a tough-looking guy," said Charley. "I never saw a real estate salesman with a face like that."

"He can't help his face. He's very kind."

"And you said he was old."

"Well, he is, but he doesn't look it. I think he said he was sixty."

Charley stood shaking his head. "That's an odd one. I guess I didn't come home any too soon."

"What do you mean by that?" cried Myrta, her anger rising.

"Oh, nothing," said Charley; then: "Are we ever going to eat? What's holding things up?"

Myrta went to the kitchen and started banging pots around. Charley turned on their radio and stretched out on the sofa.

In the bedroom Shirley said: "I wish he would go away."

"Who?" asked Bobby.

"You know," said Shirley, then she talked to her doll for a while, and both finally fell asleep.

Dooley went to a movie. It was a Western with a lot of riding and shooting and it kept Dooley fairly well absorbed, but occasionally his mind would return to the scene at Myrta's: Charley, the kids. Hell, it was the perfect ending. He couldn't have asked for anything better. Fine—then why did he feel so depressed about the whole thing? Was he changing? Was it a matter of the arteries? It was time to leave obviously; to get out of Chicago—to get away from all the circumstances connected in any way with the knockover of Travelon, Inc.

He made up his mind that in the morning he'd drive down to The Loop and see about reservations on the Twentieth Century Limited to New York. Often they were sold out. Sometimes he'd been told by the porter, you had to wait three or four days. It was an extra-fare train, much favored by affluent travelers. The train made it to New York, or from New York to Chicago, in the stated time or you got so much back for every minute late; if it was over a stated time late, you got all of your extra fare back. It was nearly always packed.

He kept thinking about Shirley and the crummy doll she insisted on keeping. Clearly, it was time to go.

It was very late. Shamus and Dixie lay in bed talking, the room faintly alight from outside reflections.

"All right, all right," said Dixie. "You broke me down. What do you want to talk about?"

She'd been evading, childishly evading, for quite a while now. She kept insisting all she wanted to do was stay in the apartment and keep house for Shamus and just loaf and "laze around."

"No more rat-race, please," she kept insisting.

"Should I complain?" asked Shamus. "This is fine for me, but it doesn't make sense and it may lead to trouble. You're a missing person. The police are looking for you. There's a stink at Chez Roma. Your husband's pestering everybody. I talked to Skip. Even Sergeant Murtaugh knows about the case . . ."

"Who is he?"

"He's a toughie that I wouldn't want after me. Not that he's after you. But he raised bloody hell at Chez Roma." Then he told her about Skip, Franco and Sergeant Murtaugh.

"All right," said Dixie. "So what do you suggest? That I go back to Chez Roma and have Angelina hanging around after me all the time? That I go back and live with that clown, Ty Willis—that sorry mooching no-good hambone? Is that what you are suggesting? Once I go back I'll have them all after me again—just like before, and then so what will happen? I'll do the pill routine or run out again."

Shamus groaned to himself. Maybe they could go away for a while. But then they'd just have to come back. Then something suddenly occurred to Shamus. Why did they have to come back? They were not tied to Chicago. He had plenty of money. Why not the Coast. Maybe Dixie could crash the movies. If she got in the right hands, she might. She'd never do it on her own. Dixie was not the smartest girl in the world, and disorganized.

"Well," said Shamus, finally, "let me think it over. We don't have to decide right away."

"That's my honey," said Dixie, then she flung her arms around him and began kissing him, little pecks all over his face . . .

Time passed . . . they slept. A heavy silence settled down over the big bedroom that was faintly, dimly alight from outside reflections. Something woke Dixie; she seemed to be rising to the surface of the water from a long immersion in the deep green of the sea—which was the deep green of sleep. In fact she wasn't sure she was awake. A figure seemed to be climbing in the window. But how could that be? The apartment was four stories up. Dixie froze, terrified. The figure, very dim, moved to the foot of the bed; a beam from a flashlight sprayed across them briefly, went out—then there were two sudden shattering spurts of flame. Dixie heard somebody screaming. Suddenly she realized it was herself. She tried to hold on tight, keep her wits about her. The figure melted out through the bedroom door, leaving it open. In a moment she heard the outer door close.

She had to force herself to turn on the light by the bed. Then she started screaming again. Shamus was obviously dead, lying half turned away and contorted as if he'd been trying to throw himself out of bed when the bullets hit him.

Dixie stopped screaming, her instincts aroused, her survival instincts. After all she had survived to the age of twenty-two in the tough half theatrical half-underworld of Chicago clubs. And it wasn't easy.

But what could she do? Merely pack up her things and leave? Nobody knew she'd been living with Shamus. But where would she go? What would she say? How would she handle this?

Suddenly she knew. She dressed quickly. Shamus's clothes were lying across a chair. Often she'd seen him consulting a little black book he carried an inside coat pocket. Nervous, fumbling, feeling cold as ice, she finally found it, took it into the living room, turned on the lights and searched through it. There were five numbers for SK—which was no doubt Skip.

Skip was the answer. Had to be. Skip was responsible for her present position—in a way—he had introduced her to Selby Reed. And then Skip was a sharpie who had all kinds of angles. He would figure things out; tell her what to do.

Dooley was pulled out of an uneasy sleep by a knocking at his door. He switched on the lights, glanced at his watch: twenty till four a.m. And this could mean only one thing: trouble.

And trouble it was: Skip on the payphone. The deserted lobby was cold and drafty, a gruesome-looking place at this hour, with its dim lighting and its emptiness. Dooley kept cursing to himself as he listened, the bad news prodding him to full wakefulness.

Finally Dooley did some talking himself—giving precise instructions, then he finished. "I'll be there just as fast as I can get there," and hung up.

Maybe it was just as well he hadn't left.

Dixie just couldn't make Dooley out. She'd been told by Skip his name was Mr. Roberts and that he was a private investigator who was going to help them. But Dooley did not look like a "private investigator" to her—hadn't Shamus been a "private investigator"?—no, Dooley looked like what she thought of as a "thug"; he looked much tougher than Franco and the other hoods who worked for Madame at Chez Rosa. But he didn't really seem tough, but kind of mild and patient.

As for Dooley he kept looking away from Dixie, who was half sitting half lying on one of Skip's big chairs. She was the prettiest girl he'd ever been this close to and he found her presence disturbing. Dooley's taste was for large mature women. He'd had no experience whatever with polished slenderness and the extremes of femininity. Dixie hardly seemed real to him. On the stage, fine. That's where she belonged, in his opinion. But sitting here in intimacy—in Skip's Evanston apartment . . . no.

"Just tell me everything," said Dooley. "Everything you can remember. From the time you woke up."

Dixie did so, nervously, looking away from Dooley who also was looking away from her, as Skip noted. The recital went on for quite a while, with Dooley asking an occasional question, until at last Dixie could think of nothing more. "Then I called Skip," she concluded.

"OK," said Dooley. "Now maybe you'd like to rest while we talk this over."

"Oh, God, would I!" cried Dixie.

She was in a hurry to get into bed and leave all the rest to them. They'd handle it. She knew they would.

Skip took her into the bedroom. "Now stop worrying, baby," he said. "This guy is the best. He'll figure a way."

"Good God, he looks tough," said Dixie. "He scares me."

She kicked off her shoes and lay down. Skip covered her with the spread.

"OK," he said. "Catch your forty winks."

"You mean we can't stay here?" said Dixie, snuggling into the pillow.

"That's what I mean. I got a place for you. Don't worry."

When Skip returned to the living room, Dooley was standing, smoking a cigarette, and staring as if lost to this world.

Skip mixed them a couple of drinks, handed one to Dooley, then sank down into the big chair where Dixie had been sitting.

"I guess maybe you got a real good look at Shamus's reason for going over the fence."

"Well . . . he's sorry now," said Dooley, then he sat down and stared at nothing for a long time.

Skip grew impatient. "What a noise this is going to make! Wait till Sergeant Murtaugh and my pal Dave Santorelli get on this one. Will they burn the asses of that Chez Roma bunch. Crazy bastards, killing Shamus over a girl. Madame must be out of her mind."

Dooley ignored the comment. "Are you sure she didn't leave anything behind in the apartment?"

"I combed the joint," said Skip. "And I know my business. I even brought a goddamn box of candy."

"All right. Did you take a look at the place where this guy might have climbed up? Outside, I mean."

Skip shook his head dubiously. "Yeah. It's an old place with a lot of angles and things jutting out and pipes and stuff. It's not straight up. An acrobat could make it, all right. I couldn't. It was a pro, what else?"

Dooley nodded. Then he said something that startled Skip. "I had the Hamm business figured wrong."

"You . . . what?"

"The pro who killed Hamm sneaked in the window while Hamm was sleeping, shot him, then went out the door, not the window, and down the stairs. Hamm fell out of bed. I found his door unlocked. Now why should he go to bed and leave his door unlocked . . .?"

"What are you saying?" Skip demanded.

"Same MO," said Dooley.

There was a long silence, as Skip sat with his drink poised.

"Goggles?" he asked, as if dreading the answer.

"Yes," said Dooley.

"Good Christ," cried Skip. "That means he knows. That means . . . we . . . all of us . . ."

"No," said Dooley. "It just means Shamus, who worked for Mike, and *me*, the guy Shamus was tailing. Some way Goggles figured out Shamus double-crossed them. He was tailing me, right? So it must have been Shamus and me. Make sense?"

"Wait a minute," said Skip, slapping his forehead. "When the shooting was going on, all of a sudden somebody turned a flashlight on in the truck. It was on Shamus's car."

Dooley nodded slowly. "Maybe that's it."

Skip thought this over for a moment. "Then why didn't he go for Shamus's money in the apartment? At least, look for it."

Dooley pondered this, then stretched out his legs and lit a cigarette. "Well," said Dooley, "It could be that he figured Shamus for merely a hired hand and me for the money. Shamus doubled-crossed them, not me; so Shamus was marked for death."

"Then you don't think . . .?"

"I think you, Doc and Chuck are in the clear."

Skip heaved a long sigh of relief, then he said finally: "And you, Dooley?"

"I'll worry about me. Killing me gets him nothing. If I'm right, he's figuring me for the big money."

"He could kill you to get it."

"He could try," said Dooley.

Long silence, then Dooley said: "As far as the knockover is concerned, there's no problem. The police are a cinch to blame the Chez Roma bunch, so we leave it that way."

"How do you mean?"

"You hide Dixie. Right? She can appear any time she likes. I don't know of any way she could be connected with this . . . unless . . ."

Skip's mind was working like a computer, with tales, cons, evasions. "Unless . . ."

Unless somebody saw her in Shamus's car the night she ran away. "Right. Right," said Skip, after a little thought, "Now how about this? She had a rendezvous with Shamus that night. I know, I helped arrange it, right? Afterwards she came over to a place I've got and spent the night and told me she was not going back to Chez Roma or her husband. Good story, right? If we need it, right away the police will jump to the conclusion that Dixie decided to let me manage her. Does it fit?"

"Why hasn't anybody seen her?"

"Because she's been hiding from the Chez Roma bunch."

"Have you got such a place?"

"I sure have," said Skip. "A little flat, not five blocks from Chez Roma. I spend more time there than I do here. For one thing, I've got this expensive broad Patsy living in the same building."

"Let's not get her into it."

"No. No chance."

"They might question her."

"Maybe. But if she knows nothing, she knows nothing. Anyway it would take a lot of figuring on somebody's part."

"All right," said Dooley, more or less satisfied. "And did you make that call?"

"Yeah," said Skip. "I even used a spaghetti accent." Skip demonstrated and Dooley was surprised how authentic it sounded. "The homicide boys have already found Shamus now. And it'll all hit the fan in the late morning papers. Not that it will make any particular noise there. Ex-cop slain, you know; buried some place in the paper . . ."

Dooley rose. "OK. Now get her out of here and to that place of yours before it gets light. And, Skip, coach her on the story, backwards and forwards, until she believes it herself."

"Right," said Skip.

Dooley left. It seemed suddenly to get very quiet in the apartment. With Dooley there all was well. With Dooley gone it was a different ball game. Skip began to worry about that crazy creep, Goggles. Was Dooley right? Suppose Dooley was wrong? Suppose Goggles was after all of them? A shadow, a building-climber, a ghost who could appear out of no place. He'd found Shamus. Would he find Dooley? Would he find them all?

Finally Skip calmed himself. Dooley was right. He was always right.

He found Dixie sleeping with one arm flung out, her head to one side, and her face almost hidden by her thick, luxuriant, midnight black hair. It was a very strange thing, but Dixie had no particular appeal for Skip, though he acknowledged that she was one of the best-looking girls he'd ever seen. For him, something was missing. What, he wasn't sure— And as far as he knew he was alone in this opinion.

"Dixie, Dixie," he said, pushing her gently. "Time to go."

"Oh no!" complained Dixie. "Can't we stay here?"

"You want the water treatment?"

"OK, OK," said Dixie.

Murtaugh, in shirtsleeves, sat in his office chair like a man ready to spring. "Where's Dave?" he yelled at young Tom Boyle.

"Well . . . the Cassini case was getting hot and . . ."

"To hell with the Cassini case. Let them bastards kill each other. Who cares? I want Dave—now."

Murtaugh was trying to keep things in perspective. He was also trying to keep his temper. The worst thing you could do in his business was jump to conclusions. But if the Mob didn't kill Selby Reed, who did? Strictly a pro job. A voice kept whispering to him that anybody might have. Selby had been in a very chancy business. Underworld shadowing was on a par with working as a steeple-jack or doing parachute jumps out of airplanes. A hundred and one guys might have had one on for Selby. He'd caused a lot of trouble here and there. So as tough as it was, Murtaugh fought to bide his time.

"But just give me one little thing. Anything," he told himself, "and I'll make those bastards crawl. *Personally* I'll make them crawl."

Tom Boyle had left hurriedly, now he was back. "Dave will be in in a few minutes, Sergeant," he said. "And Selby Reed's brother is in the outer office. He wants the effects."

"Soon as the lab gets through," said the Sergeant; then: "What's he like?"

"Just a guy," said Tom. "He runs an auto accessory store on the near North Side. Nothing like Selby."

The handling of the case was a jurisdictional matter. Strictly speaking it was Homicide's. But all hoodlum activity was under the supervision of the Metropolitan Hoodlum Squad, of which Murtaugh was the boss—and this definitely came under that category until proven otherwise. So it was up to Homicide and Murtaugh to get together. Dave Santorelli, formerly of the Hoodlum Squad, was now in Homicide—so naturally Murtaugh wanted Dave in charge of the case. Some homicide guys tried to bypass the Sergeant.

Finally Dave arrived.

"I talked to the Lieutenant," said Murtaugh. "It's yours."

"Sergeant, I could break this Cassini case in a couple days."

Murtaugh just sat looking at him.

"All right," said Dave.

The disturbing news had arrived by way of the grapevine and Madame Chez Roma just didn't look like herself today. Even her hair was mussed, an unheard-of thing. Giovanni, her husband of many years, was more shook by the mussed hair than by anything else. He brought her a Napoleon brandy, and said: "Here, dear. This will . . ."

She threw it on the floor. "We have enemies," she cried. "Who are they? Get my cousin. I must talk with my cousin."

"How can I get him? It is impossible. He will not bother with such little matters." Giovanni was distracted. He didn't know what to do as Madame just sat staring.

In a backroom Franco and Packy were trying to play cards. But it was no use and finally they gave up the game.

"What do you say?" finally asked Packy.

Franco shrugged and raised his hands up slowly and sadly; then he made a gesture an operatic tenor might have envied, conveying despair, distraction, what's to do.

"How do you figure it?"

Franco gestured once more, conveying "how could you figure such a thing" with movements of his head, shoulders and hands.

"Yeah," said Packy.

Skip played it as if it was just another night. Dixie had a flat of her own now, down the corridor from Skip, and when he kept warning her not to go out, she got very irritated with him and finally said: "I wouldn't go out if I got paid. I want to stay in, goddamn it."

Some strange girl, thought Skip, trying to understand her.

So he took Patsy to Gunter's Back Stage, an open-all-night eating place on the nearby boulevard, where an older guy with plenty of money could get a look at her. The older guy was at the bar; he was big and heavy and in a way looked like a young guy who had suddenly aged—with remnants of both stages apparent. He owned a Cadillac agency in the suburbs. One of his friends, a satisfied customer, had recommended Skip to him.

Patsy was having one of her "young" nights. She didn't look over sixteen, and in a legitimate place—if there were any—she wouldn't have been served liquor. The owner of the Cadillac agency was visibly shaken—and gave Skip the old Gung Ho sign from the bar. Then he paid for his drinks and went out.

"You passed the test, honey," said Skip.

"Good, good," said Patsy. "I'm hungry. I want a club sandwich and some chilled asparagus with mayonnaise."

"Oh," said Skip, "I thought we'd go down to the Duke's and have chiliburgers."

"That's not funny," said Patsy.

So Skip put in their orders.

Gunter's Back Stage was a hangout for musicians and theatrical people and others of that kind. The food was excellent, if a little expensive—and you could get almost anything at any hour of the day or night, including excellent sea food. It was generally crowded late at night, especially on weekends, and tonight was no exception. Service was slow tonight.

But their food finally arrived and Skip was starting to eat when a guy stopped nearby and just stood there. Skip finally looked up at him. It was Ty, Dixie's husband. He was a large young man, who had his hair curled at a beauty parlor, and sometimes played tough guys on the stage. Apparently he had decided to play that part tonight. He was glaring at Skip.

"You want something?" asked Skip; then Patsy turned, studied Ty disdainfully and returned to her club sandwich.

"Yes, come on outside. I've got something to say to you."

"Run away, ham," said Skip.

Ty's face turned red. He had an audience watching, some of his friends, and he'd been bragging about what he'd do to Skip, so he grabbed Skip by the lapels and jerked him to his feet. A dish crashed someplace. People were looking.

"So you won't come outside," cried Ty.

Skip stamped on his foot hard. Ty jumped back in pain, and Skip said: "How would you like to have a gun stuffed up your nose, you big hambone? Now get the hell away from me before you get hurt."

Ty was badly shaken, but he stood his ground. "Where's Dixie? I want my wife."

"What did you do," said Skip, "mislay her?"

Patsy almost fell into her mayonnaise laughing.

Ty was about to blow his top completely when a guy came into the scene in an unconcerned manner and sat down at Skip's table. It was Detective Dave Santorelli. He spoke briefly to Ty:

"Beat it, son."

And now a hostess arrived hurriedly and said very pointedly but politely to Ty: "Would you mind returning to your table? We do not allow this sort of thing in here, as Detective Santorelli knows very well."

"Right," said Dave.

Ty not only returned to his table; shortly thereafter he faded from the scene entirely.

"What'll you have, Dave?" asked Skip. "This is Patsy."

"Hi, Patsy," said Dave. "Oh . . . cup of coffee. Why don't you give him back his wife, Skip?"

Skip wagged his head from side to side. "I talk to this broad once in Chez Roma and everybody thinks I ran off with her. I get threatened by hoods—Murtaugh knows all about that. Now this clown. It's crazy."

Dave laughed. The waitress brought his coffee. He slipped it in silence for a moment, then he said: "You knew Shamus pretty well, didn't you?"

"I saw him around," said Skip. "Yes. I knew him."

"Any ideas?"

"About the same as what you guys have got, I imagine."

Dave studied Skip for a moment, then went back to silently sipping his coffee.

"Who's Shamus?" asked Patsy.

"Eat your sandwich," said Skip.

Patsy shrugged and from then on ignored them.

"What we need is raw evidence," said Dave finally. "We've got our ideas, as you say. But we could be wrong."

"That's right," said Skip. "You never know."

"Well, you get around. If you hear anything . . . I might spring for a couple more chili-dogs."

"Oh, gee!" said Skip.

Dave laughed, and got to his feet. "Goodnight, Patsy," he said, then he left.

He'd caught Patsy with her mouth full. She couldn't reply but she turned and looked after him. Finally she said: "A nice copper. What do you know?"

"On the surface," said Skip. "On the surface. But he used to be on the Hoodlum Squad."

That meant "tough" to everybody in Chicago.

"Him?" cried Patsy. "Well, what do you know!"

It was a busy night. A few hours later Freddie Kling was having a chili-dog at Duke's. Freddie was known as a bad boy, though he was far from a "boy," being in his early 40s. As a youth he'd been a club fighter, then a bouncer and then a guy suspected of many things in the rip-and-tear penny-ante robbery line; he had quite a police record, and was generally avoided because of a quarrelsome disposition. Yes, Freddie was having a chili-dog at the open fronted diner when a radio car drove up, two cops got out, slammed Freddie up against the diner, frisked him thoroughly, then handcuffed him and took him away. Nobody had said a word. Everybody stared blankly at this swift visitation, then went on eating their chili-dogs.

Back in the station the cuffs were removed and Freddie was shoved into Dave Santarelli's office, where Dave was waiting.

"I said I'd talk to the Sergeant, not you," said Freddie.

"He'll be through in a minute. How did the boys do?"

"They did fine," said Freddie. "Rough as hell. I could get killed for this, you know."

"Don't worry, Freddie. The act should work. Lot of people see the bust?"

"Yeah. Some of the night regulars. It'll get around. It's OK I think."

After about half an hour a buzzer sounded and Dave took Freddie into Murtaugh's office. The sergeant was still in his shirtsleeves, his shirt all sweated. The steam heat was on full, the windows closed.

"God, it's hot in here," said Freddie.

"Hot? What?" asked Murtaugh, who obviously hadn't noticed. "OK. Open a window, Dave."

A window was opened and the cold Chicago night air rushed in.

Freddie sat down in front of the Sergeant's desk.

"Like I was telling Dave," said Freddie, "I could get killed for this. And I'm no fink, and you all know it."

"Right," said Murtaugh, "What is this all about?"

"It's about Shamus."

Dave and Murtaugh exchanged a quick look.

"Yes? What?" Murtaugh prodded.

"Them dago hoods killed him, that's what. Look, I'll level. That night I had a joint staked out. A guy did me some dirt. I was waiting for him to come out. I was going to work him over. Nothing serious, you understand. Just a few souvenirs."

"Oh sure," said Dave. He'd seen some of Freddie's "souvenirs."

"Shamus was a friend of mine," said Freddie. "And I ain't got too many. When things got real tough I could always go to Shamus for a fin, or more. Sure I tried to help him in his work. But how many guys can you go to any time and say 'Look! I'm strapped!' and he hands you a fin—maybe more, if you've got the guts to ask . . ."

"Right, right," said Murtaugh impatiently.

"You were waiting for this guy . . ." said Dave, urging Freddie on.

"Yeah, in a doorway. Right across from the what-do-you-call-it. Where the chorus broads come out of Chez Roma at night. And there was Shamus with a car, waiting. And pretty soon this broad comes out and gets in his car and they drive off."

"What broad?"

"That broad—what's her name . . . Dixie . . . that's missing. The hoods' broad from Chez Roma."

"You are absolutely positive?" Dave prodded again, while Murtaugh said nothing and tried hard to keep a grim smile from spreading over his face.

"I know Shamus well. Couldn't be wrong. And I seen that broad's picture. A doll baby. She was wearing a man's raincoat and carrying a little suitcase. Tall girl, a little shorter than Shamus. She got in and off they went. And I thought to myself, good hunting, Shamus."

"Anything else?" asked Murtaugh.

"No," said Freddie. "That's it. And I hope you bust them bastards for killing Shamus. I never want nobody busted. Them—I do."

"We'll do our best," said Murtaugh. "Now have I got it straight? You want us to hold you the rest of the night?"

"Right, Sergeant."

"He can sleep in one of the detention rooms," said Dave, and so it was arranged.

Later Dave and Murtaugh sat down together to talk things over.

"Would they kill the girl?" asked Murtaugh, trying to convince himself of something.

"I don't know," said Dave. "Maybe she left town. Nobody can get any line at all."

"Put a man on it—nothing else."

Dave thought it over for a long time; finally he said: "I'll take it for the time being. I've got some ideas."

"All right," said Murtaugh. "It might be the crux of the whole business. Tomorrow night I sweat the Chez Roma bunch. You give 'em a little warning first, right? So they'll be shook up. But don't mention the girl. I'll spring that one."

Dave laughed quietly. There was a long silence. Finally Murtaugh spoke: "Does it ever occur to you, Dave, that there is something screwy going on in this town? Something we don't know about?"

"How do you mean?"

"George Hamm. Unsolved, nothing. Ivan, Kovacs, Lacy, unsolved, nothing. Now Shamus. All big time, in a way."

"How the hell you going put that together . . .?"

". . . and the girl missing," Murtaugh went on. "We tie the Mob in with the Detroit guys getting whomped. Now we tie the Mob in with Shamus and the girl . . . I don't know. I just get a feeling . . ."

To Dave this didn't make sense. He looked at the Sergeant who seemed bone weary.

"I think maybe you need some sleep, Frank."

"Yeah," said Murtaugh.

The next night none of the regulars strolling the boulevard or hopping from joint to joint missed the sight of Sergeant Murtaugh's Cadillac parked at the curb just beyond Chez Roma. In the front seat was a hard-eyed copper named Ridgeway, who had rousted the tenderloin on foot for years and now had been promoted to the high estate of being one of the Sergeant's right hand men. Nor did the strollers and pub-crawlers miss the mounted machine-gun in back. It was a conversation piece all over town. Had it ever been used? Or was it just a symbol? No one was sure, and no one was anxious to test the possibility, least of all the hoods, apparently.

In the foyer of Chez Roma Tom Boyle was passing the time talking to Mina, the cute little check-girl, who was propositioned fifty times a night—but had never been known to go out with anybody. The rumor was she was Giovanni's illegitimate daughter, but how the rumor had started nobody knew. She was bright and sharp and fast with a quip and had many regular admirers who always stopped to talk with her, Tom Boyle being one of them. Tom was married and had three kids. His intentions in regard to Mina were not nefarious, he merely liked to talk with her.

"Doomsday," said Mina. "What is going on?"

"Problems," said Tom.

"It's like a wake around here. It makes me sick in the stomach. Do you know what I mean?"

"Yes," said Tom.

"I like it happy," said Mina.

Mina was right. It was like a wake—in Madame's elegant office in the back, with its pictures, its bric-a-brac and its antiques. Giovanni stood with his back against the wall, as if trying to push himself through and disappear, smoking one cigarette after another. Franco, Packy, and Bimbo, three big hoods, were sitting on a couch side by side, with their arms folded, trying to look tough and unperturbed. Madame sat at her desk, elegantly attired, but inelegantly disturbed.

"You are persecuting us, Sergeant," she said. "That's what you are doing, persecuting us. We never have any trouble here. You know that. We've never had any trouble at all except with the Federal Government. We have always been friends with the Chicago police. They are welcome here. So now why do you persecute us like this?"

"I'm not persecuting anybody," said Murtaugh. "You've been doing the persecuting. Like Franco there. Barging into Clancy's—lucky he didn't get his thick head knocked off—and threatening a young guy by the name of Mahaffy. All on account of that girl Dixie. It's all up and down the street: Chez Roma is looking for Dixie. Hoods combing the joints. Where is Dixie? Threats, strong arm stuff—you name it. Do you deny that?"

"We were looking for her, yes," said Madame. "She was a valued employee. She didn't even turn up to get her paycheck. Why shouldn't we look for her? But, Sergeant, what has all this to do with the unhappy killing of . . .?"

Murtaugh was waiting for this, sitting in his chair as usual, as if ready to spring. "What it has to do with it is . . . we have a witness who saw Selby Reed pick Dixie up at your stage-door the night she disappeared. And if a witness, an outsider, could have noticed this, any one of you could have. You, for instance, or you, or you," Murtaugh went on pointing from one hood to the other.

The hoods all tried to look unconcerned—tried to keep from glancing sideways at each other. Jesus, what a make! This was bad, bad. So why plead innocent even if you are? Everybody is always innocent to hear them tell it. Just a waste of time to deny anything. They kept still.

"You, Packy . . .?" Murtaugh brought it out like a shot.

Packy moved slightly, crossed and uncrossed his arms. "I didn't see nothing, Sergeant."

Giovanni seemed to be trying to get through the wall. Madame's face was rigid and pale.

"I swear to you, Sergeant," she said, "we had nothing to do with this. Nothing at all. Sergeant—you'll ruin us. Don't you understand?"

"Why should we kill that poor man?" cried Giovanni, suddenly. "Who would it profit? For a silly girl we kill a man? Sergeant, please . . . how can you believe such a thing?"

Against his will Murtaugh was beginning to wonder. It was expensive to have a man killed by a pro—if Selby had been beaten to death, it would be a different thing: pointing to Franco, Packy or Bimbo. They're rip-and-tear boys, super bouncers, what else?—a different breed altogether. And in the underworld men were killed by pros for business reasons—no other reasons.

A kind of despair began to nag at Murtaugh . . . and at the back of his mind he began to hear the litany: Hamm, Ivan, Kovacs, Lacy, Shamus . . . there was something, something . . .

Long silence. Murtaugh noted that the hoods and Giovanni were all sweating; while Madame seemed chilled, icy, if anything.

"You are still looking for the girl?" he asked suddenly.

"No," cried Madame. "No—that ungrateful girl. No. She will never work here again. No. We do not want her."

Giovanni thought he noted a certain slacking in Murtaugh's purpose but before he could speak, try to take advantage of it, a table-captain hurried in and whispered excitedly to Madame, who smiled, for the first time, and stood up.

"Sergeant," she said, "my cousin is here. He will speak with you on our behalf."

It sounded like the Sergeant was being granted an audience. Well, bully for Cousin, he thought. Bowing, ostentatiously polite, the table-captain ushered in a slim, well-dressed man of fifty or so, with neatly combed gray-streaked hair, and an air that was almost Caesarian, with more than a touch of condescension.

The cousin was State Senator John V. Avezzano, formerly known as Johnny the Waiter—in the bad old days, of course, long gone, long forgotten.

Madame was almost beaming, if you can imagine it, as the Sergeant got up to shake hands.

"This is Senator Avezzano, my cousin," said Madame.

So this was the fix, thought the Sergeant, shaking hands; everybody has always thought it went pretty high up, maybe even to Washington. Had the Senator been able to call off the Feds? Looked like it.

"My compliments to the Chief and to the Chicago Police Department, the best in the land," said Johnny the Waiter, who should know. Murtaugh bowed slightly acknowledging the compliment, then the Senator went on: "Sergeant, I have talked to everyone connected with Chez Roma. I assure you any suspicion of their having anything to do with the death of that man . . . Reed, is it? . . . is false. I give you my word, Sergeant. The word of a Senator from the great state of Illinois . . ."

When Murtaugh emerged, Tom Boyle, talking with Mina, noted that his face could be likened to a thundercloud. Naturally he said nothing. Ridgeway, after a glance, was equally silent. Murtaugh got into the front seat and slammed the door, ignoring his fans. Tom got into the back with the machine-gun. They drove over a block before the Sergeant said anything, and when he spoke he spat out only one word.

Ridgeway seemed to be struggling with some emotion. Tom noted his shoulders moving suspiciously. Tom had an almost hysterical desire to laugh.

But they rode back to the station in silence.

"God, what a girl for sleep," thought Skip, contemplating that odd phenomenon known as Dixie. And no trouble at all, no bitching, no impossible scenes, no beefs—it was incredible. Of course maybe it was partly due to the fact, Skip considered, that there was nothing between them except a kind of mild friendliness—but this was unusual in itself. Skip had the habit, as he said, of sampling the product. But Dixie was special in every respect. He had big plans for her. He intended to get her an agent, for modeling and club work. No more dancing in the chorus. Maybe she could whip up a single—she could sing and she could dance and she was a knockout. What more could you ask? And there was no hurry to grab a job, any job. Skip had plenty of money and in Dixie he saw the possibility of plenty more. And if some big shot money guy just couldn't resist—it was going to cost him— unbelievably—or no play. Nobody was hungry—hungry days were over.

Many girls found Skip attractive—Dixie did not. But strangest of all Skip had no more feeling for Dixie than if she was a child, and that's what she reminded him of at times, he didn't know why. Once Ty had got furious at Dixie and had called her a neuter—and Ty in his rage had got near to the truth. Sex meant very little, if anything, to Dixie. With her it was not a necessity at all, it was a weapon—a lure.

So . . . Dixie, after a bird-like supper, had returned to bed and was now sleeping peacefully, while Skip, in his own flat, drew up plans for the future. He saw it largely as unlimited.

Skip was deep in thought of the future when the phone rang. It was Dave Santorelli, and he asked Skip if a meeting was possible, and when Skip replied, "Why not?" Dave named time and place.

Half an hour later Skip found Dave sitting in an unmarked car on a little side-street, just off the brilliantly-lighted boulevard. It was early and very busy, with cars hissing by in an almost continuous stream. Skip got in the car, they lit up cigarettes, and Dave said "Murtaugh put me on the Dixie case, special. It's a must, definitely tied into the killing, Murtaugh thinks. And I need help."

"Well . . . you know me, Dave."

"Skip—I think you know a hell of a lot more than you're saying."

"Why do you say that?"

"It's a feeling."

"Everybody's got a feeling, right? The Chez Roma hoods. That dumb thespian with the curly locks. And now you. You don't say where there's smoke there's fire."

"You don't know anything even for a chili-dog?"

"Like what?"

"Like where she is."

"God, I've heard that enough." There was a long pause, then Skip asked: "And if you find her?"

"Skip," said Dave, "I'm going to level with you. We've got an eye witness who saw her get into Shamus's car the night she ran away."

Skip resisted a jump. Oh, that Dooley! What a smart, crafty bastard! And here they were, all prepared. He had done just as Dooley had instructed him; he'd drill the story into Dixie till she actually seemed to think it was true. Skip sat rubbing his chin and thinking, then he noticed a phone booth just down the street near the corner.

"Got to make a phone call," he said. "I'll be right back."

In the booth Skip dialed Dooley's hotel payphone, knowing the number by heart, and thinking, "If the Gorilla's there, I'll put it to him. If he's not, I'll stall."

The Gorilla was there. He took in the situation in a moment, asked if Dixie had been thoroughly drilled, and then gave Skip the go-ahead.

"Business or pleasure" asked Dave, ironically, as Skip got back in the car.

"I promised to check with Patsy and I forgot all about it," said Skip, knowing Dave wouldn't believe him in any case, and was certain Skip had checked with a principal of some kind.

But it didn't matter. He hadn't taken time enough to set up a complex story and nobody would be more aware of that than Dave, who knew his business.

So, after they had lit up again, Skip told Dave the whole long tale, even elaborating slightly here and there.

Dave thought it all over for a moment, then asked (oh, that Dooley): "Why hasn't she been seen?"

"She's ducking the Chez Roma people. She's had it with them. She didn't even go back for her check."

Dave sat lost in thought. Finally he said: "It's a very plausible story, Skip. But where's the girl? This is a missing person thing, remember?"

"Want to see her? Be my guest."

Frankly, Dave was startled. "Just like that, we go see her?"

"Why not? She may be in bed, but she's always in bed or thinking about going to bed or talking about going to bed—I think she'd live in bed if she could. We can get her up."

As a matter of fact, Dixie was lying on a couch in her flat, eating candy from the same old box, and reading the same *Harper's Bazaar* and listening to music on the radio. She was wearing her Japanese kimono and little else, her thick black hair loose and hanging.

Brought in by Skip and introduced, Dave didn't know where to look. He felt all shook and disoriented. No wonder there had been such an uproar over this broad.

Skip said nothing, no prompting, nothing; he just lit a cigarette, leaned back in his chair and watched Dave out of the corner of his eye. Dave didn't seem to know whether to be the big tough cop, the big brother, the sympathetic friend or what . . . it was pitiful. Skip got up and started to walk about to keep from laughing.

After a few questions from Dave, Dixie told the tale. She'd bragged she was a quick study, and she was right. She didn't miss a thing; in fact, to add realism to the recital, she seemed to hesitate at times, as if not quite sure she was remembering things exactly right.

Once she asked, at a point dealing with Skip: "Is that right Skip?"

And he replied: "Well, it's close enough."

Finally the tale had been told, and Dave studied Dixie at length, then rose. At that moment Dixie found it necessary to lean far over and rescue her *Harper's Bazaar* from the floor. Dave fled into the hallway.

"Satisfied?" asked Skip.

"Yeah," said Dave. "Well, that clears up a missing persons case—and leaves us out in left field. I'll spring for the chili-dogs."

"I'll take a raincheck," said Skip.

"It figures. I don't blame you." He jerked his head back toward Dixie. Skip didn't disillusion him.

Skip called Dooley back and gave him a quick account of how it had gone. The Gorilla seemed pleased, Skip thought.

Going up in the rickety self-serve elevator, Dooley said to himself: "Well, that's it. Tomorrow I get out of here. The only loose end is Goggles and there's nothing I can do about that." Meaning he didn't think it was worth the effort to try to track him down and eliminate him from the scene.

"That Mahaffy's a slippery bastard" said Murtaugh. "Hiding her all the time, right?"

Dave nodded, feeling tired and somehow dissatisfied with life.

"Well," said Murtaugh, "I can understand it with those stupid hoods tramping around."

A long silence fell. It was late. They could hear a clock ticking some place.

They were at a dead end.

"How about home?" asked Murtaugh finally.

Dave yawned and got up. He often wondered what the Sergeant's homelife must be like with seven kids, and another one on the way, or so he'd heard. As for himself, a widower; he had remarried and now had an odd family: a son, 14, a daughter, 12, and another daughter not yet one year old. It made at times for strange upsets and tensions. And he wondered briefly what it was like to be a Skip and have a broad like Dixie available next door; to live a life of sin openly, unashamed. Dave was a good Catholic; he had an aunt who was a nun, his mother's sister. Who had the right of it after all?

"God knows," thought Dave, yawning again.

As they walked down the corridor together, Murtaugh said: "Well, Dave—start over tomorrow."

"Right, Frank, right," said Dave, restraining his yawns.

And the litany kept running through Murtaugh's mind: George Hamm, Bill Lacy, Frank Kovacs, Mike Ivan, Selby Reed . . . someway it made sense, but the Sergeant didn't have an inkling how. It was an instinct. A hunch—

It had just begun to rain and the damp shine was now spreading all over the pavements. Ridgeway was waiting with the Cadillac.

"Did you ever see that girl?" asked Dave.

"What girl?" said Murtaugh, irritably.

"Never mind," said Dave.

Chuck sat at his apartment window watching the rain fall. What could have happened to Ingeborg?

Every Saturday night as soon as she finished work at the rathskeller she came to his apartment and they had a night and two days together, the rathskeller being dark on Sundays and Mondays. She usually arrived by one; now it was nearly two thirty. It was too late to phone her, as she lived at home and he didn't want to wake up the family.

Half an hour ago he'd driven over to the rathskeller and cruised the nearby streets: nothing.

In his heart he was pretty sure what had happened but he couldn't bring himself to get it out in the open and examine it. Things had not been going too well with Ingeborg lately. At times she'd sound indifferent and abstracted and not as anxious to go to movies or out dancing as in the past. There were long intervals of silence between them. And

Ingeborg, who used to love cooking in Chuck's apartment (it was more modern in every way than her antiquated home), now seldom cooked at all—said it bored her and why not run down to Winkel's and get it over with? In the past having dinner together did not come under the category of "getting it over with." It had been pleasant and fun . . . as they dawdled and talked and drank German beer and listened to the records usually played at Winkel's, mostly polkas and such, very lively, cheerful music.

Chuck saw a car coming and got hopefully to his feet . . . but it just drove indifferently past and the street was empty again. Now the rain began to fall heavily, making puddles into which the raindrops plunged, then bounced.

Chuck got out his bottle and poured himself a stiff drink. All week long at the used car lot, irritated by customers and niggling business details and old Ed Weed, he looked forward to these weekends. He actually didn't feel that he was living otherwise. Was selling and repairing cars living? Was listening to Ed Weed living? He'd rather be sleeping, so the days would pass faster and the weekend would arrive.

He tossed down his drink—then he couldn't stand the suspense a second longer. He called Ingeborg's home. After a long interval, one of the kids came on—a kid sister. She seemed astonished that it was Chuck calling.

"Isn't she with you?" asked the kid.

Now Chuck could hear the uproar and finally an older girl came on. "If I wake poppa he'll shoot me," she said. "Isn't Ingeborg supposed to be with you?"

"Well . . ." said Chuck. "Maybe there's been some kind of mix-up. Don't tell your father."

The girl seemed relieved. "All right," she said. "But where could Ingie be? I'm worried."

Chuck hung up, wincing away from the certainty, though he'd been pretty sure of what had happened all along. Ingeborg was getting tired of the whole business . . . as she had warned him she might.

Ingeborg had obviously gone elsewhere.

Chuck sat down, stared moodily out at the rain, and poured himself another drink. It was always this way—sooner or later. It always had been.

"What's the matter with me?" Chuck asked himself. "Why don't girls like me? Am I some kind of crumb? I don't get it!"

He felt both anger and despair; in fact, he wasn't sure how he felt.

The phone rang and Chuck upset his glass making a grab for it.

"Chuck," cried Ingeborg, "I didn't know how late it was. My God, it's going on three. And here I thought . . ." He could hear laughing and some kind of music; there seemed to be many voices, which was a relief in a way. "I met all these old friends of mine at the rathskeller and we had such fun and . . . Chuck, are you listening?"

"I'm listening," said Chuck. "Call home. I already called there, and the girls are upset."

"Now why did you do a silly thing like that?" cried Ingeborg.

"I got worried," said Chuck after a pause.

"Chuck, that is no way to act and now I'm sorry I called you. Goodbye."

"Wait, wait . . ." pled Chuck.

"Well . . .?" Ingeborg sounded cold, very cold.

"Will I see you tomorrow?"

"Yes, why not?" said Ingeborg. "Pick me up around noon." She hung up.

Chuck felt vastly relieved, though in his heart he knew it was no good, no longer any good. It was just a question of time now . . .

He mopped up the spilled liquor, showered, and went to bed. It was very quiet. All he could hear was the rain falling.

He felt very much alone, with Ingeborg receding and his father up in Canada, hunting moose. Chuck tried to visualize the Canadian scene as pictured in his father's last letter: the immense snowfields, the dark pines here and there, the guys on snowshoes, tracking the moose. Chuck wished he was there, away from all the trouble of the gasoline-stinking, used car lot . . .

At long last Chuck fell asleep.

Early morning, Selby Reed's brother, Dawson, made up his mind that today he'd break into that lock-box of Selby's. The funeral was over and the odds and ends were being tidied up. For years he hadn't been at all friendly with his brother; he'd seldom seen him. They lived in different worlds: Selby on the boulevards of downtown, he in a small suburb with small houses, small lawns and small trees. And with a small accessory business that was making him small money, hardly enough to maintain his house, his wife, and his two small kids.

But Dawson was a happy man who had slowly bettered himself, married a fine girl he loved, and now had two kids, a boy and a girl, who were cheerful, laughing—hard to take at times because of exuberance—but basically damned fine. He loved them.

The problem had always been money; and now that problem had been solved, certainly for the time being. To his surprise, his careless, no-good brother, Selby, had left a will, naming him as sole executor and beneficiary, as his only living relative (except of course for the kids.).

One day Dawson, taking the kids to a big downtown toy store (it had been the holiday season) had run into Selby who was standing in the doorway of a jewelry store talking to a tall blonde girl, who looked like an actress to Dawson, who had little knowledge of such things. Selby had seemed rather pleased with the kids, to Dawson's surprise. "They look just like you, Daw," he said. "No doubt who their father is." The tall young lady knelt down and hugged the kids and was very nice to them. On the way home Ernie said: "Phew! She smelled funny." And his sister laughed at him: "Silly, that's French perfume . . ."

It was the only time Selby had ever seen the kids.

Dawson had been amazed to find over twelve thousand dollars in a savings account, and over a thousand in a checking account. Windfall! Bonanza!

And now he was in the garage trying to open the big lock-box he'd found in Selby's closet.

Alice, his wife, was out in front with the kids, playing ball with them—there was much running and falling down and screaming and Dawson was enjoying the uproar.

He had found many keys—but this box seemed to have a secret system of some kind. He tried every possible combination of keys— nothing worked.

"Well, it's probably a lot of junk and old records and stuff anyway," thought Dawson, aware that his brother ran some kind of an investigative business.

But his curiosity got the better of him, and getting out his car tools, he went to work on it. It was a tough job. He was called in for a very big, very elaborate Sunday breakfast, then he dawdled over the Sunday papers, played with the kids—and finally remembered the lock-box. He went back to it reluctantly, far preferring—

But at last he wrenched it open, ruining the box, which he had been striving not to do. Dawson was a careful man, not a wrecker, and he hated to see anything demolished. Just as he had thought: stacks of films, papers, clippings—nothing. But finally his hand encountered something fat, leathery and bulging. It seemed to be a stuffed briefcase; more papers no doubt. Dawson lifted it out—sprung it open and got the shock of a lifetime. Stacks and stacks of money, big bills—a fortune.

His hands shaking, he closed the outer garage door, turned on the light, and counted the money, complete disbelief growing in him. When the tally reached one hundred thousand dollars, he stopped and just sat there.

Where did it come from? What did it mean? Should he declare it as part of the estate? Where in God's name could Selby have got a sum like this?

"Daw," he said to himself, "you've got to think and think hard. You've got family to worry about."

After a long time, he decided he would put the money in safety-deposit boxes while he decided what to do about it. You couldn't settle something like this on the spur of the moment. It took time, time . . .

Dooley was about ready to leave. He had decided not to go to New York after all; instead he intended to drive to Milwaukee, where he had another "home"—a small obscure hotel on a side-street—stay for a day or so, or until he had made up his mind what to do with himself, and then perhaps sell the car, which might turn out to be a burden, and then go, wherever he intended to go, by train. Go someplace and with some purpose in mind he shortly would. With Dooley it was always, what's next?

His bags were packed; the oil had been changed in the car and there was a full tank of gas, and now there was nothing left to be done but eat and take off. It was nearly three p.m. of a very gloomy, cloudy, threatening day. What used to be called in the Midwest "snow-clouds" were massed all over the sky. In some windows lights were already showing.

Dooley went down the street to the diner and had fried steak, hash brown potatoes and a salad—and as he ate he sat looking out the window at the street he had stared at for so long—a street that from now on no doubt would merely be a vague, a very vague memory, like the many other streets he'd stared at from various hotel windows in many many other towns over the last twenty-five years.

"I guess they never did catch them gangsters," said the cheerful counterman.

"I guess not," said Dooley.

"They never do. And so what? Somebody'll kill 'em sooner or later. Why waste taxpayers' money?"

"Right," said Dooley.

He drank a second cup of coffee, smoked a cigarette, gestured goodbye to the counterman and left. It had been quite a stay. Would he ever see any of his co-workers again? It was doubtful; though if he came back to Chicago for another job, he would certainly check with Skip, who was worth his weight in gold. He could find things out for you, he could operate, and you could depend on him. In twenty-five years of experience Dooley had never before seen a junkie like Skip. They were usually jumpy and extremely undependable.

As he walked down the hotel corridor to his room Dooley was running over in his mind the highlights of the record hit, starting with the discovery of George Hamm's body . . . what a weird chain of events. Any one of a dozen things could have blown them out of the water . . . but his thoughts broke off suddenly and he became still as only an animal can become still. His door was unlocked and he knew damned well he had locked it when he left. He hesitated, then pushed the door open slowly and reached in and switched on the lights. But the room was empty, and the bathroom door was closed, as usual. Dooley closed the outer door and locked it, then he carefully opened the bathroom door and reaching in switched on the lights. Nothing.

Then he examined the room. It had been frisked, but by an expert who had carefully put things back the way he had found them—only not carefully enough for Dooley's eyes. And he was certain the wardrobe had been moved, if only slightly—maybe the frisker hadn't got around to moving it fully, surprised by his arrival. Or maybe he had a lookout some place who had tipped him off and he'd been forced to relinquish his search.

Dooley moved the wardrobe, rolled back the carpet, and lifted the lid. All was well. Still not certain what he intended to do, Dooley got out his gun belt, strapped it on, and holstered the loaded .45. Then he replaced the rest, and got the wardrobe back in its normal spot.

Then he stood in the room lost in thought. Finally he nodded to himself, went out, locked the door behind him and returned to the lobby.

He had an irrational feeling that he was being watched; a slight crawling of the spine, an uneasiness, a kind of instinctive fear. He went to the payphone and appeared to talk on it for a moment, then he crossed to the dayman behind the desk.

"Have you checked any strangers in here lately?" he asked.

"No," said the dayman. "Nobody has checked in here for four days. We're mostly permanents, you know."

"Have you seen any strangers hanging around here today?"

"No, sir, Mr. Dooley. What's the matter?"

"I thought I saw somebody up in my hallway when I got off the elevator. He sure disappeared fast."

"You're thinking of sneak-thieves, I suppose. Well, we've had no trouble here. It's the rich hotels that have that kind of trouble. Anybody can get in here. The whole back part's open, with the garage and all, and there's the work-elevator in the back. We've never had any trouble."

Dooley thought this over, then he put a five-dollar bill on the desk— the dayman eyeing it hopefully—and slipped it under the blotter. Then he gave the dayman precise instructions on what he wanted him to do. The dayman was puzzled but was only too eager to help.

"And don't pick up the money," said Dooley. "Leave it there till later."

The dayman thought this was all pretty weird but he complied.

Well, thought Dooley, as he rode upward in the creaky old elevator, this is one advantage of not having a phone in your room. Many of the rooms in this hotel had no phones; you were charged extra for phones and many people didn't need them. On arrival Dooley hadn't needed one either; anyway, he preferred to talk on payphones and not go through switchboards—you never knew when you might run into a switchboard jockey with a long nose and big ears—but when things got hot, as at his listening-post in The Loop, then you had to take chances—no other way.

Dooley unlocked his door, whistling. Once inside, he continued to whistle and move about, as if changing his clothes, and he even sang a bar or two. If there were eyes about there might also be ears.

Five minutes later the dayman knocked on his door, and when Dooley opened it, the dayman said: "The garage man called back. If you bring the car down right away he can fix it. Says it will only take maybe fifteen minutes."

"How far is that garage from here?" asked Dooley.

"One block," said the dayman. "South, toward town."

"Thanks," said Dooley, then he shut the door, stalled, then came out wearing his overcoat, whistling, and putting on gloves.

In the lobby he gestured in a friendly manner to the dayman, who was puzzled but dedicated and returned the gesture, then Dooley went down the back stairs to the garage, got into his car, left the garage and started off south down the alley. At the end of the alley he turned into a side-street and parked. Smoking, biding his time, he just sat there for a long moment.

Finally he left the car and went back up the alley, keeping close to the buildings, then back into the underground part of the hotel where he found the work-elevator the dayman had mentioned. The dayman was right. Anybody could get into and out of the hotel with very little chance of anybody seeing them.

He got out at his own floor and took off his shoes, and left them outside a door, as in a big hotel where they came and shined your shoes, then he moved down to his own corridor, made the turn, and if anybody in the hallway had been blind or with their eyes closed they would never have known Dooley was there. It was almost unbelievable that a man of his size could move without making a sound but it was a fact; he had learned it the hard way, as a young sneak-thief.

Little by little he crept to his own door. Finally he reached it and pressed his ear to it. No doubt about it, somebody was in there. He didn't know whether the door was locked or unlocked and he couldn't take any chances experimenting. If it was Goggles, you could find yourself dead very quickly. Trapping Goggles was like trapping a deadly snake; you'd better strike first. Bracing himself, he drew back his right foot and gave the door a powerful kick. It burst open at once. And there was Goggles with the wardrobe moved aside, on his knees, with the carpet rolled back and the lid in sight. Goggles' gun was on the floor beside him; he made a frantic grab, but Dooley was on top of him. He hit Googles once, twice, three times about the head and neck, vicious powerful chopping blows, and Goggles fell forward with a groan and lay flat on his face. His hands moved as if he was trying to grasp something, anything—then in a moment they stopped moving. Dooley closed the door, then stood looking down at Goggles. Now he was lying very still.

Dooley tested the artery in Goggles' neck. No doubt about it. Goggles was dead.

Dooley left, locking the door after him, retrieved his shoes, went down in the work-elevator . . . and a few minutes later, having retrieved his car, he appeared in the lobby and said to the dayman, who gave him a rather bewildered look: "Everything's all right. I'll be leaving shortly. I just have a few errands to take care of."

"It's going to seem funny without you, Mr. Dooley," said the dayman, now capturing his five-dollar bill. "Many thanks."

Dooley gestured and went out the front door. He remembered seeing an Army surplus store just down the street at the corner, and there he bought a coil of rope, several large blankets and three heavy belts.

Dooley came in carrying bulky packages and again waved to the dayman.

In his room, Dooley tied Goggles' arms and legs securely with the rope, rolled him into the blankets, making a large blanket-roll, then he strapped it all up with the belts.

Throwing the big Goggles-bundle over his shoulder, he carried it down the corridor and into the work-elevator. In the garage, he dumped it into the back of the car, then he returned for the rest of his luggage, including the duffle-bag that had cost Goggles his life.

A few minutes later he reappeared in the lobby, from the back, and waved to the dayman: "I'm going," he called.

"Good luck, Mr. Dooley," called the dayman.

The day was gloomier than ever as Dooley drove up the lake highway toward Milwaukee, very few cars out, all with their lights on. Dooley drove with one hand on the wheel, smoking and thinking. A slick one, that Goggles! How had he run Dooley down? Quite a job: except by some strange mischance—maybe by a mere matter of only five minutes—he'd got caught.

Finally Dooley came to a stretch of road that was very close to the beach. He pulled over to the side, got out and put the hood up, as if he was having engine trouble. Then he opened the back door on the beach-side, lifted the Goggles-bundle out, and heaved it down in among the tufted dunes, where it rolled, then stopped.

A car went past. But who pays attention? Nobody, as Dooley in his long-checkered career had found out. Nobody. Drop dead. Who cares?

He lowered the hood, got back in, and drove off in the gathering gloom, toward Milwaukee.

Dooley was long gone, but Chicago was still there and operating just as if it had never received the questionable boon of Dooley's presence. It was night, cold and clear, but there was gloom in Murtaugh's office as the Sergeant and his driven men continued to get nowhere with the Selby Reed case—it was an all-around total blank, though they kept doggedly trying, as the same litany continued to run through the Sergeant's head: Hamm, Ivan, Lacy, Kovacs, Shamus . . . he was certain it meant something. But what? He might now have added another name to that strange collection except that the body of Goggles had been found far from his jurisdiction and was unknown to him. And the suburban police could make nothing of the discovery: all they had was the body of a young male Caucasian, and a Toronto (Canada) driver's license issued to one Armand Kahr, 26, six feet tall, weight 145, blue eyes, blond hair . . . they had checked with the authorities at Toronto but as yet had received no reply. So the body of Goggles still rested, unclaimed, in a drawer in the morgue.

With Skip and Dixie things were going well. Ty had removed himself from the scene by going to California where he hoped to astonish those in Hollywood with his talent and charm. Before leaving, however, he had taken great pleasure in selling all of Dixie's clothes, including half a dozen expensive dresses, many expensive accessories and a fairly good fur coat. Ty now had a bankroll and left with no regrets. "I hope I never see that Polack bum again," he told his friends, who were very sympathetic.

Skip had decided on what he called a test run. It was said of Skip that he hadn't been raised a bum but that he was a bum at heart. Anyway, his raising came in handy. He was accepted anyplace, a rather conservative-looking young man correctly dressed and with good manners. And when he appeared with Dixie at the formal dining-room of a Gold Coast hotel he was received as matter of course, and after a generous—but not too generous—tip, they were seated in a favored center booth with a good view of the whole room.

Dixie's luxuriant black hair was up, but loosely arranged, and she had put a few brilliants in it, in the shape of stars. Skip liked those stars and he was proud of Dixie in her simple shimmering white dinner dress. They ordered and had wine with their dinner—real wine, compliments of this elegant hotel which naturally never had any trouble with the law. Unthinkable.

Skip observed all without seeming to. He noted several of the men were being excessively attentive to their lady friends to mask the fact that they were falling out of their clothes over Dixie. Skip could hardly restrain his giggles. It was a very polite civilized place—naturally none of these guys was going to get up, come over and say: "Hi, baby. How about you and me go tear one off?"—but that is the way they were feeling, and feelings don't differ, only manners.

Dixie had made quite a quiet impact in a quiet place. Even the women were now criticizing her.

"Stars in her hair? That's silly," said one matron and her husband hastily agreed.

At last the maître d' bowed them out.

"I like that place," said Dixie. "Did you see the dinner I ate?"

"Almost enough for a small child," said Skip.

The doorman whistled for a taxi. As they were waiting, Detective Tom Brenner came out of a side door and crossed toward the parking lot. He was tired after a long boring stint of supervising the guarding of a jewelry collection that was on display in the hotel. Now he'd been relieved and was anxious to get home and relax and listen to the radio. He noted the elegant couple, blinked—then crossed to them to see if he was seeing right.

Skip turned and noticed him.

"Hi, Tom," said Skip.

"Hi, Skip," said Detective Brenner.

Their taxi arrived and bore them off. Brenner just stood there looking after the taxi, then he slowly shook his head.

"Some town, Chicago," he said.

THE END

Man With a
Thousand Enemies
....
W. R. BURNETT

CHAPTER ONE

Jack, the chauffeur, swung the big limousine into Upper Pelham Road, then, turning and smiling slightly at his boss, who was lounging comfortably, smoking a cigar, he stepped on the gas and the speedometer moved to 70 then 75 then 80.

The boss, Gordon Minot, a man of forty-five with greying hair and a long, rather handsome, sunburnt face, turned to the man sitting beside him and grinned maliciously.

"Ah," he said, "this is what I like. Speed! Speed! What's the matter, Jimmy? You don't seem to be enjoying yourself."

Jimmy said nothing. He was a medium-sized, sober-faced young man of about thirty. He was well-dressed and did not look out-of-place in the huge, ornate Minot limousine, but a certain toughness showed through his unobtrusive exterior and a close observer might have wondered what he was doing with such an evident swell as Gordon Minot.

"Sometimes," said Minot, smiling, "I think you've got a yellow streak, Jimmy."

"And sometimes I think you're a fool," Jimmy replied quietly.

"Please! is that any way to talk to a multi-millionaire? And one of the lower classes, too!"

"You pay me six grand a year to see that somebody don't tag you, then you let that curly-haired delight of the parlor maids drive this hearse as fast as it will go. Is that sense?"

"No. Not to you probably."

"You never make sense to me."

"I'd be insulted if I did."

"All right. You're smart. I'm dumb. But you've got to pay me more money if you're going to let that ape drive like this when I'm in the car."

"I gave you a raise in January. I'd like to know what you do to earn your money. This is just a sinecure."

"A what?"

"All right. I see I've got to talk down a little. A soft snap. You're practically on a pension. Slow down a little, Jack, or I'll have to raise Mr. Devore's salary."

Jack grinned and the speedometer showed 87, then 90. Two motorcycles shot out of a side road, a siren roared, and, laughing, Jack slowed down gradually, then drew up and sat waiting.

The cops came up, grinning.

"Hiya, Jimmy," one of them said.

Jimmy nodded without smiling.

"Excuse me, Mr. Minot," said the other, "but if I ain't mistaken your boy, here, was doing forty-five or better. Now that's pretty fast on this road. A couple of bridle-paths cross it down a ways and I got strict orders . . ."

"We were doing 90," said Jimmy, "at least. Maybe more."

"Humor him, gentlemen, humor him," said Minot, giving the cops his best smile; "he's a little drunk, and when he's drunk he's dangerous."

"Anyway," said one of the cops, looking dubiously at Jimmy, "can't you have this boy here drive a little slower, Mr. Minot? We got strict orders."

"Certainly. Jack, what do you mean taking advantage of me and driving like that? It won't happen again, I assure you."

"Thank you, sir," said one the cops. They touched their cap and Jack drove off.

The cops stood for a moment watching the limousine disappear down the road, then one of them spoke:

"Nutty as a fruitcake, that guy."

"Got the city in the palm of his hand. What a life! Wouldn't I like to see myself riding around in one of them Mercedes, laying back with a cigar in my face. And how about Jimmy Devore? What a snap!"

"Done time, ain't he?"

"Yeah. He was two years in stir. They tell me he took a rap for Mr. Minot's brother; you know, the guy that was supposed to have bumped himself off, only they hushed it up and said he died of a stroke!"

"Sure. Political scandal, wasn't it?"

"Yeah. Bribery. Jimmy took the rap and now he lives on the fat of the land. He's head of all the Minot plant police and he watches Gordon Minot like a hawk."

"Has he got anything? You know what I mean."

"I hear so. They tell me that he's tough and smart. Plenty tough. Plenty smart. I always liked him. He's a pal of Cap Berger's and I used to see him every day down at the old Canal Street Station. Cap thinks he's the berries. Hey!" yelled the cop, as a car turned in from a side road and swept past, the driver not seeing them. "Why, that so-an-so's doing sixty. Let's get him."

Mike, the caretaker, unlocked the big gates and swung them wide, then he took off his hat and held up his hand to keep Jack from driving on.

"Good evening, Mr. Minot! Excuse me, please. Mr. Devore, Captain Berger wants to see you. He'll be here any minute now."

"Thanks, Mike. Did he say what he wanted?"

"No, Mr. Devore. Sorry to hold you up, Mr. Minot."

Minot waved the apology aside and smiled very graciously. Mike glowed with pleasure. The boss was sure one swell guy and anybody that didn't like him was nuts, that's all. They said he had so many enemies you couldn't count them. One time the *City Call* had come out with an article saying the boss was a man with a thousand enemies. That was too much for old Mike; he couldn't understand it.

"I'll drop off here," said Jimmy, indicating his own little bungalow, which was west of the caretaker's house. "Okay?"

Minot threw back his head and laughed.

"You look a little glum, Jimmy, my lad," he said. "You're not taking me seriously, are you? I was joking. I couldn't get along without you, Jimmy. You know that. Anyway, I put you in for a raise three days ago. You'll get it in your next check."

Jimmy smiled.

"I might've known . . ."

"Yes, you might have known. But you're a cop at heart, Jimmy. Which means you aren't quite bright. By the way, I'll want at least three men in the house tonight. Jean's giving a party. All the darling young folk will get drunk all over the place. You know how it is."

Jimmy flushed.

"Why do you talk that way? Jean never even takes a drink. You ought to be proud to have a daughter like that, instead of running her down. She's too good for you; that's my opinion."

"Ah ha! Are you getting romantic about my daughter?"

"Me? Say, she wouldn't look at me. She thinks I'm a comic. Anyway, I'm as good as married, so don't worry about that."

"I never worry. So you're as good as married. You've been good as married for two years, I understand. Scott Bayliss tells me you've got a mighty good-looking girl. Scott's secretary, isn't she?"

"You know too much."

"I know my own business. Scott works for me; your girl works for Scott. I make it my business to find out things."

"Well, Eve's a nice kid, so don't worry about me being romantic."

"See you tonight."

"It's my night off. I'm going to a movie with my girl. I'll be back around eleven."

"Will O'Brien be in charge?"

"Yes. Ed's all right."

"He'll do. Well, let's go, Jack. What are we waiting for?"

Jimmy watched the limousine drive up the tree-bordered drive toward the huge Minot house, then he turned up the gravel walk toward his bungalow. Sometimes he thought that Gordon Minot was the best man that ever lived; sometimes he thought he was a silly fool. Either way, he liked him. In Steel City, which was practically owned and controlled by the Minot interests, they said that Gordon was "eccentric"; meaning, as Jimmy well knew, that he was screwy. Jimmy often laughed about this. Gordon forgot more every day than most citizens of Steel City would ever know. Still, his manner was unfortunate. He seemed too frivolous and he was too familiar with everybody, including all the men who worked for him. To the gentry of Steel City and its suburbs, all ultra-conservative Babbitts, he was a portent. They feared and disliked him. He was even accused of radical tendencies in spite of his ruthless handling of the strikers in the big general strike of '32, when there had been martial law in the city and he had acted as Director of Public Safety. No, the gentry thought that the Minot blood had run thin and sighed for the days of Gordon's father, Andrew. Gordon's brother, Judge Thomas Minot, had disgraced himself and committed suicide, and Gordon's sister, Catherine, a widow at forty, had married a young man of twenty-five, Bush McEvoy, who had come from God knows where, and then she had died under very peculiar circumstances, and now at a little over thirty, young McEvoy was a power in the city, second only to Gordon. The gentry thought that Gordon had the same tendency toward irrational behavior manifested by his brother and sister. But their hands were tied. They were afraid. Gordon held the whip hand. The John Minot and Company interests controlled not only the biggest steel plant in the state, but four of the largest newspapers, a brokerage house, a chain factory, a hotel, several theaters, and innumerable smaller concerns. "He's got them where the hair is short," Jimmy often said, laughing.

On his way up the gravel walk, Jimmy paused suddenly. He saw Jean Minot coming across the lawn, accompanied by two men: Bush McEvoy and Scott Bayliss, head of the accounting department at the plant. Jimmy disliked McEvoy and liked Bayliss. But he did not give them even a passing thought. All that he could see was Jean. She was to him the smartest, the best looking, the nicest, the kindest girl in the world. She was tall and straight and it was a pleasure to watch her walk. Her hair was blond and thick and always a little tumbled. Her eyes were blue and very sparkling and frank. She did everything well. She was an excellent rider, a fine tennis player and a good swimmer. Best of all, she ran her father's house for him and ran it well. She was twenty-three years old. Everybody said that she looked like Gordon and was a true Minot. To Jimmy, Gordon was a ridiculous caricature of his daughter

Jimmy quickly lit a cigarette. He knew that Jean was going to speak to him and he wanted to appear at ease. He was always angered by the disturbance she aroused in him. Him! He was no blushing young kid. He'd been places and seen things. He was tough in the real sense of that word. And yet . . .

"Hello, Jimmy," she said. "Dad home?"

"Yes, Jean."

The men nodded to him. McEvoy stiffly; Bayliss smiling and without constraint. McEvoy was a medium-sized man with unusually broad shoulders and narrow hips. He looked strong and tireless. His thick black hair curled tightly all over his small, well-shaped head. His face was pleasing, especially when he smiled ("the ten-million-dollar smile", as Steel City cynically put it); his eyes were a pale gray, contrasting strangely with his dark complexion. Bayliss was an entirely different type: very tall and angular with a high color and a boyishly handsome face. He had done well and had risen fast but there was something rather unsophisticated about him, puzzling in such a successful young man. Jimmy's girl said that he was 14 karat and that was good enough for Jimmy.

"Don't you get tired being a watch dog, Jimmy?" asked Jean. "Isn't Dad rather a handful?"

"At all times."

Jean laughed.

"Oh, he's terrible."

There was a short silence. Jimmy was very embarrassed and kept his eyes lowered.

"Been playing tennis?" he brought out finally.

"Yes," said Jean. "I beat both of them."

"I don't wonder. I watch you every once a while. I'm glad I'm not playing you."

"Why, Jimmy, do you play? I didn't know. You must play with me some time."

"Haven't got time." Then, grudgingly, fearing he had been too abrupt: "But, thanks. I couldn't warm you up, anyway. You're too good."

"Much too good," said McEvoy; then: "Shall we go in, Jean? I want a shower before dinner."

"Oh, sure. Bye, Jimmy."

"Goodbye," Jimmy mumbled.

Jean and McEvoy started away, but Bayliss came up to Jimmy.

"I let Eve off early this afternoon. She said she was going out with you tonight and wanted to go to a beauty parlor first. What is this strange power you have over women, Devore?"

"It's my great conversational ability," said Jimmy, shrugging.

"Yes, I noticed it a minute ago." Bayliss smiled. "Well, take good care of Eve. She's the best secretary a man ever had."

Bayliss joined the others. Jimmy mumbled to himself: "Good guy, that Bayliss. Was he trying to tip me off about Jean? Could he see what was the matter with me? Maybe. Anyway, that McEvoy guy didn't notice anything. He was too busy worrying whether his hair was curled right. Damn his hide! What's he trying to do, get next to Jean? Why, he's her uncle; by marriage, anyway. Gordon thinks he's pretty hot stuff. He married Gordon's sister; I guess it would be all right with Gordon if he married his daughter." Jimmy cursed softly, then he went on: "If she's got to marry somebody I hope it's Bayliss. She's young, though; got lots of time yet . . ." Suddenly, he laughed sardonically. "Poor old Jimmy! Got it bad and ain't got a chance."

Somebody touched his arm. He turned.

"Well, talking in your sleep?" It was Captain Berger.

"Hello, Frank. When did you get in?"

"I saw you talking with the swells. I waited. I want to talk to you."

"Come in. Have a drink. Anything serious?"

"No drink for me. I wouldn't say it was serious, but there's some funny stuff going on some place."

They went into the living-room of Jimmy's bungalow and sat down. Frank Berger was a man of fifty, big, grey-haired and solid-looking. Jimmy had been a detective under him and they had been friends for years. Berger was now chief of detectives in the city and was soon to be promoted to police commissioner.

"All right, Frank. Shoot."

"I came clear out here on Mr. Minot's account. I thought it might be wiser. If I asked you to come in the office, somebody might try to find out something."

"Find out what?"

"Don't ask questions yet. Give me a chance, Jimmy. I'll try to give it to you fast. Now in your opinion what kind of a suburb is Willow Wood?"

"It's lousy with rich people. Taxes are sky high. Everything's high."

"Exactly. Gordon Minot started it; built his own house here and all the codfish aristocrats followed him. The place is so ritzy the traffic cops give you the broad "A". All right. Would you think of living here if you weren't working for Mr. Minot?"

"I should say not."

"Right again. Neither would I, and I make pretty good dough. We just wouldn't fit. All right. Did you know that Roxy Doyle was staying at the Willow Wood Plaza?"

"What! That Youngstown chiseler?"

"Private detective, if you please," laughed Berger. "Yes, one of my boys, Ed Schiff, ran into him, and Roxy told Ed he was on a vacation. How do you like that?"

"That's the bunk."

"Exactly. Roxy's gone now. As soon as I found out he was in Willow Wood, I had him watched. He got wise right away, of course, and blew. Funny, eh? This is even better. Ed Schiff was taking a look-see down the road from here a piece the other night and he sees a guy walking a wire-haired fox terrier across Grey's Meadow down there by the trout club. Nothing wrong in that, of course, except that when Ed stepped up to him kind of a sudden the guy pulls a gat. This guy's all dressed up in tweed and is staying at the Plaza. He didn't have a gun permit. But Ed went back to the Plaza with him and everything seemed okay so I didn't do anything about it. He's got his orders, you know."

"It looks mighty bad," said Jimmy. "But it's sure a jigsaw. There are a lot of guys that would like to see Gordon knocked off; but they haven't got any underworld tie-up. At least, they'd never know how to get hold of a hot guy like Butch Crump."

"That's what gets me. Maybe we're barking up the wrong tree. Maybe there's a big bank job or something like that. The only reason I connected this with Mr. Minot at all is because these guys are out of place in the Willow Wood picture."

"I'll say they are. Well, there goes my date. I'll never leave these grounds tonight."

"Need any help let me know. All this is sub rosa, Jimmy. I'm not even letting the police reporters in on it. They'd head-line Butch Crump. Just stir up a lot of unnecessary trouble. "Well, I've got to get home to the wife and kids."

They shook hands. Jimmy looked a little pale.

"Thanks, Frank."

"Don't let it worry you too much, kid. It may be just one of those false alarms."

Jimmy was pacing the floor in his living-room, muttering to himself, when Big Ed O'Brien came in.

"What's the matter, boss?" asked Ed, grinning and showing his gold teeth. "They got you talking to yourself?"

"Yeah. I had a date tonight. Had to call it off and did I get an earful!"

"Someday you'll get wise to yourself. If I had a dame like yours, I'd sure hang on to her. Sure is a pip. Nice girl and she knows all the answers. I run into her the other day. She sure was nice and friendly. You wouldn't think she'd take the trouble to be nice to a big lug like me. But she did. Why, don't you get wised up, boss? That girl's worth all the jobs there is. You work like a dog and what thanks do you get for it!"

"Oh, hire a hall. Did you get the men?"

"Yep. Got ten boys from the plant. With the two regulars that makes fourteen. Say, what's this all about? Why, we could hold off the militia in this joint with fourteen men."

"Don't ask questions. Just do what I tell you."

Big Ed studied Jimmy's unsmiling face for a moment, then he said:

"Okay, boss. Don't get sore. You know me."

"Don't do so much thinking. You're not supposed to think. You're a policeman."

Big Ed roared with laughter.

"You kill me!"

"All right. All right. Don't overdo. It wasn't that funny! Are you ready to settle down now and listen?"

"Yeah, if you don't pull any more of them fast ones."

"Good. First, I want all the alarms checked. That's your job. You're responsible. Next, I want Bill and you to check all the electrical equipment. I'm going to put some heat in those wires tonight and anybody that climbs the estate wall is going to look like burnt toast . . ."

"But, Jimmy! Mr. Minot says we're never to use them wires any more since that gardener burnt his fanny . . ."

"I'll take the responsibility. Just do as I tell you. I want two men on the gate besides old Mike and if anybody goes to sleep they're fired. I'll tell you guys when you can sleep. I let Rogers get away with it last time but . . ."

"His wife had a kid. He hadn't slept for three nights."

"I know all that. I want six men around the house, and you in charge there. I'll be around myself all night either here at the gatehouse or over at the servants' quarters. If anything comes up you don't understand send a man to each place. Scatter the rest of the fellows through the grounds. Tell them to keep their eyes open and their mouths shut."

Big Ed was silent for a long time. He began to look very grave.

"This must be a bad one, Jimmy."

"And it may be a false alarm, but we're taking no chances. All right,

Ed, get going."

"I'm on my way. What if Mr. Minot sees all these guys and gets on his ear like he does!"

"Refer him to me."

"How you get away with it, Jimmy, I don't know. Why, you talk to him like a Dutch Uncle. You're a funny guy."

"Listen, Ed, this job of mine is enough to put a guy in a straitjacket. Soft snap! I can't help it if I get jittery now and then. The boss makes allowances, that's all."

"Well, here I go. See you later. Suppose Mr. Minot sees us checking the wires and tells us to stop it?"

"Go right ahead with your work. Refer him to me."

Jimmy shrugged wearily and nodded indifferently when Big Ed grinned and waved goodbye, then he poured himself a straight drink of whiskey, and drank it down in one gulp, grimacing. Finally he slipped a small, blunt automatic into his right coat pocket. He was just going out the door when old Mike came hobbling up the gravel walk.

"Well, Mike!"

"There's a girl at the gate in a roadster. Says she's got to see you, Mr. Devore."

"Girl? Tell her to go away. Nobody gets in here tonight except guests. Have you got the guest list, Mike?"

"Yes sir. Excuse me, Mr. Devore, but this girl, she's pretty mad. She said if we didn't let her in she'd climb over the wall."

"Tell her to beat it," said Jimmy, indifferently, vaguely wondering what dizzy dame was having a brainstorm now. Before he started to go around with Eve Barry he'd played them all and some of them still pestered him. Also a lot of little chiselers, who knew how he stood with Gordon Minot and wanted to cut in, would bother him from time to time. "Maybe it's that Akron redhead. She's just utsnay enough," he muttered.

Mike persisted.

"She says she just talked to you on the phone. She . . ."

"What! Pretty girl with dark hair? Small, you know. Nifty?"

Mike grinned, showing his tobacco-stained teeth.

"Yes, sir."

"Where'd she get a car?" Jimmy shrugged, then he ran past Mike and hurried to the front gate, where two of the plant cops were arguing with somebody in a battered black roadster.

"Jimmy! I want in." It was Eve! Jimmy cleared his throat and looked uncomfortably at the two guards who turned to stare at him.

"Open the gate," said Jimmy, finally. "Eve, let Johnson park your car on the road. Leave the keys with him. I can't let you bring that car in here."

"He can drive it over a cliff if he wants to," said Eve, hurrying through the gate. "And I'll send you the bill."

Johnson went out to park the car. Mike and the other guard stood in the gateway watching him. Jimmy took Eve by the arm and escorted her toward the bungalow.

"We've got to get inside, honey," he said. "What you trying to do? Get me fired?"

They crossed the veranda silently and went into the living-room. Jimmy shut the door.

"Now," he said, "What's this all about?"

"That's what I want to know," said Eve. "There's something going on here and I'm going to find out what it is."

Jimmy stared at her. He had never seen her angry before. Her pretty face was contorted with rage. What a honey she was! What a swell kid! He felt ashamed of himself. He had been giving her the runaround, all right. But it wasn't on account of another dame, or yes it was, too; but not a dame she needed to worry about.

"What do you mean, babe?"

"You know what I mean. You never used to give me all these excuses. You couldn't get to my house fast enough. Now you got to do this; you got to do that. Tonight we were going to the Brentwood and see Joan Crawford; then we were going over to the New Dilling and dance and have supper. I get all dolled up for you and even buy a new dress—how do you like it, by the way? And what happens? He has to work! Why don't you come right out and tell me you want to give me the air? I can take it."

"Now, honey, you're all worked up over nothing."

"I know. And that nothing's name is Jean Minot. I guess these rich girls like to kid around with the hired help. At least that's what they tell me."

"Don't be silly. She wouldn't look at me."

"Oh, she wouldn't. Well, why not? You're not so hard to look at. I know. I've been looking at you long enough." Eve turned away suddenly and burst out crying.

Jimmy put his arm around her.

"Now wait, honey. You're all worked up over nothing. Listen, didn't you notice three men on the gate? We never have more than one. Something's come up, honey. I was sure looking forward to seeing you tonight, but things broke bad. I can't tell you about it. Just take my word for it. And all that silly talk about Jean Minot! Why, she's got every young punk in Willow Wood chasing her. All of them rich. Most of them swell looking young fellows. Even if I went for her, it wouldn't do me any good."

Eve tossed her hair back out of her eyes and pulled away from Jimmy.

"No? You don't look like a wallflower to me. I don't know a girl that wouldn't go for you if I gave them half a chance. I hear things, that's all. A lot of people think this wonderful Jean girl, that's got everybody chasing her, goes for you in a big way. I heard all about it a long time ago. Tonight I just got burnt up, that's all. If you're tired of me, just let me know. I'll get myself a new boyfriend; two or three in fact."

She began to cry again. Jimmy put his arms around her and kissed her. He felt very tender toward her because she was making such a show of herself. She was nuts about him, that's all; and he didn't have sense enough to appreciate it. What a chump! Crying for the moon with a girl like Eve Barry nuts about him.

"Please, kid," he said. "Have a heart. This is all imagination. I'm sorry you got so steamed up. For two cents I'd quit my job tonight and take you out. Like to show off the new dress, wouldn't you?"

Eve looked up at him, smiling slightly.

"Jim! What's wrong with me? I never should have come out here bothering you. It was just because . . ."

The living-room door was pushed open suddenly. Gordon Minot stepped in, followed by Jean and Bush McEvoy. Jimmy and Eve drew apart. Gordon's face was red with anger; he smiled sarcastically.

"I hope I'm not intruding," he said. "Excuse me, Mr. Devore, but could I prevail upon you to pause a moment in your love-making, and explain to me why all these men are running about? And who told Ed O'Brien to check up the equipment? I gave strict orders about that. And by the way, if I'm not too inquisitive, who is this girl, who seems to be distressed about something; one of the maids?"

"I quit," said Jimmy, turning away.

"He quits," said Gordon.

"Dad," said Jean, "you're insufferable. What's the matter, Jimmy? Don't mind Dad. I'm pretty sure you can explain everything. Don't quit. You know how we feel about you around here."

Eve looked at Jimmy accusingly. He flushed.

"It's no use, Jean," he said. "I quit. I'm sick of this slavery. And this girl, Mr. Minot, is not one of the maids as you know very well. It's Eve Barry. The girl I'm going to marry, if she'll have me."

Eve smiled and glanced at Jean triumphantly.

"Oh, my error," said Gordon, still sardonic. "Still, I'd like to have an explanation about all those strange gentlemen running loose on the lawns. It looks like an Elk's picnic. Did you order a keg of beer?"

"It's all very irregular," said Bush McEvoy, examining his nails.

Jimmy glared.

"All right. I'm taking extra precautions, Mr. Minot, because of a tip I got. I'm just trying to protect you and your family, that's all. I had a date tonight and had to break it. Eve, here, got all upset, thought I was two-timing her and came out to see. But I still quit!"

"I told you, Dad," said Jean. "You leave Jimmy alone. He knows what he's doing."

"Very irregular," said Bush McEvoy.

Gordon hesitated. His anger had worn off. He seemed slightly embarrassed.

"Well," he said, "maybe you know what you're doing. I suppose you do. Let's go, Jean. You'll forgive me, Miss Barry. I didn't mean to be rude."

"Wait a minute," said Jimmy. "I mean what I say. I quit."

"All right," said Gordon. "See me a week from today. I'll have a check ready for you then. Meanwhile, you're still in charge. A week's notice is customary, I believe." He turned away to hide a smile when he saw Jimmy writhing.

Jean smiled at Eve.

"I'm glad to meet any friend of Jimmy's. He's practically indispensable around here. Dad wouldn't know what to do without him. Shall we go, Bush?"

"I still don't like the business about the wire, but . . ." Gordon went out, talking to himself.

When they had gone, Jimmy said:

"You see?"

Eve shrugged and turned away.

"She surely is a mighty good-looking girl."

"That's one of her boyfriends."

"Bush McEvoy? Why, he's her uncle. He knew me all right but never a peep."

"Her uncle by marriage. Your boss is her best boyfriend."

Eve shrugged.

"I wouldn't trade both of them rolled into one for you, Jimmy."

"Thanks."

"I guess I better go."

Jimmy grinned, feeling better.

"Where did you get the hack?"

"At a U-Drive-It place. Oh, the trouble I had in the Broad Street traffic!"

Jimmy laughed.

"Let's have a drink. Stick around, Eve. Since they know you're here, you might as well stay. We can have a little party. I may have to run out on you from time to time, but . . ."

Of a sudden, Jimmy stood stock still, cocking his head.

"What's that?" he cried, paling.

Somewhere beyond the estate wall in the direction of the business center of William Wood there was a shattering burst of machine-gun fire followed by shouts of "help! help!", then silence.

"You stay here," cried Jimmy, leaping toward the door. "I've got to look into that. Thank God it's outside the wall, anyway. Hey! Do you suppose Gordon sneaked out some place?"

CHAPTER TWO

Running down the road toward the gate, Jimmy almost collided with Ed O'Brien.

"Where's Gordon?"

"He's in the house, Jimmy. Did you hear that typewriter down the road? Good God!"

"Come on, Ed."

Jimmy hurried to the gatehouse and got Rogers on the telephone. Rogers had charge of the house while O'Brien was checking the electrical equipment. Jimmy told him that he was in full charge temporarily and not to let Minot get out of his sight till he got further orders. Then Jimmy turned to Ed.

"Let's go see what this is all about, Ed. Johnson, give me the key for Eve's car."

Looking a little scared, Johnson handed over the keys. Old Mike was standing with his mouth open, staring at Jimmy, who leaped into the car, followed by Big Ed, and drove off toward the business center.

They saw a crowd gathering under an arc-light down the road. Beyond, the electric signs of the business center blazed under the summer sky. They heard a police siren and saw a squad car skid into the main road and stop just ahead of them. Jimmy parked the car and they got out.

"Why, it's right close to Mr. McEvoy's house," said Big Ed.

"Yeah," said Jimmy. "I didn't think it was that near us. This is something new. Machine-guns in Willow Wood."

They saw three policemen shoving the crowd back. Then Jimmy saw Frank Berger and went over to him. Frank was looking down at two men who were lying, shot to death, on the sidewalk.

"Well?" said Jimmy.

Frank turned.

"I got a tip," he said. "Butch was seen again. He sure fixed these two mugs up. Recognize the one with his coat off?"

"Roxy Doyle!"

"Yeah. I guess he didn't leave after all. Neither did the other guy. That's our friend John C. Harter. Ed Schiff just identified him."

"Well, this beats me."

Big Ed stammered:

"They sure punctured them birds plenty. Is that their car parked in front of Mr. McEvoy's drive?"

"We think so," said Frank. "We've got to check. This is a funny one, Jimmy."

"Well, anyway, it looks like we're in the clear. That takes a load off my mind. These rats don't matter. Roxy Doyle's been asking for it for ten years. Now he's got it."

"My sentiments exactly. And the other guy is probably in the same class."

A policeman came up with a wirehaired fox terrier under his arm.

"This pooch was in the car, chief."

Frank turned.

"Ed, is this the dog that guy was leading?"

Ed Schiff came up and stood staring at the terrier, which barked sharply and tried to wriggle out of the policeman's arms.

"I think so, chief. Them dogs look pretty much alike."

"I'm pretty sure that's their car. We'll check. Jimmy, drop over to my house late tonight, will you? I may have something that might interest you."

"About Gordon?"

"I wouldn't say that. But I've got a theory, I'm not ready to talk now. But I'm pretty sure of one thing. You don't have to worry about Butch Crump anymore; he's probably over the State Line by now."

"I feel ten years younger."

The policeman with the dog under his arm, cleared his throat, then said:

"Chief, what am I going do with this animal?"

"Put him in the car. Take him to the pound, I guess."

Jimmy glanced quickly at the dog, then averted his eyes.

The dog was looking at him, wagging his tail.

"What'll they do with him, Frank? Gas him?" he asked, trying to appear unconcerned.

"Maybe, if they don't find a home for him." Frank turned away slightly to hide a smile.

Jimmy lit a cigarette and turned half away.

"Well, I'll be getting back," he said. "Suppose I drop over to see you about eleven. Okay?"

"Yeah. That's fine. Goodbye, Jimmy."

Ed started toward the car but Jimmy still hesitated; finally he said:

"You know, Frank; I always did want one of those fox terriers. My girl did, I mean. She's crazy about dogs."

Frank smiled.

"Give Jimmy the dog, Burns. If we want him we'll let you know."

Jimmy cleared his throat uncomfortably and took the dog under his arm. The dog barked loudly and tried to lick Jimmy's face.

"Cut it," said Jimmy, harshly, then: "Eve sure will be crazy about this dog." When they got into the car the dog jumped upon the back of the seat and began to bark sharply.

"Cute, ain't he?" said O'Brien, petting him.

"He's all right," said Jimmy. "Dogs are a damn nuisance, is what I think. But Eve's crazy about them."

Ed laughed.

"Now I'll tell one."

When Jimmy entered the living-room of his bungalow with the dog under his arm and followed by Ed O'Brien, Eve was sitting on the lounge talking with Jean Minot. Gordon, Bush McEvoy and Scott Bayliss were walking up and down talking, and Sid Rogers was looking on uneasily, his face haggard.

Gordon turned.

"He goes out to investigate a murder or something, and comes up with a dog. What a man!"

"What's all the excitement?" asked Scott.

Jimmy ignored them.

"Honey," he said to Eve, "look what I brought you. Go see your mama, pooch."

He let the dog down and it ran over to Bush McEvoy, barking joyfully. Jimmy straightened up and stared.

"Hello, Tommy," said Bush. "Where did you come from?"

"He your dog?" Jimmy asked.

"He used to be," said Bush. "I sold him to a fellow named Harter."

"I see. Did you know Harter very well?"

"Didn't know him at all. He was a stranger. From Chicago, I believe. He was staying at the Plaza. Somebody told him I raised wires so he came over and I sold him Tommy. Where did you find the dog?"

Jimmy turned.

"Jean, would you mind taking Eve into the next room? You can read all about this little mix-up in the paper tomorrow. I want to talk to these men."

"Why, no," said Jean. "Come on, Eve. We're not a bit curious, are we?"

"Oh, not at all," said Eve. "Anyway, Jimmy, thanks for thinking about me. Maybe Mr. McEvoy'll let me have the dog after all. Oh, isn't he cute?"

"You can have him," said Bush. "I've got too many now."

Eve called Tommy and, wagging his tail and leaping playfully, he followed her and Jean into the next room.

"Rogers," said Jimmy, "you and Ed can go. Let the plant boys go home, Ed. We won't need them any more tonight. Keep Johnson, though."

Both Rogers and Ed looked disappointed, as they wanted an earful, but they went out without a word.

"Hitler, old boy," said Gordon, putting his hand on Jimmy's shoulder, "do you mind if I interrupt for a minute?"

"Go right ahead."

"Thank you. He's almost the perfect autocrat, but occasionally, gentlemen, he remembers who signs the checks. So much for that. Now, Jimmy, is the little surprise party over? May we circulate freely now without danger of stumbling over your choice collection of G-Men?"

Bush laughed.

"Very clever, very clever."

"I don't think you'll be shot tonight," said Jimmy, "if that's what you mean."

Gordon started slightly.

"You mean somebody's been shot!"

"Yes," said Jimmy. "A couple of guys got bumped off right in front of Mr. McEvoy's house. Or almost in front of it." Jimmy watched McEvoy carefully but he didn't turn a hair.

"You're joking!" cried Gordon. "What, in Willow Wood!"

"I'm sorry to say a chopper cut them down. It was a very professional job. One of them was your friend Harter, Mr. McEvoy."

"Can you imagine that! Why, it actually sounds like a gang killing. Harter seemed like such a nice fellow."

"No doubt. The other guy was a mug from Youngstown that's been trying to get it for years."

Gordon laughed.

"It seems you knew something was going to happen, Jimmy. You really scare me sometimes. Two men actually killed!"

"Very dead. They're lying down there practically in Mr. McEvoy's front yard with their toes toward the sky. It was a nice job. A thousand-dollar job. Maybe more."

Scott Bayliss laughed uneasily.

"It doesn't seem possible."

There was a long silence. Bush McEvoy took a little comb from his pocket and began to comb his coarse, curly black hair.

"That Harter fellow gave me a check for Tommy. I suppose it's no-good."

"Very likely. It's too bad you're hooked up with this, Mr. McEvoy. Captain Berger will want to see you, I'm sure."

Bush put his comb away.

"I'll give him any information I can. Glad to."

Gordon was still incredulous.

"This is just like a bad dream," he said. "Imagine, two men murdered, almost in front of the place. Why it's simply unbelievable."

Jimmy smiled slightly.

"Maybe you won't give me the runaround so much now. Maybe you'll just let me handle things."

"That's what he likes, gentlemen. He wants to handle things. That's his middle name. Alright, Jimmy. I still don't understand how you knew so much. It's really uncanny."

"Nothing uncanny about it. I was tipped off."

"I hope your tipsters keep it up. I want a drink. Bush, let's go get a drink. Anyway, I was almost forgetting I was a host. People are arriving. Let's go."

"I'll get Jean," said Bush.

"Let Scott get her. Come on, Bush."

Gordon went out; Bush hesitated, then followed him. Scott got up.

"You're a whiz, Jimmy," he said. "I'm mighty glad you're around to look after the boss. He needs a lot of looking after."

"I do my best. But he gets under my hide sometimes."

"He's a very irritating man. But he's all right. I couldn't stand him at first." Then: "Jean! Conference is over. We'd better go. Some of your friends are already here."

Jean came into the living-room, followed by Eve and Tommy.

"He can sit up," said Jean. "And he'll roll over if you take a little time with him. He's quite a smart little dog."

Eve picked Tommy up and kissed him.

"He's my little fuzzy baby," she said

Tommy barked and stared at Jimmy with his little dark varmity eyes.

"You ugly little no-good mutt," said Jimmy.

The women protested loudly and both Jimmy and Scott laughed.

"Jimmy," said Jean, "I've got to run. But Eve and I are dying of curiosity. Was somebody killed?"

"Scott can tell you about it if he wants to. Anyway, it'll be front page in all the papers."

Jean shrugged, then she took Scott's arm and they went out. Jimmy did not like to see her so familiar with Scott, or with anybody for that matter. He turned away to hide his annoyance. Eve sat down on the lounge and began to play with Tommy.

"What do you think of Jean?" he demanded.

"All she did was talk about you."

"I don't believe it."

"She thinks you're perfect."

"She thinks I'm a swell policeman. She's glad I'm looking after her rattlebrained father, that's all."

"Didn't Scott look handsome tonight? I never noticed how good-looking he was before. I guess Jean really goes for him. At least that's the impression I got."

"Come on, Eve. I'll take you home."

"In my car, you mean?"

"Yes. I'll take a taxi back."

"Were there many people killed?"

"Two."

Eve stared.

"Really?"

"I wouldn't kid you. I'll tell you about it on the way home."

But Jimmy didn't say a word until they'd driven almost into the center of town. Eve was playing with Tommy who barked every time they passed a car, then turned to glare, as if to say: "Slow poke!" She was delighted with him.

"Eve," said Jimmy at last, "I've been thinking. I'm going to try to get a week's vacation next month. Let's get married."

"All right."

"You don't seem very excited."

"Why should I? I've heard this about ten times before, and here I am still a maid."

"I mean it."

"When the preacher says, 'I pronounce you', then I'll get excited. You big lug! You think I'm blind." She turned away suddenly and began to cry.

"What do you mean, honey?"

"I mean you can't look that girl in the face."

Jimmy sighed and stepped on the gas.

The clock in the Derby Street fire-engine house was just striking eleven, when Jimmy rang Frank Berger's doorbell. The door was opened immediately, and Frank said:

"I heard the car stop. Taxi?"

"Yeah! Eve was out to the place in a U-Drive-It. I had to take her home. Well, Frank."

"Come in. The wife and kids are asleep so we'd better keep our voices down."

They sat down in the big comfortable living-room. Frank gave Jimmy a cigar and poured him a drink.

"I got news for you," said Jimmy.

"Yeah?"

"You remember the dog? He used to belong to Bush McEvoy. He went right up to him."

"How did he take it?"

"Calm as ever. That boy's got something on the ball. I mean, of course, if there's anything wrong about him. Maybe there isn't."

"What did he say about the dog?"

Jimmy told him.

". . . a dog for?"

"You got me. But a lot of tough guys like dogs."

"Including yourself." Frank laughed and lit a cigar. "I wouldn't have minded having that dog myself. But seeing you wanted him so bad . . ."

Jimmy writhed.

"I gave him to Eve."

Frank laughed and poured himself a drink.

"I'm glad to hear about that dog business, Jimmy. It sort of goes along with the things I've been thinking about. Now, about McEvoy . . ."

The phone rang and Frank answered it. When he came back he was smiling broadly.

"Things are adding up, Jimmy." He sat down and crossed his legs. "They identified Harter. His name's Edmundson. He's a blackmailer. Did a stretch in Joliet. But he's been loose since '29."

"Blackmailer, eh. That's sort of in Roxy Doyle's line too, isn't it?"

"You took the words out of my mouth."

Jimmy sat up suddenly.

"Maybe they had something on this McEvoy guy. Maybe they

pressured him once too often . . . but, no . . . where does Butch Crump come in? Nobody but an underworld big shot could get hold of him. It's got me. All the same, this McEvoy guy needs watching."

"I agree with you. Jimmy, how much do you know about McAvoy?"

"Why, I . . . that's funny. To tell you the truth, I don't know anything about him."

"Oh, you must know something. Think. Tell me what you know."

"Well, Gordon's sister married him when he was about twenty-five or six. It was an old dame going for a handsome young guy. One of those things. He married into money and a good job, and he's been going up ever since. Smart. Got something on the ball. I understand they're going to make him vice president of John Minot and Company, and if I'm not mistaken, he's trying to get next to Gordon's daughter, the heel!"

Frank studied Jimmy's face but said nothing.

"Oh yeah. He passed the Ohio Bar examination just after he was married. That's all I know."

"But where did he come from?"

"Wait a minute. Let me think. Oh, yeah. He came from Phoenix, Arizona."

"Sure?"

"That's what Gordon says. It just happened to come out once when we were talking."

There was a silence; then Frank said:

"I wish I knew how he got next to Gordon's sister. How she met him and all that. You know, the Minots and that crew are hard to meet. An outsider wouldn't have a chance unless . . ."

"Yeah?"

"Well, he either had letters of introduction or he picked the old girl up. Either way, I'm going to check. In fact, I'm going to call Phoenix, Arizona, right now. Meanwhile, pump Gordon. I'll get in touch with you later tonight."

They got up and shook hands.

"We may be barking up the wrong tree, Jimmy," said Frank, "but a lot of things point McEvoy's way. But we've got to tread lightly my boy, very lightly. The Minots and all their relations are practically untouchable in this man's town. Look at Tom."

Jimmy smiled sarcastically.

"I took his rap for him. I was well paid and all that. But I'll never shake off the stir jitters as long as I live. Sometimes, Frank, I wake up at night thinking I'm still behind those grey walls. Oh, well. We'll go light. But if that McEvoy's a phony we'll put him where he belongs.

Why, Jean might even marry him. You never know what a dame's going to do."

Frank shook a finger at Jimmy.

"Listen, boy; I'm old enough to be your father and I'm your friend. Don't worry about that girl too much."

"It's my job," said Jimmy, flushing.

"Don't work at it too hard."

Jimmy shrugged and turned to go.

"Wait a minute," he said. "I almost forgot. Listen, I took this dog back for Eve like I told you. She was in my bungalow with Jean and Gordon and Bush McEvoy. Here's what I mean. McEvoy told Eve she could have the dog before I'd let him know about the killing. See? How did he know that Harter hadn't just lost the dog?"

"I get you. That's not evidence. But it helps the total. Goodnight, Jimmy."

Jimmy sat on the verandah of his bungalow listening to the music which was swelling out from the ballroom at the big house. It was a still summer night. Lightning bugs were flying in and out among the huge, old trees along the drive. It was hot. The trees stood rigid. Jimmy took his coat and shoes and, putting his feet up on the railing, lit a cigarette.

A stringed orchestra was playing "Did I Remember" and Jimmy listened for a long time, feeling very sad and young loverish, then his lip began to curl and cursing himself, he took his feet down from the railing, put his shoes back on, then got up and began to walk up and down.

He tried to concentrate on the problem he and Frank had to solve, but it was no use. He kept seeing little irrelevant pictures of Jean: Jean on horseback, managing a bullheaded horse she insisted on riding and laughing at his antics; Jean playing tennis, lithe and active, tossing her hair back out of her eyes; Jean in a bathing suit, one of those strip numbers that these damn fools were wearing now—but, no; he rejected that picture. It made him very uncomfortable. "Oh, hell," muttered Jimmy; "you'd think I was a twenty-year-old kid. I better marry Eve and settle down. No use being a fool . . ."

An imitation-Crosby was singing:

"Did I remember
"To tell you that I adore you...?"

"Nuts!" muttered Jimmy. "It's a wonder these Tin Pan Alley guys couldn't find something better than all that love junk to write songs about. To hear them tell it you wouldn't think there was anything in the world but a lot of dumb clucks bellowing around after a bunch of frails. It makes me sick. Why can't they write about . . . well, anything . . ."

He heard somebody coming up the walk. He hoped it was somebody looking for trouble or somebody he didn't like. It was one of the negro houseboys.

"Mr. Devore, please."

"What do you want, Sam?"

"I got a tray of food and everything for you, sir."

"Well, you know what you can do with it."

"Excuse me. Miss Minot told me to . . ."

"Oh, she sent it."

"Yes, Mr. Devore. She picked everything out herself."

Jimmy felt like crying.

"Well, take it inside. Put it in the dining-room. What are you standing there for?"

When Sam came back out onto the porch Jimmy stopped him and gave him a half dollar.

"Thank you," said Sam. "Mr. Devore, you is the funniest man. Just now I thought you was sore at me about something. I always been all right with you, ain't I, Mr. Devore?"

"You sure have, Sam. To tell you the truth, you woke me up. I didn't know what it was all about for a minute."

"Yes sir. I hope you like that food. Better eat that creamed chicken with mushrooms right now; it's nice and hot. Goodnight, Mr. Devore."

"Goodnight, Sam."

As soon as Sam had gone, Jimmy went into the dining-room and stood looking down at the big silver tray loaded with food. Creamed chicken in a patty shell; vegetable salad in aspic; orange sherbet, a pot of coffee; golden brown biscuits; little balls of butter iced in a silver bowl. Jimmy sat down and poured himself a cup of coffee.

"At least I can get this down," he said, smiling to himself; and wondering what he would have done to get a meal like this when he was in the penitentiary. "I'd've done anything," he told himself, "I'd've killed a guy for grub like this, preferably a guard. Now I can't eat it."

As he sipped his coffee, vaguely philosophical ideas began to run through his mind. "When I was in the joint, I thought if I could ever get out again everything would be rosy. Just to get out, that's all. I used to see cripples going past the joint and envy them. I used to even envy the garbage man. I would've traded places with him any day. And now look! I'm out. I got a swell job. I got a swell girl. And I'm not any more happy than I was in stir. So what?"

He finished his coffee and got up.

"I better ditch this grub. She might ask if I ate it. I know. I'll give it to old Mike."

He carried the tray to the gatehouse and gave it to Mike, who looked up at him with the eyes of a grateful dog.

"They sent it out, Mike. I wasn't hungry. Bring the tray and dishes back when you get through. Mum's the word."

"Oh, boy," said Old Mike, licking his lips; then restraining his gluttony, he said: "Kin I give Johnson some?"

"If you want to split it. But mum's the word. Might get in bad."

"You're a prince, Jimmy."

Jimmy started away; over his shoulder he demanded:

"How do you spell it?"

Old Mike roared with laughter.

Coming up the walk, Jimmy saw that there was somebody on his veranda.

"Jimmy!" It was Jean. He saw that there was a man with her.

"I heard you were back," said Jean. "We wanted to see you."

"That you, Bayliss?"

"It's me. Can we talk to you for a moment?"

"Sure. Come in and sit down."

They went into the living-room. Jimmy glanced from Jean to Bayliss. They looked a little agitated. They paced the floor for a moment, then they sat down.

"Did Sam bring you the tray I fixed?" asked Jean, smiling.

"Yes," said Jimmy, clearing his throat loudly. "It was sure fine. I enjoyed it. I sure did. Did you want to see me about something?"

"Yes," said Jean; "it's about my poor old Dad. I'm afraid he's cutting up again."

Jimmy's face sobered immediately. He glanced at Scott.

"Oh, it's all right, Scott being here," said Jean. "I'll tell you something confidentially, Jimmy. I think maybe Scott is going to be Dad's son-in-law."

"At least I hope I am," said Scott with a boyish grin. "But Jean changes her mind so often."

"Silly!"

Jimmy got up and, pacing the floor, kept his back to them as much as possible. Bayliss, eh! Well, it was a good choice. Leave it to Jean for sense. He might have known she wouldn't fall for that slick uncle of hers with the nice crinkly hair. All the same, he was hit hard; and he knew that his face was red and stony. Damn it! He'd have to control himself.

"Well?" Jimmy demanded.

"I wouldn't come to you about this, Jimmy," said Jean, "if I wasn't pretty sure that you had Dad's best interests at heart. I know you have. You don't need to say anything. Well, it's about a woman."

Jimmy was dumbfounded. He sat down.

"Woman! Why, the boss never looks at a woman. It's always tickled me because it made my job that much easier. Women are tough to handle. And they can sure cause a guy grief . . ."

"Hear! Hear!" said Bayliss.

Jimmy flushed. "You see!" he told himself silently. "What are you shouting about? Want to give your game away?"

"You're right, Jimmy," said Jean. "Ever since I can remember, Dad's had nothing do with women. He's nice to them, that's all. He's a strange man, you know. So many tried to marry him after mother died. It made him a little cynical, I think. But now . . ."

"Yeah?"

"Well, a woman with a very sweet voice is always calling him up."

"His private number?"

"Yes."

"That's a good one. Well, he's certainly been putting one over on me."

"Tonight she called. About an hour ago. I heard him talking. He insisted on going out. He'd been drinking a little . . ."

"Don't worry about that," said Jimmy, grimly. "He can't get out without me knowing it."

"I talked him out of it. All right, Scott. Now you say your piece."

"Well, it isn't much, but since Jean confided in me, well, it seemed to have a certain significance. You see, what Jean's afraid of is that some mercenary woman will get hold of her Dad. He's such a queer one, you know. Nobody knows what he will do next."

"And he's getting to the right age," said Jimmy.

"I see what you mean," said Scott. "Well, there was a very charming girl that worked at the plant in the stenographer's room. Her name was Novak. She was a rather peculiar type for a stenographer. More like an actress. But she knew her work, right; because she helped out in my office one day . . ."

"Eve may know about her."

"A good idea. Well, she was promoted. She was sent up to McEvoy's suite of offices, and then suddenly she was fired."

Jimmy stared at the floor. Always this McEvoy guy!

"To tell you the truth," said Scott, flushing, "I noticed her particularly because she was so terribly good-looking."

"How old is she?"

"About twenty. Well, for a few days she was always sitting in the employment office trying to see Mr. Minot. She claimed she hadn't got a square deal. One day she caught him. He wouldn't talk to her at first. But pretty soon he was smiling all over his face. I thought he was going to give her back her job. Of course, I couldn't hear what was being said. But she never turned up again. Not so long ago I saw the boss talking to her in the lobby of the New Dilling Hotel."

Jimmy pondered.

"That must have been the day of the Manufacturers' Association luncheon."

"It was."

"Is that all?"

"That's all. Jean and I were just putting two and two together. As a matter of fact, this girl had a very attractive voice."

"You say she was fired from Mr. McEvoy's office?"

"Yes. Of course, he probably had nothing whatever to do with it. He's a very busy man. He hasn't got time to bother with stenographers. I just mentioned the fact."

Jimmy got up.

"Well, thanks for the information. I'll get to work on this right away. Anything else you get a hold of, why, let me know. Jean, could I see you alone a minute?"

"Why, certainly." She and Bayliss got up. "You wait on the veranda, Scott."

Bayliss went out.

"Well, Jimmy?"

"I want some very private family information, but it's necessary."

"If I can give it to you, I will."

"How did your aunt meet Bush McEvoy?"

"What?" Jean laughed. "That was certainly unexpected. I thought it would be about Dad. Let me think. Why, he had letters of introduction to Uncle Thomas, I believe. I'm a little hazy. Oh, yes. He's a lawyer, you know. The District Attorney at that time was a classmate of Uncle Thomas's. He recommended Bush. Dad gave him a job at once, everybody liked him so. Why? Is Bush suspected of something?"

"Don't ask questions. No, he's not suspected."

The living-room door opened and Mike came in with the tray; the dishes were so clean they looked as if they had been licked by dogs.

"Thanks Jimmy," said Mike. "Oh, excuse me, Miss Minot." Jimmy flushed heavily.

"Put it down any place, Mike. I'm busy."

"Yes sir." Old Mike put the tray on a table. He sensed the tension. Glancing from one to the other, he said: "You see, Devore wasn't feeling well. He couldn't eat. So he thought of us. It was mighty thoughtful of him."

"Yes, wasn't it," said Jean.

Mike went out quickly.

"I don't know why I lied to you about it," said Jimmy. "Except that I knew you fixed up the tray. I just wasn't hungry, Jean."

Jimmy was very much upset.

"Think nothing of it," said Jean. They shook hands. "Goodnight, Jimmy."

In an agony of embarrassment, Jimmy pressed her hand and said: "Goodnight, honey."

Jean started, then smiled.

"Aren't you afraid Scott will hear you?"

"Boy," cried Jimmy, "I surely am up in the air tonight. I guess I thought I was talking to Eve."

"I imagine. Eve's nice. I'm going."

When she had gone, Jimmy shut the door and flung himself into a chair and sat cursing himself. What a ridiculous ass! He writhed, thinking what a spectacle he had made of himself. He couldn't bear the thought of appearing ridiculous in her eyes. But he had seen how amused she was, all right; how she had struggled to keep from laughing!

The phone rang. Jimmy almost knocked it to the floor, he grabbed for it with such violence.

"Frank speaking. Find out anything?"

"Not a thing. He's O.K. Letters of introduction."

"Same here. His father was Judge Edmund McEvoy of Phoenix, Arizona., a Federal judge and a big bug, I understand. Deceased. Bush has no other relatives that I can find out anything about. He graduated from the Law School of the University of Arizona. It's a stonewall all around, Jimmy."

"I got a new one on my hands with a slight McAvoy tie-up. That guy's getting in our hair."

"I'm sort of stupid. But here's something to think about. I got good reason to believe that Butch Crump is still knocking around."

CHAPTER THREE

It was Saturday afternoon and in Steel City everybody who could knocked off work on Saturdays. Gordon Minot, who had a slight cold, said that he was going to lie down till dinner so Jimmy left O'Brien in charge of the estate, called up Eve and arranged to meet her at the New Dilling, then he drove his new sport phaeton, of which he was very proud, into town and went up to Frank Berger's office.

Berger kept him waiting in the outer office for nearly twenty minutes. Jimmy paced up and down impatiently and smoked one cigarette after another. This was going to make him late. Eve would jump on him again; the old dance would start all over. "What a life! What a life!" Jimmy muttered.

Finally he got in. Frank looked tired. His collar was wilted and he kept mopping his face. It was a hot day and the electric fans did not freshen the office at all; they merely stirred up the dead air.

"Sit down, Jimmy."

"Hot, eh?" said Jimmy, sitting down.

"It's killing me and on top of that the last few days they've been running me ragged. The mayor's all up in the air over that Willow Wood killing. It's a headline all over the state. Willow Wood is being built up as a ritzy summer resort; good for the town. The mayor and everybody else is just raving about all this unfavorable publicity. As if I could help it. There goes my big job."

"No fooling, Frank?"

"The mayor put it in a very nice way, of course. Oh, the hell with it! I'm getting too old to worry about things like that. Sorry I kept you waiting, but I was giving Blackie McGraw a going over."

"That rat!"

"He told me he was a friend of yours."

"I served time with him. He was the worst stool in the joint and the screws' pet."

Frank smiled wearily.

"Well, anything new?"

"No. I'm stuck. I'm working on a McEvoy lead but it's got nothing to do with this job. At least I hope it hasn't. It's confidential, anyway. What did you get out of the stool?"

"Nothing. But I will. He's out on parole. I'm holding a minor violation over his head."

"What did you expect to get out of him?"

"Butch Crump is hiding here someplace. Bemis, the Federal man, was in to see me this morning. They think the Willow Wood business was a Crump job. If those boys get close to him he'll never pull another trigger. I'm hoping maybe Blackie can find out where Butch's hiding. We can't prove this one on him, but at least we can turn him over to the guys that want to see him hanged. That is, if the Feds don't get him first."

"Anything new on McEvoy?"

"He's clean as a hound's tooth."

"Somehow, I think that guy's dangerous."

"Jimmy, a guy doesn't turn crooked overnight. Of course, a guy might do a little embezzling, but that's not what we're up against. We're trying to prove that McEvoy was being high pressured by Doyle and that other rat and hired Butch Crump to knock them off." Frank smiled. "Sometimes, when I'm in bed thinking, I begin to get an idea that you and me are a little touched. Get me? I know you don't like McEvoy. But what does that prove? All the same we'll keep going. I've got a man up in Youngstown, looking up Roxy's pals. We might get a lead."

Jimmy got up.

"If I get a hold of anything I'll let you know. I just hope we can locate this Crump guy; then you can pinch him and get your police commissioner job. Eh, Frank?"

"It wouldn't hurt me any."

They shook hands and Jimmy went out. As he was getting into his car somebody took hold of his arm. Jimmy turned. He saw Blackie McGraw grinning at him.

"Hiya, kid."

"Hello, Blackie."

"His Nibs gimme the works."

"That's something new for you."

"Huh? Oh, you mean I'm a stool. I thought you was a friend of mine. You was mighty nice at the big house when them other guys was gunning for me."

"I felt sorry for you. You were such a lousy rat. Let go of my arm."

"Now, look, Jimmy. I know the guys was all down on me. But I wasn't as bad as they made out. I protected youse guys lots of times. Course on the big things I stooled. I admit it. I hate them bars. I get the stir horrors. I had to get out."

"Go on. Beat it. I'm busy."

"Listen, Jimmy; I know you're a tough guy and got guts. But them bullets ain't made of charcoal."

"You full of hop?"

"Gimme a fin, Jimmy. I got a good tip for the third at Arlington. I'm busted."

Grimacing, Jimmy gave Blackie a five-dollar bill.

"Thank you. I always said you was a gentleman and not like them other lousy bums. Okay. Now listen. There's something big going on in this town. I ain't wise yet. But I will be. Berger can't scare me. I won't rat on this one. It's too big. But maybe I can give you a tip. Who knows?"

"Stalling again, eh?"

"On the square, Jimmy. On the picture of me mother, God bless her. See you around."

Jimmy got into his car and stepped on the starter. He was ashamed of himself for having allowed Blackie to bilk him so easily. He turned. Blackie was grinning at him.

"Pretty soft for old Jimmy," he said. "Maybe I can help you keep that nice cushy job."

Jimmy drove away. He was already nearly a half-hour late. He could see Eve standing, tapping her foot, getting madder and madder. And he had allowed a cokey old stool to hold him up. Suddenly Jimmy snapped his fingers. "He may know something at that," he muttered. "He was Red McMahon's cellmate in stir. Red used to be one of Butch's buddies. Maybe I didn't waste a fin after all."

Just as he had expected, Eve was standing near the cigar-stand looking angrily off over the big, ornate lobby, tapping her foot. He hurried up to her.

"Sorry, babe."

"Why, you're almost on time. Only thirty minutes late. That's practically perfect for you. What's the matter? Did you have to give Jean's horse a bath? Or was it Jean?"

"I'm sorry, honey," He tried to explain, but she turned away, shrugging.

"Well, buy me a drink, anyway. A sidecar car might soothe me a little."

They started toward the cocktail bar. Jimmy took her arm, but she pulled away. He could see that she was really very angry.

"Oh, let's forget it, babe," he said. "Let's have a good time for once. Let's sit in one of these little booths and sort of visit."

They sat down and Jimmy ordered two sidecars, then she said:

"You are the most exasperating man. Do you think I like to stand in this lobby with all the old guys from out of town thinking I'm looking for business? It's embarrassing to say the least."

"I'll bet you have plenty of trouble at that, a great-looking honey like you."

"Blarney! I'm still mad. But not as mad as I was. Jimmy, you do think I'm what you said, don't you?"

"On the picture of me mother, God bless her, as a friend of mine just said."

"You meet the nicest people. Jimmy, I wish I could kiss you. Do you? Do you think we'd be seen?"

"Let's try." But the waiter returned with their drinks and Eve laughed.

"Always interruptions!"

"Here's looking at you."

"Down the hatch."

"Honey," said Jimmy, after a pause, "did you find out anything?"

"What about?"

"Why, about that Novak dame."

"Not a thing. I did just as you told me. I called McEvoy's office from the outside and asked his secretary if she could help me locate Marie Novak. I told her I was speaking for the merchants' Credit Association. Couldn't find out a thing. Jimmy, listen. Can't we forget business for just one day? Let's go to a movie and hold hands and let the world go by."

"All right. Have another drink?"

"No, thanks. One is plenty for me."

Jimmy rubbed his chin and hesitated. Finally he said:

"What about this Novak dame, anyway? What was your reaction?"

"She was a beauty. She makes Jean look like a comic."

"Are you still harping . . .?"

"Gee, it's nice to know you can always annoy your boyfriend so easily. It's fun, annoying boyfriends. Why, you're blushing, James. You kill me!"

"It was the drink. Did you notice anything phony about this dame?"

"Nothing except that she wore her clothes too tight for a John Minot and Company stenographer and business ceased when she walked to the water-cooler."

"One of those things."

"Yes. She had it and was proud of it."

Jimmy sighed.

"Oh, well. I'm getting fed up. Let's go to a movie. I'm just going round and round."

Jimmy paid their check, and they went out into the lobby. They stood for a moment looking at the theatre bulletin board, choosing a movie, and Jimmy was just going to suggest that they go see Clark Gable when glancing up he saw Gordon Minot walking hurriedly across the lobby. Gordon was looking from side to side and seemed a little uneasy.

Jimmy's hand tightened on Eve's arm and she turned in surprise. Then she saw Gordon and Gordon saw them.

"The party's off, I see," said Eve.

Jimmy groaned.

"I thought he was home in bed."

Gordon stopped. He was very red in the face. Frowning, he motioned for Jimmy to come over to him.

"Sit down a minute, honey," said Jimmy hastily. "Please don't be sore."

"I'm going back and get myself another drink," said Eve, walking away quickly.

"Well," said Gordon, his eyes glinting, when Jimmy walked up to him.

"Well what? You called me over, didn't you?"

"No insolence today, please, or I'll fire you on the spot."

"I already quit. I'm just working an extra week to help out."

"Fine. Don't be so diligent."

"What do you mean?"

"Jimmy, I talk about you being dumb. But I know you're not. You're smart. Too smart. How you found out about where I was going, I don't know. But now you've seen me, forget about it. That's all."

Jimmy smiled to himself.

"All right."

"Anything else?"

"Yes. She's got dark hair, hasn't she? Pretty nifty number, I understand. Wears her clothes so tight she has to take them off with a shoe horn. Used to be a stenographer."

Gordon blinked, then recovered.

"Does that mean you think I'm coming here to see a woman? Ridiculous! Now, Jimmy, we've always been pals. I'll let you in on a secret. I'm writing a book."

"Is that so?"

"Don't grin, you idiot. I really am. It's a history of the Minot family. Goes clear back to Colonial times. I've got about two hundred reference books up there in my suite. That's where I work. I'm going to surprise everybody. Anyway, I can't work at home with all those young idiots running about all over the place."

"Leave it to you to think up a screwy alibi. I'd like to see those two hundred volumes."

"Take my word for it, I've got them. Better yet, ask the manager, Ed Worth."

"All right, boss. It's nothing to me."

"Then quit following me. Run along. Get your girl and have a good time. Take her to dinner. Take her to a show. Be your age, Jimmy. Get a smile on your face. You're only young once."

"I'm not so young."

"You're as young as you feel. Look at me."

"I'm looking. You got me up a tree. I don't know what to do. I'll bet O'Brien threw a fit when you drove out."

"I fired him. I fired everybody."

"That's nice."

"I'm sick of this eternal interference."

"Well," said Jimmy, "I guess a man that's been shot at half a dozen times does get sort of used to it."

"What's all this talk about me being shot at! That was during the strike, and once a lunatic shot at me. You're getting an obsession, Jimmy. Now run along." Gordon turned away, muttering: "Just because a couple of thugs were killed down the road a piece." Then he turned back. "We had a terrible row at the factory this morning. Did Pelkey tell you?"

"Yeah. I heard all about it." Jimmy hadn't heard a thing, but he was playing it safe.

"You would. Terrible row. I never knew that Bush had such a temper. What's wrong with the man, anyway? It was a step up for him and a step up for Scott. Any ideas?"

"Maybe he was sore because Jean's going to marry Scott."

"I thought of that. But why should he kick up such a vulgar row? He's first vice president now, confirmed by all the directors, and when I retire he'll be active head. And I may retire any day. But that's a secret. Anyway, Scott was entitled to the leg up. He'll make just as good a general manager as Bush. It's too much for me. Well, goodbye, Jimmy. Maybe I was a little harsh just now. You're still my favorite employee."

"What did McEvoy have to say?"

"Oh, he thinks Scott is too young. He wanted this Welborn man in the job."

"Welborn? Oh, yeah. He's from Colorado, isn't he?"

"Yes. Mining engineer. Very brilliant. But I wanted Scott in the job and that was that. I'm going and don't follow me and look through the keyhole."

Gordon turned and walked swiftly toward the elevators. When he had gone up, Worth, the manager, who had been standing nearby, came up to Jimmy.

"Could I see you a minute, Mr. Devore?" he said.

"Why, sure." Jimmy glanced into the cocktail room in passing. Eve was smoking a cigarette and reading a magazine. "Be with you in a minute."

They went into the manager's office and sat down.

"I'm glad you're here, Mr. Devore," said Worth, a small, well-dressed, middle-aged man with a dark face and a waxed mustache. "I've been intending to have a talk with you for a long time. Mr. Minot's a great responsibility, isn't he?"

"You said it."

"His having this suite here worries me. Of course, it's his own hotel and all that, but a public place is a public place."

"How long has he had this suite?"

"About a week. Maybe a little longer. He's writing some sort of a book, I believe. Says he can't work at home. The boys took up a whole truckload of books."

Jimmy smiled to himself.

"Anybody helping him? Stenographer, or anything?"

"Not now. He used our public stenographer for a day or so, Mrs. Wilson. Very nice woman. She thinks Mr. Minot is a god. She's a widow with two children. Mr. Minot gave her twice what she asked, and also gave her money to buy the children some presents."

"How old is Mrs. Wilson?"

"About forty."

"Good looking?"

Worth smiled.

"Very plain. I hired her for that reason among other things."

"I see. Nobody's been helping him lately?"

"No. He's been alone up there nearly every afternoon."

"What's the layout of the place?"

"Only one entrance. Huge sitting-room and a very large bedroom with twin beds. It's on the fourth floor on the north side. Of course Mr. Minot is perfectly safe here. No one can get in that room except through the one door. But still . . ."

Worth lowered his eyes. Jimmy felt pretty sure the manager had something on his mind.

"Whatever it is, you can tell me."

"I know it. Well, one of the maids, very dependable girl, too, thought she heard voices in the suite several times when Mr. Minot was supposed to be alone."

"Men's voices?"

"She couldn't be sure."

Jimmy got up.

"Thanks. I've got to think this over." Jimmy wrote the number of his bungalow telephone on a card and gave it to Worth. "If anything should come up, you can get me there. Goodbye."

"You don't know what a weight this takes off my mind," said the manager, sighing.

When Jimmy got to the cocktail room he looked every place for Eve but she had gone. Finally a waiter came up with a note.

"You Mr. Devore? A lady left this for you."

Dear Sleuth:

I ran out of crossword puzzles so have gone to the Palace to see Gable. It's pretty dark in that theatre but if you can find me you can have me. No clues.

Eve

Jimmy shrugged, then he turned the note over and scribbled a line or two. Tipping the waiter, he went out quickly, crossed the long lobby to the east entrance, and, after a short search, found Gordon's car parked down the street from the marquee. Jack was sitting at the wheel reading an adventure magazine and smoking. When he saw Jimmy looking at him, he flushed slightly.

"Don't look at me!" he exclaimed. "I work for the boss, not you."

"All right, Jack. I'm not blaming you." He handed Jack the note. "In a few minutes take that down to the Palace theatre and leave it at the box office; then tell the manager to let Eve Barry know that there's a note for her."

Jack brightened when he saw that Jimmy wasn't going to bawl him out, and smiled and nodded, anxious to be obliging.

"You bet."

"Jack, have you been driving the boss down here from the plant every afternoon?"

"Yes."

"How is it worked?"

Jack hesitated.

"I'm no snitcher, Jimmy."

"Well, okay. But if anything should happen to the boss when you're driving him around without me knowing anything about it . . . well, draw your own conclusions."

Jack took off his cap and carefully scratched his head.

"It's like this. The boss leaves his office by the back stairway and I drive him over to the railroad entrance. The guy at that gate don't know anything. He just bows and scrapes and never a peep."

"Very nice. Sid Rogers arranges everything, eh?"

"I don't know. It's none of my business."

"It'll be some of your business if the boss gets knocked off."

"Well, my guess is, Sid does."

"All right. You keep this under your hat, and see that you get the boss home safe for dinner."

When Jimmy got to the estate the guards were thoroughly disorganized. The big gate was standing open and he saw old Mike and Johnson arguing in the roadway. Further along, in front of the caretaker's house, Jean was talking with Ed O'Brien, whose face was almost purple. Jimmy drove in, parked his car, then got out and yelled:

"Shut that gate, Mike. And you, Johnson; what do you think this is, your birthday? Haven't you got something you can do?"

Johnson opened his mouth to speak, but hesitated, then turned to help Mike shut the gate.

"We're all fired," called O'Brien. "You, too."

"I quit long ago," said Jimmy. "What's the trouble, Jean?"

She hurried over to him, looking very pretty and very much distressed.

"Oh, Dad's just turned this place upside down," she said, trying to smile. "I don't know what's got into him. Just because O'Brien wanted to know where he could be reached, he blew up. O'Brien was very polite to him. I heard the whole thing. I don't blame O'Brien for saying he'll never work for us again no matter how much I beg him."

"Oh, he said that, did he?" said Jimmy, his eyes glinting. "O'Brien."

"Yes, sir." The big Irishman hung his head sheepishly.

"Get back on the job. Nobody's going to be fired. And when I quit next week you'll be the boss."

"God forbid!"

"Oh, you're not really quitting, are you Jimmy?" said Jean. "Why, we couldn't get along without you. Willow Wood would never be the same. I'm sure you're joking. Why, Dad was just getting ready to raise your salary and he told me he was going to buy you a big car so you wouldn't be driving that rattle-trap around."

"I just bought a new car," said Jimmy, "Don't you see it?"

"How stupid of me. Of course."

"Anyway, Ed, get back on the job. By the way, call up Mr. Borchers. Tell him to fire Sid Rogers. I'll take the responsibility."

O'Brien stared, then disappeared into the gatehouse, where they could hear him talking with Johnson and Mike.

Jimmy stood looking across the enormous expanse of lawn which sloped down toward the big house; a dozen sprinklers were sending up clouds of silvery spray.

"You mustn't quit, Jimmy," said Jean, at last. "Please help me with Dad. Something's wrong with him. I can't make out just what. He's much more stubborn than he used to be. I'm worried."

Jimmy mumbled:

"I'll stay if you say so."

"That's fine. Jimmy, try to be patient with Dad. He's a very brilliant man, although most people don't think so, and he's very nervous. Gets up in the air over nothing at all and in five minutes he's forgotten it. Have you found out anything yet?"

Jimmy hesitated. Why worry her?

"No: not yet. Say, I understand that Mr. McAvoy and Mr. Bayliss had a row."

"Yes. I heard so. But it's all made up now. At least they're coming over for tennis this afternoon."

"I see. Just one of those factory rows, I guess. At least that's what your father told us. But I told him maybe McEvoy was sore because you were marrying Bayliss."

Jean smiled.

"The bright boy doesn't miss anything, does he?"

"Not if I can help it. Listen, Jean; I'm not just trying to pry, but did McEvoy propose to you?"

"Yes. Several times."

"I thought so. You don't like him much, do you?"

Jean laughed.

"I know *you* don't," she said.

"Do *you*?"

"Well, I don't know. He fascinates me, sort of." Jimmy growled under his breath and turned away. Fascinated her, did he? These dames! All alike. He never knew it to fail. If a guy wasn't worth his salt, he fascinated them!

"I hate to hear you talk like that," Jimmy mumbled.

"Why?"

"It sounds so cheap." The words were out before he knew it. He glanced up fearfully. Jean was flushing, but her face was calm.

"I was joking in a way. Do you like Scott?"

"Yes. And excuse me for what I just said. I didn't mean it at all. I get so used to riding people . . . I . . . it's my job."

"Yes; you seem to make a habit of being unpleasant as if you were afraid people weren't going to like you. I'd like you much better if you'd try to be more pleasant."

Jimmy flushed deeply.

"I want you to like me," he said, avoiding her eyes. "I sure like you."

Jean smiled a little awkwardly.

"Well," she said, "I'll be running. I know things will calm down now that you're here."

Jimmy nodded and turned away. He was a plain damned fool. He'd tipped his hand. Very sensibly, Jean was putting him in his place. After all he was hired help, and a jailbird at that! Jean had the Minot gift of clearing the air of all ambiguity and putting things on their proper levels. Just like Gordon only with more finesse. It was great to be born with a pile of jack; it gave you such a feeling of superiority.

"By the way," said Jimmy. "Don't worry about your Dad. I know where he is. It's all right."

"If you say it is, I know it is," said Jean. Then she waved and walked toward the house across the broad lawn.

"That settles it," said Jimmy, savagely. "I'm going to marry Eve next week. Vacation or no vacation. A man can get the silliest notions."

He went into the bungalow, took a shower and put on polo shirt and a pair of slacks, then he went out on the veranda and sat for a while staring into space. At three o'clock McEvoy and Bayliss drove in together in Bayliss' car; they were talking and laughing. Jimmy looked the other way so he wouldn't have to speak to them. He was feeling low.

After a while he heard shouts of laughter at the tennis courts. Lighting a cigarette, he walked a little ways beyond the bungalow and stood staring off across the lawn toward the courts. Jean was playing with McEvoy, beating him.

"This McEvoy guy!" thought Jimmy. "As a matter of fact, I never paid much attention to him. Never even looked at him very close. He always struck me as a cross between a gigolo and a big-time chiseler. I'd like to study that guy a little." He walked closer to the courts and stood with his hands in his pockets, watching.

Finally Jean saw him.

"Jimmy," she called, "come sit down. Watch me. I'm beating him nicely."

Jimmy went over and sat down beside Bayliss. McEvoy turned and smiled at him very agreeably, then they went on with their game.

"Good, isn't she?" said Jimmy, trying to watch McEvoy but with little success. Jean looked so pretty and she was so graceful!

"Too good," said Bayliss. "It makes a man feel inferior when a woman beats him at tennis."

"Mr. McEvoy doesn't seem to mind."

"Oh, he thinks it's a sissy game. He plays for exercise."

Jimmy began to concentrate on McEvoy. In spite of his handsome, rather pleasant face he had a certain vague air of brutality which Jimmy had never noticed before; his brow was a little too low, his cheekbones a little too prominent; his wrists and ankles a little too thick. His shoulders and back looked powerful; surprisingly so for a rather sedentary business man.

"He don't add up right," thought Jimmy, still studying him. Gradually he began to notice that every time McAvoy seemed on the point of winning a game, he invariably made an error. He was letting Jean win! And Jean, with all her smartness and all her tennis experience, had no idea he was. "He's slick," thought Jimmy. "Too slick." Occasionally, McEvoy would seem momentarily to lose his temper. This delighted Jean. Jimmy smiled to himself. "Smart and slick, that guy."

"Is he playing his best?" Jimmy demanded of Bayliss.

Bayliss stared at Jimmy.

"Of course. Can't you tell? Look! He's furious because he drove that lob out. He feels just like I do. Jean can be very exasperating on a tennis court."

Jimmy thought: "Bayliss doesn't know the score either! This guy is too smart."

Jean finally beat McEvoy in a love set, although every game had been close, several of them deuce.

McEvoy threw his racket disgustedly on the grass and sat down beside it.

"This is too much," he said. "Why don't you play her, Devore? I want to see if she can make you look as silly as she does me."

"No thanks. I haven't played for years. I couldn't warm her up. She'd better play Mr. Bayliss."

"I want to sit for a minute," said Jean, flushed and triumphant. "That first ball of yours, Bush! I simply can't see it. If you'd hit it in oftener I couldn't get a point on your serve."

"If," said McEvoy, shrugging.

A very suave, a very plausible mug: Jimmy summed him up. He turned. He saw Johnson hurrying across the lawn toward them.

"Well," he said.

"Man wants to see you, Mr. Devore. Says it's very important."

"What's his name?"

"William McGraw."

Jimmy glanced at McEvoy, whose right hand had made an involuntary movement of some kind. McEvoy looked up; their eyes met. McAvoy smiled calmly.

"They keep you busy, don't they, Devore?"

"Yes," said Jimmy, thinking: "Yes, you slick mug, they keep me busy. Maybe too busy for your liking. If I'm not mistaken you've heard the name of McGraw someplace."

He got up, smiled at Jean, and hurried to the gate, where old Mike was talking through the bars to Blackie McGraw. Jimmy opened the gate and shut it behind him. Blackie was pale and bleary-eyed. He looked scared and as if he was going to burst out crying. Jimmy swore to himself: full of whiskey and hop! Probably getting ready to start picking them out of the air.

"What are you doing out here, Stool?"

"You got to help me!" cried Blackie. "You got to help me! Gimme some dough. I got to blow this burg. Them bullets ain't made of charcoal."

"Stalling again! How much this time?"

"Jimmy, old pal, I got to blow. They're after me because Cap pulled me in. They're afraid I'll stool. Hell, this is too big. I'm no sap. I wasn't gonna stool, but Red, he says . . ."

"Red McMahon?"

"Yeah him and Butch, they're afraid, see? Look, Jimmy. They're gonna get me sure if I don't blow. Could I hit you for a hundred!"

"You had enough dough to get a snootful," said Jimmy. "Are you talking about Butch Crump?"

"Holy Mother! I didn't say nothing about Butch, did I? No, I don't even know the guy."

Jimmy took a roll of money from his pocket and counted off ten tens.

"Come clean, Blackie," he said, "and I'll give you this dough and you can get out of the State. What's Butch and Red doing in town?"

"I don't know, honest. But they're here. Red is, anyway." Blackie looked from side to side, fearfully. "That Butch! He gives me the creeps. He's got eyes! Jeez, what eyes! Why, he'd bump me just to see me fall! He likes it. Look, Jimmy. This is a big one. Biggest one since Denver, Red says. I heard him. They thought I was dead drunk, but Blackie's always got his ears open. Only think! They knocked over this bank in Denver and got eighty grand, and they never took a chance in the world. Am I talking all right? My head's sort of going round and round. Yeah they never took a chance in the world. They was hired. Is that hot? Payroll money. There's a big smelter there. Eighty grand. That's dough. Look; there was a crook in a bank. He was the cashier or something, see? He and a couple of other softies hired Red and Butch to knock over the bank, then they all split the dough. The money was insured. What the hell did the cashier care, get me?" Blackie rocked with laughter. "That's smart. Butch won't turn a hand for less than ten grand. Red says they got the same setup here. I heard him. They got a couple of jobs here to do for a guy, then this guy's gonna turn 'em loose on another big payroll job. A hundred grand or better that's what I hear."

"What do you know about Roxy Doyle?"

"I can guess. Butch knocked him off. Butch or Red. Red calls his gun Roxy, get what I mean? I think he knocked Roxy off with that gun. He says: 'They better walk chalk or I'll turn my Roxy loose.' Get me? Am I talking all right? I'm hopped to the ears."

"You're doing well, Blackie," said Jimmy. "You're sure earning this money fast. I'm going to make it a hundred and fifty. Do you remember anything else?"

Blackie pulled at the peak of his cap, thinking.

"I ain't got nothing else straight. Only I heard them guys talking about you. That's why I buzzed you outside Cap's office. You see, they was holing up at a joint where I lived. I used to know Red. Him and me was trusties at the State joint. Red was the biggest stool in the joint and I got all the blame for it. You see, Red was a number one man. None of the guys ever thought he'd stool. That's how he got his parole, not through his mouthpiece. Jesus; I can't seem to remember nothing else. Only, Jimmy, look out. I heard them talking about you. Now do I get that money!"

"Yes; here you are. Listen, Blackie; walk down the road about half a mile. You'll see a little garage and filing station. I know the guy. He's all right. I'll call him up. He'll get you to Indianapolis in three hours, then you're okay."

Blackie stuffed the money into his pocket, then he put his head down and began to blubber.

"You're a pal Jimmy, old boy. You're a pal."

"Hurry, Blackie."

"Goodbye, pal; goodbye," sobbed Blackie, starting down the road.

Jimmy ran into the gate house and called the garage.

"Earl?"

"Yeah. That you, Jimmy?"

"Yeah. I sent a guy down to you. He wants to get to Indianapolis. Start with him. Keep on the Madison Highway. A squad car will pick you up before you get very far. I'll fix everything. No trouble for you. Give me that license number."

Then Jimmy called Frank Berger and explained to him about Blackie. When Frank found out that Blackie was in the know with regard to Butch and Red McMahon he cried:

"God bless you, Jimmy. If I can ever do anything for you just let me know."

Jimmy walked back toward his bungalow shaking with excitement. It seemed fantastic, but he was pretty sure now that McEvoy and Butch were mixed up together some way. Denver? Hadn't McEvoy letters of introduction from Denver? Jimmy's head was buzzing with ideas.

Calming himself he walked past his bungalow and glanced at the tennis courts. Some other people had arrived; Jean and Bayliss were playing doubles against another couple. McEvoy had disappeared. In a moment, Jimmy saw him hurrying across the lawn from the big house. Jimmy nodded to him, then went into the bungalow and got Smith, the butler, on the phone.

"Smith? Devore speaking."

"Yes, Mr. Devore."

"Confidential, Smith. Did Mr. McEvoy use the phone when he was in the house?"

"Yes sir."

"Any idea who he called up?"

"Yes sir. He called the plant. Talked to Mr. Welborn. Something about welfare work. I could hear him distinctly."

"Thanks, Smith."

Jimmy sat down on the veranda and tried to arrange his vague suspicions into some sort of pattern, but with very little success. Finally the phone rang. It was Frank.

"Jimmy. Bad news."

"What! Didn't you pick up Blackie?"

"He never got to the garage. But he almost got there. We found him about a hundred yards from the place. He'd been shot with a rifle. Funny! Nobody around heard any shots."

"Silencer, maybe. That's tough Frank. My fault too. I should have been more careful. Is he dead?"

"Very dead. Boy, the heat goes on again. Another crook knocked off in Willow Wood. I can hear the mayor's voice now."

"We'll have to get together. I've got some dope for you."

"Drop by tonight. Thanks anyway, Jimmy. You did your best."

Jimmy hung up and stood staring at the wall.

"Welfare work, eh?" he muttered.

CHAPTER FOUR

At six o'clock Jimmy, who was sitting on the veranda, saw Gordon's big limousine drive through the gate. Gordon smiled at Mike and Johnson and was very friendly as if he hadn't discharged them four or five hours before. There was a man in the backseat with Gordon. Craning his neck, Jimmy saw that it was Dr. Sanders.

"What's this?" Jimmy exclaimed, then he hurried down to the driveway and held up his hand for Jack to stop.

"Hello, Jimmy," said Gordon, smiling a very tired smile. "Everything's shipshape again, I see. This man, Doctor, is a regular little Hitler. He makes men jump by wiggling his finger. Very able young man, but too self-important."

The doctor smiled at Jimmy.

"What's the matter, boss?" asked Jimmy. "Why the croaker?"

"And he speaks English of a remarkable purity," Gordon went on, laughing. "Croaker is good, eh, Doctor? But don't let him fool you. He knows better. He pretends he's really very tough. He uses all the newest slang. As a matter of fact, he's soft as mush, especially in regard to dogs and women. Jimmy, to tell you the truth, I'm not up to much. I had a dizzy spell so I stopped by to see the doctor. He's having dinner with me." Gordon turned and glanced at the crowd of young people at the tennis courts. "And so, I suppose, is everybody else."

"I want to talk to you," said Jimmy.

"I want him to lie down for a little while," said the doctor. "He must rest before dinner. The heat got him, I think. It's been frightful in the city today. Nice out here though."

"Jump in, Jimmy," said Gordon. "I'll talk to you and get it over with, then I can rest."

Jimmy got into the front seat with Jack and when they reached the house, Jimmy got out and opened the car door for Gordon.

"You'd make a nice footman, Jimmy," he said with a smile; "very nice indeed. Come in the library. Excuse us for two minutes, Doctor."

Smith opened the door and smiled at his master and nodded coldly to Jimmy. Smith didn't approve of Jimmy at all; thought that Mr. Minot was making a mistake being so familiar with him. Smith was an imitation Englishman and a stickler for all the niceties. Jimmy's informality made him wince.

"Hello, Smith," said Gordon. "Anything turn up while I was gone?"

"Yes sir. The mayor's been trying to get in touch with you."

"What does he want?" said Gordon. "The election isn't till this fall."

Jimmy laughed.

"I know what he wants. That's one of the things I want to see you about."

Gordon went into the huge library and sank into a chair, sighing.

"Sit down," he cried suddenly. "Stop fidgeting."

Jimmy sat down.

"Little jumpy, eh?" said Jimmy.

"I guess so. Well?"

"Did you get much work done on the history of the Minot family? Looks to me like you overworked."

Gordon's mouth tightened.

"None of your insolence. We've got to have an understanding, young man. First, did you fire Sid Rogers?"

"I did."

"Why?"

"I'm his boss. He's responsible to me. I won't have two-timing."

Gordon shifted and sat thinking. Finally he spoke:

"I think you're quite right there. I see your point. You're hired to do a job and you're doing it. All right. I wish I had more men like you. If you hadn't resisted education so successfully, you might get someplace in the plant. In fact, Jimmy, I've been thinking about making you Director of Welfare."

"You want to get me out of here. Is that the idea?"

Gordon groaned but said nothing.

"Boss," said Jimmy, "you've got to listen to me. Do you know what the mayor wants? They knocked off another chiseler down the road a piece. That's the third crook that's been knocked off in Willow Wood this week. Naturally the mayor's scared you're going to rake him over the coals. Everybody knows he does just as you tell him. Now, listen. The mayor's been taking it out on my pal, Frank Berger. He's a great guy and is doing his best. Do me a favor. Tell the mayor to give him his appointment and lay off him."

"What appointment?"

"He's been promised a police commissioner job."

"All right. But what's this about somebody being killed?"

"A no-good tramp by the name Blackie McGraw came here to see me. He was in the jug when I was. He borrowed some money. Shortly after he left here, somebody shot him with a rifle."

Gordon rubbed his chin thoughtfully.

"Did you know that McEvoy had warned me against you?"

Jimmy flushed.

"I don't wonder. Things are getting a little hot for him."

"What! Bush? Ridiculous! However, I've been warned against you before. That's nothing." Gordon pondered. "What's this nonsense about Bush?"

"I'm not ready to talk."

Gordon looked at Jimmy keenly.

"Are you sparring for time?"

"What do you mean sparring for time? I'm trying to keep you from being shot. There's a lot of things I don't like going on."

"Will you stop talking about me being shot! Listen, Jimmy, you detectives are all alike. I ought to know. I've hired enough. You suspect everybody. It's an obsession. Now quit it."

Jimmy shrugged.

"Boss, I wish you'd stay home for about a week. Pretend you're sick. Let me supervise things."

"Impossible."

"What's the matter? That skirt got you down?"

Gordon got very red in the face.

"Damn your impudence. I see we'll never get any place until I tell you the truth. I didn't like that remark you made about me overworking. It was very vulgar and uncalled for. I'm in love, Jimmy. That's the long and short of it, so make the best of it. Stop trying to interfere with me when I want to go out. Stop making a nuisance and prying into my affairs. Just do what I tell you. That's all. Is that clear enough for you?"

Gordon started. Jimmy was doubled up with laughter.

"Oh, you're killing me!"

"What's wrong with you, you idiot? Don't you think I can be in love? What's so funny about that?"

Jimmy calmed himself.

"Excuse me. But it just struck me as so funny."

Gordon jumped to his feet and began to pace the floor.

"I might know a jailbird like you would think it funny."

Jimmy sobered immediately.

"I resent that remark."

"I withdraw it. Stop irritating me. I don't know what I'm saying."

Suddenly Jimmy remembered that Gordon had been ill that afternoon. He got up.

"Well, boss, if that's how it is there's nothing I can do about it. Just be careful. Be like you've been doing. See her in the afternoon at the hotel. Don't go anyplace with her."

Gordon whirled.

"You idiot! I'm not doing that to protect myself. I'm doing it to protect her. What would anybody say if they saw a poor young girl going about with me? You know what they'd say. And it wouldn't be true. Not by a long shot. I'd marry her tomorrow if . . ." Gordon paused suddenly and turned away.

Jimmy hesitated.

"Why don't you?"

"She's married. She has to get her divorce."

"I see. Well, excuse me, boss. I had no idea it was anything like this. I apologize. I'll help you all I can if you'll just wise me up and not play against me."

A happy smile lit up Gordon's face.

"Fine. Shake on it."

They shook hands.

"Excuse me, boss. Would you tell me her name?"

Gordon shook his head decisively.

"Not yet There are a lot of things you don't understand. I will later."

"All right. You're the doctor. By the way, there's a little item of one hundred and fifty dollars that I've got to add to my expense account. Okay?"

Gordon stared at Jimmy, then laughed.

"Bribery?"

Jimmy flushed.

"If that's what you think, forget it." He turned and walked out.

Gordon ran to the door and called after him.

"Don't be a fool. I was joking."

But Jimmy paid no attention. He went into the entrance hall to see the doctor.

"Is he all right?" he demanded.

The little doctor got up and stood fumbling with his glasses.

"As far as I can make out. He's a rather healthy man, I think. But very nervous. He has had a dizzy spell and some palpitations. The heat, I think. Or he may be overworking. Nothing alarming. But he should rest more."

"Thanks, Doc."

When Jimmy got through telling Frank Berger all the things Blackie McGraw had told him, Frank sat for a long time in silence, staring at the wall. Jimmy could hear a clock ticking in the next room. Finally, Frank said:

"I kind of remember that big bank robbery. Wait a minute. It was the Canyon Run Bank. A little place just outside of Denver. There was an investigation, if I'm not mistaken. Some official was suspected of connivance, but was exonerated, if I'm remembering this thing right. I'll wire the chief of police out there for information."

"Get the names of all the officials."

"What have you got up your sleeve?"

"Nothing but my shirt. I'm playing hunches. Something tells me Bush McEvoy was mixed up in that robbery some way. Don't laugh. Bush went to the telephone and Blackie got knocked off. Is that right?"

"Yes. But it might be a coincidence."

"Good Lord! Didn't I see his hand jump when Johnson told us McGraw was outside?"

"You might have imagined it. So far we haven't got a scrap of evidence. I mean real evidence. You know that as well as I do."

Jimmy lowered his head and sat thinking. Frank finally spoke.

"I got a bigger mystery than this one. When Blackie McGraw got knocked off in Willow Wood I was almost afraid to go to the phone. I expected to be asked to resign. But, no; the mayor clams up and you'd think he owed me money. That's a funny one."

Jimmy grinned.

"I put a bug in Gordon's ear."

"You did? What a pal! Good old Gordon and good old Jimmy."

"You'll get your appointment pretty soon now; that is, providing I get all the service I ask for."

"You'll get it, don't worry."

"Good. I'll start now. I want you to put two good men on at the New Dilling Hotel. One day and one night."

"All right. But what for?"

"Just in case."

"All right. What instructions?"

"Report to the manager. He knows what I want." Jimmy got up. "Now I got to run over and see Eve before I go home. I had to walk out on her this afternoon. She never called me. So I guess she's sore."

"She's a nice kid, Jimmy. Hang on to her. They're scarce. I was lucky. I managed to get me the nicest wife in the world. Take a tip from me. I'm a happy man. At home, anyway."

The traffic was heavy in the downtown district and as Jimmy was an impatient driver, his blood was boiling long before he got out into the residential section. As he turned into Eve's street, he saw in the rearview mirror that there was a car about a hundred feet behind him with noticeably yellow headlights.

"That's funny," thought Jimmy. "I saw those lights half a dozen times in the traffic. Do you suppose . . .?"

He took his big automatic from the shoulder holster and put it on the seat beside him within easy reach, then he patted his right coat pocket where he kept his little emergency gun. He stepped on the accelerator and drove past Eve's going about fifty. Glancing into the mirror, he saw that the car behind him had speeded up. He turned a corner on two wheels; in a moment the car with the yellow headlights turned the corner also. Jimmy turned another corner and another; the car kept a hundred feet or so behind him.

"If those guys are so handy with a rifle, why don't they use it!" he muttered.

Losing his temper suddenly, he leaned out the side of his car and driving with his left hand and taking a chance on crashing into a light-pole or a tree, he fired two shots at the yellow headlights. One of them went out. The car swerved; there was the shriek of violently applied brakes and the screaming of tires, then the car turned and Jimmy saw its red taillight disappearing.

"That wasn't Butch or Red," he told himself grimly. "What a chump I was!"

It was a warm summer night. People were sitting on the porches along this residential street. Jimmy heard men running. He pulled over to the curb and getting out, began to examine his car. Two men came up.

"Was that shooting?" one of them asked.

Jimmy laughed.

"No. I think I blew my muffler. I got to get this hack looked at. I never had so much trouble with a new car in my life."

The men laughed.

"Boy, we thought we were seeing something. The way that car turned around and the way them flames shot out."

"What car?"

"Oh, a car turned right around in the middle of the block."

"I didn't see it. Well, I hope this hack gets home. Goodnight."

Jimmy drove off, turned into Eve's street again, and parked his car half a block away from the apartment house where she lived. Her apartment was second floor front; her windows were dark. He tried the outside door; it was unlocked. He went in, climbed the stairs to the second floor, and knocked at Eve's door. There was no response. Jimmy glanced at his watch. Quarter after ten. Where could she be? He hesitated, then, taking out a card began to write her a note.

He heard somebody coming up the stairs and turned, still a little jumpy, and put his hand in his coat pocket. It was Eve. She was coming up the stairs with a rather good-looking young man. Jimmy swore under his breath. When Eve saw him she started slightly, then she smiled.

"Hello, Jimmy."

"Hello. I was just writing you a note."

"You write lots of notes, don't you? You seem to love writing notes. Jimmy, this is Mr. Carter. We were out getting a drink. Isn't it hot tonight?"

Jimmy compressed his lips and grudgingly shook hands with Mr. Carter, who had nice curly hair and was tall and slender. Jimmy hated him on sight.

"Didn't catch the name," said Mr. Carter.

"Devore," said Jimmy, frowning. "Well, since you're busy I'll run along, Eve. I was just driving past, thought . . ."

"Some other night perhaps," said Eve, smiling calmly.

She meant it! Jimmy couldn't believe his ears. He hesitated. Yeah. She was giving him the air and he'd almost got himself shot up trying to see her. How do you like that!

"Sorry I couldn't get back this afternoon," he said, flushing.

"Oh, that's all right. I understand. You know, Bill," Eve went on, turning to Carter. "Jimmy works so hard. Never has a minute to himself."

"That's tough," said Carter, indifferently, resenting Jimmy's manner and wishing he'd go on about his business.

Bill! Now isn't that a hell of a name for a guy that looked like a panty waist. And who was this guy anyway, and how come Eve was so familiar with him?

"I want to see you a minute, Eve," he mumbled.

"Won't some other time do?"

"Now listen . . ."

Eve glanced uneasily at Jimmy; then she said:

"Bill, here's my key. Would you mind waiting inside?"

"Not at all. Very glad to have met you Mr. Defoe."

"Thanks Mr. Carp."

Carter glanced sharply at Jimmy, then he unlocked Eve's door and went inside.

"This is sweet!" said Jimmy.

"I told you."

"I came up here to ask you to marry me next week."

"I don't think I can get around to it."

Jimmy was so angry he couldn't speak; he just stood there staring.

"You've stood me up for the last time."

Jimmy jammed on his hat.

"Okay!"

He started for the stairway. Eve hurried after him.

"I found out something for you."

Jimmy turned and started back up the stairs. He walked past Eve and was trying to open her door when she caught his arm.

"Listen, Jimmy, I found out something for you."

"I don't care what you found out. I'm going to paste that guy one for luck, just to sort of finish things off right. Mr. Defoe! Where does he get that stuff?

"Who is he, anyway!"

"He lives down the hall. He's been after me for a date for months."

"Well, he finally caught up with you."

"He's a nice fellow. He's a gentleman."

"He's a sister."

"Jimmy, you tend to your own business. If I want to have dates I'm going to have them. You and your Jean! You can't fool me. I'm through playing second fiddle. If you want to have dates with me like the other fellows, all right. But I'm back in circulation. And if you go in there and cause a row, I'll call the manager and have you arrested."

"You win." Jimmy turned and started back down the stairs. "Next time you want to see me, call me up."

"I lost your phone number," said Eve, tossing her head. "Wait. Since I went to all this trouble I might as well tell you about it." She took a card from her purse and handed it to him. There's the address of that Novak girl."

Jimmy's mouth dropped open.

"Yeah? How did you get it, honey?"

Eve's lips trembled slightly. She turned away to hide her agitation. She wouldn't give in! She just wouldn't.

"She came in the picture show right after I got your note. She met some man. A man I'd never seen before. Pretty soon she went out and I followed her, that's all."

Jimmy hesitated.

"Listen, honey, I'm sorry . . ."

Eve turned away abruptly and rang her doorbell. The door was opened almost immediately.

"Well," Jimmy heard Carter say, "you took a long time, Eve . . ."

Jimmy heard Tommy, the wire-hair he'd given Eve, barking joyfully. Then the door was shut. Jimmy turned and went slowly down the stairs.

He felt low. Scarcely thinking about the car with the yellow headlights, he drove into town at a very slow pace, worrying about Eve. There was no doubt in the world that he had been taking her for granted. He hardly ever gave her a thought when he wasn't actually with her. He felt that she'd always be waiting for him to call up and ask for a date. Women were keen about those things. Eve had sensed something in his behavior lately; he'd certainly never said anything that would lead her to think he'd been cooling off. And as a matter of fact, had he been cooling off? He had just been too sure of Eve, that was all. Then there was Jean. Jimmy laughed grimly. "Yeah. A lot she cares about me. Why, she'd just as soon get mixed up with Jack as me. What I need is a drink!"

Suddenly thinking about the Novak girl and the address Eve had given him, Jimmy snapped his fingers and, turning off into High Street, went past the New Dilling, noticing that the cocktail bar was crowded, then he pulled up at a cheap apartment house at the end of the block.

"This must be it," he told himself.

He parked his car, then he went up to the door of the apartment house and tried it and found it locked. Turning, he studied the list of names. There it was. Miss Marie Novak. Apartment 2A. He noticed that the slip bearing her name had been carelessly shoved into the slot and under it was the slip of the former occupant, Geo Grady.

Jimmy hesitated, then pressed the button for 2A. Much to his surprise, the door clicked immediately and he shoved it open and went in.

The girl's apartment was the first on the right. Just as Jimmy got up to the door, it opened. A girl dressed for the street stepped out into the hallway. Jimmy whistled to himself. What a pip! The girl started when she saw Jimmy; her dark eyes got big; she drew back a step.

"Oh," she said, "I thought . . ."

Jimmy took off his hat.

"Excuse me," he said, "but could you tell me where Mr. Grady lives?"

"Mr. Grady?" The girl stared at him suspiciously. Her nostrils quivered with some sort of emotion. Was she scared or sore? Jimmy couldn't make out. But he knew one thing already; this baby would take some handling. There was a certain something about her face, pretty as it was, that said: Meddle at your own risk!

"Excuse me," said Jimmy, as politely as he could, "I'm sorry to bother you. Mr. Grady used to live here in 2A. I'm trying to locate him."

"Oh," said the girl, "I see. Well, he was gone some time before I moved in. You might ask the manager. 2B."

"Thank you very much."

The girl smiled mechanically, then turned and went back into her apartment.

"That dame's got a dangerous eye," thought Jimmy as he stood hesitating in the hallway. Somebody was coming for her, that was certain. It might not be such a bad idea to try to get a look at whoever it was. Turning, he rang the manager's bell.

A rather tough looking fat man opened the door. Jimmy didn't like the way this bird narrowed his eyes. What a nice friendly joint he'd stumbled into!

"Excuse me," said Jimmy, trying to make his voice sound high and harmless. "I'm looking for the man who used to live in 2A."

"Looking for Grady, eh?" said the manager, roughly. "One of his friends?"

"Yes."

"That's all I wanted to know." Suddenly, the manager made a grab for Jimmy's coat lapels, evidently with the idea of pulling him into his apartment. But Jimmy knocked his arms aside with a quick blow of his right fist.

"Wait a minute guy. What's the hurry?"

The manager hesitated. He saw that he had underestimated Jimmy and, though he was evidently enraged, he sparred for time.

"That Grady guy," he muttered. "He not only got the police down on me. He lammed, owing me about eighty bucks."

"He owes me money, too. What are you grabbing me for?"

"I thought maybe you was one of his buddies. He had them coming here. A lot of no-good tramps. I was going to shake it out of you, get me?"

"Glad you changed your mind," said Jimmy. "I might have to drill a hole in your vest."

The manager started.

"Now wait a minute, pal," he said. "Excuse me. But I'm so sore about that Grady guy I can't sleep at night."

"Don't know where he is, eh?"

"I wish I did."

Jimmy heard the buzzer in the girl's apartment. A moment later the front door opened. Jimmy started. Welborn, one of the big shots at John Minot and Company, was coming quickly down the hall. Jimmy ducked into the manager's apartment.

"I don't want that guy to see me," he said hurriedly.

"Okay," said the manager.

They stood just behind the half-opened door, listening.

"Hello, Frank," said the girl.

"Hello, Marie. Ready?"

"All set. Listen, Frank, there was a man here a minute ago. Funny! I think I better . . ." They went out. The front door slammed.

Jimmy turned. The manager was regarding him with a smile.

"Looking for Grady, eh? You don't look like Grady's kind to me."

"I'm not, I guess. Forget it. What do you know about that dame over there?"

"Nothing except she ought to be in pictures."

"No wisecracks."

"Wait a minute," said the fat man. "This is my joint, or am I wrong? Want me to call a cop?"

"All right. Look. Get me a picture of her and I'll give you twenty bucks."

"That's the easiest twenty bucks I ever earned. Wait right here."

Jimmy stepped out into the hallway. The manager unlocked the girl's door with a master key and in a moment came back with a little framed snap shot.

"Nice work," said Jimmy, slipping the picture into his pocket. "I'll be going." He took out a twenty-dollar bill and handed it to the manager.

"I may get into a jam over this," said the fat man, ruefully.

"If you do, call Frank Berger. Tell him to call the bungalow. Maybe we can work together."

The manager was staggered.

"Number one Berger? Jesus; I didn't know you was a copper. You don't look like no copper to me."

"I'm not. If I happen to call you who should I ask for?"

"Ben."

"All Right. Play ball. An 'in' with Berger wouldn't hurt you any."

The manager mopped his brow.

"I'll say it wouldn't."

Jimmy nodded and went out and drove to the New Dilling. The manager, Mr. Worth, he was told, was in his apartment sleeping. Would Mr. Devore like to see the night manager?

"Okay," said Jimmy.

The night manager was a very nervous young man with blond hair and thick-lensed glasses. He fidgeted in his chair and kept nervously clearing his throat.

"Know me?" Jimmy asked.

"By reputation. We all know how you stand with Mr. Minot."

"You can trust me. You know that."

"Oh, certainly. No question of that."

Jimmy gave the night manager the picture.

"Know this girl?"

"Yes, Mr. Devore. She lives here."

"Under what name?"

"Ann Jocelyn. A very charming girl. She just came in and went to her apartment."

"Anybody with her?"

"No. She was alone."

"Did she have on a dark suit and a small black hat?"

"Yes."

"Sure she went up to her apartment?"

"I think so. I happened to be near the desk. She got her key."

"Thanks. What floor is her apartment?"

"Third."

"You don't have floor clerks here, do you?"

"No, Mr. Devore."

Jimmy left the manager's office and walked toward the cocktail bar. As he turned to go in, he came face to face with Marie Novak, who was coming out. She glanced at him sharply, then smiled.

"Did you find Mr. Grady?"

"No. The manager didn't know where he was."

"That's too bad, Mr. Devore. That's really too bad."

She laughed, and, turning, walked swiftly across the lobby toward the elevators.

Jimmy sat on a stool at the bar and ordered a Scotch and soda. He was just drinking it when somebody touched his arm. He turned. Sid Rogers was standing with his hat off looking very penitent.

"Jimmy, old boy."

"Hello, Sid. Have a drink."

"Thanks." He sat beside Jimmy and ordered. They were both silent till the bartender came with Sid's drink, then Jimmy said "Here's how!"

Smiling sadly, Rogers said: "To the best sleuth in town. No fooling, Jimmy."

Jimmy grunted.

"No soft soap, Sid. You're fired and you're going to stay fired."

"What could I do, Jimmy? The boss called me in his office and said it was either that way or else."

"You should have come to me."

"I know it now. But the boss had me scared and there was a rumor going around that you were going to get the sack. So I didn't know . . ."

"Sorry."

"Look, Jimmy. I got three kids. Jobs are hard to find. Especially after you've been kicked out of John Minot and company."

"Sorry."

Sid slowly finished his drink.

"Listen, Jimmy, I could give you a tip that would make your hair curl. I get around. I hear things. I'll gamble with you. If I can give you a lead that would put you in solider than ever and maybe save Mr. Minot's life would you be interested in giving me back my job?"

Jimmy turned and stared at Sid, whose eyes did not waver.

"Yes. With a raise."

"Okay. And you don't need to promise nothing till you hear what I got to say."

"That's fair enough."

Sid leaned forward as if to speak, then he glanced about him at the crowd and said:

"You're the doctor, Jimmy. But can't we go someplace else? This is pretty public."

"We can get in my car and drive around."

"Yeah, we could. But why not go down to Joe's on Front Street? Nice quiet joint. Anyway, I'm hungry, and Joe puts out the best steaks in this man's town."

"I could stand a steak myself. Come on." Jimmy paid the check and they went out. Joe's was only a block and a half away so they walked.

"You'll never regret this," said Sid. "I better wait till we sit down before I start. It's a long story."

Joe's was deserted except for a couple at a front table. The proprietor, a big Italian, was sitting behind the cash register picking his teeth.

"Hello, Joe," said Sid. "We want two of your best sirloins with all the fixings. Anybody in the back?"

"No," said Joe. "You like to sit in the back? Very cozy and private." He glanced questioningly at Jimmy.

"Okay by me," said Jimmy. "And Joe, a big stein of beer. Nearly midnight and it's still hot."

"Yeah. Look at me sweat," said Joe with a grin. "Go sit down, gentlemen. I fix you up."

Sid pushed aside some dirty portieres and they went up two steps into a little wood-paneled room where there were two tables, a few chairs, lighted candles stuck into oddly-shaped wine bottles, and pictures of prizefighters and racehorses on the walls. Jimmy sat down facing an alley window. Sid sat on his left.

"I hope he hurries with that beer," said Jimmy. "I've had a hard night. I need a little refreshment. Whiskey just makes me hotter." He turned toward Sid, smiling. But Sid's face was white and he looked very scared.

"What . . . ?" Jimmy began, then he happened to glance at the window in front of him. It was pitch black in the alley outside and the window was like a mirror, reflecting the room; behind him, Jimmy saw a door slowly opening. He saw reflected in the window a tall man peering at his back; a man with a black forelock and piercing pale eyes. He had something in his hands. A rifle!

With one movement, Jimmy knocked over the table and dove through the window with a splintering crash of glass and sash wood. He lit on his hands and knees in the brick alleyway. He heard voices behind him. Getting to his feet he ran at breakneck speed up the alley toward the big buildings and the reassuring lights of High Street. A bullet whined over him, then another. But he heard no report. "Silencer!" he muttered, turning at right angles and crossing a cement areaway, stumbling over trash and garbage cans and making a tremendous racket.

A big Greek put his head out of a side door.

"Hey, wassa molla you!"

But Jimmy swore at him and ran on, emerging finally into West Broad Street. He had lost his hat; his face and hands were cut and bleeding and his clothes were torn. Several people stared at him with amazement. But he didn't care. He was safe!

Turning, he saw a patrolman at a call-box down the street. It was midnight. The cop was phoning his precinct. Jimmy rushed up to him. The cop stared.

"Is that you, Murphy?"

"Heavens above! Jimmy Devore! What they been doing to you?"

"Never mind that. Get Berger. Tell him it's time for the dragnet. Butch Crump just tried to kill me at Joe's Place. Tell him Sid Rogers from the plant put the finger on me. Tell him to pinch Joe Cianelli and give him the works. Tell him to knock over every underworld joint in town, and tell him to hurry. I got to get home."

"Yes sir, Jimmy."

"Have Berger call me and let me know how things turn out."

CHAPTER FIVE

Every once in a while during their conversation, Frank Berger would suppress a smile and finally, Jimmy, his face disfigured by strips of court plaster, his left wrist bandaged and in a light sling, his neck stiff, his head aching, and his temper very short, burst out:

"What the hell are you grinning at?"

"It's you," said Frank, laughing. "I went down and took a look at that window. Jimmy Devore, the human projectile! I'd like to have seen you going through that glass. You ought to join a circus."

"Very funny! A guy tries to kill me and you laugh. Old soft-hearted Frank!"

"Oh, don't be a sap. You're safe, aren't you? Butch and his bunch are probably in Chicago now. A least if they kept on the way they're going and weren't picked up. Eddie Shea had his car wide-open and they pulled away from him like he was standing still. You talk! Say, Eddie won't be out of the hospital for three months. Of course that tire would bust when he was crossing a culvert. How he kept from being killed I don't know."

"You're pretty sure Sid Rogers was in the car?"

"Yeah. Didn't he turn blackleg in a hurry!"

"He never was any good. I only kept him on because of his wife and kids. What about Greasy Joe?"

"I don't think he had a thing to do with it. I never saw a man so scared in my life. We weren't gentle with him. We had him begging for mercy but I think it was all news to him."

"You sure handled the papers nice. Everybody thinks Sid tried to kill me because I fired him. It's a good story. It gives us elbow room."

"Yeah. But will the Feds burn if they ever find out you caught a glimpse of Butch and never said a word to them! However, we've got other fish to fry. I've got some news for you. Bush McEvoy was adopted by Judge McEvoy when Bush was nine years old. His name is James Selby. Here's one that may help. The name of the Canyon Run cashier was W. W. Welborn."

Jimmy jumped up.

"That's it. That's what I wanted. Look, Frank. It's a straight line now."

"I'm glad you think so. And wait a minute. This Marie Novak is in the clear as far as we can find out. We've checked and re-checked. I've had every old-timer in the City Hall look at her picture. That snapshot you sent me had Kansas City, 1934, on the back. I wired the chief of police and got all the dope. Her father's got a shoe store. She graduated from high school there in 1930. Very nice family, and according to all records, she's okay. In fact she was an honor student."

"All right. Let's forget her. She may just be taking Gordon and playing on the side with Welborn. Frank, what a doll she is! She's an absolute knockout, but I'd put my watch in my inside coat pocket if I had anything to do with her. All right. Let's forget her and Gordon, too. It's a straight line with them out of the picture. Look! Red and Butch knocked over this bank at Canyon Run. Frank Welborn's brother was the cashier. He hired them to do it. Blackie says a couple of softies helped them. When Blackie says softies he doesn't mean sissies; he means non-professionals, outsiders. All right. Suppose McEvoy and Frank Welborn were the outsiders. They keep under cover. Nobody suspects them; they're still good citizens as far as Denver is concerned. All right. They cut eighty grand five ways. McEvoy has a nice pile to start out with; he gets letters of introduction and turns up here. When he's in solid, he has Welborn come along. All right. Here they are living on the fat of the land. Not a worry in the world. Pretty soon things get around along the grapevine and Roxy Doyle gets wind of it. Well, you know what kind of rat he was. He gets one of his pals, that Chicago mug, and they come here and high-pressure McEvoy. He's in a spot. Maybe he pays off a few times, but these blackmailers can't stand prosperity; they never can; they want all he's got. Okay, says McEvoy, you'll get it. So he gets hold of his old pal, Butch, who brings Red along with him. McEvoy has a little talk with them. If they'll knock off these rats, he'll not only give them a nice hunk of gelt but he'll put them in the way of something big . . . like the John Minot and Company shop payroll which runs close to $300,000 a month . . ."

"Give me time. Who has final charge of transporting the dough from the bank? The general manager. All right, McEvoy had the job, but he got promoted. He kicked about it and Gordon couldn't understand why. Seeing the jig was up, McEvoy does his damndest to get Welborn appointed in his place. But Gordon gets bullheaded. He wants Scott Bayliss in the job because Scott's going to marry Jean and is a good guy. Meanwhile, Blackie spills something to me; they don't know what. But they're not taking any chances. First they knock Blackie off, then they try to knock me off. What they're going to do about the payroll, I don't know."

"I'm glad there's something you don't know. You've got a nice story there, Jimmy, but it's too pat. Listen, here's one for you. You know how hot Butch Crump is. He's the only so-called Public Enemy left. How could that crooked cashier get hold of him in the first place, and how could McEvoy get hold of him in the second place?"

"That's the one you've got to answer."

"Thanks."

"Anyway, I'm beginning to think Gordon's in the clear. This girl's just playing him for all he's worth, maybe. I don't like the Welborn hook-up, but on the other hand a girl like that could never go knocking around a place like Minot and Company without some of the bigshots trying to make her. Anyway, Gordon's getting beyond me. I can't control him any longer. You can't tie a guy up. If he wants to run after this dame, that's his business."

Frank got up.

"Well, I've got to be moving. Every man on the force has got strict orders about Butch Crump or Red. They've all got pictures and dope. If they turn up in this town again, they'll have to hole in and stay there. It's going to be too hot for them to show."

"Thanks for coming out, Frank. And think over what I told you. Do you agree with me about Gordon?"

"Looks logical."

"I'm glad you think so. I was getting to the point where I seriously considered knocking McEvoy off."

"Don't be a damn fool, Jimmy. You did one stretch. How did you like it?"

Jimmy shuddered but said nothing.

Shortly after Berger left, the phone in Jimmy's bungalow rang. It was Smith, the butler. Mr. Minot wanted to see Jimmy right away in the library. Jimmy groaned and put on his hat.

"Just when I was getting ready to call Eve," he muttered.

Crossing the lawn on his way to the big house, he saw Jean coming toward him. This made him very uncomfortable as he was in such a state. He knew that he looked comical plastered, bandaged, and with a sling. Even Frank had laughed at him.

"Why, Jimmy," said Jean, looking prettier than ever and very much concerned, "what have they done to you? I read where they'd tried to kill you but I didn't know . . . I mean I thought you got away unhurt."

"I'm all scratched up, but nothing very serious. Dove through a window."

"Really? Glass and all?"

"Yeah. I didn't have time to open it."

Jean hesitated, then said:

"Jimmy, Dad's all up in the air. He's furious. I don't know what about. He sent for you, didn't he?"

"Yeah."

"Jimmy, promise me you won't quit. No matter what he says to you."

He lowered his eyes and stared at the grass.

"I don't know why I should take all this grief. He's my boss. If he fires me today, I quit on the spot. None of that week's notice stuff this time. I can only stand so much."

"I don't know what's got into Dad. Nobody can do anything with him but you."

"And I can't do much."

"Have you found out anything?"

Jimmy hesitated. There was nothing Jean could do. She might just get in the way. As a matter of fact, he'd just about given up himself on the girl angle. If a man like the boss wanted this girl as bad as he seemed to there wasn't much anybody could do. Gordon was healthy and in his right mind. And when you come right down to it, it was nobody's business but his own.

"No, Jean. Nothing of any importance. But if your Dad has got a girl what can I do about it? I'm just hired help."

"I see what you mean. I'm not just trying to interfere and run Dad's life for him. I'm only thinking about his best interests. He doesn't really know much about women, you know. He's pretty innocent."

Jimmy said nothing. He stood staring off over the lawn, trying not to look at Jean. Oh, but she was an eyeful today!

"Anyway, please don't quit. Try to soothe him down. We need you around here. Everything goes wrong when you're not around. Even the servants get on their high horses. Would you like more money, is that it?"

"I'm not worrying about the money," said Jimmy. "I just never have any time to myself; never a minute's peace. I can't live a normal life."

Jean hesitated.

"Eve gets very angry with you, doesn't she?"

"Yes."

"Well, why don't you marry her and bring her here to live? I liked her. She could play tennis with me and go swimming. Wouldn't that settle your problem?"

Jimmy winced. Yes, it was all very simple. It was just a casual matter to Jean. She cared no more about him than she did about the gardener or Jack! Why couldn't he wake up and forget his dream?

"Thanks, Jean. We'll talk it over."

Jimmy saw Smith beckoning to him from the porch.

"Eve seems like such a charming girl," said Jean. "Just the sort for you to marry. Both sensible and pretty. I imagine you're rather wild. She could hold you down."

"I'm getting tamer," said Jimmy, wearily. All Jean wanted was to arrange things so nicely for him that he'd stay in spite of the discomfort and look after her father! "Smith's giving me the high sign. I'll have to run."

"Please don't quit." Jean gave him one of those soft lovely looks. Giving him the works! Women were all alike. If they wanted something, they gave you the works.

"I'll do my best to keep my job," he said, then returned, crossed the lawn without looking back, and stepped on the porch beside Smith. "Hello, high pockets. How's the boy?"

Smith sniffed.

"Mr. Minot is very anxious to see you, Mr. Devore. In the library."

"Go to movies much, Smith?"

"Occasionally. The better sort. I don't care for those crook and police dramas."

Jimmy laughed.

"You're the perfect movie butler, Smith. Been studying 'em, eh?"

"Not that I was aware of. In the library, please."

Smith was very much hurt and turned away to hide his annoyance. "Just plain vulgar!" he muttered.

Jimmy found Gordon pacing the floor.

"Hello you gorilla," cried Gordon "If you will play around with toughs you'll occasionally get hurt. Made the front page, eh? What's all this nonsense about Sid Rogers trying to kill you?"

"He tried, but I was one jump ahead."

"You're sure her husband didn't come home and you had to jump from a second story window!"

"No, I leave that kind of stuff to you."

"Damn your insolence. There isn't another man in the world I'd take that from."

"You started it. I'm just two jumps ahead of the undertaker and you call me a liar."

"I was joking. However, you are a liar. Didn't you promise us you'd leave me in peace? I confided in you. You, of all people! And what happens? You go snooping around, trying to find out things that are none of your business. What do you mean going down to Miss Novak's apartment?"

"Which one?"

"Both of them."

"How many houses has she got?"

Gordon strode up and down, fuming.

"Don't try to put me off."

"And why the alias? Only crooks use phony names. And what about Welborn?"

"Welborn? Well, what about him?"

"He was down to see her last night."

Gordon whirled.

"What!"

"I saw him, but he didn't see me!" Jimmy explained.

Gordon looked at Jimmy for a long time, then he sat down.

"That's funny . . ."

"Boss," said Jimmy, "excuse me for saying so, but in my opinion this Novak dame is bad medicine."

Gordon was calm now.

"Why do you say that?"

"That's the way she strikes me. I'm not bragging, but I've known a lot of women. She sure is a knockout. Best looking dame I ever saw, I think. But it's skin deep. Not like Jean. She's out for what she can get."

Gordon waved all this away.

"Spare me this back-alley cynicism. In other words you've got nothing definite?"

"No, sorry to say. As a matter of fact, just the opposite. She's okay all-around as far as we can make out. I had her checked. She's from Kansas City. Graduated from the high school there. Honor student. Her old man runs a shoe store."

"That's funny." Gordon got up and began to pace the floor.

"Don't this check with her story?"

"To tell you the truth, no. I was under the impression she was from Cleveland. In fact she told me she was born there."

"Of course that don't mean much. You're big stuff to her, boss. She maybe was trying to make an impression."

"Maybe. She said she studied at the art school up there. She paints. Pretty well, too."

"Well, that don't make much difference. It's this Welborn business I don't like. She might be two-timing you, boss."

"Twenty minutes ago I'd've slapped any man's face for a remark like that. Except yours of course. That would just be a waste of time. But right now . . . it's funny! Especially about Welborn."

"You may have to get out the old checkbook to straighten this one out."

Gordon ignored this.

"You're sure that was Welborn?"

"I saw him. She called him Frank. I was behind the door right across the hall like I told you. When they were going out she said: 'Listen, Frank, there was a man here a minute ago.' Meaning me. She was suspicious."

"There's something mighty strange here."

"Maybe not. She may have been playing Welborn right along. Maybe she had a fight with him and she had him canned. Then she gets a chance to go for you and does. Maybe she makes up with Welborn."

"That's all very possible. But, Jimmy, you don't understand. I thought she was a very superior girl. Not a gold digger, or anything of that kind. I still can't believe it."

"Brace her about Welborn. You'll get a reaction if I know dames. I'll bet she can stand up for herself and talk smart and fast. But she may talk too smart and too fast if you see what I mean."

"I see. You know, Jimmy, you're not so dumb after all."

"Thanks. I've got another twenty to add to that expense account. That makes a hundred and seventy for miscellaneous expenses already this month."

"Go as far as you like. You're worth it. I'm sorry I talked to you the way I did. After all you're trying to protect me. If I were you, I'd get on the good side of Bush McEvoy. He's got no use for you whatever and to tell you the truth he's been prejudicing me against you. However, if Marie . . . well, time will tell!" Gordon sighed and stared out the window. "Don't laugh now, Jimmy. But this is sort of a blow for me. I'm so goddamned sick of mercenary women. If you had twenty or thirty million you'd know what I mean."

Jimmy smiled.

"You don't need twenty or thirty million. In some places you can find out with twenty or thirty dollars."

Gordon smiled wanly.

"Wise Guy Devore! I've lived a pretty sheltered life. Too sheltered, I guess. Well, run along, Jimmy. Take the afternoon off if you like. I'm staying home. I've still got a touch of something or other. Sanders thinks it's nervousness."

"Listen, if Eve will go out with me this afternoon do you suppose Scott would let her off?"

"I'll have Smith call the plant right away. You talk to Eve; then I'll talk to Scott."

It was good to hear Eve's voice.

"How about a show, honey?" said Jimmy. "Fred Astaire's at the High Street. Then some dinner at the New Dilling. Sound good?"

"I thought I had to call *you*, you big bluffer! Anyway, what's the matter with you? I got to work."

"Mr. Minot says you don't."

"Oh, got influence, I see. Well, if you'll promise not to fight with me or leave me in the middle of the show and disappear for hours, I'll come. Otherwise, no. And I'm still mad at you, anyway."

"Did you know a guy tried to kill me?"

"I heard about it."

"How come you didn't call me up?"

"Why should I? I told you I wouldn't."

"Well, Lord; when a guy almost gets killed . . ."

"I called Mr. Berger."

"Honey, I can hardly wait to see you. Got a proposition to make."

"Meet me at one? In front of the theatre?"

"I'll be there at twelve-thirty so I won't get bawled out."

After Jimmy had made himself as presentable as possible and had taken off the sling because he felt that he looked ridiculous enough without that, he glanced at his watch. Plenty of time. He'd show Eve that he could be punctual for once. But when he hurried down the steps of his bungalow he almost collided with Bush McEvoy, who had just come up the gravel path. McEvoy's big foreign car was parked on the road in front of the bungalow.

Jimmy started slightly with surprise.

"Hello," he said.

"Hello," said McEvoy. "Could I see you a minute, Devore?"

Jimmy groaned inwardly but said:

"Sure. Come in."

"No. This will do. We can sit on the porch."

They sat down. McEvoy studied Jimmy's face.

"Something about the plant?" asked Jimmy, lowering his eyes; McEvoy's pale intent gaze made him a little uneasy. Where had he seen eyes like that before?

"No. Personal matter. You don't like me much, do you?"

"I don't know you very well. Why should I like or dislike you?"

"Can't we do a little better than this?"

"In what way?"

"Let's speak our minds. You've been working against me with Gordon."

Jimmy smiled slightly.

"Why shouldn't I? You've never liked me. You've tried to prejudice Gordon against me. What do you expect?"

"I see. Suppose I were to tell Gordon that I'd changed my mind about you. That you were a swell fellow. What would your attitude be?"

Jimmy smiled, sparring for time. He made up his mind to play ball to a certain extent with this slick and dangerous guy. Maybe he could find out something. Maybe he could allay McEvoy's suspicions of him.

"I'll tell you how it is. If a man's friendly with me; I'm friendly with him."

"Speak more directly."

"Mr. McEvoy, I'm hired for one thing: to protect the boss. I try to do a straight job of it, and I think he'll tell you I'm worth what I get. When you try to throw a monkey-wrench in the machinery, I don't like it. Naturally he trusts you and likes you. You're his brother-in-law and a smart guy . . ."

"I know all that. What I want to know is, what am I suspected of and why do you persist in warning Gordon against me? Why are things getting too hot for me? Let's talk this out, Devore. You're a tough guy and I know it. I'm surprised to hear you rambling around like this."

Jimmy hesitated, then laughed.

"All right. I'll tell you. But it's old stuff now. I've given up on you. When those guys were killed practically in your front yard and then that dog came and jumped on you, me and Cap Berger began to get ideas."

McEvoy stared at Jimmy, then burst out laughing.

"Go on."

"Well, you must admit it looked mighty funny. We figured those guys came to blackmail you and you had them knocked off. Well, if a couple of rats like that were blackmailing you, there was something behind it. We wanted to find out what that was." Jimmy laughed. "We burned up the telegraph wires trying to find out something, but you were clean as a hound's tooth. Still we weren't satisfied till the Feds told us the thing looked like a Butch Crump job. Well, if it was a Butch Crump job, we felt pretty sure you didn't have anything to do with it. As he's a hot potato. You have to know your grapevine and you have to be somebody to get hold of him."

McEvoy laughed again. He seemed very much amused.

"Go on."

"Well, that's about all. We've practically given up. We haven't got a leg to stand on. But," said Jimmy with a grin, "naturally I wasn't going to make myself look like a chump to the boss, especially when you were putting a bug in his ear about me."

"So that's it. I'm clean as a hound's tooth but as far as Gordon's concerned, I'm still suspected of shooting people et cetera. This is very funny. However, Devore, maybe I can help you. I didn't say anything to you before because I didn't trust you. Besides, I didn't want to worry Gordon. This is confidential. As a matter of fact, I am responsible for the death of those men . . ."

"What!" Jimmy tried to look as pop-eyed as possible.

". . . indirectly. I don't understand it myself. But I've had threats of kidnapping for the last three months. I didn't do anything about it for several reasons. In the first place, I'm not easily scared. I always carry a gun and I'm a dead shot. In the second place, I didn't want to worry Gordon. He's much bigger game than I am, and he might expect the same. These two men both managed to talk to me. The Harter fellow bought a dog. The other fellow got to see me on some pretext; I forget what. I was just getting ready to take it up with the police when they were killed. I have no doubt they were killed due to some mix-up over the attempted kidnapping. By that Butch what-ever-his-name-is that you mentioned or by some other gangster. Their friends, I've no doubt. They might have had a row over the division of the money. They were demanding three hundred thousand. Maybe you can straighten it out. But there are the facts."

Jimmy laughed.

"Well, I always said as a detective I'm a good hod-carrier."

"Oh, I don't know. It probably did look rather bad for me. That's why I didn't mention the fact that I'd seen and talked to both of them. Now, Devore, you see? Maybe you'll stop riding me."

"It beats me."

McEvoy took a piece paper out of his coat pocket and handed it to Jimmy.

"Maybe this will help to convince you."

A few lines of coarse handwriting were scrawled in pencil on a sheet of cheap yellow paper.

> You may be godalmighty in this town but your just a duce
> to us. We will lay you out right on that same lawn where
> Roxy and the Dude got theres maybe you think we're
> kidding but you and some others is going to get a surprise.
> pay off like Roxy said or else.
>
> Tracer

"I see," said Jimmy. "Want me to look into this?"

"I'll handle it," said McEvoy. "I was supposed to take the money in fives, tens and twenties, and drive to McConnelsville alone. Then I was supposed to pick up a hitchhiker at a certain time at the third culvert between McConnelsville and the next little town. God knows from then on. They gave me ten days."

"Better watch your step."

"Things don't worry me. I can always look after myself," said McEvoy icily. "All I ask is that you don't tell Gordon any of this. He's very nervous right now." McEvoy got up. "I'd consider it a favor if you wouldn't even mention this to Berger. If I need your help I'll let you know. Now, let's shake hands, Devore, and stop fighting each other."

Jimmy shook hands, grinning.

"It's a deal."

But when McEvoy had climbed into his car and driven off, Jimmy muttered, "That was a mighty swell performance, Mr. McEvoy. I'm glad I saw you playing tennis with Jean and pulling your punches so she didn't even have the slightest suspicion. It's a good thing I'm bullheaded. What a smart guy!"

Then Jimmy glanced at his watch, and crying: "Oh, Lord!" He jumped into his car and almost ran over O'Brien, who appeared suddenly from the gatehouse.

"I'll be at the High Street," yelled Jimmy, "for about two hours, then I'll be at the New Dilling. Cocktail bar, Doric Room, or dining room. Open that gate, Mike. What's holding you back?"

"Okay, Jimmy," O'Brien shouted, then he burst out laughing. "You look like you'd been in a catfight. That cat must have had long claws."

Jimmy said something to O'Brien which made him wince, then he drove out, waved at Mike, and turned west on Pelham Road, already going very fast. He did not slacken speed when he reached the shopping center of Willow Wood. He hit the green on two traffic lights and ignored the third, which was red. At the edge of town he pushed the accelerator to the floorboard and the little car almost jumped out from under him. He was doing nearly 70 when he heard a siren. Glancing into the rearview mirror, he saw that a motor-cop was after him. Groaning, he pulled over to the side of the road. He'd have to humor this cop as he didn't want to be taken to the jug.

It was Tom Parker, an old friend of his.

"What is this, Jimmy, a test run?"

"Listen, Tom. Every time I meet my girl I'm late. She's going to give me the gate this time."

"You just sort of ignore red lights, don't you? And I didn't know one of those cheap hacks could do sixty going downhill. It must be your personality."

"Have a heart, Tom."

"Where you bound for?"

"Town. High Street Theatre."

"In a hurry, eh?"

"And how!"

"Well, old Cap told the boys to keep an eye on you and help you out if you needed it. I'm roving, anyway. Still trying to pick up that Illinois car. Follow me. I'll escort you in, bigshot!"

Parker started off with his siren going. Jimmy followed him, pushing his car for all it was worth to keep him in sight. Cars appeared from side roads, stopping suddenly with a violent yowling of brakes. People came out of their houses to stare. Jimmy began to feel like a fool. Parker went faster and faster, glancing back from time to time. Once, bursting through a suburban intersection, Jimmy barely avoided a lumber truck. Curses were hurled after him. He was thoroughly scared now but he wasn't going to let that wise guy Parker make a monkey out of him. At the edge of town, Jimmy sighed with relief when he saw

Parker slow down, then draw up to the curb and stop.

"There you are, Jimmy. But what delayed you?" Parker laughed, bending over his motorcycle. "You look funny enough without looking scared to death. What a pan!"

"All right, laugh! But you probably saved me from getting the air. Thanks."

Jimmy was feeling very high. He had met Eve on time and they had seen a good picture, and Eve was in a very good humor. Of course, they had quarreled a little about curly-headed Mr. Carter and Jimmy had talked so loudly several times in the show that people around him had stared and when he persisted had bluntly told him to shut up. Turning, he had said: "Shut me up." But Eve had soothed him and held his hand.

Now they were dancing in the Doric Room to a marimba orchestra and Jimmy had already drunk four cocktails and wanted another one.

"Jimmy," cooed Eve, with her cheek against his shoulder, "to look at you nobody would think you could dance like this."

"How come? What's wrong with my looks?"

"Why, you look like a cross between a scoutmaster and a bouncer."

"Thanks. I suppose you think *you* bowl 'em over."

"Don't I bowl you over?"

Jimmy laughed.

"You sure do. And can you dance! Yoosts like a fedder!"

"Fred Astaire's pretty good, too."

"He's not bad. But that's his racket. Of course if I'd really put my mind to it . . ."

The orchestra stopped. Eve stood laughing while Jimmy applauded. But the orchestra leader, acknowledging the applause, shook his head repeatedly, then said: "No more, friends. No more till later."

Jimmy and Eve walked off the floor arm-in-arm. Jimmy looked somewhat contemptuously at the tea dance crowd.

"Eve, how do you suppose all these lounge lizards live? Hanging around here every afternoon. Somebody must be keeping them."

"Nobody's keeping you. You're here. Anyway, what do you care? It's none of your business. Forget it. Let's have a good time for once."

"Okay. But these slick guys put my back up. That pretty boy of yours would look right at home here."

"He works hard. Please let up on him, Jimmy. He's just a side issue."

"I don't like side issues. And before I forget it. Will you marry me next week?"

"I don't think the boss will let me off." They sat down. Jimmy was so much on his good behavior that he remembered to place her chair for her and gently shove it under her. Although why an able-bodied woman couldn't sit down without help was a mystery to him! Eve loved all those little attentions: she often raked him over the coals because he was such a "boor" but when he wanted to be especially agreeable, he did his best, clumsily of course.

"Thanks, James. You're improving."

They had another cocktail.

"No fooling, Eve. Let's get married. We can live in the bungalow. You can quit your job. I'm making plenty. Jean says . . ." He bit his lip, but it was too late.

"Jean says what?" Eve's eyes gleamed.

"Well, I told Jean we were getting married," said Jimmy, stretching the truth a little, "and she said fine. You could swim with her and play tennis . . . she said she thought you were charming."

"Really, did she?"

A bellboy stepped up to the table.

"Wanted on the phone, Mr. Devore."

"This isn't Mr. Devore," said Eve. "He just left."

The bellboy smiled uncertainly. Jimmy hesitated, then got up.

"I'll be right back."

Eve compressed her lips.

"I'll give you fifteen minutes."

Jimmy smiled at her, then went out into the lobby. Mr. Worth motioned him to one of the desk phones.

"Hello," said Jimmy.

"O'Brien speaking. I just talked on the phone with a fellow who said his name was Ben. He said to tell you that girl you were asking about moved out just now. Paid her bill and blew, leaving no forwarding address."

"Thanks." Jimmy hung up and stood pondering.

"How are you today, Mr. Devore?" said the manager. "Did you come down with Mr. Minot?"

"No. I took an afternoon off. Drove down myself." Jimmy was turning away. A thought struck him. "Is Mr. Minot here?"

"Didn't you know? Yes, he came in about half an hour ago."

"Is he upstairs?"

"Yes."

Jimmy leaned on the counter and thought. There was something about this he didn't like. He wanted to ask about "Ann Jocelyn" but hesitated. Maybe he'd better keep his mouth shut. He was letting the manager know too much.

He was just getting ready to go back to the cocktail room when he saw Herb Atkins, one of the detectives Berger had assigned to the New Dilling, coming toward him across the lobby, walking very fast.

"I'm glad you're here, Jimmy," said Herb. "There's something I'm a little worried about."

"Spill it."

"I'm sort of moseying along the fourth-floor hall and I hear something fall. I don't know what. I listen. Nothing more. It was kind of faint, see, so I thought maybe I was hearing things. I take a stroll toward the High Street side; then I turn and come back. When I get kind of near Mr. M.'s apartment, I see a dame running down the hall. She turns at the end of the corridor and I lose her. This joint's all crisscrossed with hallways and so ..."

"How long ago was this?"

"Maybe fifteen minutes ago."

"Well, why didn't you say something to somebody!"

Atkins began to shake. This assignment had worried him all along. He began to stammer.

"But, Jimmy, Jeez, a lot of dames play tag in them halls. You know what I mean. I can't ..."

"Be quiet." Jimmy turned to the operator. "Ring Mr. Minot's apartment." The girl rang. No answer. She kept ringing. Still no answer. Jimmy got as pale as death. But presently the girl smiled and said: "Here's Mr. Minot for you." But instantly her smile faded and she stared at Jimmy, her mouth dropping open.

Jimmy grabbed the receiver.

"Boss! It's Jimmy ..."

"For God's sake, Jimmy. Come up at once. I've been ..."

There was a loud clatter. Jimmy stared, then hung up. He motioned for the manager to come over. When the manager saw the expression on Jimmy's face he began to tremble.

"Come with me," said Jimmy. "Bring a master key in case we need it. Come on, Atkins." Then he turned to the telephone girl who was still staring. "You didn't hear a thing, sister. Not a thing." On the way to the elevators, Jimmy touched first the manager's arm, then Atkin's. "Not so fast. Look calm. We don't want this all over the place."

CHAPTER SIX

Jimmy found the door of Gordon's suite locked. He turned to the manager.

"Try your key. If there's key on the other side I'll get it out for you."

The manager's hand shook so that Jimmy finally took the key away from him and unlocked the door himself. Turning, he saw a couple of women coming down the corridor, chattering, and laughing.

"Come in a minute, boys," said Jimmy, winking, then he opened the door and went in quickly, followed by the manager and Herb Atkins, who was pop-eyed with excitement and dread, and kept mopping his face with a dirty white handkerchief. Jimmy shut the door, then ran over to a huge lounge where Gordon was lying in a faint. Gordon's coat was off and his white silk shirt was covered with blood. He was very pale and was breathing heavily. "Don't touch anything," said Jimmy, sharply, as the manager, purely out of nervousness, began to rearrange some ornaments on a little side table.

"They tagged him," said Atkins, half crying, "they sure did!"

"North," said Jimmy, "get Dr. Sanders on the phone and tell him to come here right away. Atkins, when Worth gets through you call Berger and tell him I'd like to see him in Gordon's suite. Don't tell him anything else. Is there a phone in the bedroom? This one is busted."

"Yes," said Worth.

"Both of you use the one in there then, and don't touch anything else."

When the other two men had gone into the bedroom Jimmy looked around the big living-room till he found a bottle of whiskey in a wall-cabinet, then he poured out a stiff drink and tried to force some of it down Gordon's throat. At first Gordon lay limp, groaning and breathing heavily; but finally his eyelids fluttered, his lips opened, and he drank nearly all the whiskey Jimmy had poured out.

"Boss!"

"Jimmy . . . did you . . .? She ran after it happened. I don't think . . . yes, you were right . . . just another gold digger . . ."

"Did she shoot you, boss?"

". . . in my shoulder . . . terrible pain . . . I can hardly bear it . . . just like somebody hitting me with a sledge hammer . . . but she ran . . . that's what I . . ."

"Was it her, boss? Did she let you have it?"

"I don't think so. But I had my back turned. She ran when I asked her to . . ." Gordon turned his head away and tears started from his eyes and ran slowly down his cheeks.

Jimmy compressed his lips.

"Don't worry, boss. I'll get the so-and-so that did this."

"Is the doctor coming?"

"We're trying to get hold of him. I could get the hotel doctor but I'm not sure yet that I want him. What do you think, boss?"

"Wait for Sanders. We've got to hush this up."

"Right you are."

Jimmy paced up and down in an agony of worry. He could see that Gordon was very weak and seemed to be suffering terribly. But he was no doctor; he didn't know what to do. He felt absolutely helpless.

In a moment, North and Atkins came back.

"They will be right over," said Worth. "Is there anything I can do?"

"Yes," said Jimmy. "Go downstairs and threaten the telephone girl's life if any of this leaks out. I'll call you if I need anything."

"All right, Mr. Devore," said Worth, brightening, obviously relieved to be getting out of the room.

When he had gone, Jimmy turned to Atkins.

"Well?"

"Captain Berger's on his way. Will be here in a few minutes."

"Good. You go downstairs and wait in the lobby. Stay near the phones. If you want me, ring me up."

When Jimmy was left alone with Gordon, Gordon turned his head slowly to look at him.

"I should have listened . . ." he said.

"Everybody makes mistakes, boss. How you making it?"

"It's stopped bleeding, I think . . . but my shoulder . . . it's broken. I'm all numb on the left side . . ."

"Keep a stiff upper lip, boss. Doc'll be here in a minute."

An ambulance had been backed quietly into the big cement areaway behind the hotel and a stretcher had been taken up the freight elevator. Dr. Sanders gave Gordon a sedative, then he was put on the stretcher, covered completely with a sheet, and taken down to the ambulance without one guest in the hotel knowing a thing about it. At the door Jimmy spoke with the little Doctor, who seemed as upset as everybody else.

"What about it, Doc?"

"It's a curious wound. But shouldn't prove fatal. Gordon's a healthy man. Was he lying down when he was shot?"

"I don't think so. Why?"

"Call me later. I'll be able to give you some precise information then."

Jimmy closed the door and turned to Frank Berger, who was sitting on the lounge, staring thoughtfully at the floor.

"Well, they made a chump out of me," said Jimmy. "I was pretty sure Gordon was out of the woods."

"This is a funny one, Jimmy."

"It is. Listen, Frank, I'll tell you what I know. The door was locked. Gordon was in no shape to lock a door and didn't have any reason to, after the dame ran out on him. Poor guy! He's all cut up because the dame ran out on him when he was seeing the lights go out. He's a trusting kind of bird. Oh, well! I'll get on with it. Here's what I think. The dame locks the door on the outside, then pushes the key under it. It can be done. I tried it. I don't know how she got the key so far in, but that's a detail. Here's what beats me. There wasn't anybody in here except her and yet I'm pretty sure she didn't shoot him. He doesn't think she did. He said he had his back to her. Listen, Frank, I got a brainwave. It might have been just as big surprise to her as it was to him. Follow me?"

"I see what you're driving at. Well, if she gets out of this town I'll be surprised. Let me get my hands on her once and she'll talk."

"Okay by me. Frank, I been over this place with a fine-tooth comb. There's nothing except one of her gloves or one of somebody's. It's a little glove and she was kind of a little dame, but that's all one, anyway."

"Did you smell any gun smoke?"

"No, I didn't," said Jimmy. "But that big window over there is down all the way from the top."

Frank glanced at the window.

"Blank wall outside, eh?"

"Yeah. Of course somebody might have hid in here, or something like that. Only it don't seem logical. Anyway, if somebody had hidden in here why would they wait till the dame was here with him?"

"Might be a jealous boyfriend."

"It might. But that's too easy. No, there's something behind all this. I've got a feeling, a hunch."

"Play your hunches and go broke."

"All right. But I just feel that that dame was scared to death and got out without wasting any time."

"According to what you've told me, she took time to pitch the key under the door."

Jimmy shrugged and began to pace up and down. Frank shifted and lit a cigar.

"What worries me is how I'm going to hush this thing up. That's a real chore. I gave orders to hold the girl incommunicado if they nabbed her and if anybody gets wind, to stall them off. We've got to do a little stalling ourselves, Jimmy. Atkins is okay. But how about the doctor's people? And Worth?"

"He's all right. I'm not worrying about that. I'm only worrying about one thing." Jimmy turned toward Frank, his eyes glinting. "All I'm worrying about is getting the so-and-so that did it."

They sat talking and arguing for a while, getting no place, when the phone rang. It was Dr. Sanders. Jimmy talked to him.

"Well?"

"Devore, Gordon was either lying down when he was shot or he was shot from above."

"Yeah? How's he doing?"

"He's sleeping. He has a very good chance."

Jimmy hung up the receiver and stood staring at the floor. Suddenly, with an exclamation, he ran over and looked out the window. The blank wall stopped one story above the window. The building next door was an old one, five stories high.

"Well?" Frank demanded.

"He was shot from above or else he was lying down, the Doc said. Well, I'm pretty sure he was standing up from something he said. A guy could have shot him from that roof over there if he'd been standing at the window. I got an idea. You stay here, Frank. I'll be back in a minute. Take a look-see if you like. You're a real detective. You know all that S. S. Van Dine stuff. I don't."

Jimmy went down in the elevator, crossed the lobby hurriedly without looking to right or left, then he went into the building next door and asked the elevator man where he could find the janitor.

"Right at the end of the hall. In that little office."

Jimmy knocked on the office door and after a moment there was a surly "come in." Jimmy opened the door. He saw a big man about sixty sitting with his feet up on a battered desk, reading a form sheet. He didn't even look up.

"What do you want?"

"You the boss here?"

"I run the building. If you're selling anything, I don't want it."

"I'm looking for a little information. Get your nose out of that paper a minute."

Jimmy didn't like the man's attitude.

"Want to get tough, eh," said the janitor, lowering the paper and getting slowly to his feet. He was a huge man and towered over Jimmy. "Listen, I've throwed guys twice as big as you out of this building.

We're always being bothered with somebody. Scram, get me?"

"Wait a minute," said Jimmy, trying to calm the man down, "all I want is a little information. Have there been any guys on your roof today?"

"Who wants to know?"

"I do."

"You a copper?"

"No."

"Well, scram then. I don't answer questions around here unless I feel like it."

"You asked for it," said Jimmy, drawing a gun. "Want to talk?"

The man drew back a step, startled.

"Now wait. I don't want to get myself in no jam."

"You'll get yourself in a jam if you don't talk."

"Lower that gun a little, buddy. It makes me nervous. Now what's this all about?"

"I'm asking you not telling you."

"About those guys on the roof, they had badges. I thought they was okay."

"Describe them."

"Well, there was two of them. One was a little fellow, smaller than you yet. He had brown hair and a kind of pale complexion. Just an ordinary looking guy. Dressed about like you. The other guy was husky. Medium-sized guy. Kind of a red face. Had on a blue suit. Looked like a detective. Brother, I try to keep out of trouble, so when they flashed them badges, well, I told them to go as far as they liked, and forgot all about them."

Jimmy pondered. These descriptions didn't tally at all. He glanced up. The janitor was getting restless.

"Say, can I sit down?"

"Sure, sit down," said Jimmy, putting away his gun.

The janitor sat glancing nervously at the form sheet. Jimmy's silence worried him. Finally he looked up.

"Listen, mister, no matter what happened I didn't have nothing to do with it. I tend to my own business."

Jimmy was turning to go when a thought struck him.

"Anybody else on the roof this afternoon?"

"Yes," said the janitor, "there was. But he was working for the city. Something about the light wires. He was up there all afternoon."

"Describe him."

"Well, he had on overalls and his face was kind of dirty. Big tall fellow with black hair. Kind of gangling. Real nice fellow. We had a drink together. Don't need to worry about him. But he had the funniest tool kit or whatever it was. Looked almost like a golf bag."

Jimmy began to smile.

"What kind of eyes did he have?"

The janitor glanced up with a puzzled look on his face.

"Funny you'd ask me that! His eyes kind of had me worried at first. Sharpest, piercingest I ever saw on a human."

"Pale eyes?"

"Yessir. Nearly white they was."

Jimmy grinned.

"Thanks."

"Something wrong with that guy?"

"Don't ask questions." Jimmy turned to go. "Say, you don't care who runs around your roof, do you? You ought to charge admission."

The janitor winked.

"I do at night. You can see right in them hotel windows. Oh, boy!"

Jimmy put a five-dollar bill on the janitor's desk.

"Under your hat," he said.

The janitor was grinning now.

"What a surprise you turned out to be!" he said.

Jimmy rushed back to the hotel. He found Frank pacing up and down.

"I can't find a thing," said Frank.

"I found plenty. Butch Crump was up on that roof all afternoon. Say, what kind of a bunch of detectives have you got, Frank?"

Frank flushed slightly.

"I sometimes wonder."

"Anyway, we know what we're doing now. We got to nail that guy."

"We'll try the dragnet again about eleven tonight. We sure turned up some interesting specimens the last time. We found three guys wanted for murder."

Jimmy was just driving through the big estate gate when he remembered. Slapping his forehead, he cried:

"My God! Eve!"

Mike and Johnson stood looking at him, but without speaking to them, he made a U-turn in the drive, running over the edge of the flowerbed ("Oh! Oh!" cried Mike, knowing what the head gardener would say) and started for Pelham Road.

"Wait!" cried Johnson. "Message for you"

Jimmy paid no attention, so Johnson jumped on the running board.

"Headquarters called. They said to tell you they've got that girl. She was trying to leave town. Got her at the depot, I think."

"Thanks. Get off, Johnson. Got to go back to town."

Jimmy drove back to town faster than he had driven when Parker escorted him in. He miraculously avoided accidents and was cursed from one end of Steel City to the other. It was five o'clock when he parked his car near the New Dilling. Eve had been waiting for hours! Or maybe she'd gone home. He was in Dutch right now!

He ran across the lobby and hurried into the Doric Room, but the tea dance was over. Several couples were sitting in the almost deserted room. The musicians were just filing out.

"I need a drink," said Jimmy and hurried into the cocktail lounge. It was crowded. A four-man orchestra was playing—harp, violin, clarinet, and cello—and a blond girl was singing: "These Foolish Things." But nobody seemed to be listening. The place was a hubbub of loud chatter. A few couples were dancing among the tables. Jimmy stopped in his tracks. Eve was dancing with Carter, who looked very nice with his marcelled hair and his white linen suit.

"Eve!" called Jimmy, walking rapidly toward them.

She looked at him and shrugged.

"Well?"

"I'm sorry but I . . ."

"It doesn't matter. Please go away. Can't you see we're dancing?"

"Is that what you're doing?"

Carter looked at him sharply.

"Hello, Defore."

"Hello, Carp. I'm going to cut in."

"Oh, no you're not," said Eve, decisively, and when Jimmy insisted, she turned to one of the waiters. "Waiter, will you put this man out. He's bothering me."

Jimmy's face got brick red. People stopped talking to stare at him.

"If you please, sir," said the waiter, smiling.

Jimmy turned and stamped out of the lounge. He heard people laughing behind him. He ground his teeth and clenched his fists. But this was no time for a rough house. He had work to do.

"If she wants to play that way, all right!" he muttered as he got into his car.

There seemed to be considerable activity at Headquarters. Phones were ringing loudly all up and down the corridor. The door of the office of the homicide squad was open and Jimmy heard loud talking, which sounded like an argument. An old friend of Jimmy's, Lieut. Brady, stepped out into the corridor from Berger's office. He grinned when he saw Jimmy.

"Hello, Mike," said Jimmy. "What's all the excitement?"

"Red McMahon was seen in the Willow Wood district but he got away and Ed Schiff and Parker are getting a dressing down. Boy, was the chief burning! He and Berger almost had a fist fight. Frank got his police commissioner job today and the chief told him he ought to be demoted instead of promoted. Frank took off his badge and threw it on the chief's desk. Then the chief called the mayor and for some reason the mayor gave him hell. We're all going to get kicked around till we run them rats out of town or plug them. I'd like to have that Crump guy in the front office with me for ten minutes, no holds barred. I'll bet his own mother wouldn't know him." Mike was six-foot three and weighed two hundred and fifty pounds; he was the strongest man on the force and a great amateur hammer thrower.

"I want to see Frank."

"He said to go right in. Say, if I ain't too inquisitive, who's that doll Frank's got in there? I'd sure leave my happy home for that baby."

"It's a secret, Mike," said Jimmy, smiling.

"I might know you'd be in on it. I never did get any of the breaks. Women don't like me, anyway. They always want me to be a father to them."

Jimmy laughed and slapped big Mike on the back.

"Wouldn't mind having a father like you myself. I could call everybody all the names I pleased."

"Oh, you don't do so bad as it is. I never saw you backing down much. When you first came on the force I thought you was the most impudent little devil I ever saw. Boy, how you've come up in the world. How do you like associating with the rich?"

"I like the boys around here better."

"Blarney! But we like it."

Jimmy grinned at Mike, then he opened the door of Berger's office and went in. Several policemen were sitting around staring at nothing. A clerk was busy pounding a typewriter.

"Shall I go in the boss's private office?" Jimmy asked the clerk.

"Sure, Devore. Go right ahead."

Jimmy knocked on the glass-paneled door, then he went in. Frank was sitting at his desk, smoking a cigar and looking very tired and thoughtful. Marie Novak was pacing the floor. Jimmy glanced at her quickly.

"Well, Frank?"

"Hello, Jimmy. Miss Novak, I believe you know Mr. Devore."

The girl turned and looked at Jimmy. Her face was pale and slightly haggard, but her eyes were beautiful, large, dark, and shining.

"Oh, yes. We've met."

Jimmy cleared his throat uncertainly. He was afraid of this girl's power. Afraid of the appeal of that magnificent body tightly sheathed in silk. Afraid of the shrewd feminine brain he sensed behind those lovely eyes.

"We weren't formally introduced," said Jimmy with a sneer, "but I know this dame pretty well. Too well. And so does Gordon." Much to his surprise he didn't feel at all antagonistic toward the girl. He was putting on an act with some difficulty.

"She doesn't choose to talk till she sees her lawyer," said Frank with a slight smile. "She can't seem to understand that she's not going to see a lawyer for at least twenty-four hours and that she's being held for murder."

"That's absurd," said the girl. Then she turned to Jimmy and looked at him appealingly. "He's the most heartless man," she went on, pointing at Frank.

Jimmy turned his back. He had begun to glow all over. She was giving him the works, like Jean, like Eve, like all women; and she was doing a mighty good job of it. He'd always been a sucker for women. But this time he'd have to steel himself and forget his own feelings. He turned to Frank.

"Come outside. I want to see you a minute."

Frank got up and they went into the outer office, ignoring the girl. When Frank had shut the door, Jimmy said:

"Well?"

"I can't get anything out of her. I swore I'd strongarm her if I had to, but I can't. I just can't. Women and police work just don't mix."

"I know. But this is damn serious. We know now that Butch was after Gordon. That puts a new face on things. We got to work fast. God knows what McEvoy's up to. I don't get the point of having Gordon shot at all. My head's going around."

"Everybody's heads are going around down here. Red McMahon slipped through the boys' fingers and the Old Man is about to commit suicide."

"Did she admit anything?"

"She admitted she was living at the New Dilling under an assumed name. That's all. She implied that Gordon was keeping her. Paying all her bills, and that it wouldn't look well in the papers, that we'd better go easy. One of those things."

"Are you clear on the newspapers?"

"Absolutely."

"Let me talk to her."

"Go to it, Jimmy. If you need help, yell." Frank smiled grimly. "And don't lock the door."

Jimmy flushed and avoided Frank's eyes. He would hardly admit to himself that he was anxious to be alone with this girl. Without another word, he went back into the private office and shut the door.

Marie was sitting on the edge of Frank's desk swinging her foot, and displaying a good deal of leg. Jimmy stared past her resolutely.

"Sister," he said in his toughest voice, "the chief gave me a free hand with you and if you knew me better, you'd know what that means."

Marie laughed.

"I don't think you're very tough. I think you're cute."

Jimmy took a step toward her.

"Listen, sister . . ." He clenched his right fist. "For two cents I'd spoil that mug of yours. Getting my boss knocked off. You don't know how I feel about Gordon Minot. He's the best guy that ever lived. He . . ."

Marie put out her hand and touched his arm.

"I'm not afraid of you. Don't keep pretending. I like Gordon as well as you do."

Jimmy hesitated and drew away from her. All the heat had gone out of him. A guy just couldn't bulldoze a dame like this.

She had two strikes on him before he started. "Why couldn't we have picked up Red McMahon?" he uttered. "I'd've wiped up the office with him." Then he looked at her: "Sister, you don't seem to realize what a spot you're in."

"I realize only too well. I'm trying to think what to do. I know I'm in a spot. But will talking help me? That's what I'm wondering." She got up, crossed the room, and came close to Jimmy. "I know how you stand. Gordon often talked about you. He said he couldn't like you any better if you were his own son. Gordon wouldn't want anything to happen to me. You can help me, Jimmy. Will you?" She smiled very sadly; there were tears in her eyes. "You'll never be sorry."

Jimmy recoiled. In that simple sentence and with that sad smile she had conveyed so much, Jimmy's scalp tingled. He was almost irresistibly drawn toward her. He turned roughly away from her, trying to control his desires, which were clambering, and to take an objective view of her. She was all artifice: a woman cunningly designed to make suckers out of all men. He kept telling himself that.

"Oh no," he said, harshly. "Gordon wouldn't want anything to happen to you! You almost broke his heart when you ran out on him after he'd been shot."

Marie looked at him with interest.

"Then you don't think I shot him?"

"I know who shot him."

She came toward him again, all smiles.

"Well, sweetness," she said, "why didn't you say so?"

Jimmy started. She put her hands on his shoulders. They stared at each other for a long time.

"It looked bad, didn't it?" she demanded.

"Yeah," said Jimmy, pulling away from her hurriedly. "And this would look worse if Frank would happen to come in."

"You know," said Marie, sitting down, "I like your type. Hardboiled and good-looking. Most men are one thing or the other. But you're both. Too bad I didn't meet you at the plant."

"It was a break for me. Say, sister, how about this Welborn guy. Which was he? Or was he both?"

"You put Gordon up to it, didn't you? Oh, he was furious with me about Welborn."

"What lies did you tell Gordon about him?"

"I told him the simple truth."

"Tom never told the simple truth in his life."

Marie laughed.

"Oh, you funny man. I like you."

"If you aren't the screwiest dame! Don't you know you're being held for murder?"

"Why, you just said you knew I didn't do it."

"Yes. But I'm going to have a warrant sworn out for complicity."

Marie jumped up.

"I want to see a lawyer."

Jimmy laughed.

"You'll see no lawyer, and we'll bury you in that jailhouse till we see fit to let you out. You'll see nobody. You meddled with the wrong guy this time. Gordon owns this town. Get me?"

There was a long silence.

"Jimmy," she said in a little-girl voice, "if I talk will you protect me?"

"Yes, if you didn't have anything to do with getting Gordon knocked off."

"Oh, I didn't. I swear I didn't."

"If you'll help Frank and me there isn't anything we won't do for you."

Marie smiled.

"Is that a promise?"

Jimmy turned away.

"Sure it's a promise. We'll see that you get the best while you're in this joint, and we'll protect you when you get out. Come on. Talk. I haven't got all day. McEvoy had you canned. Go ahead."

"Don't you want a stenographer to take this down?"

"No. I'm handling this. Talk."

"Well, I met Frank Welborn at a party on the South Side. I was out of work. I told him I was an expert stenographer and he got me a job at the plant . . ."

"And went for you in a big way."

"Why not? I was promoted several times. Mr. McEvoy went for me in a big way, too, and there was a row. Jimmy, excuse me for interrupting. I said you were tough. But you're really just an infant with a gun in your pocket. McEvoy is really tough. How a man like him ever got so tough I don't know. Well, pretty soon, being just a stenographer, I got the worst of the row. I was fired. I'm not used to getting the worst of things, so I didn't take it very well. McEvoy tried to bluff me but I'm not easily bluffed. I waited around till I saw Mr. Minot. I'd always heard how unapproachable he was. It makes me laugh to think of it now; he was so easy! He said he wouldn't give me my job back in the plant. He had something better for me to do. He was going to write a book and wanted me to help him. He offered me a hundred dollars a week. Well, I was pretty sure what that meant, but we worked for three days before he even smiled at me. He's such a nice man." She sighed and stared at the floor.

"Go ahead," said Jimmy.

"Pretty soon Welborn found out about it. How, I don't know. He began bothering me, so I had to take that place where you saw me; that dump, you know. I couldn't take a chance on Gordon seeing me with Welborn in the hotel."

"Kind of go for this Welborn guy, eh?"

"I used to till I met Gordon. Gordon sort of makes other men seem like such awful creatures. Don't look at me like that. I'm not trying to be ladylike. I mean it. Well, Welborn started giving me money. Lots of money. Too much. I got suspicious and began to ask questions. Welborn told me to shut up and keep right on the way I was going. By the way, what sort of men work for John Minot and Company? Welborn is another tough one. Almost as tough as McEvoy. Of course around the office they're all smiles. But when they're themselves, they're really astonishing. Anyway, I began to get worried about Gordon; I really did. Today I almost told him to be careful. But he started on me as soon as he saw me and I never could get a word in."

"Tell me how he was shot!"

"I don't know. We were having a row and we were both pacing up and down. He was going one way and I was going another. We had our backs to each other. Suddenly I heard sort of a click, then an awful sound like somebody tearing a thick piece of cloth. I looked around. Gordon was staggering and pretty soon he fell. He begged me to help him. I saw the blood all over his shirt. I can't stand blood. I just lost my head. I put my hat on and ran out."

"Did you lock the door?"

"Yes. I locked the door and put the key under it and gave it a kick."

"Why?"

"I don't know. It was just a wild idea. What scared me most was, I had forgotten one of my gloves."

"I've got it in my pocket."

"Oh," cried Marie, "it was awful, seeing him like that. Poor man. He thought I was such an angel till today."

Jimmy got up.

"Thanks, Marie," he said. "I'm glad you had sense enough to talk. This is just what we need. Sorry, but we're going to have to lock you up again. But don't worry. I'm handling this. There'll be no charges against you, and when we get this thing cleared up, Gordon will take care of you. Plenty of dough, I mean. I'll see to it."

Marie gave a little laugh, then she came toward Jimmy so quickly he couldn't avoid her. Before he knew it he had his arms around her and was trying not to kiss her. The door opened suddenly, Frank stepped in, then shut the door quickly. Jimmy moved away from Marie, flushing.

"Well," said Frank, frowning, "you seem to be doing all right. Through?"

"All through," said Jimmy. "Marie told me the whole story. She's in the clear, but I've got some swell dope for you."

Frank sat down at his desk and, without looking at Marie, rang for a matron. When she appeared he said:

"Take Miss Novak back to her cell. Nobody's to talk to her or see her, understand?"

Jimmy touched the matron on the arm.

"She can draw on me for anything she wants."

"Yes, Mr. Devore."

Marie smiled, then came over to shake hands with Jimmy.

When the matron had taken her out, Frank jumped to his feet and confronted Jimmy.

"You damned little pushover! I might have known . . ."

Jimmy flushed with anger.

"Sit down. Not so fast. I got the story. What are you kicking about?"

"You got *her* story. I'll bet she tied you in knots."

"Maybe. But her story checks with my own hunch. You couldn't get a line out of her."

"I don't comb my hair the right way, I guess!" Frank began to pace the floor. "Well, let's have it."

Jimmy told Frank the story from beginning to end.

"Sounds all right. She's got no record. Can't find a thing against her," said Frank, grudgingly. "You did a pretty good job at that, Jimmy. But I think I came in at just the right time. You idiot! I thought you were done with all that stuff since you've been going with Eve."

"I am! I am!" muttered Jimmy. "But that dame . . . I don't know . . . No wonder she had Gordon eating out of her hand!"

Frank sat down wearily.

"This is getting to be too much for me. What do we do next?"

Jimmy started to pace the floor. Vague plans were running through his mind. Walking to a table at the far end of the office he began absently to finger some papers. After a while he glanced down at them. They were handbills from various cities and states, carrying descriptions and mug shots of Butch Crump and Red McMahon. He stared at them vacantly, still trying to evolve some plan of action. Suddenly he clapped his hands together.

"Frank," he cried, "I've got it. I've got the thing that's had me down all this time."

Outside, phones began to ring; there was the sound of men running in the corridors. A gong rang some place. Frank got up.

"What's all the uproar?" he cried. "And what are you smiling about?"

"Butch Crump is McEvoy's brother. I knew I'd seen those eyes someplace. But that's not it, Frank. I've got something better than that. Listen: 'Wallace C. Crump, alias Butch Crump, alias Walter Wallace, alias Blackie Wallace, alias Wallace Selby.' Didn't you say McEvoy's name was Selby?"

"Good Lord!" cried Frank.

"It's an old Omaha handbill. You must have overlooked it."

The door burst open. Mike Brady rushed in followed by Ed Schiff.

"Boss . . ."

"What's up?"

"This is the worst yet. Somebody tried to kill Mr. McEvoy, Mr. Welborn and Mr. Bayliss."

"What?"

"Mr. Bayliss got it the worst. Mr. Welborn got shot in the hand. They missed Mr. McEvoy."

"Were they all together?"

"No. This is the pay-off. All in different places."

Jimmy stared at Frank, then sank into a chair.

"Where do we go from here?" he demanded.

CHAPTER SEVEN

Jimmy sat with his feet on the desk staring glumly out of the window. It was dark now. All along High Street the electric signs were blazing. On the desk in front of him was a tray of food which he had left untouched. He had a coffee cup in his hand from which he took an occasional sip. Frank was eating from his own tray very fast and very hungrily.

"I wish I could eat like that," said Jimmy, sighing, "but my stomach's all tightened up."

"I never let anything interfere with my meals. A man's got to stoke up every so often."

The phone rang. It was the operator in the outer office.

"Sorry, Mr. Devore. I can't locate Miss Barry."

"Keep trying." Jimmy hung up with disgust.

"In Dutch as usual, I see."

"Yes, and this time it's not my fault. She just got sick of me leaving her around places. Well, Frank, what's next?"

"We'll have to wait till Brady comes in. I've got every man I can get my hands on looking for Crump, McMahon and Sid Rogers. I've got three men out at Gordon Minot's helping O'Brien, just in case. I don't know what else I can do. Say, Jimmy, about Crump being McEvoy's brother. That handbill business might be a coincidence, and you might have imagined it about their eyes looking alike. Anyway, how can we prove it without going to a lot of trouble?"

"Forget it. The way things are now, it wouldn't do us any good, anyway. I'll just keep it up my sleeve."

"Besides, both McEvoy and Welborn have requested a bodyguard. They surely act scared. What a mess!"

"You know, I told you about that threatening letter McEvoy showed me. We both thought it was a phony. Now God knows!"

"Yeah. But what about Crump gunning for Gordon?"

"I wish I knew the answer."

Mike Brady knocked and came in.

"There's only one good point about the whole business," said Frank. "We were able to release the story about Mr. Minot being shot and tie it up with the others. But what a row, Jimmy? Have you seen the papers? 'Citizens demand martial law. Attempt made to wipe out all high officials of John Minot and Company.'" He glanced up. "Hello, Mike. Sit down. Look at this in *The Call*: 'Aftermath of the general strike. Wholesale butchery of the men who handled the strike situation attempted. Police apparently helpless. Expert reporters term it work of professional killers. Mr. Minot and Mr. Bayliss in critical condition. Mr. Welborn escapes with slight wound. Mr. McEvoy displays great presence of mind. Citizens are telegraphing the Governor for troops. In our opinion this situation borders on anarchy.' How do you like that?"

"Since you think I'm screwy," said Jimmy, glumly, "you tell me what it's all about."

Frank shrugged and turned to Brady.

"Well, Mike?"

Big Mike shook his head sheepishly.

"We can't find out a thing. Nothing much, that is. Bayliss was shot from a balcony window. He'd just got through taking a bath. Nobody saw anybody or heard anything. Somebody took a few potshots at McEvoy from behind his front hedge. The bullets broke two windows and I'll bet they didn't miss his head two inches considering where the glass was busted. Welborn got a look at the guy that shot him. Said he was tall and he had black hair and looked like a workman. Had on dirty overalls. Had dirt on his face, too. Welborn had a gun and shot back. That's what saved his life. This other guy was too busy ducking. I guess you know all about Mr. Minot. I couldn't find out a thing at the hotel. But Herb said you had the dope, anyway."

Frank grinned at Jimmy.

"Looks like our old friend was shooting at Welborn. No, Jimmy; you're all up in the air."

Jimmy thought for a long time, staring at the floor; finally he muttered:

"Do you suppose those guys are that smart?"

"What's that?" Frank demanded.

"Nothing, nothing."

The phone rang. It was the operator again.

"Miss Minot to speak to you, Mr. Devore."

Jimmy sat up and showed a little interest.

"Yes, Jean."

"Are you all right, Jimmy? So many people have been shot and I'm so . . . oh, I hardly know what to do."

"How's the boss?"

"Pretty bad, I think. But Dr. Sanders says he thinks he has a chance. Gordon keeps talking about you. Telling how smart you are and how he should have listened to you."

Jimmy flushed.

"I'm not so smart. Tell him I said so. Tell him if I was so smart he wouldn't be lying there in bed. It was my job to keep him out of trouble and I fell down on it."

"You mustn't take it like that, Jimmy. Gordon says if he gets well the first thing he's going to do is make you Director of Welfare."

"Tell him to forget it. How's Mr. Bayliss?"

"I had him moved over here. They were going to take him to a hospital but I wouldn't let them. He's safer here and I can look after both him and Dad."

"You're a great kid, Jean. Excuse me for saying so, but I don't mean anything fresh."

"I know you don't. I think the same about you. When will you be out?"

"I can't say. O'Brien and the Headquarters men doing all right?"

"Yes. I feel pretty safe now, but I'd feel safer if you were here. You don't know how dependent we are on you, Jimmy."

Jimmy cleared his throat, then he took out his handkerchief and ostentatiously wiped his nose.

"I'm going to get my hands on the guys that did this if it takes a year. You tell Gordon."

"Don't get yourself killed, Jimmy; and call us up from time to time. Bye."

Jimmy hung up the receiver slowly and sat looking at the desk. Lucky Bayliss!

"Well?" said Frank.

Jimmy exploded.

"Stop 'Welling' me! That was Jean Minot. She just wanted to know if everything was all right."

Frank shrugged.

Jimmy took up the receiver again.

"Are you still trying to locate Miss Barry?"

"Yes, Mr. Devore. I'll ring you if I get her."

Mike stared.

"Miss Barry?" he said. "You mean Eve, that girl you go around with, Jimmy?"

"Yes."

"Why, she's sitting out there in the hallway."

Jimmy jumped up.

"Sure you know her?"

"I've seen you with her. In fact, she spoke to me. I thought you knew she was waiting for you."

Jimmy ran out, crossed the outer office in three strides, opened the door into the hallway. Eve was sitting on a bench reading a magazine. Two policemen, sitting across from her, were staring at her sleepily. When she saw Jimmy she got up quickly.

"Eve! What on earth!"

"Well, I knew you had to come out some time."

"But why didn't you let me know? I almost drove the operator in there off his nut trying to get you. What's the big idea?"

"Still mad?"

"I'm way too busy to be mad. But, Eve, that was a dirty trick you played on me at the New Dilling."

"Oh, I was burning up. I thought you were just giving me the runaround again all on account of some little thing. Maybe Jean wanted some flowers delivered or something. But I see by the papers . . . Gee, isn't it awful!"

"I'm up to my neck. But I still don't see why you didn't let me know you were out here."

Eve smiled, looking very pretty, Jimmy thought.

"I just wanted to show you I could wait for you."

Jimmy grinned, then his face darkened.

"Where's our handsome friend Mr. Carp?"

"He's outside in his car. I told him to go away but he wouldn't. He's still waiting. I looked out the window and saw him."

"Let me handle that guy. I'll bet he'll go away when I get through talking to him."

Eve took hold of his arm.

"No, now, Jimmy. It's all my fault. He left his office early to meet me at the hotel. He's really a very nice fellow. Honest. He wants me to marry him. He asked me tonight."

"You're going to marry me if I can ever get around it, so that's flat and I don't want any arguments. I'd sure like to talk to that guy a minute."

Eve's face darkened.

"If you go out there and make a row, I . . . I don't know what I'll do. I'll let him take me home, that's what I'll do. Don't think he's afraid you; he isn't."

"We'll see." Jimmy started down the corridor but Eve grabbed hold of him and held on.

The policemen on the bench couldn't contain themselves any longer. They burst out laughing. Jimmy turned, his eyes blazing.

"You think it's funny, eh?"

The policemen roared. Eve blushed, then she began to laugh, too.

"You awful idiot!" she cried.

Jimmy stood staring at the policemen for a minute, then he began to laugh. How ridiculous they must have looked tugging each other up and down the hallway of a police station! They were all laughing when the door opened and Frank Berger glanced out into the corridor. The policemen froze immediately.

"Jimmy," said Frank. "I've got some funny information."

Jimmy hesitated.

"Is it all right for Eve to wait in the outer office?"

"Why, sure."

Jimmy took Eve firmly by the arm and escorted her in.

"You're not going to get away from me tonight."

Frank smiled.

"What's the matter children, fighting?"

"He's doing the fighting as usual," said Eve.

"Oh, sure," said Jimmy. "Have a chair, Eve. Don't let these hard-looking mugs around here scare you. They're harmless. Sorry we haven't got any old Police Gazettes for you to look at. But there's all the evening papers."

She smiled up at him looking very happy. He smiled back, then followed Frank into his private office and closed the door.

"Nice girl, Eve is," said Frank.

"You bet. I'm going to get married as soon as we get this mess straightened out."

Big Mike grinned.

"Talk about trouble. You ain't seen nothing yet. Wait till you get married. Then the fun will really begin."

They sat down.

"Remember Joe Cianelli?"

"Sure."

"Well, you know how scared he was. He thought he was going up sure when Butch tried to knock you off, Jimmy. I felt pretty certain he didn't have anything to do with it. So I let him go. But I made him report once a week. He just called. A lot of shady guys hung around his place, you know. He gets an earful now and then. Well, he told me that he'd heard that Brick Morton just got in town . . ."

"The big-time bandit!"

"That's the guy. Joe thinks there's something up. Of course we know there's plenty up. But what Brick Morton's got to do with it, I don't know."

"Got any record of Butch and Brick ever being in on anything together?"

"Well, some of the boys thought that Red, Morton and Butch knocked over that bank in Hammond the time the three guys got sixty grand."

Jimmy jumped up.

"What day's this?"

Frank told him, looking bewildered.

"I mean date! Date!"

"Thirty-first."

"And tomorrow's the first. Frank! I've got it! Look, you've got to listen to me this time. If I steer you wrong, why, there's no damage done. I'll want some help tomorrow and some men. First of all, I want Brady, and I'll want at least three squad cars. Okay?"

Frank smiled slightly.

"Anything you say, Jimmy. This is probably just another one of your pipe dreams, but I'll take a chance."

Big Mike grinned.

"There'll be rough stuff. I know that. That's why he wants me along."

Jimmy turned to him.

"Mike, step outside, will you? I want to talk to Frank alone. And, Mike; tell Eve I'll be out as soon as I can."

When they were driving home, Eve said:

"Why so silent, Jimmy?"

"Just thinking."

"Are you going to take that vacation? I'd like to go to Marvin Lake some time this summer."

Jimmy turned to look at her.

"Yeah?"

She laughed.

"I mean, of course, if we get married on your vacation."

"That was the idea. All set?"

"I've been all set for two years."

"You women!"

"You were always getting out of hand. Jimmy, you're kind of difficult. I often wonder what kind of a husband you'll make."

"I'll do my best. That's as good as a preacher can do."

They rode along in silence. Jimmy kept to the back streets where there was hardly any traffic and he could tell very easily if he was being followed. With the town full of guys like Butch, Red McMahon and Brick Morton, Lord knows what might happen.

Finally Eve said, half to herself:

"Well, I hope you're over this Jean business."

Jimmy groaned.

"Are we going to start all over?"

"My error!"

"Look, Eve, let's forget all about Jean. That was just one of your wild ideas. Say, I wonder if there are any empty apartments at your place. I got a hunch I'd better stay there all night, and not try to drive clear to Willow Wood."

"Yes, I think they have," said Eve turning to look at him.

"Is it that bad, Jimmy? Gee, I'm getting scared."

"They tried it once. They might try it again. But don't you worry, honey. You'll be all right."

Nevertheless, when Jimmy had kissed Eve goodnight and had gone into the apartment on the front the manager had assigned to him, he turned out all the lights, carefully locked the door, then he drew a chair up in front of the big street window and sat looking out till morning.

Sitting at Frank's desk in the harsh late morning light, Jimmy and Frank were both a little pale. Neither of them had slept the night before and even Frank, who had boasted that nothing interfered with his appetite, had eaten but little. From time-to-time Jimmy took a sip of whiskey from a glass at his elbow.

Spread out before them was a large detailed map of the city. Jimmy kept running his finger along a certain roadway and they both argued at great length. Jimmy often lost his temper and shouted, but Frank was very patient with him. After a while they sat silently staring out the window, seeing nothing.

"Well," said Frank, trying to smile, "we'll be the laughing stock of the city if this is just another one of your pipe dreams. But if you've got the right hunch we'll be the talk of the town."

"I know," said Jimmy, wearily. He got up and began to pace the floor. "Somehow, since sunrise, I haven't felt so sure about it. These guys are the smartest I've ever been up against. Course they haven't got any idea how much I know. And smart guys are always a little inclined to overestimate themselves. But I don't know . . . Oh, well. Say, Frank, before the show starts (if it does start) I want to thank you for everything you've done. You've sure been regular."

Frank laughed.

"After all, I wouldn't be a commissioner if it wasn't for you. Forget it."

"If it wasn't for Gordon, you mean." Jimmy glanced at the clock. "Well, I guess we better be getting started."

The phone rang. Frank answered it.

"Yeah? Oh, that's good. Well, keep up the good work. Haven't noticed anything out of the way? I see. But you can't be sure, eh? All right.

Don't call back anymore. We're leaving right away." He hung up.

"Well?" cried Jimmy, unable to control his excitement.

"The boys are located. They've got a clean sweep of the whole street. Atkins says he thought a couple of fellows in an old Ford were on the prowl but he couldn't be sure."

"I hope he's right. Come on, Frank. If I sit here much longer I'll be biting my fingernails. Boy, that's powerful whiskey. I'm glad you told me to go light."

"You forget you haven't eaten anything. Better take a look at your guns, Jimmy."

Jimmy took out both his guns and examined them carefully, then he slipped the big automatic back into the shoulder holster and, unbuttoning his vest, put the little one down inside the waistband of his trousers.

Mike Brady knocked and came in.

"All set, boss?"

"Yes," said Frank. Then he picked up two typewritten sheets from his desk and handed them to Mike. "Here's the instructions. One for each car. Jimmy and I will be in the other car. Follow them to the letter, and watch your time schedule. Jimmy did the typing so don't blame my stenographer."

"Yes sir. I'm raring to go," said Mike. "I hope to God I get near enough to that Butch Crump guy to swing on him." Mike glanced from one to the other. "In case we're after him, I mean." Mike grinned.

"You'll never get that close to him without getting full of lead," said Jimmy. "All right, Mike. We're ready. When our car starts, the other cars are to start. All set, Frank?"

The three of them walked down the corridor in silence and out into the blazing sunlight of High Street.

"What a day!" exclaimed Mike, already beginning to sweat.

Two detectives, Carlson and Smith, were waiting for Jimmy and Frank with a squad car. Two other squad cars were parked across the street. Mike got into one of them. Frank nodded.

"All right," he said to Carlson, who was driving. "Go straight down High Street, then turn left at Wall and take the first alley to the right and keep on it."

Carlson and Smith exchanged a glance. They wondered what was up. Nobody knew the plan in its entirety except Frank and Jimmy.

The car pulled away. Behind them the two other cars made U-turns and followed. At the corner of Wall and High Street the cars diverged; Frank's car to the left, the other two to the right.

"Keep your fingers crossed, Jimmy," Frank said.

"I wish I had my rabbit's foot." Jimmy tried to appear calm, even indifferent, but he was extremely pale and from time to time a shiver would pass through him. He mentally cursed himself and finally lit a cigar Frank had given him, hoping it would steady him. He threw it violently from the car.

"That's not a campaign cigar either," said Frank, looking at Jimmy out of the corner of his eye.

"I'm just all upset inside," said Jimmy, apologetically. "All that whiskey on an empty stomach."

They rode for a long time in silence. Then Frank said:

"Stop at the drugstore on the corner of Eleventh and the alley."

Carlson double-parked.

"This okay?"

"Yes. Wait here. Come on, Jimmy."

Jimmy and Frank sauntered into the drugstore. Herb Atkins was buying a pack of cigarettes.

"Why, hello, Herb," said Frank. "Haven't seen you in a long time. How's things?"

The counterman was making change and paid no attention to the three men. When he returned with the change Frank bought a few cigars, choosing carefully, and arguing a little, then Jimmy took out a penny and weighed himself. Herb and Frank stood close by, waiting, then took their turns on the scales. The store was almost deserted. A woman was buying some perfume in the back. No one was paying any attention to the three men.

"Well," said Frank.

"We got the whole front of the place covered," said Herb. "If they try it there it'll be curtains. This may interest you. I'm pretty sure them guys in the Ford were on the prowl. I'd swear it in court. But they never give us a tumble so that's all right. Eddie and his bunch have got the whole second floor of that furniture warehouse across the street. It's perfect."

"That's fine," said Frank in a loud voice. "Well, glad to have seen you, Herb. See you around some time." Frank and Jimmy went out and got into the squad car. Herb turned down a side street and disappeared.

"Where now?" Carlson demanded.

"Straight north through the alley," said Frank. "Drive about twenty-five or thirty, no faster."

They started off again. Jimmy looked very glum and sat staring out at the backs of buildings, but not seeing them. Frank patted his arm.

"I've got a feeling, Jimmy," he said. "I'm getting like you." He glanced at his watch. "If the truck's on time we're going to make perfect connections."

"I hope the mob didn't lose their timetable," said Jimmy with an unpleasant laugh.

Suddenly Frank called:

"Stop at the next intersection, Carlson. Don't get clear out in the middle of it, but get out as far as you can without obstructing traffic."

Gradually Carlson slowed to a stop. Jimmy glanced up the alley which ran at right angles to their course. At the corner of High Street and this alley he saw the worn brownstone facade of the Drovers and Farmers National Bank. Frank leaned forward to look also. As they watched, the clock in the firehouse down the street struck twelve and a few seconds later the John Minot and Company pay truck pulled up in front of the bank. It was an antiquated old contraption at least fifteen years old. In all its long history the plant had never had a payroll robbery. Patterson, the head guard, was a man of sixty, stooped and nearsighted. He had on a faded blue uniform with silver buttons; a gun in a leather holster bumped carelessly at his hip. It had probably never been fired. With him was a boy about nineteen also in a uniform. He had a gun on his hip and a sawed-off shotgun under his arm. They got out of the truck and disappeared into the bank.

"Back the car up," said Frank, "about to where that telephone post is."

Carlson backed up, then Jimmy and Frank got out. They went to the corner of the alley, lit cigarettes and stood smoking.

After a while, Patterson came out followed by the boy and two bank guards. Patterson and the bank guards were loaded down with sacks. The boy walked beside them carrying the sawed-off shotgun loosely in front of him. They were all talking and laughing. When they reached the truck, the boy swung a door in the back of it wide and the sacks were dumped into it. The door was locked. The two bank guards stood waiting at the curb while the Minot men got into the truck and drove off.

"Well," said Jimmy, throwing his cigarette away, "that's that."

They got into the car.

"Keep straight north up the alley," said Frank.

Carlson drove off.

"I was wrong," said Jimmy.

"Don't give up yet, boy. Where's the next likeliest place?"

"At the railroad bridge," said Jimmy, "all the traffic on High Street goes either to the right or the left about a square before the bridge. The street's practically deserted from the bridge to the plant."

"How about this alley?"

"It stops at Alford Street just this side of the bridge."

"That's bad."

"Yes. We'll have to turn right at Alford and come out into the open, if they don't hit the truck before that."

Frank gave Carlson detailed instructions now, then they rode along in dead silence. Nothing happened. There wasn't a suspicious sound. As they got father north out of the business section little Italian children swarmed in the side alleys playing baseball and shouting. Twice Carlson narrowly avoided running over boys chasing balls into the main alley. Women put their heads out of upstairs windows and cursed. "Why you no blow your horn!" they shouted.

Presently they saw Alford Street ahead of them. It was a street bordering the railroad tracks and empty of houses or buildings on the track side. There were junkyards and old warehouses and an occasional garage on the other side. Carlson turned to the right. The street ran uphill diagonally toward the head of the big bridge over the railroad yards. Under the bridge tracks converged then diverged in every direction.

Jimmy leaned forward. The pay truck was approaching the bridge. Suddenly a big touring car skidded into High Street from a side street and, bearing into the truck, forced it to the curb. There was a loud squealing of brakes and the piercing rasp of the tires, then a loud burst of machine-gun fire. Jimmy, gritting his teeth, saw old Patterson slump forward, then slide sideways and hang over the car door head down.

Carlson drove straight across Alford Street and stopped behind a telegraph pole. Jimmy heard a siren going and in a moment the other two squad cars swung up into High Street from the opposite direction. Carlson and Smith jumped out with machine-guns in their hands and began firing at the bandits. Jimmy jumped out of the car and running low got into a doorway near the corner. Frank was beyond him down Alford Street in another doorway.

One bandit was already lying face down in the street. Jimmy saw Butch Crump and Red McMahon blast away at Mike and his bunch, then Butch turned and ran round the pay truck and plunged down an impossibly steep embankment into the railroad yards.

Red turned around twice and fell, throwing the machine-gun away from him with an unconsciously final feature as if to say: "Well, that's that." He tried to crawl under the truck but Carlson caught him with a deadly rain of lead. Jimmy saw Sid Rogers fall on his knees in front of the detectives, begging for his life.

"My God!" cried Jimmy, "I forgot to tell Mike. Mike!" he shouted. "I want Rogers alive! Grab him. Don't let anybody shoot him."

Three men had plunged down after Butch, and Jimmy ran over to watch their progress. He saw the detectives searching for the fugitive among the tangles of freight and equipment below. But Butch had disappeared.

Frank caught up with Jimmy who was starting down the embankment.

"Wait! He can't get away. It's broad daylight. They'll get him. You got work to do."

"Yes," said Jimmy, soberly. "But God how I'd hate to see that heel get away."

Mike came up to them, half dragging Rogers.

"They killed the old man, poor old devil," said Mike. "The boy got hit bad but he's a nervy one and never a peep. You, you murdering devil with a nice family and all!" He cried, shaking Rogers till his teeth chattered.

"They made me do it," cried Rogers in an agony of terror. "They made me. I never wanted to hurt anybody in my life. That time I took you to Joe's, Jimmy. They said they just wanted to talk to you. Thought they could fix you . . ."

"Shut up," said Jimmy. "Listen, you yellow-belly, this is a murder rap. If you want to save your neck you've got to talk, get me. Otherwise you'll get the hot squat."

"I'll talk. My God, Jimmy. I'll talk."

"All right. Put him in the car, Carlson."

Frank turned to Mike. "Take charge," he said. "First thing, get that boy to a hospital. That's the most important thing. These rats are dead, I think."

He turned Red over with his foot, then he glanced at the other dead bandit.

"Brick Norton," he said. "You were right, Jimmy. Boy, you ought to play the races."

"Yes," said Jimmy, taking off his hat and wiping the sweat from his clammy face, "I was right, but I was sure getting cold feet."

"Carlson," said Frank, "you stay with Mike. Call the plant if you get any dope on Butch. Smith, you come with Jimmy and me."

Frank and Jimmy got into the back seat. Rogers was in the front seat with Smith, who drove. Rogers sat with his face in his hands, crying. From time to time he tried to talk to Jimmy, who shut him up.

When they drove up to the main gate of John Minot and Company, Jimmy leaned forward:

"Use your siren, Smith."

The siren screamed. There was a rush of feet toward the gate inside the plant. The gateman put his head out, looking bewildered.

"They knocked over the pay truck, Harrison," cried Jimmy. "Let me in. Hit the siren again, Smith!" Jimmy turned to Frank. "Maybe that will make their hair curl."

Harrison, the head gateman, swung the big gate wide, then he stood staring in at Sid Rogers, who was pale as death.

"Sid was in on it," said Jimmy." They killed old Patterson. Tell the boys."

The gateman stood with his mouth open watching the car disappear down the big yard, then he ran for a phone.

"Pull up over here," said Jimmy.

When the car stopped Jimmy jumped out, followed by Frank, who took Sid by the arm. They climbed the stairs to McEvoy's suite of offices. In the hallway Jimmy saw Eve at the water cooler staring at him.

"Hello, Eve. Can't stop now."

Jimmy went into McEvoy's outer office. His secretary began to stammer and got very pale when Frank came in pulling along Sid Rogers, who looked more dead than alive and was covered with dirt.

"Mr. McEvoy's busy," said the girl. "He's in conference with Mr. Welborn."

Jimmy said nothing. He walked past the girl and opened the door of McEvoy's private office. McEvoy was standing up and turned to stare. Welborn, with his wounded hand in a sling, was sitting near the window.

"Well?" said McEvoy. "What's Rogers been up to?"

"He and a few other guys knocked over the pay truck. They killed the old man. I told the gateman about it on the way in. The boys are all going to be mighty sore about this."

"Can you imagine that?" said McEvoy, turning to Welborn. "Did you get them all, Devore?"

"We killed two of them. One got away."

McEvoy began to pace the floor. Berger sat down and, taking out a notebook, began to write in it. After a moment, Welborn reached for a phone, but Jimmy stopped him.

"No phoning."

Welborn glanced at McEvoy.

"Why not?" said McEvoy with a laugh. "What's this all about, anyway? Why can't Welborn use the phone?"

"I'm in charge," said Jimmy. "Mr. Minot said so. There's a lot of things he doesn't like going on around here."

"For instance."

"Well," said Jimmy, "we've got Rogers here on a murder rap. He says he don't like the idea of frying. So he says he's going to talk."

Rogers avoided McEvoy's eye. The phone rang and Welborn reached for it, but Jimmy took it away from him.

"Yes? That you Carlson? Yeah. Fine. That's mighty good news. Thanks."

Jimmy hung up then he stood, looking at McEvoy for a long time. McEvoy returned the stare without flinching. Finally Jimmy turned away and lit a cigarette.

"McEvoy," he said, "I hate to tell you this. But they just killed your brother."

There was dead silence in the room. Welborn started half off the chair but recovered quickly and began to cough. McEvoy stood staring for a long time, then he sank down in his chair behind his desk.

"It's no use," he said, turning to Welborn. Then as if to himself he added: "Everything went wrong from the first."

Welborn sat staring at the floor, getting very pale.

Rogers suddenly recovered his courage, seeing McEvoy and Welborn waiting.

"Yeah," he cried, "I'll talk. Them two guys have ruined more people. Why, they . . ."

"All right," said Jimmy. "Save it."

McEvoy leaned forward over his desk and wrote something on a pad. While he wrote, his left hand slowly disappeared below the desk. Suddenly there were two loud reports. McEvoy stood up quickly, his face contorted with pain, then he sank slowly down behind the desk.

There was a panic in the outer office. McEvoy's secretary rushed in followed by two clerks. They stood staring. Blue smoke drifted upward.

"My God, Bush!" cried Welborn. "Why did you do it?"

Jimmy picked up the pad. On it was written in wavering handwriting: "After life's fitful fever he sleeps well."

One day about two weeks later Frank Berger was sitting on the lawn in front of the big Minot house in a deck chair, talking to Scott Bayliss and Gordon Minot. Gordon and Scott were both convalescing and looked pale and thin. Jean was sitting near them, reading a book and looking up from time to time.

It was a beautiful late summer day. The sun was hot, but in among the trees it was cool. Beyond them, rows of sprinklers were playing over the lawns, sending up a rainbow spray.

Gordon was laughing.

"It beats me," he said. "How he ever figured it out I don't know. Really a remarkable young man. Too bad he has no education. But he's smart. Any man who knows his own limitations is smart. He won't take the Director of Welfare job I've been trying to give him. He says he'll have to make too many speeches. He's joking in earnest. He's afraid he hasn't got enough education for the job, and he's right. However, I'm going to double his salary so I guess that amounts to the same thing."

Frank smiled.

"I guess it does. You know, Mr. Minot, I went along with Jimmy pretty much till you and Mr. Bayliss were shot. Then I thought that he was all wrong. The thing was too preposterous. But McEvoy was a strange man. I showed you that note he wrote before he died."

Gordon smiled slightly.

"That wasn't so strange. Bush used to read a lot. That's good Shakespeare."

"Oh," said Frank, flushing. "I guess I'm like Jimmy. Not enough education."

"Yes," said Gordon, "Bush used to read a lot. His manners were excellent. He was an able fellow. But I guess at heart he was Butch Crump's brother. Funny, isn't it?"

Jean bent down to glance among the trees. The big front gate was being swung wide.

"It's Jimmy and Eve," she said getting up. "Eve wrote me they'd be home today but I didn't really expect them."

Bayliss smiled.

"You know, Jean," he said, "I'd be a little jealous if it weren't for Eve."

"Oh, silly," said Jean. "Jimmy's just like a big brother. Why, I'll bet he never gave me a thought in his life."

Jimmy drove up in front of the bungalow and, getting out, began silently to unload baggage from the back seat. They had been to the Lake and both of them were sunburned. Tommy the terrier jumped out of the car and ran up the steps, barking happily

"She'll make him a good wife," said Bayliss. "I know. She used to look after me around the office. She's a nice girl and a smart one."

Jimmy turned and waved and so did Eve.

"Be with you in a minute," called Jimmy. "Glad to see you up and around, boss."

Jimmy carried the baggage in, then he began to look through a pile of mail which had accumulated, mostly bills and advertisements. Eve sat down on the davenport and began to fan herself with her hat. Presently Jimmy held up a tiny little scented envelope and stared at it. Eve turned.

"Ah ha! Monkey business!"

Jimmy grimaced and opened the letter. It read:

Dear Jimmy:

Thanks to your kindness I'm a free woman again. I'm staying here in Cleveland and have been promised a good job. That Steel City business was like a nightmare and I hate even to think about it. You don't know how I appreciate what you did for me.

If you are ever in Cleveland and would like to see me (I'd like to see you!) inquire for me at the Atherton House.

Goodbye,
Marie

Jimmy flushed slightly and cleared his throat.

"Well," he said, putting the letter into his pocket, "let's go see everybody."

Eve jumped up.

"James, let me see that letter. I don't like the kind of perfume she uses."

Groaning, Jimmy handed Eve the letter. She read it hurriedly, then more slowly.

"Oh, our little friend Gorgeous. She'd like to see you with an exclamation mark. Now can you stand there and tell me you never fooled around with her when . . ."

"Now wait a minute, Eve," said Jimmy. "I can explain everything."

THE END

W. R. BURNETT
BIBLIOGRAPHY
(1899-1982)

NOVELS
Little Caesar (Dial, 1929)
Iron Man (Dial, 1930)
Saint Johnson (Dial, 1930)
The Silver Eagle (Dial, 1931)
The Giant Swing (Harper, 1932)
Dark Hazard (Harper, 1933)
Goodbye to the Past (Harper, 1934)
The Goodhues of Sinking Creek
   (Raven's Head, 1934)
King Cole (Harper, 1936)
The Dark Command (Knopf, 1938)
High Sierra (Knopf, 1940)
The Quick Brown Fox (Knopf, 1942)
Nobody Lives Forever (Knopf, 1943)
Tomorrow's Another Day (Knopf,
   1945)
Romelle (Knopf, 1946)
The Asphalt Jungle (Knopf, 1949)
Stretch Dawson (Gold Medal, 1950)
Little Men, Big World (Knopf, 1951)
Vanity Row (Knopf, 1952)
Adobe Walls (Knopf, 1953)
Big Stan (as by John Monahan;
   Gold Medal, 1953)
Captain Lightfoot (Knopf, 1954)
It's Always Four O'Clock (as by
   James Updyke; Random, 1956)
Pale Moon (Knopf, 1956)
Underdog (Knopf, 1957)
Bitter Ground (Knopf, 1958)
Mi Amigo (Knopf, 1959)
Conant (Popular Library, 1961)
Round the Clock at Volari's (Gold
   Medal, 1961; republished from
   author's version, 2024)
Sergeants 3 (Pocket, 1962; ghost-
   written by unknown author)
The Goldseekers (Doubleday, 1962)
The Widow Barony (UK only;
   Macdonald, 1962)
The Abilene Samson (Pocket, 1963)
The Winning of Mickey Free
   (Bantam, 1965; with Robert
   Silverberg)

The Cool Man (Gold Medal, 1968;
   republished from author's version
   as *Night Without Morning,* 2024)
Goodbye, Chicago (St. Martin's,
   1981)
The Loop (Stark House, 2025)
Man With a Thousand Enemies
   (Stark House, 2025)

SHORT STORIES
Across the Aisle (*Collier's,* Apr 4,
   1936)
Between Rounds (*Collier's,* Aug 30,
   1930)
Captain Lightfoot (*Argosy,* UK, Nov,
   Dec 1954, Jan 1955)
Dr. Socrates (*Collier's,* Mar 23, 1935)
Dressing-Up (*Harper's,* Nov 1929;
   Ellery Queen's Mystery Magazine,
   June 1947)
First Blood (*Collier's,* Apr 23 1938)
Girl in a Million (*Redbook,* Jan
   1938)
Head Waiter (*Cosmopolitan,* Sept
   1931)
High Sierra (*Five Star Western
   Stories,* July 1941)
The Hunted (*Liberty,* June 28 1930)
I Love Everybody (*Argosy,* UK, July
   1943)
Jail Breaker (*Collier's,* July 7, July
   14, July 21, Aug 4 1934)
Little David (*The Saturday Evening
   Post,* Feb 15 1947)
Mr. Litvinoff (*Collier's,* July 18 1931)
Nobody Lives Forever (*Collier's,* Oct
   9, Oct 16, Oct 23, Oct 30 1943)
Nobody's All Bad [Billy the Kid]
   (*Collier's,* Jun 7 1930; *Ellery
   Queen's Mystery Magazine,* Dec
   1953)
Protection (*Collier's,* May 9, May 23
   1931)
Racket Alley (*Collier's,* Dec 16 1950,
   Jan 6 1951)
Round Trip (*Harper's,* Aug 1929;
   Ellery Queen's Mystery Magazine,
   Dec 1950)
Suspect (Collier's, July 4 1936)
Throw Him Off the Track (*Argosy,*
   Dec 1952)

Traveling Light (*Collier's*, Dec 7
  1935; *Ellery Queen's Mystery
  Magazine*, Sep 1951)
Vanishing Act (*Manhunt*, Nov 1955;
  Mike Shayne Mystery Magazine,
  Aug 1964)
War Party (*Lilliput*, May 1954)
Youth Is Not Forever (*Redbook*, Feb
  1939)

ESSAYS

Whatever Happened to Baseball?
  (*Rogue*, June 1963, article)
The Roar of the Crowd (Potter, 1964)

SCREENPLAY CONTRIBUTIONS

The Finger Points (1931)
Beast of the City (1932)
Scarface: The Shame of a Nation
  (1932)
High Sierra (1941)
The Get-Away (1941)
This Gun for Hire (1942)
Wake Island (1942)
Crash Dive (1943)
Action in the North Atlantic (1943)
Background to Danger (1943)
San Antonio (1945)
Nobody Lives Forever (1946)
Belle Starr's Daughter (1949)
Vendetta (1950)
The Racket (1951)
Dangerous Mission (1954)
I Died a Thousand Times (1955)
Captain Lightfoot (1955)
Illegal (1955)
Short Cut to Hell (1957)
September Storm (1960)
Sergeants Three (1962)
The Great Escape (1963)

UNCREDITED SCREEN CONTRIBUTIONS

Law and Order (1932)
The Whole Town's Talking (1935)
The Westerner (1940)
The Man I Love (1946)
The Walls of Jericho (1948)
The Asphalt Jungle (1950)
Night People (1954)
The Hangman (1959)
Four for Texas (1963)
Ice Station Zebra (1968)
Stiletto (1969)